To Beth,

Dragon in the Snow

The Third in the Orkneyinga Murders Series

Lexie Conyngham

Lexie Conyngham

First published in 2020 by The Kellas Cat Press, Aberdeen.

ISBN: 978-1-910926-62-8

Cover design by Helen Braid at www.ellieallatsea.co.uk

Dramatis Personae

In Birsay:
Thorfinn Sigurdarson, Earl of Orkney and Caithness, a planner
His wife, Ingibjorg
His daughter, Asgerdr
Bolla and Groa, maidservants
Skafti, one of Thorfinn's men
Tosti, a priest
Ketil Gunnarson, one of Thorfinn's men, and his own followers Skorri, Geirod and Alf
Sigrid, a poor widow, and Gnup who works for her
Helga, her neighbour

Shapinsay folk:
Beinir, who can read and write
Vali and his household, Hamthir the boatman and his brother Ingvar
Aslak, a farmer
Leif and Hervor, and their daughter Thora
Gillaug and Eyolfr
Asta and her husband Hoskuld, a potter, their daughter Katrin and their serving maid
Osk, of whom little is known

Margad from Caithness and his dog
Sundry Westray men

I

Helga, Asmund's daughter, had many talents, for she was an excellent cook and managed her longhouse competently. But there were other things for which she was particularly well known around Birsay, notably the exact assessment of the qualities of handsome young men, and the dispersal of her husband's silver.

Both of these required observational skills and an attention to detail, and she had honed these like a smith honing a blade. It was a rare boat or ship that passed below her longhouse unnoticed, lest she should miss the opportunity of enjoying fancy goods – of whatever type – when they had rounded the Brough of Birsay to beach in Thorfinn's harbour. Thus it was that, even though the air was dotted grey with snow, she saw the boat passing west along the coast, sailed by two men she barely troubled to examine, and another, in a green hood, who was worth a second, or even a third, glance. For a moment she thought it might even be Ketil Gunnarson, but even as a smile curled her pretty mouth at the idea, she remembered it could not be him. He was safe at the Brough.

Ketil Gunnarson, warrior and general agent for Thorfinn Sigurdarsson, was indeed at the Brough. But he did not feel safe at all. In fact, he was doing his best to avoid Thorfinn.

It was true he was growing more accustomed to the islands and their eccentricities – both the land and the people. It seemed he was going to have to tolerate them, anyway. When he had first worked for Thorfinn, he had barely stayed a few months in the same place: Thorfinn's earldom extended from Hjaltland in the north down to

Hwitebi (when they could keep the locals quiet) in the south, taking in parts of Fife, most of Caithness, and reaching round to the Western Islands – and of course, it behoved Thorfinn also to have one or two trusted men at the Trondheim court, keeping an eye on the current king and making sure that any moves on Thorfinn's earldom could be countered swiftly and efficiently. That was in the days of raids and battles, murders and maimings, and a young man from Heithabyr like Ketil, with no aptitude for his father's cup-making business, could see some action.

But then Thorfinn killed his nephew Rognvald – and Thorfinn regretted it – and Thorfinn travelled to Rome to make his penance. And now Thorfinn, recently become the father of twin boys, was more interested in church building, and settlement making, and law giving, and tax raising, and since he had chosen to base this fascinating new way of life on a peninsula poking assertively into the sea off the west mainland of Orkney, Ketil knew he was going to see more of the islands over the next few years than he had ever remotely intended. Prone to fogs, windy, and impractically flat compared with what Ketil thought of as his Trondheim home, the islands were not what he would have chosen for himself.

He had returned with his own few men about a month ago, at the beginning of winter, and found Thorfinn's hall bright with new tapestries and Thorfinn's wife, Ingibjorg, smugly busy with her twin boys. Her daughter Asgerdr, possibly prettier than ever with that sweep of bright blonde hair and rounding into a woman few men could pass by without at least a backward glance, was also busy, but not at all smug: all her mother's duties of overseeing hall and longhouse seemed to have fallen to her, and anyone giving her that backward glance needed to do so from a safe distance – she had developed a handy way with a wooden spoon that seemed at least to relieve some of her impatience.

Thorfinn, away from the womenfolk, had plans, but was not explicit about them. His first question to Ketil was an odd one.

'What do you know of Sigrid's farm? What do you think of it?'

'Sigrid Harald's daughter?' Ketil asked, playing for time as he made sure there was no other Sigrid.

'Yes: you know the place, don't you?'

'A little, my lord,' Ketil conceded. 'It's small, I believe, though her sheep graze quite a wide area: she has mentioned a cow and some hens. A boy called Gnup helps her – he's a kinsman of Bjarni Hravn.'

'Longhouse in good condition?' Thorfinn asked briskly. 'Smallish, I know, for a family.'

'I've never heard her complain about it,' said Ketil, wondering what this might be leading to. Thorfinn did like to organise his men. It occurred to Ketil that perhaps he had someone marked out for a husband for Sigrid - as a young widow with a farm and no family she might seem to Thorfinn like a good match. The idea sent an uneasy prickle down his spine. He should at least warn his old friend. 'Is there anything in particular you'd like to find out? I can go and talk with her today, my lord.'

'Yes, yes, do that – just some general information, get a feel for the place, see what you think.'

'I'm not a farmer, my lord,' Ketil reminded him.

'Sigrid'll tell you all you need to know, I'm sure. Go and see her. Send her my greetings. Tell her Ingibjorg is still delighted with the tapestries.'

So Ketil went – though not immediately. He had not seen Sigrid in the couple of days since his arrival, so he thought it only courteous to take a bath in the bath house first, and change into a clean shirt, and shave. He had known Sigrid when they were children in Heithabyr, their fathers both Norwegian merchants, but they had not seen each other for years until he had discovered her recently, an impoverished widow in Birsay. She still treated him like a little brother in need of firm guidance, but he was fond enough of her, he supposed. Enough to warn her of any plans Thorfinn might have for her future.

Sigrid had other ideas.

'It's this stupid notion of his about taxes!' She stamped ahead of him into the longhouse – she had offered him a cup of ale, and he had accepted, wondering if she had brewed it herself. 'Give that fire a poke, Ketil, I can't feel my fingers. Honestly, I sometimes think you men ought to find somewhere to raid again: off you'd go for the summer and leave us in peace, and then you'd come back with enough loot to keep us going through the winter. How can I pay Thorfinn taxes from this place? It doesn't even keep me alive, not without the weaving and nailbinding and felting and … oh! Stupid man.'

'He sends his greetings,' said Ketil mildly. The ale was unexpectedly good, and Sigrid's cat, seeking warmth, had settled hard against his side, purring. 'And he said to tell you that Ingibjorg is still delighted with the tapestries.'

Sigrid snorted: there was no love lost between her and Thorfinn's wife.

'You can be grateful for it, anyway,' she told him. 'That barrel of ale was part of the payment.'

'Ah! It is good,' he said. She gave him a glare, but refilled his cup.

'So do you want to know about the farm?' she asked, resigned. 'Do you want to see round? There's not much to see. The house is small - big enough for me and Gnup, of course, and the animals down that end at this time of year. Thorsten made sure the roof was sound and the door is only a few years old, but there's an awful draught in that corner there when the wind's in the wrong direction. I have one cow who has faithfully given me a calf a year but she's going to run out of them some time soon, and I have ten sheep and eight hens and a cockerel – usually, sometimes he goes to Helga's hens for a fight. And a cat.' She nodded at it. 'The infield for the bygg is parched at the top if there's no rain for two days, and running with water at the bottom – and all down one side – if there's rain for half a morning. I've lost the occasional sheep off the cliff, but the outfield grazing is mostly all right, if wet – you have to keep an eye on the sheep's feet, check them often. The wall between the infield and the outfield needs repair three or four times a year – I think it needs widening at the base but I've never had the people to carry more stones up to do it. There's no boat noust – there's no space for one and I don't have a boat, but I suppose it's handy enough for the harbour. There, what do you think Thorfinn might think a fair rent for that?'

'I have no idea,' Ketil said honestly. He was eager to accept Sigrid's deduction that rent was all Thorfinn wanted from her. 'I suppose you can work for your rent, too.'

Sigrid sighed.

'That usually means spending time with Sheep Face – I mean Ingibjorg. But yes, when I can. I think I've done most of what she fancies at the moment, though. The new hall is half-tapestried, with the rest to be done in the summer.'

'I saw. It looks very fine.'

He could see her blush.

'Aye, well, don't look too closely at some of them. When Sheep Face is at her most annoying, things don't always go the way I want them to. And I didn't always have the most skilled assistance. Anyway,' she refilled his cup again, 'what have you been up to? Subduing the good folk of Thorfinn's earldom?'

'Only bits of it,' Ketil shook his head. 'A quiet autumn, just a few skirmishes.'

'Are you here for the winter, then?'

'Yes – with my men.'

'Your men?' She made a face. 'I hope they're better than the last one you brought home.'

'That was – he was not really one of my men,' said Ketil defensively. 'He just turned up.'

'Aye, but you let him!'

He sighed. Why did they always descend into bickering? Why did she always pull him into it? He set his cup down, though it was still half-full.

'I'd better get back to them – obviously you think they need close supervision.'

'How many of them?'

'Three. Skorri, Geirod and Alf.'

She shrugged.

'I'll keep an eye out for them.'

'I'll keep them busy. Thank you for the ale.' He rose easily from the bench where he had been perched, and towered over her as he would have done since he was fourteen, if he'd seen her then. He could not resist adding, 'No doubt Thorfinn will be in touch.'

'I'm sure,' she sniffed, arms folded. 'He'll probably send you back to collect his hacksilver and a hen or two. I'll see you soon.'

He waved a hand, and pushed out past the door curtain. The cold air grasped him at once as he paused to look about him. He had liked this view from the first time he had seen it, the gentle slope before the house, the sea close enough to the right, the curling mainland to the left, and ahead the Brough with Thorfinn's growing settlement snuggled to this side by the saddle of grassy rock that linked the headland to the mainland. The earth and grass were frosted now, but however attractive the land, the sun blued the sea, ruffled with froth, tempting him back to sail, to feel the soothing surge beneath his feet, to be away and free and faced only by sea and air, not by awkward, difficult, ambiguous people. The sea was dangerous, but it was never devious.

It was when he reported back to Thorfinn at the Brough that he began to feel that something might be amiss.

'The farm is a pleasant, well-set place,' he told the Earl, 'but scarcely very productive.' That should help protect Sigrid from taxes, he hoped. But Thorfinn did not seem overly concerned.

'Hm, that's a shame – have to find somewhere else. And that would have fitted so well.' He glanced over to where Ingibjorg was sitting, her twin boys arranged to best advantage on her lap in case anyone might not notice and admire them. Ingibjorg frowned, but took the opportunity to reach out a pale, wistful hand to Ketil. The frown turned to a smile he assumed she believed was devastatingly attractive.

'Dear Ketil, it's disappointing – it would have been so convenient! And with Sigrid leaving …'

Sigrid leaving? She had not mentioned it. Ingibjorg's smile had developed a patina of self-satisfaction – was that because she saw he had not known?

Thorfinn cleared his throat with unexpected emphasis.

'Well, we'll sort something out. Have you any work on hand at present?'

'Awaiting your orders, my lord.' Ketil accepted the change of subject: he could find out more about Sigrid later. Leaving? Going where? Why had she not mentioned it?

'Your men around?'

'Just outside.'

Ingibjorg coughed. Thorfinn's eyebrows rose, then he shook his head.

'No, come to think of it, you can do it yourself. It's a bit menial, I know, but Asgerdr has been busy with packing salt cod for the winter and she needs a bit of help shifting the barrels. I mean, she can't move them herself, obviously.' Thorfinn's eyes were not quite meeting Ketil's. He probably had his mind on less domestic matters.

'Of course not, my lord. I'll be happy to help. Where are the barrels?'

Ingibjorg described where to find them, and Ketil left the hall by the side door. He was surprised to find Asgerdr just outside the door, as if she might have been listening. She could have picked a more interesting conversation to eavesdrop on, he thought.

'I'm to help you with some barrels of fish,' he said. The winter sunlight darted off her hair, and for once she was smiling. This might not be a bad way to spend the morning.

'Oh, thank you, Ketil! I hope you don't think it too lowly a task

– it shouldn't take too long.'

'Not at all. I'm here at Thorfinn's command.'

'Well, it's very kind of you.' She had not moved from the doorway yet: she had a thick cloak about her and did not seem to be feeling the cold. Her cheeks were pink and her eyes seemed very bright blue.

'I think perhaps I need to get past,' said Ketil.

'Oh! Of course. I'll show you where the barrels are. I really just need a couple of them moved to – well, here, against the wall.' She gave him a smile that was a little like a ribbon around his neck, tugging her after him. Ketil followed obediently, wondering what she was up to. He had felt the force of Asgerdr's interest before, but she was flirtatious and fickle, he knew well, and substantially above him. If she was directing her charms at him, either she wanted him to do something – more than mere barrel-shifting – or she was trying to make a point to her parents. Which might mean that Thorfinn had finally found her a husband of her own station, but not one she approved of. He grinned to himself. He did not envy a man married off to an unwilling Asgerdr. He would lead a life of considerable suffering.

'Here we are,' said Asgerdr, opening the door of a small building. The stone walls were lined with barrels about the height of Ketil's waist.

'Any in particular?' He tipped a barrel experimentally, testing its weight.

'The two nearest the door would be best,' she said, following him into the little chamber. The hairs rose on the back of his neck. He did not like being trapped.

'You'll have to move out of the way,' he said without emphasis. 'I'll roll the barrel outside then lift it.'

'You'll never lift it!' she exclaimed. 'They're packed full!' Her eyes played a little longer than was comfortable on the muscular structure of his upper arms. She herself had not moved from the doorway, though: she was so close he had to bend his neck to meet her gaze. 'I wouldn't want you to hurt yourself, just helping me,' she added, her voice suddenly low.

'At least give me the chance to try,' he said, resisting the urge to whisper back.

She lifted a hand, and for a moment he thought she was going to – to what? The movement was hard to interpret. Then she smiled again, and backed slowly out of his way.

'Of course,' she said. 'There you are!'

He rolled the barrel on its edge through the low doorway, then hefted it with ease on to his shoulder. Any man on the Brough could have done the same, he told himself, as he walked, without looking near her, back across to the hall. He set the barrel down where she had shown him, and went back for the second one, meeting her on the way. She passed him with another little smile, a look out of the corner of her eyes. He nodded – it would have been rude to ignore her completely – and went on to the store.

When he returned with the second barrel, she was waiting for him at the door of the hall.

'Where are you going now?'

'Is there anything else you need to me to carry?' he asked.

'Well ...'

'Because I should probably make sure that Thorfinn doesn't need me,' he went on, and before she could manoeuvre into his path he slipped past her into the hall. She followed at once.

'All done? Good, good,' said Thorfinn, seeing them. Ingiborg favoured them both with one of the smiles she seemed to think of as motherly. Ketil looked from the pair of them to Asgerdr and back, discreetly: there did not seem to be any tension in the family at present. That in itself was unusual. The three of them working towards some common goal was a frightening thought. Thorfinn looked his daughter up and down, but still seemed to have trouble meeting Ketil's eye. Ketil felt a sudden urge to run for the door.

'If you'll excuse me, my lord,' he said, thinking quickly, 'I must go and speak with someone.'

'With Sigrid, I suppose,' said Ingibjorg, her smile turning a little sour.

'No, no,' said Ketil quickly, though the thought had crossed his mind. He rapidly reviewed possible acquaintances he might need to see. 'I must go and speak with Tosti,' he finished.

'With Tosti?' Thorfinn queried mildly. He exchanged a glance with Ingibjorg. 'Well, all right, then. I'll see you later, no doubt.'

'My lord.'

Who, after all, more harmless than a priest? Well, thought Ketil, remembering one or two priests he had known, who more harmless than Tosti? And just at the moment almost anyone would be more harmless than the family he had just fled in the hall.

Outside at the front door he found his men loitering, making use of their free time by seeing who could hit a particular stone in the wall most often with chips of rock from around their feet. Alf, usually the best at precise tasks, had been set further back than the others and forced to use his left hand, so Ketil reckoned he must have been winning by quite a lot. Geirod and Skorri were laughing at each other's failures, till Skorri saw Ketil watching.

'Need us for anything, sir?' he asked.

'Yes,' said Ketil, 'come with me.' They straightened their swords and fell in casually behind him as he climbed up to Thorfinn's newly-built church. Geirod grumbled as he recognised the building.

'It's not Sunday,' he muttered. Skorri cuffed his ear hard. Ketil ducked his head at the doorway, but the church was empty: the building next door, though, intended as part of a new monastic foundation, stood with the door open. Inside, Tosti sat at a low table, a thick book open in front of him. Ketil was not adept at the matter of books, but it seemed to him that the work was too rough for a Bible.

Tosti blinked as the light from the doorway changed, and looked up.

'Hello, Ketil! I saw you in the hall last night but I wasn't able to linger. You're back for a while?'

'That's the idea, till Thorfinn thinks of something else he wants me to do,' said Ketil. He found a stool near the table, and angled himself on to it. 'These are the men I've brought with me: the broad one is Skorri, Geirod's the surly one, and Alf's the one who looks like a skald.'

The men grinned, used to these descriptions. Skorri came forward and asked for a blessing, but the other two hung back. Tosti nodded them a greeting instead, not offended.

'What can I do for you?'

'I wondered if there was anything we could do for you, in fact?' Ketil asked blandly. 'You look busy.'

Tosti nodded at the great book.

'Thorfinn has taken to asking for reports to be sent from the various islands, and I'm to write them into this book. And for the most part, that's easy enough: Thorfinn's man in the area comes here, or sends someone for him, and they sit there,' he pointed to Ketil's stool, 'and tell me all the news, and I write it down. So I suppose you could, if you really were at a loose end, you could help me herd the various men coming to report? Meet them down at the harbour, show them up here, make sure they don't get lost … I mean, it's not very exciting, but –'

'We'll do it,' said Ketil at once.

'All of you?'

'Of course. You hear that, you lot? Down to the harbour, and let's see who's coming.'

His men shrugged: it would probably be more interesting than hitting stones with other stones. Harbours were always places to go and see what was happening.

'Thanks, Tosti,' said Ketil.

Anything to get away from the Brough, and whatever Thorfinn and his womenfolk were devising between them.

So they worked – easy work, sociable, a little dull – for a couple of weeks. They took time off to swim, or to practise a little swordwork, or to throw an axe or two. There were worse ways to spend the winter. Ketil had in fact just returned from a swim, his short hair bristling on his head as if it were growing frost, when he met Alf and Skorri bringing a man up from the harbour to see Tosti. Tosti offered the stranger a cup of ale, and settled him down to rest before reporting.

'By the way,' said Tosti, 'do any of you read?' Skorri and Ketil shook their heads, but Alf tilted his to one side.

'A bit,' he admitted.

'Then if you're bored, you could help me – with Ketil's permission, of course.' Tosti gave Ketil a bright grin.

'What kind of work is it?' Ketil asked.

'Well, it's Shapinsay …'

'Shapinsay?' Ketil struggled for a moment to place the island. 'What do they report? Surely nothing ever happens on Shapinsay.'

Tosti, normally the soul of patience, rolled his eyes. As a good and godly man he was evidently trying to restrain himself, but his hand reached of its own accord out to a sheaf of curling skins by the side of his table, a sheaf bound together by a leather cord through holes punched into the side edges.

'What's that?'

Tosti shook the leaves very slightly.

'That,' he said, his lips tight, 'is the report of Beinir, head man on Shapinsay. Beinir can read and write. And this,' he laid the bundle down with infinite gentleness, 'this is the result.'

Ketil was just leaning towards it to see what the problem was, when there was a little explosion of sound by the door.

'Beinir can read and write?'

It was Sigrid.

'How do you know Beinir?' Ketil asked.

'Never mind that now,' said Sigrid briskly. 'Sorry to interrupt, Tosti. Ketil, Thorfinn wants a word, and Sh – er, Ingibjorg says it's urgent.'

Ketil, heart beating as if he expected an ambush, rose from the stool. He should not go.

He thought Sigrid was speaking to him, but he could not make out the words. He felt his feet take him past her, past his men, out through the door, and back down the hill to the hall.

And less than an hour later, Ketil had frozen. He thought that even his blood had stopped in his veins.

Around him the organised life of Thorfinn's great hall continued, smooth murmurs at the back of his head. He felt his hand twitching for his sword hilt, but he knew that would do no good. No sword was going to solve this situation.

'So what do you say?' Thorfinn's voice came again, slowly penetrating the ice in his head. The words were curiously flat: surely Thorfinn, at least, should sound a bit more enthusiastic. If nothing else, it was a chance of getting Asgerdr off his hands. 'Will you marry my daughter?'

'I should be honoured, my lord,' Ketil heard himself say. 'Of course I should be honoured.'

II

Sigrid had been looking forward to a reasonably good winter.

She had worked hard for Ingibjorg, overseeing the complex weaving of the expensive tapestries as well as other odds and ends around the place, and Ingibjorg, torn between the satisfaction at having at her command the best woolworker in Orkney (Sigrid reminded herself that this was so) and the relief at finally having Sigrid out of her house, paid her with uncharacteristic generosity. Sigrid had ale, dried and salted meat, and grain to see her through a few months, and hacksilver to buy when she ran out. Or to bury under the floor, against those rainy days that seemed to litter her life, despite her best efforts.

The animals were all healthy, and Gnup had not yet suffered an attack of the sniffles that could drive a body mad as he snored behind his curtain in the little longhouse. Her neighbour Helga baked bread for her, and the cat made its contribution in mice. All boded well.

And then Thorfinn decided he needed reports from the other islands.

From as far as the north of Hjaltland they came, and as near as Rousay, and all points between and across the mainland. Taxes, Sigrid thought grimly, it would all be to do with taxes. She prayed he would find enough in his islands and not feel the need to look too close to home.

Tosti the priest was kept busy making a record of all the reports which, for the most part, he seemed to enjoy, making his own quiet enquiries into the state of the church life in each community. Thorfinn was an enthusiast for the new religion – not so new now, though still not universal – and liked to make sure his islanders were worshipping the way he felt they should. This did not always meet with the same level of enthusiasm, but Tosti nodded and noted, and kept many of his opinions to himself. Sigrid liked Tosti. In a community where cooped-up warriors and strong-minded women were quick to share their opinions and slow to accept others', Tosti was always a haven. And he was a wonder, too: he could read and write in a number of different languages. Sigrid could manage, if she concentrated, the occasional rune. Tosti was very impressive.

He did not seem to mind if she occasionally took her nailbinding up to his relatively well-heated office by the church, and worked and watched as he transformed the words of the islands' representatives into his odd little patterns on the page, pausing to dip his pen in the dark brown ink he had told her was made from oak galls – imported, of course. Oak trees were about as common on Orkney's islands as three-headed ducks.

Several of the representatives, either because of bad sailing weather or just for the interest in an unfamiliar place, stayed for a while at the hall, enjoying Thorfinn's excellent hospitality. They were made very welcome: it was easy to grow bored with familiar faces in the winter months, and some of them had new songs to sing or new stories to tell after supper, and made an appreciative audience for the hird's own tales – there was nothing like a fresh audience to give an old yarn a new lease of life. Sigrid, who could pour a jug of ale as well as most, came up to the hall to help on a few evenings, which was how she met the party from Shapinsay.

'Four of them,' she told Helga the next day – Helga was very happy to receive gossip in exchange for her delicious flatbreads, and Sigrid was pleased to oblige. 'The head man is Beinir, who talks a lot and not all of it of great use.'

'What does he look like?' Helga claimed she could ignore anything a man said if his looks were right. Sigrid had a suspicion that Beinir's looks were indeed right, and chose to tone down her description.

'He's an older man, and on the tall side,' she said, 'not very striking. Like a plant grown in a barrel: all height and no breadth.'

'Hm,' Helga shrugged him off. 'Next?'

'The fellow with him is called … um … Aslak, I think. Small, stocky, dull red hair, and a leathery kind of face.'

'Well, I'll know him when I see him,' said Helga, unimpressed.

'Then there's Margad – oh, no, wait, he's from Caithness. But he arrived about the same time.'

'Caithness? Another little dark fellow, then?'

'No,' said Sigrid with a smile, 'this one's tall and red-headed.'

'I'll look out for him!' said Helga, blue eyes widening.

'He has a yellow dog. And he's rich, I gather. I wonder if Thorfinn has his eye on him for Asgerdr?' That should make Helga keep her hands to herself – maybe.

'It's certainly about time that girl was away to a hall of her own,' said Helga, and her interest in Asgerdr's future was perhaps only partly governed by her feelings about Asgerdr's fine figure and hair – and youth, compared with Helga's.

'I think Ingibjorg has someone in mind, anyway. Now that they have the twins and Thorfinn has clear heirs.'

'If I were Asgerdr I wouldn't want to hang around. Not with Ingibjorg,' said Helga darkly, knowing that Sigrid would agree. 'I thought she might have taken Hakon last summer. The pair seemed very close.'

'Yes, well,' said Sigrid. There were several good reasons for Asgerdr not to marry Hakon, the chief, perhaps, being that he already had a wife in Norway.

'Anyway, tell me about the others! You've only named three men. Who is the fourth?'

'Oh,' said Sigrid, 'only the boatman who brought them – brought Beinir and Aslak, I mean. A young man, strong, of course, name of Hamthir, and he has his little brother with him. Well, not so little, but there's something wrong with his head, you know? I don't know if he was born that way or what. He seems a gentle boy, though. He says nothing much, and Hamthir himself doesn't say much more, but then you wouldn't expect a boatman to contribute if Beinir and Aslak are the ones making the report.'

'Too many names,' said Helga, giving the flatbreads a final flip on the hot stones. 'I'll have to go and see these men for myself. Margad and Beinir sound very promising.'

'Where's Hrolf today?' asked Sigrid innocently. Helga glanced around as though her husband might have been forgotten in a corner as she discussed the potential delights of other men.

'Hunting,' she said. 'He's taken the boys. If they bring back anything interesting I'll make sure he takes you some. In fact,' she said, scrambling to her feet to fetch a cloth for the flatbreads, 'they'll be out for ages. Why don't we carry these back to your longhouse and then I'll take a little walk down the hill and see who I might see?'

She was well-practised at preparation for her own hunting trips, Sigrid thought, watching her swiftly add a string of beads to the others on her overdress, tug a few curls out from beneath her headcloth, and arrange her cloak around her shoulders in a manner that somehow made it look more revealing than it really was – only a madwoman would wear revealing clothing in Birsay in the middle of winter.

No doubt Helga had planned to leave Sigrid at home and carry on alone towards the Brough. Helga preferred to hunt alone: whether this was through a somewhat warped sense of decency or whether she was afraid Sigrid would laugh out loud at her antics, Sigrid had never been quite sure. But circumstances intervened on this occasion: at once as they left Helga's house they saw five figures in the distance, on the path that linked the two longhouses then carried on over the hill to Kirkuvagr. Sigrid knew them at once, the tall, well-made shapes of Margad and Beinir, Aslak sturdy beside them, and to one side the more slender boatman, Hamthir, one restraining hand on his brother's arm. It looked an accustomed gesture, as if it were just what Hamthir always did when they were near cliffs or strange people, and there was no sign of a struggle from his silent brother. Almost as soon as the women had seen the party approaching, they realised they too had been spotted. Helga strolled easily towards them, quite as if they were exactly what she had expected to see, though Sigrid spotted her special little smile flitting about her lips, ready to flash in full force on the men when they were close enough.

'I've seen that man,' she murmured to Sigrid. 'The one with the green hood.'

'He's been out and about,' Sigrid agreed. 'He has various friends he has been visiting while he's here.'

'So which one is he?' Helga demanded.

'That's Beinir, from Shapinsay,' Sigrid conceded reluctantly. 'The other tall one is Margad from Caithness.'

But it seemed Margad and his yellow dog had been knocked into second place.

'You said there was nothing to Beinir!' Helga was complaining, causing her preparatory smile to twist a bit. 'Look at that! What lovely shoulders he has!'

'Helga …'

'His face – well, not bad, really. I like the short beard – that reddish tinge on a fair-haired man just lends that bit of ambiguity, doesn't it? If the wind would just flap a bit the other way we might have a better view of his thighs …' Yet all the time she seemed quite fixed on her conversation with Sigrid, as though she had barely noticed the strangers. As an afterthought she added, 'You can take Margad if you fancy him.'

'You're very kind,' said Sigrid wryly, and then the two groups met.

If Sigrid had really found either of the men appealing, she would not have enjoyed the next few minutes. Margad and Beinir turned towards Helga like flowers towards the sun, just as she knew they would, and the other man, Aslak, subjected her to a very thorough scrutiny. Sigrid was left to talk to the boatman Hamthir and his brother. Hamthir bowed without fuss.

'I remember you from the hall, don't I?'

'That's right: I'm Sigrid. I live just down there.' She gestured to the longhouse the men had just passed.

'Good place to live. Handy for the sea,' said Hamthir, and Sigrid agreed: it was usually easier to agree than to admit she did not have a boat, or even somewhere to bring one in. She hoped he was not one of those men who had no conversation unless it involved boats. 'Does your husband farm this, then?'

'He's dead. I farm it, for as long as I can afford the taxes.'

'Taxes?' Hamthir looked alarmed.

'Thorfinn's latest game. I mean, it hasn't happened yet, but he's always planning. Someone came and asked me all about the place, only today.' She did not name Ketil: it would only distract Helga.

'Is that why he wanted us all to come and report to him?' Hamthir's alarm had not diminished much. 'I thought it was just the usual check to see we had men trained in arms and good boats and so on, you know, in case of attack. Varts at the ready for sending signals. You know the kind of thing.'

'Well,' said Sigrid, ever practical even through the fear of taxes, 'I daresay he finds that useful, too. Does Shapinsay have a vart?'

Shapinsay was not the highest of islands – she had seen it from the mainland. Where on earth would they light a signal beacon?

'Of course it does!' said Hamthir proudly. 'We're the defence to the east. You need to have a vart on Shapinsay. I mean, we could tell from Shapinsay if Kirkuvagr was being attacked.'

'So could Kirkuvagr,' Sigrid pointed out. 'They could send someone up to wherever their beacon is.'

'Better safe than sorry,' Hamthir told her. 'We'd be signalling straight over the invaders' heads, right across to Redland, then to Greeny Hill, then here.'

'Hm,' said Sigrid, trying to picture this low-level beacon trail. She tried to remember if it had ever been fired in all her time in Orkney. 'Well, that's good to know. Keeping us safe.'

Hamthir looked pleased.

'We all do what we have to do,' he murmured.

'Where are you all off to?' Sigrid asked.

'Oh, just out for a walk,' said Hamthir. 'I think Beinir wanted to see something out this direction. And Ingvar here likes his exercise, don't you, Ingvar?' He squeezed his brother's arm, which he had been holding. 'He runs, and he doesn't always know where he's going. But this will tire him out a bit.'

Ingvar did not look remotely tired out – the impression was one of an irrepressible puppy - but he grinned at Sigrid.

'Hello, Ingvar,' she said. 'Do you like Birsay?'

'He doesn't say much,' Hamthir put in quickly. 'He fell when he was only a lad, hit his head on some rocks. But he always seems happy.'

'That's good. I'm glad you're enjoying yourself, Ingvar.'

Ingvar chuckled, and indeed he did seem happy. He might not have been clever, but he felt like a very easy person to be with, Sigrid thought: not something she often found with strangers.

'Oh, so you're Sigrid?' Beinir broke off suddenly from the conversation with Helga to look over at her. 'I mean, I remembered you were called Sigrid, of course,' he added quickly, though he probably had not, 'but I hadn't realised you were the Sigrid that lives up here. Ah, that explains it!'

'Explains what?' asked Helga, keen to draw him back to her. Beinir looked at Sigrid rather intently for a moment, then turned back to Helga. 'Oh, I'm sorry, it was something Thorfinn mentioned. About Sigrid holding a farm out this direction – that's right, isn't it?'

'Yes,' said Sigrid, instantly suspicious. What was Thorfinn up to? 'You're standing on it.'

'Oh, I see!' He looked about him. 'Well, meagre means are no shame, are they?' He smiled, oblivious, presumably, to Sigrid's bristling. The others, however, seemed to notice: there was an awkward little silence, then Helga and Sigrid began to speak at once. Sigrid, crosser, won.

'I'll head home. Plenty to do.' She bundled her cloak around her and strode off down the hill, doing her best not to slither in the mud. Dignity was important when one was offended.

The trouble was she agreed with him – she was not ashamed of her farm, where she worked hard and which just about sustained her. That did not give a stranger the right to say so, though. All the way down the hill she constructed damning and witty responses to what he had said, but she was still cross when she reached her own door. Helga's flatbreads were warm against her stomach, and she was pleased to find that Gnup had already prodded the fire into life with a pot of broth over it for the midday meal. Gnup was a cheerful lad, and hard to be cross with, even for Sigrid. She made herself relax and did her best to forget about ill-mannered visitors who would have gone soon, anyway. The sooner the better.

The visitors from Shapinsay lingered about the place like the smell of fish. Tosti explained that their report was very complicated, though as far as Sigrid could see they spent little time in Tosti's office. Beinir in particular seemed to wander up and down the path to Kirkuvagr, passing close to her own longhouse and often stopping to chat as she sat in the dregs of the daylight working on her tablets – no doubt he was being entertained by Helga, she thought with a grin. But it was when she realised that, on the evenings when she went to help in the hall, she was mostly directed to serve the Shapinsay visitors, she began to wonder if someone had a scheme in mind. In a quiet moment she sat back and observed them, Hamthir's quiet efficiency, his brother's hard-suppressed energy, Aslak's unapproachable silence, Beinir … yes, Beinir was most likely. Sigrid's husband had been a warrior in Einar's hird, and Einar was one of Thorfinn's closest counsellors – Thorfinn would not expect Sigrid to marry a boatman unless she really wanted to. If he were arranging something – and Thorfinn did like things to be tidy - it would be for Beinir.

Hm, Beinir.

She knew he was single, and he was undoubtedly well-built. He was the head man on Shapinsay, so he had standing – and no doubt, though she would not give up her woolwork for her own household and for friends, she would not have to work on it in every moment of daylight God gave. She knew one day either her eyes or her fingers would fail her: if she were not part of a household when that happened, then Thorfinn and Ingibjorg would have to take her in and that would be unbearable. So marrying Beinir would have its advantages.

But she had good cause to know what an unhappy marriage was like. She would not – certainly not to please Thorfinn – rush into this. She had not found Beinir particularly engaging, it was true, but maybe that was good: she was not dazzled, like some young thing in love. On first impressions she found him … well, boring and sanctimonious.

Hm.

She tried to watch him without seeming obvious: he was singing a song for the company after the meal, and had a decent, light voice, but then Sigrid was not musical enough to feel that a good voice made up for tedious company otherwise. She looked about the room. She would have liked someone to talk to about it, but Helga was certainly not the right person and Ketil was not in the hall. In fact, she had barely seen him since he had called to ask about her farm – weeks ago. He must be busy on Thorfinn's instructions somewhere, eating in someone else's hall. For a moment, she felt very slightly lonely.

She shook herself, as the song finished and Beinir, to polite applause, returned to his place. He bowed to those seated near him.

'A prudent man wields his power in modest measure,' he told them. 'With brave men he finds that none is foremost or excels in all things.'

She shuddered. After all, this was entirely speculation. Thorfinn might have absolutely nothing in mind. She might be completely wrong.

Two days later she found out she was not.

'A good bit of land running down to the shore on Shapinsay – the south side of it,' Thorfinn was saying. 'He tells me things are in good order there, nice and peaceful, good farming land. I believe he had sheep …' He eyed her expectantly. Fortunately Beinir himself was not there, which had given her a moment of hope when she was summoned to the hall. Ingibjorg was, though, looking as pleased with herself as a sheep that's broken into the infield and started on the vegetables.

'Land alone does not a good marriage make,' said Sigrid. It was the kind of thing that Beinir might say. 'Not even sheep. And what about my sheep? They might not like it.'

'You could sell them to – to whoever takes on your farm.'

This time Sigrid gave Thorfinn a look. It was pretty clear he had someone in mind. Who could it be? Maybe one of Ketil's men was looking for a place to settle down. Technically the land belonged to Einar, under Thorfinn, but Einar barely moved from his fireside these days and Thorfinn had been overseeing Einar's estates more directly for some time. Could one of Einar's men want it? She doubted it: none of them had the energy anymore. Or perhaps there were no plans at all: Ingibjorg might just want Sigrid off her doorstep, and Beinir might have mentioned looking for a wife. There might not be too many options on Shapinsay.

'Well,' Thorfinn sighed, 'nothing's settled. Give it some thought. He'll be going back to Shapinsay soon: perhaps you could go with him, take a look at the place? See what he's like on his own land?'

'Go to Shapinsay with him?'

'Yes, why not? It's winter. Gnup can look after your animals, and no doubt you can pack some wool. Meet his neighbours, talk to his friends, to the other women around. See if it's something you might consider.'

'And how does Beinir feel about this?' Sigrid asked.

'Oh, it was his idea,' said Thorfinn. Ingibjorg's expression wriggled subtly – no doubt she had put the idea into Beinir's head. Oh, heavens, was that what Beinir had been doing, pretending to walk up the Kirkuvagr path just to call in and see her? When she thought he had been visiting Helga?

'Would you take a cup of spiced wine, Sigrid?' asked Ingibjorg with honey in her voice. 'You look a little pale.'

'I think I need some fresh air,' said Sigrid. 'Thank you for the thought, my lord. I shall certainly consider it.'

And she had to. She had to consider it, unappealing as it was.

Outside, she decided she needed a good walk, and made her way through the tangle of new buildings towards the cliff edges of the Brough, watching the grey sea beating the sliced rock below. Looking back along the coast towards her little longhouse, she noticed a head in the water – a seal? No: a man, swimming. She shivered in sympathy. Arms sliced neatly through the waves, beating as efficiently as oars. He was heading back to the stepped and jagged shore where she could see a cloak lying, flapping idly in the wind to summon him back. He pulled himself out of the water with an enviable lack of effort, and as he bent to wrap himself in the cloak – Helga would have enjoyed the moment - she realised it was Ketil. He had time to swim, then, but no time to come and talk to his old friend. Sulking a little, she turned away and began a circuit of the breezy Brough, and only when she had gone too far to bother did she think she could have caught him on his way back up the hill and asked him what he thought about Beinir.

She completed her circuit and, feeling chilled, decided to drop in to Thorfinn's hall to see if she was needed that evening. Inside was Bolla, the maid, tidying the detritus left by too many men living in too small a space, and a few of the said men, apparently admiring the tapestries.

'Hello, Sigrid!' said Bolla. 'Have you ever seen anything like the mess in here? There's some of them can barely roll up their own bedding without falling over it.'

'Keeps us busy,' Sigrid agreed, managing to get close to the warm hearth and help Bolla pick up stray belongings at the same time. The two men, disturbed by their chat, looked around.

'These are fine tapestries,' said one, and she saw that it was Hamthir from Shapinsay, one arm about his poor brother. The other one, the sour-faced Aslak, had more of an eye for Bolla, but she ignored him.

'Sigrid designed them!' she said, before Sigrid could stop her. Sigrid blushed to her headcloth.

'Did she?' Hamthir stood back, giving the tapestries a more considered examination. 'That's very impressive, Sigrid!'

'I had a lot of help,' she said, mangling the words. She went across to him, hoping that not shouting across the hall would make it better. Bolla, the coward, slipped out by the side door. Aslak watched her go. 'And we haven't finished yet – the daylight was growing too short. We'll start again in the spring.'

'Expensive, eh?'

'Oh, only the best for Ingibjorg!' Sigrid was on happier ground here. 'That's gold thread, you know, even though I told her it was horrible to work with. It has a mind of its own, never sits the way you want it to.'

'So she spent the money anyway?' He had an odd little smile, though she thought he was a likeable man.

'She did, or Thorfinn did. As I say, only the best for her.'

'Sigrid!' It was Bolla again. 'Have you seen Ketil?'

'He's just out of the bath house. He was heading up to the church.' One of his men – Skorri? – had appeared at the doorway just at a useful moment. He had yet another visitor with him: Thorfinn would have to tax them all for he would be ruined trying to feed everyone.

'I'll go and fetch him,' Sigrid said.

'Tell him Thorfinn wants to speak to him – and her ladyship says to tell him not to linger,' said Bolla, vanishing back towards the side door.

It was the matter of a few moments to climb up to the church and round to Tosti's office. Tosti was waving some papers around, apparently uncharacteristically cross.

'That,' he was saying, his lips tight, 'is the report of Beinir, head man on Shapinsay. Beinir can read and write. And this,' he laid the bundle down with infinite gentleness, 'this is the result.'

She felt her heart give a little leap, and before she could stop herself she snapped out,

'Beinir can read and write?'

Ketil looked mildly startled

'How do you know Beinir?' he asked. Sigrid opened her mouth to explain, but now she did not want to: she wanted to digest this new information. Someone who could read and write? That put a different gloss on Beinir indeed.

'Never mind that now,' she said briskly. 'Sorry to interrupt, Tosti. Ketil, Thorfinn wants a word, and Sh – er, Ingibjorg says it's urgent.'

She was astonished at the effect her words had.

Ketil rose from the stool where he had been sitting. If it had not been Ketil, she would almost have sworn that he was shaking.

'Are you all right?' she asked. 'Is it a fever?' She reached out a hand. 'Ketil, are you ill?'

He pushed through the doorway, past his men, and strode down the hill. For a second she paused, shocked, then ran after him. He looked as if he were being summoned to his execution: she could not leave him.

III

The cave lay ahead of him, the rough edges teeth and claws, the black mouth gaping. Why did he have to go in? He could feel the heat from here. But he gripped his sword and drifted, somehow, towards that dark maw.

And then there was something else in the darkness, a glow, deep and red, confusing the eye. Why could he not stop? Something was very wrong here. The glow flared. Yellow and amber blazed. The dragon spun and lunged in one instant. It burned, fire from its mouth, from its eyes, from everywhere. The cave was an oven: his nostrils filled with the sweet stench of burning flesh. He backed towards the entrance, hands fumbling for support, then turned and ran.

Panting, he woke. A few paces away, the central hearth in Thorfinn's hall smouldered, but someone must have thrown in some broken piece of wood that flickered busily in one corner. The seeds of a dragon? He was sweating. He scoured his sleeve across his forehead, and turned on to his stomach, watching the little flame rise, and ease, and die. Now he could sleep again, he thought – but sleep was hard to find.

'She's going to Shapinsay?'

'That's what they're saying, sir.'

'To Shapinsay?'

'Aye, sir. Are you fighting or what, sir?'

Ketil shifted his hand on his sword hilt as if to remind himself that it was there, and attacked. He and Skorri were well used to each other's fighting style, even when they tried to take one another by surprise. The swords clattered and slid together, and Ketil grunted as he lunged and pulled back. It was good to feel the sword in his hand, good to force his muscles to move, his limbs to obey his commands even before he had thought them. Muscle and limb worked well – the same could not be said for his head.

He knew very well why Sigrid was going to Shapinsay, but he just could not take in the reality of it. It was Beinir, great lumping boring self-satisfied Beinir, that was who it was. He had met the man twice, and so he was entitled to his well-considered opinion. Why was she giving up her little farm to marry Beinir? He knew Sigrid: she would stab Beinir with a binding needle within a month out of sheer boredom. And as for Shapinsay … well, nothing ever happened on Shapinsay. Two months and if she couldn't find a boat she would swim home. It was Beinir he felt sorry for, he decided. The man should be warned before it was too late.

He slithered on the soggy grass in the sloped open field above the chapel: it was always wet up here. Skorri nicked his elbow with his swordpoint, and laughed as Ketil snatched his arm back.

'Sorry,' he said, 'I wasn't expecting you to fall over.'

Ketil inspected his ripped shirtsleeve, and felt the soggy knee of his breeches cling to his skin, cold as a fish.

'My fault,' he said, pressing his arm to stop the bleeding. 'My mind is wandering.'

'Thinking of your pretty bride?' Skorri sheathed his wiped sword and came to poke Ketil on his good arm. 'She'd keep any man distracted.'

'She's not my bride yet,' said Ketil.

'Affianced bride, then,' Skorri corrected himself good-naturedly. 'Good looking, used to running a house, and – *and* – Earl Thorfinn's daughter! What did you do, my friend? Save his life?'

Ketil shook his head. He had no idea why he had been selected for this honour: it was not the kind of question you asked, or the kind of offer you declined. The only thing he could see in its favour, just at the moment, was that Asgerdr herself seemed content with the idea. To be married to Asgerdr against her wishes – well, he might even be worse off than Beinir.

'Is the wedding date set?' Skorri asked. Ketil wished he would stop talking about it.

'Midwinter,' he said. 'Three weeks away.'

Before that Sigrid would have left for Shapinsay with Beinir.

'That'll be a feast and a half!' Skorri remarked with satisfaction. 'I'm looking forward to that!'

Ketil wished he could say the same.

Geirod and Alf were running nearby, racing each other over the sodden ground, and for a while Ketil and Skorri joined them until all four were decently tired and sweating. Alf ran like an absent-minded saint, seeking wonders, while Geirod tucked his head down and charged, armed to the teeth with his own ferocious determination. Both nodded when Ketil suggested a visit to the bath house by the cliff for some hot steam: they could already feel their faces prickling with the cold.

They had to withstand it a little longer, though, for they had arrived at a popular time for baths. They joined the queue propped against the bath house wall.

'Every man and his mother here,' Geirod grumbled.

'Does Thorfinn have his own bath house?' Skorri asked Ketil. Skorri was partial to a little grandeur. Ketil shrugged.

'I don't think so. No, I'm sure I've seen him here.'

'Aye, everyone,' Geirod nodded, as if that just confirmed his point.

'Good day to you!' came a voice from behind them. A tall, red-headed man had joined the queue. 'Margad,' he reminded them.

'Of course,' said Ketil. 'I'm afraid like us you've picked a busy time.'

'Yes, looks like it.' Margad eyed the line of people in front of him, running a hand through his fine red hair. 'I don't mind so much, but the dog will get restless.' He kicked the yellow dog sharply with his heel. 'I don't like him barking and annoying people.'

The dog looked like the last creature in the world who would set out intentionally to annoy anyone.

'I'll take him off for a walk if you like,' said Alf. 'If you want to wait.'

'Oh, no, no,' said Margad, looking at the state of their clothing after their exercise on the hill, 'I think your need is greater than mine. Come on, dog. I'll try again later.' He encouraged the dog with another kick, and added a few more for guidance as he and the dog headed back towards the hall. The dog walked close behind him as if it hardly dared breathe.

'That is not a man I like,' Alf remarked quietly.

'He seems popular enough,' Ketil said.

'Aye, with the ladies,' added Skorri. 'But half that will be to do with the money. He's rich, they say. That's a nice belt he has.'

'That he's taking off,' Geirod said suddenly, still watching Margad. The others turned, and watched with disgust as Margad lashed out at the dog with the belt, three times, as if he had deliberately chosen the number. He wiped the belt off as a warrior would with his sword, and replaced it at his slim waist. The dog cowered behind his ankles. Margad grabbed it by its collar, and hauled it off and out of sight.

'I should not like to be under his command,' said Alf, and the others nodded.

'Is he one of the Shapinsay crowd?' asked Geirod.

'No, though he has been a good deal in their company. He's from Caithness,' said Ketil, 'and if Thorfinn sees him there will be trouble. He does not care for those who hurt dogs.'

'He has that wee lapdog, has he not?' asked Skorri, interested in anything the high heidyins did. 'It's a strange choice for a great man.'

'The dog belonged to Rognvald, his nephew,' said Ketil shortly. 'After Rognvald's death he took it. And cared for it,' he added.

The queue made a sudden surge forward, and in a few minutes they were all undoing their frozen muscles in the steam room, their muddy clothes abandoned at the door for washing. It was bliss, and with a bath to follow they felt collectively ready for anything – even for supper in the Great Hall. Ketil braced himself to assume his position as Thorfinn's prospective son-in-law – the words still echoed unconvincingly round his head. He loathed sitting up at the head of the hall by Thorfinn and Sheep Face – Ingibjorg (he needed to stop listening to Sigrid if he were to survive this marriage), with Asgerdr perching at his side, clutching at his arm and pouring him more wine every time he took as much as a sip. He much preferred an obscure bench, with or without his own men, quiet near the door, where he could watch and not be watched.

Why had he said yes?

Because he could not have said no.

The hall was filling up, busier than usual with all the visitors to the Brough. He lost track of his own men, but thought they might split up anyway: Alf and Geirod, like him, preferred obscurity, while Skorri could not resist the attraction of being where he could at least see the great Earl Thorfinn and his family, as if a little of the glory would polish his own sword. Margad, he noticed, was also near the head of the hall, quite at his ease, brushing his hair back out of his face. Beinir was further down, in what seemed to be his best clothes for the occasion, and his Shapinsay friends were with him – the angry-looking Aslak was already downing ale as if it might run out. The woman serving him sighed in a way visible even from this distance, and refilled his cup. She turned to deal with the next man, and he saw that it was Sigrid, her hair already struggling out from under her headcloth, her sleeves rolled up ready for a hard evening's work. Her expression was nothing better than resigned. He wondered if she were marrying for money – there had been all that talk about taxes and woolwork, after all. Was that her only reason? Reason good enough, though, if it meant survival. And Sigrid had always struck him as sensible.

An elbow in his ribs distracted him. It was Asgerdr, of course.

'Do you like the way this pork is cooked?' she asked. 'Someone from Hoy brought the recipe.'

'It's – very good,' he said, though he took another bite just to check. He had not even noticed that he had eaten some of it already. She smiled.

'I'm glad you like it. I thought we might have it at our wedding feast.'

'If it pleases you, then of course.'

Wedding feast. He let the words slither back out of his head again, almost unrecognised.

Sigrid had followed him down to the hall when Thorfinn had summoned him – of course she had, for she was always nosy, even as a girl. She had not quite come into the hall itself but he knew she had lingered at the doorway, just out of sight of Thorfinn and Ingibjorg. Sensible Sigrid, she had not fallen into a state of shock at the news like a man struck on the head in battle.

'Now there's advancement for you!' she had said at once when he came out. She slapped him on the arm. 'Well done! You're going up in the world!'

He had tried hard to smile. Perhaps for once she had even admired him.

'No longer a worry to you, eh?' he had said. 'That will please you.'

'Exactly,' she had said brightly. 'I can pass any responsibility for you over to Asgerdr. I'm sure she can cope.'

Yet she had seemed a little distant, all the same. No doubt even then her thoughts were full of Beinir and her own future, away on Shapinsay.

The elbow in the ribs again. There was little excess flesh on his affianced wife: she could go into battle with those elbows.

'More wine, my dear?' she asked. She was not too shy to stare straight into his eyes, making the most, he thought, of her own very fine eyes. Or making sure he was paying attention. He could not help noticing a note of triumph in her expression, and it puzzled him. Surely he was not a very good catch? She could have been married off to some great man in Caithness, or Norway, or further afield, and he had never had the impression that she was particularly fond of her home and family. He was just one of her father's men, one with whom she had occasionally felt it useful to flirt, but not one, he thought, in whom she had had much interest. So if she did not love him and she did not consider him a trophy, why did she – and Ingibjorg, now he came to think of it – both look as if they had won a particularly complex game of King's Table?

The evening dragged on. The food was cleared from the tables, leaving only some bread and cheese to soak up any excess wine or ale. Tosti quietly absented himself, as did some of those with homes to go to, and others took the chance to head for the midden for relief, or out for a breath of fresh air. Suddenly feeling suffocated, he stood and with the least bow to Asgerdr he headed out too. The wind engulfed him as he stepped outside the hall, and for a moment he stared into the darkness of the sea to the north, feeling its pull. Would he be allowed to go away again? Would Thorfinn be allowed to send him off to work for him? Or had Asgerdr and Ingibjorg more plans for his future? What could they possibly need from him?

The hall seemed to have emptied around him: he wondered if everyone else had felt the meal as dull as he had. Skorri slapped his shoulder on the way past, and Alf and Geirod called a greeting. He glimpsed Beinir, and his angry-looking companion Aslak, and, he thought, the boatman who had brought the others from Shapinsay. Aslak broke away from the other Shapinsay men with some short comment – the wind caught it and whipped it far from Ketil's ears. And as if it were important that no one should be left to attend Thorfinn in the hall, the tall Caithness man Margad appeared, smiling at nothing in particular, and wove his way off in the general direction of the midden, the yellow dog skulking behind him. An appreciator of Ingibjorg's ale, then, Ketil thought, or perhaps he had been further enough up the table to be offered wine. Whatever he had drunk there had been a little too much of it.

Ketil took a few steps closer to the cliff, letting the wind buffet his linen-wrapped arms and slap his shirt against his skin, cooling him. The hall was always too warm when it was full, with the fire blazing in the centre. He would let the others finish their business and return before he went to the midden himself – he told himself he would round up any strays who might have lost their way in the dark. In truth, though, he was not keen to return too quickly to his place by Asgerdr's side. No doubt it was the novelty: he was not accustomed to being kept so close to someone. He would grow used to it.

By the time he wandered over, there was no one left by the midden except one elderly man making laboured use of two crutches.

'Are you all right, there?' Ketil asked, seeing the man sway.

'Aye, lad!' said the man, clearly a bit offended. 'I've been pissing on my own since I was a bairn!'

Ketil grinned.

'Just making sure you weren't so drunk you'd fall in after,' he explained. 'But I can hear you're sober enough to manage.'

'It's true I'm not so steady on my feet as I used to be,' the old man conceded, 'but that's age and battle, not ale, I fear. Time was I could have drunk all night and still taken up my axe with a reliable hand, but these days – aye, well, it doesn't take much to make my head light. I go easy, you know?' He took a moment to arrange his crutches. Ketil could feel his sideways glance. 'You favour a sword yourself, though, don't you?'

'I do,' Ketil agreed. 'What's your axe like?'

'Oh, it's fine, lad! And still polished every day, I promise you!'

Talk of weaponry took them, at the old man's pace, back to the hall and with a sigh Ketil followed him inside, back to the heat and the bright lamplight. He caught Asgerdr's eye and made a little fuss of helping the old man back to his seat, then having a word with each of his men, before returning to her. It was a small act of defiance, he knew – childish, no doubt Sigrid would call it. But it felt somehow necessary.

'All well?' Thorfinn asked, leaning down from his great chair as Ketil returned.

'Yes, my lord.'

'No need to worry about old Hrut – he wears a path to the midden every night,' Thorfinn explained. 'He could find his way there drunk and asleep.'

Ketil nodded acknowledgement. Asgerdr handed him his cup of wine, as if pinning him into his seat. He was not sure why she was not helping serve with the other women – she was usually in charge these days, while her mother sat in state – but perhaps her new status of affianced bride allowed her some leeway. But if she could not serve everyone else, he wished she would stop trying to serve him. He preferred not to drink much: he liked to keep an eye on what was happening around him. It was a policy that had saved his life more than once.

And even now he was glad to be alert. Across the hall there was some disturbance, just around the Shapinsay men. The little cross man, what was his name? Aslak? He was on his feet, fists raised, ready to do battle. Ketil looked to see who had provoked him. A tall man, older than Aslak, stomach sagging like an elderly yow, stood before him, fists on his hips, head back in laughter. Ketil recognised him as a visitor from … Westray, wasn't it? Wherever it was, Aslak had had enough of him.

The little man launched himself against the Westray lump, fists like rocks pounding into the man's slumped stomach. The Westray man stopped laughing, belatedly, and grabbed Aslak by the shoulder, trying to hold him far enough away that Aslak could not reach him. But he was not entirely sober, and his grip kept slipping, letting Aslak land enough blows to make the big man howl.

Ketil was already on his feet, making his way round to the Shapinsay men. But from next to where Aslak had been sitting, Beinir rose, an expression of concern on his handsome face.

'Aslak, Aslak, pray stop! I'm sure the man meant nothing by his words – it was only a jest!'

With some authority he stepped between the two fighters. Ketil had just an instant to catch sight of Sigrid standing, open-mouthed, prepared to be impressed, when there was a nasty thump and Beinir fell to the floor. Which of the quarrelling men had hit him was not entirely clear, but they were obviously not at all concerned to see him go. Beinir rolled over and pulled himself on to his hands and knees, retreating, dazed, to his seat. Ketil stepped over and took the tall man swiftly backwards with an arm around his neck.

'Enough, or you'll finish your evening on the other side of the hall door,' he hissed in the man's ear. When he let go, the man sat, suddenly, on the floor. Aslak looked from him to Ketil and chose to return to his seat. The incident was over in a matter of moments, and Ketil, checking to see that both men were compliant, turned to go back to his own place.

On the way he met old Hrut, shuffling to the door for the third time. Ketil watched him go, and let his gaze swing on around the hall as he returned to his seat. He had a niggling feeling someone else was missing – had been for a while.

'Where's that fellow Margad?' he asked, of no one in particular.

'Margad? The man from Caithness?' Asgerdr looked about. 'I haven't seen him since before the food was cleared.'

'But he's sleeping here, isn't he?'

'Yes, he is, certainly,' said Asgerdr. 'I don't think he really knows anyone else in Birsay. He's probably at the midden.' But she continued to study the emptying tables, concerned.

'He can't have been there all this time,' said Ketil. He thought back over the evening. 'I saw him go out when the food was cleared, and he was not at the midden when I came back in. But you're right: I don't remember seeing him since, either.'

'Who have you lost now?' A familiar voice came from over his shoulder. He turned away from Asgerdr to find Sigrid behind him, holding a newly-filled jug. She twisted to support it on her hip.

'Have you seen Margad?' he asked.

'Thought you'd have your mind on other things. No,' she went on, looking about the hall. 'Mind you, I don't see Bolla either. Coincidence? I gather your friend Margad has some success with the girls. Perhaps it's catching.' She swung the jug back in front of her, and walked off.

'What did she say?' asked Asgerdr, a hint of irritation in her voice

'She said she hadn't seen him for a while,' said Ketil.

'I'm sure Margad can look after himself,' she said, then added with slightly too much appreciation for a newly-affianced woman, 'He looks strong.'

'Strong, yes, but perhaps he has lost his way in the dark.' Even as he said it Ketil realised it sounded unlikely. The light spilling from the hall door could easily be seen from just next to the midden: it would take someone to be extraordinarily confused to miss their way. 'If you'll excuse me, I think perhaps I should go and look.'

'But the music is about to start!' said Asgerdr. For a moment she looked very like her mother, her face twisting between irritation and an intent to charm. At the thought that Asgerdr might really take after Ingibjorg Ketil shuddered, and jumped to his feet.

'I won't be long,' he said, and hurried out of the hall, taking a torch as he went.

Outside he found himself pausing for breath, as though he had run uphill. The torch flame bent across and threatened for a moment to go out, and he angled it to save it, the few seconds' concentration helping to focus his mind. Had Margad gone to the midden? If he had, where could he have lost his way? If not, where might a man, who knew few on the Brough and knew the Brough ill enough, have decided to go in the dark, in the middle of a feast?

He pictured his memory of Margad standing there in the doorway, taking in the fresh, dark air, his yellow dog at his feet.

Perhaps he had just wanted to stretch his legs. Why not? And if he had, and had been properly wary of losing his way in an unfamiliar settlement on the edge of a cliff, then where might he have gone? Well, thought Ketil, the most sensible thing to do would simply be to walk around the great hall.

He turned right, and began to do likewise.

Walking with the torch flame tilted, he stepped with care from flag to flag, trying to watch the ground and keep aware of anything else that might be going on around him. The wind was always a barrier between attacker and attacked: one had to be extra careful. But who would attack him here, right outside Earl Thorfinn's hall? He laughed a little to himself: he could probably make a list.

He had almost reached the corner of the hall when the torchlight jumped and rolled about something dark and lumpy against the outer wall of the hall. Bolla the maid sat with her back against the wall, her skirts rucked up about her thighs, and a look in her eyes that was very far away. Beside her lay Margad, face down in the mud, two bundles cast aside. One more glance around in case it was a trap, and Ketil approached, blinked, and knelt to touch Margad's throat.

Whatever had been the intention here, at least for now Margad was   still   alive.

IV

The middle of winter. The perfect time, of course, to take a tour to inspect a potential new home.

New people, a new settlement, new – what was Beinir? Not betrothed, barely friend, but still potential husband? Thorfinn had kindly backed off from actually arranging a betrothal between Sigrid and Beinir – he knew better than to cross a woman when it came to marriage – but Ingibjorg at least seemed to think it was only a thread's breadth away from being a done thing. And whichever it was, here she was now, loading a selection of her limited possessions (weaving tablets, binding needles, wool baskets, and a few clothes) into Hamthir's sturdy little boat, and trying not to catch anyone's eye, to look cheerful. It was a Sunday, but the tides were right and the weather fair – they had all gone to church as Thorfinn's followers should, then made their last preparations. Gnup at least had come to see her off.

'Now you know what to do, don't you?' Sigrid asked him, possibly for the twelfth time.

'Yes, Sigrid,' he replied with a grin.

'Send me word if you need me. I'll come back, you know, quick as I can.'

'I know.' He was a cheerful lad, but she knew he had a knack for seeing behind words. He knew she knew she could rely on him: it was her own future, not her farm's, that made her anxious.

'Are you ready, Sigrid?' Hamthir was eager to go with the tide: it was understandable. But her feet seemed somehow reluctant to shift from the flat stones of the beach, as if they were weighted down. She cast a glance upwards, towards the buildings on the Brough. The path to the harbour was busy, as usual, but there was no one in particular she could see hurrying down to see her off, to wish her well. She felt, for a moment, tears rise in her eyes – after all, the wind was cold, and it had been a late night last night, it was nothing to do with any kind of emotion except, perhaps, mild frustration at Thorfinn's eagerness to organise people. Why couldn't he let well alone?

'Sigrid!' called Hamthir.

If she did not board now, her wool would go without her. That was an alarming prospect. She scrambled over the gunwale, helped by Beinir and the boy Ingvar, and slid across to find a comfortable perch, tugging her cloak around her against the sea winds. She gave one more look upwards to the Brough – and yes, there was someone standing to watch as Hamthir and Ingvar pushed off from the beach. Tall, still, gaze fixed on Hamthir's little boat, cloak catching the wind and billowing behind.

It was Ingibjorg, come to make sure she left.

'It seems awful to leave when we don't know whether or not Margad and the girl will be all right,' Beinir commented, as they rounded the headland of the Brough to head east. His deep, soft voice was a little hard to make out but she tried not to frown. He rowed easily in these conditions, Sigrid noted, matching his stroke to the shorter arms of Aslak on the other side. Hamthir and Ingvar saw to the steering – well, Hamthir did. Ingvar mostly smiled.

'It was quite a knock he had, whatever happened,' Sigrid agreed. A late night indeed.

Ketil had appeared at the hall doorway, calling for hurdles: he could not clearly see Margad's injuries in the dark and had not wanted to move him on his own. When they had brought the man in, it turned out to be a cracked head, though whether he had tripped and hit it on the wall of the hall, or had had some assistance in the injury was not clear. Sigrid, though, had been one of the women detailed to take care of Margad in the quiet of Thorfinn's longhouse: with Ketil standing by, detailed by Thorfinn to look into incidents such as – well, anything out of the ordinary – she and a couple of other women had removed Margad's damp, cold clothes, cleaned his head wound and dressed it, and noted with some interest the broad, long bruises that were developing across Margad's back. There were four or five of them. It seemed Margad could be grateful for his fine sealskin kirtle, for it had taken the brunt of the damage – he had been whipped.

Bolla, though, was more of a worry.

She had been assaulted, that much was clear, but by whom? By Margad? She had no other injuries anyone could find, but while they had undressed her and wrapped her in blankets and laid her in a warm bed, and given her hot wine, she had said nothing. Not a word. Sigrid wondered if Bolla had said anything this morning. It was horrible to have to leave when poor Bolla was in such a state, and not to know what was happening. But she would be in good hands, amongst the rest of Ingibjorg's household.

Ketil had decided, some time in the early hours, that Margad's whipping should not be mentioned publicly: the other women were well-practised at discretion, being the ones who saw to births and deaths, and they seemed to respect Ketil. She had wondered, though, why Ketil had wanted to keep the whipmarks secret: she would have asked him, but at that point Asgerdr had come in, and the moment passed.

'I think he'll be all right, though,' Sigrid said to Beinir. 'I mean, you never know with head injuries, but he hadn't been hit too hard, whether it was accident or design. He'll not be happy for a few days, I should think. Bolla, though, I'm not so sure …'

'By design?' Beinir queried in alarm. 'You mean you think someone might have attacked him? Right outside Thorfinn's hall?'

'Fights happen,' said Sigrid with a shrug. 'Particularly after a feast – and in the winter, when men are bored.' She should not have to be telling him that. Perhaps life on Shapinsay was really very quiet.

When they had rounded the Brough, a nippy wind allowed Hamthir to raise the flapping sail and they sped along the sound between the mainland and the northern islands. On a good day you would be able to see them clearly, but today was damp and cold, the mists that Ketil disliked so much blurring outlines and carrying rain back and forth – rarely just down – to dribble under one's hood and up one's sleeves. Glistening grey seals, guarding their yellow-white pups, regarded them from tiny skerries as they passed. Sigrid kept tight hold of the carved boards of her bag, the one with the best wool and the sets of weaving tablets and the binding needles. Yes, the needles and the tablets could be replaced, but it took years to work them down to just the right smoothness, to wear off any little snags that could catch a thread and spoil it. Her best needle was reddish brown pearwood, given to her by a grateful warrior years ago from some orchard further south: it ran beautifully across the skin, and never snagged. She would swim hard before she would allow that to go to the bottom of the sound.

She thought she ought to try to make conversation, now that Beinir did not have to row, but her mouth felt tight and unsure of itself.

'How are you after last night? Were you badly hurt?'

Beinir smiled and nodded, acknowledging her concern. He even put out a reassuring hand that almost, but not quite, touched her knee.

'Just winded, really! As they say, it makes sense to set off home when guest mocks guest, Who can tell at the table if he laughs with angry men?'

'Ah, yes, of course,' said Sigrid. She had heard it somewhere before. Perhaps Beinir had read it somewhere – the thought sent a little shiver up her spine. Imagine learning things from a piece of sheepskin? From little squiggles made of oak galls? A thought occurred to her: if he really did know how to read and write, and they married – would he teach her? Maybe she could even make it a condition of marriage? What an idea! She sneaked a look at him, trying to assess if he might agree to such a thing. He met her eye and smiled again, encouragingly, and she turned away. The wind would hide her blushes.

They reached Shapinsay at nightfall – not that that was late, at this time of year. They had made good time in the wind, and Hamthir steered them neatly around a small headland into a sheltered dip in the coast, with a beach barely big enough to be called a harbour but good enough, certainly, for the selection of small vessels pulled up there. These were the boats that kept working through the winter: others would be tucked into nousts, under repair or undergoing maintenance, like mice in their burrows. Above this bay, the land barely rose at first: as far as she could see the nearest longhouse was about at the height of her nose. The island stretched out to her right, where there seemed to be low hills, and ahead of her, too, but it was flatter there. True to form, the inhabitants mostly seemed to have built their longhouses along this low coast, ends on to the water so that those to her right faced away from her and those ahead of her had their doors in this direction, as far as she could see. She had been told the land was good, rich and fertile – as to that she would have to wait and see, for just now it was starting to disappear under a thickening layer of white.

'Well!' said Beinir, standing on the beach with his fists on his hips, 'there's a sight you don't often see! I'll reckon it as a blessing on your visit. What do you think, Sigrid?'

'I think,' said Sigrid, jumping over the gunwale with her precious bag clutched under her arm, 'that a warm fire would be most welcome.' Then she thought that sounded rather rude, and added, rashly, 'And I'm looking forward to seeing where you live, Beinir!'

If she blinked through the falling flakes she could still make out the comfortable rounded bundles of longhouses set along the line of the shore, up above the tideline. She thought she counted four or five but she would have to look again later: the snow was growing thicker and it was nearly as much as she could do to keep track of Beinir's green hood. Aslak grunted farewell and headed straight up from the harbour, disappearing beyond the houses she could see, so there must at least be one more house in that direction. Hamthir loaded their baggage on to a handcart left above the tideline and started to roll it up to the path in front of the houses.

'Snaw!' came a cry, and Ingvar sprang past him, dancing like a March hare in the falling flakes, bounding from one to another of them. 'Snaw!' He pointed wildly at the sky, as though they might have missed the phenomenon. Arms wheeling, he ran round them, then to the boat and back, laughing and calling with delight, face upturned to catch as many flakes as he could, his long tongue licking off the ones he could reach. It was hard not to enjoy his joy: Sigrid found herself grinning even as the flakes stuck to her own face.

'Come on, you fool,' grumbled Hamthir, though it was easy to see he was smiling, too. 'You'll freeze out here.' He seized Ingvar by the arm, abandoning the handcart, and waved farewell to Beinir and Sigrid. 'I'll have to get him indoors or he'll dance all night!'

Ingvar continued to twist and turn at the end of Hamthir's grasp, but eventually Hamthir pushed him in through the doorway of a darkened house near the harbour. Beinir took the handles of the cart without rancour and pushed it further along the path. Sigrid followed, blinking away snowflakes, clutching her bag to her stomach. She abandoned the effort to take in the layout of the area, and simply watched where her feet were going. It was growing darker every moment as if the night was in a hurry to slide down over them. Surely it could not be much further?

Beinir paused to make sure she was close behind, then waved a hand to the left.

'Here we are,' he said. 'No doubt Katrin will have the fire lit.'

'Katrin?'

'She's the servant – didn't I mention her? You're not going straight into a cold house, I should think! What a way to welcome you that would be!'

'Oh, yes.' Sigrid nodded. Some mention of a servant had indeed been made – at the time she had only taken it as reassurance that she would not be stuck with Beinir in a longhouse on her own. In the rush to pack and sort out Gnup and leave, she had not given Katrin further thought, but in a moment she would find out what like of a woman she was.

Katrin stood at the fire when she heard the door open, with a smile to welcome her master home.

Hm, thought Sigrid. Young and pretty, and rather a nice smile, too. Should she turn around straightaway and sail back to Birsay? She had absolutely no wish to look a fool.

'You're back!' said Katrin in surprise. 'Does that mean Hamthir's back too?'

'He is, and quite safe,' said Beinir, his tone generous, as if he had been personally responsible for Hamthir's safe return. 'But it's snowing heavily out there: best to leave him till tomorrow.'

'Snowing?' Katrin's eyes widened in awe, and she gave Sigrid a little shy grin as she skipped past her to the doorway. 'Oh my! Snow!'

She stood there until Beinir suggested the house might warm faster with the door closed.

'You can stay here tonight, Katrin: there's no sense in you walking home in that, and anyway, I'd like you to stay with us for a while, for decency's sake.'

At that Katrin looked at Sigrid with even more interest, taking in the snow on her cloak, her carefully mended skirts, her headcloth that indicated a married woman.

'Beinir!' she breathed, and Sigrid realised that Katrin thought Beinir had brought back a wife.

'I'm Sigrid,' she said quickly. 'I've come to visit Beinir and see what Shapinsay is like. I'm a woolworker from Birsay.'

'Oh!' said Katrin, and her eyes went once again to the headcloth.

'I'm a widow,' Sigrid added, smiling helpfully. Katrin might not ask many questions with her lips, but her face did all the talking for her. Sigrid quite liked her, on first impressions. 'So I'm very glad you'll be in the house as well, or people might talk!'

'Oh!' said Katrin again, and giggled. Perhaps she thought Beinir was too old for that kind of thing. 'I'm Katrin, and I live up the hill – my parents do, anyway, and I work here. Oh! I wonder if there's enough food? I'm sorry, Sigrid, I wasn't expecting Beinir to bring back a guest.'

'I'm sure we'll manage, Katrin,' said Beinir comfortably, taking his own cloak and Sigrid's and hanging them near the fire to dry. He settled on the only chair, and gestured Sigrid to a fur-covered bench beside him. Sigrid hoped they would more than just manage. She was starving, and the smell of whatever Katrin had started to concoct – presumably for her own supper, as she could not have known Beinir was about to arrive – was very tempting. Katrin brought wine for both of them, then went to where the food was stored to add to her cooking pot, and Sigrid took the opportunity to look about her.

The longhouse was not huge, but it was substantially larger than her own one and Beinir must have had a different building for his animals: the whole house was set out for human habitation. All was kept very neatly, a credit to Katrin, no doubt, though Beinir did not seem an untidy man. The hanging shelves were free from dust and seemed orderly. The floor was swept, a feat Sigrid did not manage every day in her own house, she had to admit, and the cooking pots all looked clean, even polished. Under the cooking smell was a cool fragrance of dried herbs. She searched around for something where she could feel superior, even briefly. There: the blankets and hangings she could see, defining the different beds, were of good quality but not particularly new: they were probably the ones he had been brought up with, his mother's work, and as there had been no woman resident in the household since they would not have been replaced or augmented without necessity.

No woman resident in the household, though: the question niggled in Sigrid's mind as to why a well-set-up man like Beinir, undoubtedly handsome and, to judge by the longhouse, prosperous, had not married before. He did not look inclined to wear long shirts, or any other effeminate styles, and there was no hint of an overbearing mother who might have put him – or a prospective bride – off. She would have to try and find out. No doubt there would be a gossipy neighbour she could sit with some day soon, and get all the information she could about this man before she committed herself to anything. Thorfinn was too far away to rush her: she could take her time.

In the meantime it was pleasant sitting here, drowsy from the voyage, warming after the snow, her skirts steaming gently in the heat from the fire. Beinir and Katrin were exchanging news of his journey to Birsay and what had happened in his absence on Shapinsay: his low voice was curiously soporific, and she could feel her eyelids heavy, her shoulders slumping. Katrin had to rouse her a little to put a bowl of broth in her hands: she ate it with gratitude, and then was very happy to be shown to a clean bed space, helped to roll out bedding, and curtained about to be left in privacy. She quickly pulled off her outer layers and laid them to one side, afraid that otherwise she would simply fall asleep in them. Katrin had had the forethought to tuck a hot stone amongst the bedding earlier: the old blankets were soft and the newer furs thick, and in a moment she was cosy. Snow never lasted long in Orkney – the thought drifted through her mind like the snowflakes. Tomorrow she could have a proper look at the place she might consider calling home.

But the next morning, when she woke to the sounds of the household stirring, she heard Katrin's gasp of delight when she opened the door and knew they were still under snow. Bright air spiked through the smoke vents above her as Sigrid rolled on to her back: it might be one of those bright, cold days that were her favourite weather, even if she might struggle to warm her fingers over her weaving.

When she heard Katrin's soft footsteps crunching on the snow near the door again, she pulled a blanket about her shoulders and, with a nod to Katrin, headed off to follow her footprints to the privy. Outside she had to pause: everything was blue and white, like slices of the most perfect precious stones. Snow lay almost down to the waterline: beyond that the water was azure until it met the low slopes of the mainland, pearled white and neither near nor far, somehow, a land with no dimensions, the snow tricking the eye. And above that the sky was rich blue too: they must have slept late for the sun to be so high at this time of the year.

'Beinir went out early,' Katrin told her when she reappeared. 'He'll be wanting something hot soon, I should think.'

'Is this a good place to work, Katrin? Do you like your place?'

'I do,' said Katrin without hesitation. She smiled up at Sigrid from her perch by the fire. 'Beinir's kind, I like the house and it's easy to keep it clean. Have you known him long?'

'Only a few weeks,' said Sigrid, slightly surprised. She slipped back behind her bed curtains to change her shift and dress: her face felt jagged from the cold water she had washed in outside, and she was definitely awake now.

'And are you staying long?' Katrin called after her.

'I'm not sure yet. Would you mind taking me about a bit today? I'd like to meet people, and if Beinir's busy …'

'He'll be off making sure the sheep are all right,' said Katrin, smiling again as Sigrid emerged, clipping her beads to her shoulder brooches. Sigrid sat by the fire to brush her hair: it was always a bit of a job. 'But yes, I'd be happy to take you around. I'll need to see my parents, anyway: no doubt they know I didn't go home last night because of the snow, but if I'm to stay here while you're here I'll fetch some clean clothes.'

'I hope it's not too much trouble.'

'No, not at all! I share with the maid at home: it makes a nice change to stretch out a bit at night, even if it's not so cosy.'

Sigrid blinked: she could barely remember the last time she had shared a bed. It seemed an age ago. Would she and Beinir share a bed one day? Would they have children? Could she bear it if, like her own little Saebjorn, they died?

Katrin did not seem over-concerned when Beinir did not reappear for a hot drink: his sheep, it appeared, wandered broadly. She banked the fire up to keep the midday meal warming, seized her spindle and wool and tucked them into a pouch at her belt, and pulled a cloak over her thin shoulders.

'Ready?' she called Sigrid. Sigrid had her own pouch and cloak, and her headcloth firmly wrapped about her recalcitrant hair: she wanted to make a good first impression, anyway.

'Yes, I'm ready. Let's go – I want to see what this place looks like!'

It was only a few steps from the door down to the common path. It would be slippery if it froze, Sigrid thought, but in thick snow, not much trodden, it was safe enough. Beinir's long, confident strides were well marked heading in the opposite direction, up the hill. Ahead the blues and whites that had glared so precisely earlier were already blurring, the air out of the wind was almost mild, and it was clear that there would be more snow before long. The people she could see on the lane and about the houses had a sense of mild urgency about them, trying to finish their outdoor tasks while they could. Towards them, in the very centre of the path, strode a tall woman holding her headcloth and cloak in place at her throat. She slowed when she saw them.

'Good morning, Gillaug!' said Katrin brightly. 'This is Sigrid –'

'You're the one who's here to marry Beinir Ulfson,' said the woman at once, her face like a battle axe. 'I suppose you know how his last betrothed died?'

V

'So you have no idea who did it?'

'He doesn't remember anything about it himself. Not yet, anyway. And Bolla's not saying a word.'

Ketil squatted on the floor beside Tosti's table, staring out at the view of the church beyond. Margad from Caithness had spent the last two days in bed, being tended to by Thorfinn's various womenfolk, partly at least to assuage Thorfinn's guilt that one of his guests had been attacked. Ketil had a niggling suspicion that Margad was enjoying himself far too much to try to remember what had happened the night he was thumped on the head. But Thorfinn needed Ketil to find out. He sighed. 'It wasn't Beinir, anyway.'

Tosti gave him a quick, bright look from under his fringe of hair. 'No?'

'No. I remember noticing how little he went outside.' He did not elaborate.

'And he's gone now, anyway, with Sigrid,' said Tosti, innocently.

'Yes. I wouldn't have let him go if I'd thought he had anything to do with it.' He had seriously considered detaining the Shapinsay party anyway, for there was something about Aslak that he found worrying: so much pent-up anger. And some of it not so pent-up, either, though it was not Aslak who had started the fight in the hall. He called to mind for a moment the way Beinir had folded on to the floor, and managed, as he usually did, not to smile.

'And it was nothing to do with the fight? I heard there'd been a fight.'

Ketil wondered if Tosti could read minds: it would be helpful, for a priest.

'It doesn't look like it. The fight started when one of those louts from Westray made up some poetry about Shapinsay.'

'What on earth could you say about Shapinsay?'

'Well, Shapinsay men. And sheep.' Ketil shifted a little. 'A love poem. Apparently it was quite clever. Lots of witty kennings. About sheep.'

'So that Shapinsay man –'

'Aslak, the one with the short temper.'

'Yes, Aslak – he lost his short temper, and attacked the Westray men, is that how it happened?'

'It is – and I could not see how it involved Margad or Caithness at all. I don't think he was even talking with Aslak when the matter began.'

'Unless one of the Westray men took revenge on someone he thought was of the Shapinsay party, after Aslak attacked him?'

'Well, possibly, yes,' Ketil conceded. 'Except that to all intents and purposes, the Westray man won. And I spoke to them, or my men did, and the Westray men are not the kind of men who rely on dark alleys and sneak attacks to take any revenge they might feel entitled to. They would walk up to the man in broad daylight and do what needed to be done.' He gave a sharp nod: he liked that kind of straightforward attitude. Fighting, and revenge, and even murder, should be publicly accounted for. It was the only way it made sense.

'Is Margad a popular man?' Tosti asked. His fingers were busy stitching together pages of parchment, all his notes on the visitors from the other islands. He had run out of space in his great book.

Ketil considered.

'He's very popular with Margad,' he said. Tosti's mouth twitched. 'As for anyone else, well, people seem to find him good enough company. He's handsome, and reputed to be rich, so I suppose that helps.'

'A woman?'

'A woman could have attacked him – that might explain the need to take him by surprise, in the dark. That or theft, but nothing seems to have been taken. Would a woman attack him? Could he have raped Bolla, then Bolla attacked him? But why did she stay there, then?'

Tosti sat back for a moment, and considered.

'I would have thought he would be more likely to annoy a man,' he said. 'Though if perhaps a woman had thought herself overlooked, or betrayed …'

'I've talked to the women who were in the hall, too,' said Ketil with a sigh. 'But maybe I should talk to them again. I hadn't thought of that. Though none of them behaved as if they had any special interest or claim.'

'Oh, did you talk to Sigrid, too? She was there, of course.'

'Well, it wouldn't have been her,' said Ketil shortly. Tosti said nothing. 'It could have been almost anybody, though.'

'It could have been me, of course,' said Tosti after a pause. Ketil raised his pale eyebrows, and nodded.

'It could have been. It happened after you left. You might have waited outside … I'm not sure I can see it, though.'

Tosti sighed, humorously.

'No, I don't think I could do such a thing. Not without a bit of a warm-up first.'

'And I'd have to ask you why you might have done it, too.'

Tosti frowned, concentrating, then shrugged.

'No, I can't think of a reason. He wasn't very receptive when I popped down to ask if he needed any kind of blessing said over him –'

'But that's not the kind of thing you usually resent,' Ketil agreed.

'No,' said Tosti, briefly regretful, 'I'm not a very fierce priest.'

'What's all that you're trying to stitch together?' Ketil asked. 'All the reports?'

Tosti made a face.

'If I don't sort them now I'll never make sense of it. It's mostly Shapinsay.'

'Couldn't Beinir just have left his report here? He'd written it, hadn't he?' He tried to keep the note of envy out of his voice.

'He wanted to take it home with him. His handwriting is – quite – well, I struggled with it, I had to tell him. It's a different school from what I'm used to.'

Ketil suspected Tosti was being charitable.

'And is it worth it? Is it interesting?'

'Interesting?' Tosti looked at him. 'Not in the least. Nothing ever happens on Shapinsay.'

The question of who had beaten up Margad could not be avoided for long, though, and Ketil left Tosti to his work and strode up through the new longhouses spreading behind the church, up the steady slope of the Brough, as if by the time he had reached the top of the hill he might also have reached the solution to the problem.

He really was fairly sure that Beinir could not have had the opportunity to attack Bolla. Most other people who had been in the hall that night – even Thorfinn and his wife and daughter – even Sigrid - could have done so. Everyone had been drinking freely and the need to slip outside every now and again had been universal. Ketil had only been outside once, the time he had helped the old fellow back from the midden, since despite Asgerdr's best efforts he had as usual drunk very little. Perhaps if he had gone out more often he might have seen something useful, someone behaving suspiciously …

But with so many people having the opportunity, he supposed he should turn instead to try to find a reason why someone would attack Margad. For he had definitely been attacked: the head wound might have resulted from a careless step and a sudden contact with the hall's stone wall, but the stripes across his back had been deliberate and specific. And hard, too: a woman could have done it, but not a feeble girl, or a tired old man – he thought fleetingly of old Hrut on his two crutches. Could someone have found him with Bolla and taken revenge? But whoever might do that would surely have brought Bolla in to safety. Could Margad have been attacked in error, instead of someone else? Ketil thought about it, staring at the sky ahead of him without really seeing it. The light down the side of the hall was not good, but it was likely that Margad had been identified near the hall door, where he would have been clearly visible by the torches there, and then followed. Once away from those he would not have been distinctive. Why had he gone up that dark alley in the first place? Had someone drawn him in there? Chased him in there? Had he gone to Bolla's rescue? Margad would have to try a bit harder to remember.

Back at Thorfinn's longhouse Ketil rapped on the doorpost and ducked to enter. Another maid, a pretty girl, was crouched beside a bed near the door end of the house, and looked round at Ketil's appearance.

'Asgerdr's over at the hall,' she said, setting down her spinning to fetch Ketil a cup of wine. Good, he thought. He had expected Asgerdr to be attending to the patient, and had wondered how to get rid of her while he questioned him. This maid was less intrusive.

'I've come to see Margad, actually,' he explained. Margad's head rose, tousled and content, from the furs around the bed: he was lying on his stomach, so his back must be painful. Ketil stepped over to look down at him. It was true that the bruising was still quite bad, but Ketil could see no reason why Margad could not at least sit up and put his shirt on. Unless it was something to do with the appreciative glance that the maid cast on his well-muscled back. Ketil sat down and leaned against the bed frame.

'Any more thought about what happened the other night?' he asked. Margad had to twist slightly to look at him.

'The last thing I remember was standing at the hall door, taking in some fresh air,' said Margad.

'You don't remember speaking to anyone? Walking to the midden?'

'You didn't find me at the midden.'

'No, but I assume that was the main reason you left the hall, wasn't it?'

Margad pursed his lips.

'I suppose so. It makes sense,' he added kindly.

'But you don't remember it?'

'No.'

Ketil shifted, adjusting his long legs.

'Have you, deliberately or inadvertently, offended anyone while you were here? Anyone on the Brough, or around Birsay?'

Margad's eyebrows rose in surprise.

'No! How could I have done that?'

Well, you annoy me, Ketil thought.

'Could something of the sort have followed you from Caithness? Is there anyone here you know from elsewhere?' But already Margad was shaking his head.

'I came on my own, as it happens: the men who sailed with me from Caithness, good friends, all of them, went on up to Hjaltland after they made their reports. They're to join me later, on their return.'

Ketil wondered briefly why the good friends had left him here and not taken him with them up to Hjaltland.

'No one here you might have met before?'

'Not that I've recognised.'

Ketil reminded himself that Margad did not seem to be intending deliberate obstruction. It looked as if he simply could not believe anyone would dislike him enough to take him into a dark corner and whip him. Yet nothing had been stolen: Margad's rings and bracelets were all still accounted for, even the brooch in his cloak, which was a good topaz. Ketil sighed.

'Did anyone from Westray pick a quarrel with you?'

Margad laughed.

'That lot? They'd quarrel with their own cloak if they couldn't find anyone else! But no, they found no fault with me.'

'And the men you've spent time with while you were here – the men from Shapinsay.'

'Yes?'

Ketil had been over it before, but he had to go back to it.

'Did you disagree with any of them? With Beinir, perhaps?' He had to start there, then bring in Aslak.

'Beinir? How could anyone quarrel with the most boring man in existence?' Margad chuckled again, then remembered to wince just a little. The maid noticed at once, and set down her spindle to apply some sweet-smelling salve to Margad's scars. Ketil felt vaguely sick.

'Aslak, then?' Ketil went on.

'Aslak and I got on all right,' said Margad. 'I'd tease him about coming from Shapinsay, and he'd laugh.'

Hm, thought Ketil, that did not sound likely. Aslak did not look like the kind of man who would take teasing well, and of course there was evidence that he had a history of reacting badly to it. Perhaps he should follow Aslak to Shapinsay and question him again.

'That lad Ingvar, though,' said Margad. 'What about him? He could easily have done it, couldn't he? I mean, you don't really ever know with people like that, do you? Hamthir keeps an eye on him, I know, but he could easily have lost him for a minute or two.'

'Why would you have gone into a dark alleyway with Ingvar?' Ketil asked. As it happened, Ketil had already wondered if Hamthir's brother Ingvar had been prone to sudden unexplained violence, but Beinir had said it had never been known. Ketil had been disappointed –

it would have made an easy solution with no complex motives – but at the same time pleased. Ingvar, however peculiar, was somehow a very likeable boy. It was touching to see how his brother Hamthir looked after him.

'Would Hamthir have had any reason to attack you?'

'Now that I don't know,' Margad acknowledged. 'He doesn't say much. I mean, I didn't give him any reason to attack me. Jealousy, maybe?' he mused.

'Jealousy of what?' Ketil asked. It was true he had not been able to get that much out of the boatman, or not enough to form an idea of his character: he was very quiet. Pleasant, inoffensive, perhaps. Margad shrugged, though.

'He's such an ordinary man,' he offered.

Ketil was beginning to see several reasons why someone might have wanted to take Margad into a dark alley and knock him senseless. Beinir could not have had the opportunity. Aslak, though …

If Ketil had been the least bit more convinced by Aslak's involvement, he would have kept him back and not allowed him to return to Shapinsay. But there was no reason at all to link him to the attack except that he had already been in a fight that evening, and was known to be touchy. Any man in that room was capable of fighting: they did not have to prove it to Ketil. But in the time that Margad spent with the Shapinsay men, might there not have been some squabble, some affront that might have led to a short walk in a dark laneway? It seemed more than likely, but Beinir, questioned, had not been able to think of anything, and Aslak was a surly man to ask, quick to take offence and slow to give any information at all. If he and Hamthir were typical of the society on Shapinsay, Ketil reckoned Sigrid would be back within the week.

'You're sure nothing was stolen from you?' he tried once again. Margad shook his head.

'Nothing that I can think of.' He flexed his fingers to admire his rings.

Ketil drew breath, trying to think of another question, but at that there was a sound at the door, a slim figure against the light. Ketil jumped to his feet.

'Asgerdr?'

'Ketil!' It was not Asgerdr: it was Sigrid's neighbour, Helga, carrying a basket over her arm.

'Helga!' Margad's voice had taken on a pathetic edge as he tried to reach out a hand. She darted forward and knelt to take it in hers. The maid rose, tight-lipped, to fetch wine for the visitor. Ketil propped himself against one of the roofposts, and surveyed Helga's rear view as she reached to examine the progress of Margad's scars. Helga, of course: any good looking, vain young man visiting Birsay would somehow find himself in her path. He felt he should have thought of it himself.

'I've brought some honey bread,' Helga was saying, removing the fragrant bundle from her basket. 'I know Ingibjorg has some honey in the house but it's very peculiar stuff. This will be much better for you. Groa, what have you been using on his poor back?'

The maid muttered something.

'Helga, could we have a word?' said Ketil.

'Oh! Ketil, ah …'

'Outside, I think would be best,' he said firmly. And somewhere public, he thought to himself: Helga in private was nothing but trouble. Helga squeezed Margad's hand and glared at the maid, then stood up.

'Oh, all right,' she said, and picked up her basket. He allowed her to go to the door before him.

'Oh!' came Margad's voice. They both looked back, but Margad was waving at Ketil. 'Can you find out who's got my dog? I haven't seen him since that night.'

'So, Helga,' Ketil said, though his head was full of thoughts about Margad's yellow dog. 'What have you been up to with Margad?'

'I'm just being friendly to a visitor to Birsay!' said Helga in surprise.

'Your idea of friendly is perhaps more generous than some would have it,' said Ketil. 'Is he the only man in your life at the moment, or have you been being friendly to any of the other visitors?'

'I'm a married woman!' cried Helga, then glanced about her. They were near the bath house, a busy enough path, but no one seemed to be paying them much attention.

'Where was your husband Hrolf the other night, then?'

'He was at home,' said Helga, sulky now.

'Did he know about Margad?'

Helga shrugged, giving up.

'I don't know. I don't imagine he would do anything about it if he did.'

That was probably true. Hrolf was more of a sheepskin than a sheep.

'Might anyone else have been jealous?'

'Jealous of what?' Helga had one last attempt at looking innocent.

'Helga, you know what happened to Margad. I'm trying to find the man who did it.'

She sighed.

'I have no idea who might have been jealous of Margad. It might have been almost anyone. He's a very fine man, you know. Very fine indeed.'

Ketil tried not to show his exasperation.

'If you think of anyone, anything that might help, you'll tell me, won't you? If someone did this once, they might well do it again – and he might come off worse next time.'

'Oh!' That was something that had clearly not occurred to her. 'But I really don't know anything!'

'And you haven't seen Margad's dog?'

'His dog? But isn't someone looking after it?'

'I don't know that anyone has seen it. But I'll be asking around.'

But there was limited opportunity to ask around that evening. Even as Helga turned to go back to her longhouse beyond Sigrid's on the mainland, thick flakes of snow began to fall, and he saw her pull her hood up over her headcloth and huddle around her empty basket. The wind had dropped, as if sagged and weighted with the snow, but it would rise again soon: he had enough sea sense to know that. He looked up into the pinkish sky, his face quickly covered with chilly down, then wiped his eyes and glanced about him. The snow looked settled, somehow, a fall with the intent of persisting. And even if it did not, there was no sense just now in getting wet and cold. He turned, and headed back to the main door of the hall.

His men, with the instinct of old soldiers, had already sensed the change in the weather and had found themselves a good spot by the fire. Geirod was taking the chance to clean and oil his axe, concentrating on each sharp stroke as fiercely as he would on each blow he dealt with it. His jaw was clenched, and Ketil hoped he was not nursing a quarrel: no one could bear a grudge like Geirod. But the others seemed relaxed.

Skorri, too, was involved in maintenance, but this time he was scrubbing his beloved silver cup, which, regardless of its security, he took to every feast. Skorri nursed dreams of one day being a great earl like Thorfinn, though how precisely that was going to happen was never quite clear. His ambition seemed harmless enough, and he was a man who could bear to be teased about it. Alf, the third man, was sprawled on the floor – like Ketil, he was often too tall to be comfortable on other people's benches - working away at his current delight, a sheepbone flute. He had scraped and polished the bone, inside and out, and bored holes along the front, but the tone, though sweet enough to everyone else's ears, was never quite right for him and he continued to worry at it, slicing minute scrapes of bone away with his knife and trying a note again. Ketil sometimes wondered how a man of such delicacy as Alf had ever decided to be a warrior, and not find himself a position as a skald somewhere, particularly in these days when men were not so much expected to fight. But the same exquisite precision which made Alf so particular about the flute also made him deadly accurate with any throwing weapon, even an ordinary stone. He was a dreamer, but when he was put to a task he fulfilled it exactly – or if he could not, he wore himself away apologising. He was, as a soldier, a mixed blessing. But then they all were: Geirod's ability to pick fights made Ketil wonder now if he had some connexions to a Westray ancestry.

'Snowing, then, sir?' Skorri looked up as Ketil approached, and gestured to Ketil's cloak. 'Any luck finding out about Margad?'

'Nothing,' said Ketil.

'Aye, Thorfinn'll not be happy, a grand man like Margad coming here all the way from Caithness and getting skelped like that.'

'He's less grand than Thorfinn, Skorri. You make him sound like some visiting overlord,' said Alf absently. Skorri made a face at him without acrimony.

'They're both grand men,' he acknowledged. 'But Margad is Thorfinn's guest, and he's the one lying there with his back flayed.'

'I think he'll recover,' said Ketil. 'No one will admit to a quarrel with him, though, and he claims none, either. Did any of you see anything pass between him and another?'

The men looked at each other and back at Ketil, shaking their heads.

'Not a thing,' said Alf.

'Not that I'd say folks liked him,' added Geirod.

'But he is a great man,' Skorri finished, nodding. 'No one would touch him.'

'But someone did, Skorri,' Ketil reminded him. 'Someone was less impressed by Margad than you.'

'Did he take an interest in someone's wife?' asked Geirod.

'Why do you ask?' asked Ketil. 'What have you heard?'

'Nothing,' said Geirod. 'He just seemed the type that might.'

'Aye, there's that,' Skorri agreed. 'That would certainly make someone attack him. And not steal from him, either, for didn't you say he hadn't been robbed?'

'His rings and bracelets were untouched,' said Ketil. 'But there is one thing missing, and I cannot trace it.'

He stared at the floor between them, and waited.

'What's that, then?' asked Skorri at last.

Ketil lifted his gaze.

'His dog.'

VI

Gillaug, Sigrid decided, was in the running to be the most annoying woman on Shapinsay. At least, she hoped she would find no one more annoying, or she would row back to the mainland herself.

It had probably not helped that Sigrid had disliked the woman on sight: even though her face looked as if she probably sharpened it on a whetstone once a week, the rest of her appearance was pretty much what Sigrid would like for herself. It had none of the edge of flashiness that Helga sometimes veered towards, with a string or two too many beads, and her neckline a touch low for decency. This woman was respectably dressed but all the cloth was – well, it was as much as Sigrid could do not to go and finger folds of it. Did Gillaug work it herself? If so, there might be little opening for any interesting woolwork for Sigrid on Shapinsay. But if she did not work it herself, then she was likely to be a valuable customer like Helga. Sigrid braced herself to be pleasant.

'Good day to you, Gillaug,' she said politely. 'Any arrangement between Beinir and me is not yet fixed: I'm here to see what Shapinsay is like and so that we can become better acquainted.' She took a deep breath: Sigrid was not the kind of person who admitted ignorance easily. 'Did you know this poor woman who was to marry him? What was she like?'

Gillaug gave Sigrid a shrewd look – it stung like a skinned knuckle.

'Unlucky, I should say, wouldn't you? Good day to you, Sigrid: no doubt we shall meet again soon.' With a wordless nod at Katrin, Gillaug stalked on, leaving Sigrid wide-eyed in the middle of the path. She turned to Katrin, who made a face.

'Gillaug is married to Eyolfr, and they live over there.' She pointed to a well-kept longhouse set a little further back than most of those along the shoreline, as if it were holding its skirts out of the midden.

'What did she mean about the, um, the woman who was to marry Beinir before?'

'I honestly don't know,' said Katrin. 'I don't remember him going to marry anyone, I don't think. I might have been young at the time.'

You're young now, thought Sigrid. Katrin could not have been more than fifteen.

'She made it sound as if there was something peculiar about her death, didn't she?'

'That'll just be Gillaug,' said Katrin with a smile. 'She always likes to know more than everyone else, and I don't know how much of what she says she knows is real. Come on, I need to go and tell my parents that I'm alive and staying at Beinir's – with you. They'd love to meet you, and anyway, they might know a bit more for you about anyone else Beinir planned to marry.'

She led the way, stumbling occasionally in the snow, between longhouses and up the hill. When they were on slightly higher ground, she turned, waited for Sigrid to catch up, and pointed out the different houses now just below them.

'That big one, nearest the harbour, that's Vali's house.'

'That's where Hamthir and Ingvar went,' said Sigrid, remembering their arrival yesterday.

'That's right. Hamthir is an orphan, but he's Vali's sister's child.' Her pretty face took on a rosy tint, and Sigrid was fairly sure it was not the wind causing it. Hamthir must be of interest to her. 'He and Ingvar live with their uncle.'

'A prosperous-looking house.'

'Yes: the land here is good,' said Katrin. 'We're fortunate. And we're well looked after.'

So Beinir's headship was appreciated: that was good to know. Sigrid put the fact into her 'all right then, marry the man' box in her head.

'Over there,' Katrin pointed to their right, 'is Aslak's place. He's there on his own: his parents died a year ago and they had no other children. So if you decide against Beinir …' she added, with a glint of mischief in her eye.

'I'll bear it in mind,' said Sigrid, with a twist of her eyebrows. Aslak did not appeal.

'Of course this house here is Gillaug and Eyolfr's,' Katrin went on, pointing to the house she had indicated earlier. 'I heard she brought money in from somewhere, a wealthy father on the other side of the island, maybe? Anyway. Next house belongs to – oh, they're nice, Leif and Hervor. If we have time we should call in and see them. They'll be your nearest neighbours, too. Then there's Beinir's house, of course, and then – well, there's a bit of a gap, you can see, as the village starts to spread out a bit. Down there is the smithy and a leather worker, the bath house is over the other side of the harbour, and my father is a potter up here, so you see we have everything we need.'

'It's a neat little place,' Sigrid acknowledged.

'What's Birsay like? I've never been further than Kirkuvagr,' Katrin said, shaking the snow off her boots to continue up towards her father's house.

'Well … not as flat,' said Sigrid. 'There always seems to be building work going on these days, and it's always busy up on the Brough. Thorfinn has a great new hall, all finely decorated, and then there's the church with all its buildings - we had an abbot from Colonia staying there last summer.'

'Church?' Katrin must not have heard properly.

'Has Thorfinn not built one here yet?'

'What's that for?'

'For, you know, when the priest is doing a mass. Ours can be packed on a Sunday. The priest's a nice man, very clever. He can read and write and speak, I don't know, five or six languages!'

'Sundays? Ah! Yes, sometimes a priest comes here, but we just go to see him outside. There's no special building for it.'

'Oh, well.' Thorfinn's reforms were not as fast as they could sometimes seem in Birsay.

In a few moments, despite the snow, they had reached the doorway of Katrin's father's house.

'Mother!' Katrin called. When Sigrid had followed her into the house, she could see a generously-built woman setting aside her spindle by the fire to come and greet her daughter.

'Katrin! Katrin, you're safe! Where were you?'

'I was at Beinir's last night, mother – he came home and brought someone to stay, and he asked me to stay, too.'

Katrin's mother's eyebrows were in danger of disappearing under her headcloth, so Sigrid stepped forward.

'I'm an acquaintance of Beinir come to visit Shapinsay,' she said. 'I was very grateful to Katrin for agreeing to stay – and anyway, the snow was falling very thickly by then. I think Beinir was anxious she might not have a safe walk home.'

'This is Sigrid, mother, from Birsay.'

'From Birsay? My! Here, sit down and take a cup of wine.' She bustled about comfortably, fetching the wine, while Katrin went to what was presumably her own bed space, and rolled some clean shifts and hose into a bundle. Sigrid eyed the spinning, but it was nothing out of the ordinary.

'Here! How was your journey? I went to Birsay once myself – cold, cold it was! The way the wind runs over it! But I saw Earl Thorfinn, from a distance. Are you staying long in Shapinsay? Do you like it? What have you seen so far?'

'It seems a fine place,' said Sigrid, 'though since I've only seen it in the snow so far it's hard to tell!'

'Mother, we met Gillaug this morning,' said Katrin quickly before her mother could launch another fleet of questions. 'She said something very odd.'

'She thought I was here to marry Beinir,' said Sigrid, almost as prompt, 'and she asked if I knew how the woman died who was last to marry Beinir.'

'Oh, dear,' said Katrin's mother. 'Did she?'

'You mean there was someone?' asked Katrin, coming over at once to sit by the fire with her bundle. 'Someone who died?'

'Yes,' said her mother. 'It was very sad. Her name was ... oh, what was it? It's so long ago, and we barely knew her. She came here from Hoy, was it? Or was it further afield and she had come by Hoy? Oh, it was years ago! Anyway, somewhere sort of south.'

'It must be years,' Katrin agreed. 'I don't remember anyone at all going to marry Beinir.'

'Years, aye,' her mother repeated, nodding sadly.

'But what happened to her?' Sigrid asked.

'Are you really here to marry Beinir?' asked Katrin's mother. 'That would be good: he needs a wife, really.'

'But what happened to the woman from Hoy?'

'If it was Hoy,' Katrin put in.

'Oh, she fell sick and died, that was all, I think,' said Katrin's mother. 'I believe Beinir was really in love with her. It was ages before he even seemed to think about finding someone else.'

So he's been looking for a while, Sigrid noted. She put the thought in her 'Stay where you are and risk the poverty' box in her head.

'Has he arranged to marry anyone else, then, in between?' she could not help asking. Katrin's mother thought hard, her eyes glazing slightly.

'I don't believe so. Oh, what was the girl's name? I took to her myself, I remember, she was a nice lass, lively and chatty. And was it Hoy, or was it somewhere else? Anyway, you can always ask Beinir. He'll know.'

'Would Father remember?'

'Your father? I doubt it,' said Katrin's mother. 'If she wasn't a pot he wouldn't have noticed her.'

'Is he up in the workshop? I'd best go and tell him what I'm up to,' said Katrin, jumping to her feet again.

Katrin's mother shook her head as Katrin disappeared.

'So much energy, that one!'

'She's lovely,' said Sigrid, for she did quite like Katrin. 'Any sign of a husband for her yet?'

'Oh, aye,' said her mother. 'We're hoping she and a fellow called Hamthir will make a go of it. He's setting up as a boatman – maybe he brought you from Birsay?'

'He did, that's right.'

'He's an orphan and had nothing from his parents but the boat, but he lives with his uncle Vali who's prosperous enough and won't see the lad go short. You'll have seen he looks after his brother – poor Ingvar – but Ingvar's a good soul, he'll be no trouble, and he likes our Katrin.'

'I wish them joy, then,' said Sigrid. Would anyone wish her joy with Beinir? And would she have it?

When Katrin came back from talking to her father she was in a hurry.

'I should be cooking the midday meal for Beinir – and you, of course,' she said breathlessly, scrabbling back down the gentle hill to

Beinir's longhouse. 'I bet your servants are better than me!'

'I don't really have any,' Sigrid admitted. 'Just a lad who helps with the farm. He can heat things up, though, if I'm late. I'm not very good at making meals at the right time, either,' she added, and they exchanged a smile.

'You have your own farm?'

'It's very small,' Sigrid explained. 'The land was granted to my husband by Einar Einarson, because he was Einar's man – and Einar was Thorfinn's, of course.'

'Then how is it yours?' asked Katrin, confused.

'We had a son,' said Sigrid. It was very slightly easier to say it now. 'My husband died, and then – and then Saebjorn died, too.'

Katrin put a gentle hand on Sigrid's arm.

'I'm sorry.'

Sigrid drew a steadying breath.

'But it's a small place, so I do woolwork to make ends meet. You know. I mean, I was born in Heithabyr, so trade comes easily!' She finished lightly, and held the door of Beinir's house for Katrin so she could wriggle in with her bundle.

They nearly tripped over Beinir at the door.

'Good day to you both!' he said, rising politely to greet Sigrid. 'Have you been showing Sigrid around, Katrin?'

'Aye, sir, we've met my mother and also Gillaug.' She made a face, and Beinir smiled.

'Some would say that's the best and the worst, then, Sigrid: everyone else will be somewhere in between!' He nodded, agreeing with himself. How annoying would she find that over the years?

'How was your morning, then, Beinir?' Sigrid asked while Katrin hurried to the fire to set the midday meal to heat. The overwintering vegetables would have benefitted from that long slow cooking last night. She wondered if Katrin would stay on as their servant if she married Beinir – or would she just go and marry her own Hamthir?

'Up early – no battle's won in bed! - making sure nothing was amiss in my absence,' Beinir was already telling her. 'I'm just making a few notes now of what people have told me.'

'And was anything amiss?'

Beinir smiled.

'No, it's a quiet place here, and we're a peaceable community.

But I thought of some excitement we could have. I thought I might ask the priest from Birsay, Father Tosti, to come and take a service here before Christmastide. I know he'll be wanted at Birsay at Christmas, but the week before might suit him.'

'Oh, that would be nice,' Sigrid agreed. About two weeks' time: she might well be glad to see a friendly face. And if she had decided by then, and decided against Beinir, she could perhaps travel home with Tosti.

'I'll write to him. A shame I did not think of it before or I could simply have asked him. But his visit would be much appreciated, locally.'

After the midday meal, despite the steadily falling snow, Beinir went out again. Left to her own devices, and for once in her life with no urgent woolwork on hand, Sigrid found herself joining in with the household spinning, ordinary spinning she had not had to do for herself for a long time. It was a strange feeling – that, and sitting there with another woman working on the same thing, quietly at the hearth. Work on Ingibjorg's tapestries so far had taken a team of women but she had always worked a little apart, checking that they were following the designs that Ingibjorg had approved, using the expensive threads as economically as possible. When she made braids she worked alone in her longhouse, or out on the step to catch the light, and if someone came past and stopped for a chat sometimes she barely knew what to say to them. Sitting here with Katrin, telling her a bit about Birsay and, going back in time, about Heithabyr, listening to Katrin's quiet tales of her own Shapinsay childhood and her neighbours, was like a holiday from real life.

Would Beinir teach her how to read and write? She could make a few runes and read them, the ones in her own name, at least. Her favourite one was the two triangles joined together at the end, like a spiky twist of wool you would make round two fingers and use for the little details in a tapestry. They made a D sound. How did they do that? Did the squiggles Beinir put on the paper do the same kind of thing? Was there a D sound there, too, and did it look anything like her D?

She carried on spinning while Katrin prepared the evening meal. Beinir appeared promptly, taking the excellent food with appreciation.

'Sigrid, our neighbours have asked us to visit after supper if there is no more snow – it is only a step along the path. I mentioned that you had come to stay for a while and they were keen to meet you.'

'Oh! Which neighbours are these?' Sigrid asked, trying to remember Katrin's tour around the longhouses.

'Leif is his name – their house is just the next one along here. He's a decent man, and as wife of the head man you'll have to get used to visiting other houses regularly: they'll expect to see you by my side.'

Sigrid nodded. She would have liked a quiet evening with Beinir to ask him about the woman to whom he had been betrothed before, but that would have to wait.

The two longhouses were not exactly jammed up against each other: it took a generous five minutes in the snow to slither to Leif's door. Beinir knocked on the wood, and in a moment the door was flung open generously.

'Come in, come in!'

Leif was blond and, for his age, a little given to tubbiness, his face baby pink and smiling. Hervor, his wife, by contrast, was skinny and dark, not pretty exactly but undoubtedly attractive, for she had a smile that made even Sigrid want to smile back. It took Sigrid a moment, in the flurry of greeting and taking the cup of hot wine and being found a seat by the fire, to realise that there was another person in the house: perched on the edge of a bed platform was a crone so ancient that for a moment Sigrid took her for some kind of strange carving. Then she moved slightly and her beads clacked. Hervor, taking a seat beside Sigrid, glanced over.

'Oh, that's Osk,' she said. 'Now, you're from Birsay? That's exciting – Thorfinn's court!'

'Well, nearby,' Sigrid qualified, though she supposed she was familiar enough with the court.

'And Beinir says you've been working on some tapestries?'

'Yes,' said Sigrid. 'But I mostly make braids, or do nailbinding. Well, any kind of woolwork, really.'

'Oh, don't we all?' Hervor laughed. 'The work of a household is never done, is it?'

'Well …' Sigrid was about to explain, but it was difficult: to describe what she did do was also to admit what she did not do, which was mostly cooking and housework. Did Beinir realise what a terrible housewife she actually was? She might be poor, but she had mostly been able to please herself on her own, only doing the work that appealed to her, bartering for the rest. She would not be able to do that as Beinir's wife, would she?

On the other side of the hearth, Leif, ignoring the chair he could have occupied as head of the household, was squatted eagerly beside Beinir and, like some kind of reflection, was asking him about Birsay.

'They say the new hall's very fine,' he encouraged Beinir.

'It is,' said Beinir. 'All the new buildings are splendid – the church, the steam room, all that. Though I think we are more comfortably sited down here, more sheltered than up on that headland.'

'Someone told me Thorfinn's wife was a very grand lady,' said Hervor comfortably. Sigrid opened her mouth, then closed it sharply again. Perhaps now was not the time to voice her opinions of Sheep-Face.

'Oh, yes, she is!' said Beinir, apparently sincerely. 'And a wise one. I was fortunate enough to have some conversation with both Earl Thorfinn and Lady Ingibjorg, and to see their little boys – fine fellows, the pair of them.'

Sigrid cast him a sideways glance. Perhaps assessment of character was not his strong point.

'They have a daughter, too, have they not?' Hervor persisted. 'Passing beautiful, I heard.'

'Yes, I saw her, too, though I don't believe I heard her name. She was very busy overseeing arrangements for the guests.'

Well, at least there was one man in creation who was not eager to throw himself to his knees before Asgerdr. For it was true she was beautiful: Ketil had fallen on his feet in that respect, anyway.

'I hear Aslak got himself into a fight again,' Leif said, keen for the gossip.

'Sadly, yes,' said Beinir. 'Some fellows from Westray taunted him and he rose to it. No doubt he had provoked them beforehand.'

'I hear there are some big fellows on Westray,' said Leif, eyes wide at the thought. He did not look like a man who would seek out a fight himself. Sigrid had a sudden image of him in battle, stopping his opponent mid axe blow for a chat.

'It's true, they were quite tall,' Beinir admitted. 'I had to go and reason with them.'

Sigrid glanced over at him. Was he going to take credit for stopping the fight?

'Did that work?' Leif looked dubious, too.

'No,' Beinir admitted. 'One of Thorfinn's hird came and sorted it out.'

One of Thorfinn's hird – Ketil, that would be, Sigrid thought firmly to herself. Give the man his name. He's going to be Thorfinn's son-in-law, after all.

'So Aslak lost?'

'Well, the fight was stopped.'

Leif made a face, a kind of shrug.

'Anyway, I made the acquaintance of another man,' said Beinir, 'and it's given me an idea. He's the priest at Thorfinn's church.'

'Oh, aye?' Leif's expression turned even more dubious.

'Yes, I thought I would ask him if he would come over here and take a service or two just the week before Christmas. Wouldn't that be good? He's a scholar, a really interesting man.'

'Well …' Leif seemed to be calculating the disadvantages.

'A couple of services – the whole island could come! And we could have a bit of a feast for him. I know it's a fasting time but, well, if he's come all this way. I'm sure Sigrid and Katrin can organise the women to bring food to my house.'

A feast in Tosti's honour – Sigrid could picture the modest little priest's face at the thought.

'But what about Vali's bonfire?' Leif asked at last.

'His bonfire? Well, obviously he can't have that while the priest is here,' said Beinir reasonably.

'Well, yes,' said Leif. He seemed to swallow. 'Will you be the one telling him that?'

'Vali's Yule bonfire is the highlight of the winter!' cried Hervor. 'It's not just Vali you'd have to answer to. There would be serious trouble if you stopped the Yule bonfire!'

There was much laughter at this, though Sigrid thought she detected a note of anxiety beneath it. But Beinir was the head man: he would know how to handle these people. There would be no problem, whatever he decided, she was sure.

The evening had gone on gently for a couple of hours before Beinir had decreed it was time to go home. He guided Sigrid carefully through the thick snow, and bade her goodnight at her bed place, tugging the curtains shut after her.

Sigrid was not sure how long she had been asleep when she began to dream about Yule bonfires. She was confused, in her dream, because the great dancing fire before her did not seem to be warming her, though she could smell the smoke quite distinctly

She was woken by a sound – footsteps, the door opening, then a block of cold air entering the house. More footsteps, outside now, mutterings, then at last one tremendous shout.

'It's Aslak's longhouse – it's on fire!'

VII

It was surprising, thought Ketil, how long a hungry dog could go without attracting attention to itself.

For either Margad's dog had been spirited away from the Brough in the couple of days after the attack, or it had been well hidden, and Ketil favoured the latter. None of the guards who manned the gateway had remembered seeing anyone pass with a yellow dog – they were not infallible, particularly at busy times, but Ketil reckoned they were fairly observant. So instead he had sent his men, Alf the dreamer, Geirod the bad-tempered, and Skorri the seeker after worldly glory, to see what they could find. He was not entirely surprised that they returned with shrugs and frowns, and with no dog.

Likewise he had eased his questioning of Margad. It was no particular pleasure to him anyway to sit and watch Helga and the others dancing attendance on the idiot. Even Asgerdr, though she kept a degree of dignified distance, seemed a little more eager to ensure his comfort than a good hostess needed to. Or was that perhaps just because Thorfinn was still feeling guilty that his guest had been attacked? Ketil found him one morning outside the longhouse where Margad lay nursing his injuries, looking more uneasy than an earl ought to.

'Have you found his dog yet?' he asked Ketil. He had his own little lapdog with him, the one that had belonged to his nephew Rognvald. Thorfinn had had Rognvald killed, but had stopped the blade when it came to the lapdog. That had been Christmastide: another year's mind was coming up. The dog must be ancient now. Thorfinn carried it close to his chest, wrapped in a fold of his cloak.

'No, no sign of the dog, my lord,' Ketil told him.

'He's taking a long time to heal.' Thorfinn jerked his head towards the longhouse.

'He might do better with worse treatment,' Ketil suggested. Thorfinn's eyebrows rose, and Ketil knew that the message had gone in. Thorfinn was not a stupid man. Ketil suspected that Margad would have made a marked improvement by the end of the day.

'Keep an eye out for that dog, though,' Thorfinn added as he made for the longhouse door. 'I wouldn't want a dead dog on my hands.'

'Yes, my lord.'

Before he had the chance to move away, Asgerdr, his affianced bride, appeared at the door.

'Oh, Ketil, were you waiting for me?' She managed a flirtatious smile even as Ketil was sure her father had just chased her from Margad's bedside. 'You should have come in. You know you are always welcome – and you'll soon be part of the household!'

'I was on my way,' said Ketil ambiguously. He could not help wondering at her enthusiasm for the prospect of marrying him. He still could not understand what was happening: Thorfinn could have made a much better match for his daughter, with those looks and that domestic competence. A sensible man would value her intelligence, even her forthrightness. How had he come to be awarded this prize? A prize, too, that he had no particular interest in. He had no wish to be tied to court life, to politics, to machinations, however lovely his bride (and he still feared he would wake up one morning and find she had turned into her mother). Even Skorri would have appreciated it more. 'Can I be of assistance in any way?' he asked, for her company was easier when he had something to do.

'I don't think so,' she said, 'not just at the moment. Shall we go for a little walk?'

Now what did that mean? Did she want to speak to him in secret? Or did she just want to admire the views of the Brough in the snow?

'Of course,' he said, and offered her his arm for support.

She was light, and nimble on the slippery flags where the passage of all the Brough's inhabitants scoured the snow away. Yet she leaned in against him in a way that was, in itself, very pleasant. He sighed, and thought that he should be grateful: if a lord arranges marriage for you, you can do a lot worse than a beautiful girl who can run a household.

They walked as slowly as the cool air would let them, saying nothing, until they were a little beyond the main press of buildings at the Brough's edge. It was less busy here, of course, and the snow lay thicker, undisturbed. The sea was a mystery, shrouded in fog.

'You've been travelling around my father's earldom for the last few months, haven't you?' Asgerdr asked eventually. Ketil stopped staring into the fog, and returned his attention to her.

'Yes – south, mostly.'

'Hm. Not north?'

'I was briefly in Hjaltland, in the late summer.'

'I meant to ask if you had been in Norway.'

'No! Not for a while.' Not since he had started working more closely for Thorfinn: he had once been a minor representative of the earl at the Trondheim court.

'Still, I suppose news travels. Have you heard anything of that man Hakon? The one who came here in the summer.'

'No, nothing.' Ketil felt his skin crawl. He would be interested in knowing where Hakon was, and what he was up to. 'He's probably back at Trondheim, or on his farm.'

Asgerdr made a little sound which could have been a laugh or a sigh.

'Not a very pleasant man, was he?'

'No,' said Ketil. It was brief, but heartfelt.

That sound again: he was sure it was a laugh this time. She paused, and pointed over to a hut nearby. There were one or two people around, he noticed.

'I've thought of something you could do for me,' she said, smiling. 'You could bring down another barrel of that salt fish. Would you mind?'

He realised that the hut was the same one they had visited before.

'Not at all,' he said, more comfortable with being useful than with walking and talking. He almost strode straight over, before remembering that he was supposed to be supporting her through the snow.

'You're eager!' she laughed. She opened the store room, and let him inside. He turned in the confined space to ask which barrel to take this time, and found she was already far too close, the door slamming behind her. The darkness was suddenly stifling – and warm, as she pressed, full length, against him.

For a moment he froze. This was his affianced wife, yes, and a stunning woman, but she was also Asgerdr, Asgerdr Thorfinn's daughter. What would happen if Thorfinn found out what he had done? Helping himself before it was his time? But what would happen if he didn't? Already a teasing, questioning look was touching Asgerdr's bright blue eyes.

And then, before he could even draw breath to make some kind of argument, some kind of excuse, there came a very solid knock on the closed door.

'Hi, Ketil? Want a hand with the barrels, sir?'

Asgerdr slipped away from him, though not without sliding a hand down his chest. She opened the door. Outside stood Skorri, Alf and Geirod.

'Good day to you, my lady,' said Skorri. 'We saw you heading in and thought we could give you a hand. Won't take a minute with the four of us carrying. Which barrel would you like taken first?'

It was impossible, afterwards, to thank the men for their excellent timing: that would have been to admit there was something amiss, which would not have looked well for either Asgerdr or himself. Fortunately, all three men acted as if nothing out of the ordinary had happened at all, and it was a little while before it occurred to Ketil to wonder why his men might have thought he needed rescuing from a pretty girl who was also to be his wife.

'I see that fellow Margad is up and about,' Geirod commented sourly when they sat at their midday meal in the hall. Margad had seated himself carefully on the backless bench opposite. Ketil had taken the opportunity of Asgerdr's absence to sit more comfortably with his men. Asgerdr had in fact been absent for the rest of the morning, allowing Ketil the opportunity to put her out of his thoughts. It was more easily said than done.

'Has he said anything more about how it happened?'

Alf's words were so soft that for a moment Ketil did not hear them. Then he shook himself and looked across at Margad again.

'Not to me, anyway. He can't bring himself to imagine anyone would dislike him enough to injure him, unless they were jealous of him.'

'Jealous of that thing?' Geirod spat on the floor, though Skorri looked thoughtful. Alf extended a delicate toe and rubbed away the spittle into the flagstones.

'He's rich and he's handsome,' Alf remarked. 'Anyone might be jealous of that.'

Anyone who felt an affection for Helga, Ketil thought, but an attack like that would not explain what had happened to the yellow dog. He stood and went over to Margad.

'I'm glad to see you so much recovered,' he said politely. 'Is your memory likewise restored?'

'Not a bit of it,' said Margad ruefully, 'and to tell the truth I could have done with a few more days in that comfortable bed. It beats sleeping on the floor in here, I can tell you! And I have to say that Thorfinn keeps a very high standard of women around him. That young maid, Groa! Very attentive, take it from me!'

Ketil felt he would rather not.

'So no further thoughts as to who might have attacked you? Or Bolla?' Bolla had still not spoken, and her gaze was always on something no one else could see.

'None at all. Jealousy, as I said, that's the only reason I can think of, and that could be almost anybody. Have you found my dog?'

'No, we haven't.'

'Most extraordinary thing. Creature was devoted to me, you know: someone must have taken it by force. And then what? Where is it? I won that dog in a game, you see, so I'd like it back.'

'We're still looking,' said Ketil. 'I'll find it.' He was sure he would.

After the meal, he took his men out for some skiing up on the headland: it had been a while for them, and the snow was not what they would have wanted – and Thorfinn's store of skis had suffered from lack of use here on the islands. But it gave them some exercise, and Thorfinn's steam room really showed its worth on a snowy day. Afterwards, in a clean shirt and dry breeches, Ketil thought he had better call at Thorfinn's longhouse to see if Asgerdr was all right, or angry with him, or embarrassed at what she had done. He did not relish the thought.

But he was stopped, his hand stretched out to the door, by voices from within.

'No word from Shapinsay yet?' It was Ingibjorg, sharp and demanding.

'Only that Beinir wants Tosti to go and take some services before Christmas,' Thorfinn's voice returned.

'A marriage?' Ingibjorg sounded hopeful.

'He didn't mention it. And you know he would have. He mentions everything. In detail.'

An unpleasant sound followed: Ingibjorg snorting.

'She has to marry him. You made that plain to her, didn't you? Sigrid has to marry Beinir.'

'But …'

'It's perfect. I might never have to meet her again. She can just go and be superior on Shapinsay. And then, I mean, as far as I'm concerned Ketil can take Asgerdr to Trondheim and leave her there, but as you are so keen to have them both nearby …' Her voice tailed off into a sarcastic echo.

'I am. I value Ketil.' Ketil himself, still motionless outside the door, made a face and started to move away, silent on the flags. 'If they could take Sigrid's farm – I'd rebuild the longhouse, of course, and make reparation to Sigrid. But it would be perfect.'

Ketil had had no idea that Asgerdr's father was so fond of her – if that was what he meant. He hoped it made up for Ingibjorg's opinion of her daughter. For once he actually felt sorry for Asgerdr. Take her to Trondheim and leave her there! Who would run Ingibjorg's household then?

But she would have her own household if they took on Sigrid's farm.

And how would Sigrid feel about that?

In fact, the more he thought about it, the more he began to wonder if he were sleepwalking into this whole arrangement – an arrangement that clearly involved Sigrid's marriage to Beinir as well as his own to Asgerdr. Why did Thorfinn want to keep his daughter near? He had shown no great sign of fondness for her before. Why did Thorfinn want Ketil to marry Asgerdr? She was the daughter of an earl and he was no one in particular, the son of a cupmaker from Heithabyr, however much Thorfinn might value him. Daughters of earls were not intended for matches according to their own affections. Daughters of earls, as Ketil knew well from his time at the Trondheim court, were intended for establishing alliances, forming bonds, linking families – occasionally for apologies. Daughters of earls, especially ones with beauty and intelligence, were assets to be disposed of with care and with a good reckoning of the return. He could not even pay in cups.

And then there was Asgerdr's attitude. Asgerdr, Ketil was sure, knew her own worth, and her own duty. Ketil would have expected her even to relish the thought of leaving the uncomfortable shadow of her mother for a grander establishment, far from the Brough. However attentive she might have been to Ketil in the last few days – he tried to put out of his mind the incident in the barrel shed – he could not convince himself that she found him attractive enough to give all that up for marriage with him.

Yes, the more he thought about it, the more it seemed to him that the whole business was peculiar – and if his side of it was peculiar, where did that leave Sigrid and Beinir?

He found himself leaving the Brough as his mind worked, striding over the snowy causeway, and up to the snuggled hump of Sigrid's longhouse, almost lost in the white air. It had begun to snow again. The locals were saying they had seen nothing like it.

There was smoke coming from the roof vents, he noted when he grew closer, and he almost expected to see Sigrid there by the fire when he knocked at the door and pushed it open. She would be working on something complicated and tangled, and would squint at him against the light from the door, refocussing crossly.

But no: Gnup, the lad looking after her farm, was seeing to the cow at the animal end of the house, while hens murmured their private songs at him. He was growing tall, Ketil realised, more man than boy, but still with a good helping of boy.

'Hello, Ketil,' said Gnup, a wary eye on Ketil's sword. He had always been a little in awe of Ketil. 'There's no wine.'

'That's all right,' said Ketil. 'I was just passing, and I thought I'd call in and see if you were managing.'

'Oh!' Gnup looked even more nervous. 'Tell Sigrid everything's fine.'

'And is it?'

'Mostly …' Gnup shrugged, then swallowed. 'I've lost the old yow in the snow, but I doubt she'll probably turn up when it melts, or when she's hungry. Sigrid would be out looking for her, and I did, I walked miles yesterday after her but it had snowed again and there were no tracks. Not even Sigrid could have found her. But she needn't fret. She's tough: it'd take more than a bit of snow to kill her.'

It was not wholly clear towards the end which 'she' was which, but Ketil had the impression it did not really matter.

'You haven't had any word of Sigrid yet then?' Ketil asked.

'No, not yet. She's only away a few days.'

'True.' Somehow it felt longer. He had not said goodbye to her, either. 'Do you think she'll stay there?'

Gnup grimaced.

'I hope not. If she does, what'll happen to this place?'

What indeed?

'Was she pleased to be going, do you think?'

'She was a bit excited. She said she hadn't been anywhere further than Buckquoy for ages.'

Buckquoy was the settlement nearest the harbour. It was less than an hour's walk. Ketil was amused to see that even Sigrid could suffer from itchy feet.

'Not that Shapinsay is that exciting,' he said.

'No,' said Gnup, 'I don't think anything ever happens on Shapinsay. But perhaps Sigrid will change that.'

It was still snowing when Ketil left shortly afterwards. Thorfinn had said he would rebuild Sigrid's longhouse, but Ketil liked it as it was: it might be small, but it was somehow welcoming. But it would not be grand enough for Asgerdr, that was true.

He blinked his way over to the Brough, and felt as if the snow were inside his head, soft and muffling, swallowing rational thought. Nothing was making sense. He wished Thorfinn would find some problem somewhere for him to go and solve, some local uprising, some teasing puzzle, where he could take his men and get off, away from Orkney and its fog and its mysteries. Finding himself making for the hall, he turned abruptly and headed for the church. He was fairly sure he would not find Asgerdr there.

He did not: the interior of the church, dulled by the snow, was dim, with only one lamp lit up at the rounded apse. Candles were precious things, kept for special occasions: the oil-fed lamp was fine for everyday use. The shadows it cast allowed him to slip to one side, kneel on the stone floor, and sink into something between prayer and thought.

It was a comfortable state.

He was not sure how long he had sat there in silence when he became aware of someone else entering the small building. He sneaked a look to one side, wanting to choose whether or not to be disturbed. But it was Father Tosti, eyeing him to see if he was all right, and he sat back and gave him good evening.

'I didn't mean to disturb you,' said Tosti, tending to the failing lamp.

'I've probably been here too long.' Ketil rose, rubbing life back into his knees.

'Everything all right?'

Ketil made a sound which could have been almost anything.

'I hear you're off to Shapinsay before Christmas.'

Tosti turned, surprised.

'Yes, I had a message from Beinir today. I'm waiting to hear if Thorfinn wants me to go – or is this him telling me?'

'No,' said Ketil, 'I don't know what he's decided. Had Beinir any other news, then?'

'Nothing. Well, you know, the illness of a sheep, an injury to a dog's paw, unexpected snowfall -' he gestured with a grin to the church door, to their own unexpected snowfall. 'He had only been home a day or two.'

'Of course.' Ketil stared out at the snow for a moment. 'Have you been to Shapinsay before?'

'Oh, yes,' said Tosti. 'I went with Thorfinn once, but he doesn't go there much. Beinir seems to keep things under control, so there's been no need for the Earl to step in.'

'So really, nothing happens?'

'Not that I've ever heard.'

Sigrid will hate it, Ketil thought.

'What if something does, though? Are they defensible? Anyone who held it would threaten Kirkuvagr, wouldn't they?'

Tosti considered: among fighting men, even a priest could assess such things without blinking.

'It would be hard to defend the island with the people living on it, but of course they have a vart – they can signal for help.'

'To Kirkuvagr?'

'No, that's not much use. Kirkuvagr's all merchants: they can fight, but only to defend Kirkuvagr. No, if they light the vart on

Shapinsay then they would see it on Redland, then on Greeny Hill, and we can see that from here.'

'Has it ever been tried?'

Tosti chuckled.

'The man on Shapinsay got drunk one night with his girlfriend a couple of winters ago and dropped his torch on to the vart fire. Thorfinn was away on his pilgrimage so we only heard about it later. Einar was in charge and he took three longships round the coast as fast as you could think it. So yes, it worked beautifully. The vart man got a whipping, though.'

'As he should,' said Ketil, raising his eyebrows. 'Such things cannot be played with.'

'No, indeed. How is Margad?'

'Up and about, at last.'

'Good,' said Tosti, and in the dull lamplight Ketil was sure he saw a flicker of Tosti's eyebrows, as if he too thought it was about time. 'What about his dog? Have you found it?'

'No one has seen it at all,' said Ketil carefully.

'No one?'

'No one who is prepared to say anything, anyway.'

For a moment they met each other's gaze, then Tosti nodded.

'I'll not keep you,' said Ketil. 'I'd better get down to the hall and see what's happening. I'll see you at supper, no doubt.'

'Of course.'

Ketil headed out into the snow. Away from the well-used paths, it had banked up to above his knee height, and the dark air around him was thick with white, like great moths circling him. For a moment he felt disorientated, head spinning like the flakes around him, not knowing which way he should go, what lay in front of him. Then he shook himself, dislodging white fluff from his shoulders and head, and turned to make his way down to Thorfinn's hall.

He had hardly flicked the accumulation of snow from his cloak again in the doorway when a man rushed past him, lurching against him and stumbling into the bright light of the hall. Thorfinn, standing near his high chair, spun at the sound, and Ketil stepped quickly after the newcomer, already alert.

'What is it, Skafti?' Thorfinn was already braced for news. Skafti staggered to a halt, breathless. He paused as the hall fell silent, finding the words for his tidings.

'It's Shapinsay, my lord. They've fired the vart.'

VIII

Sigrid found herself in a chain of men and women passing pots and buckets of water up from the sea to Aslak's burning house. Perhaps it was the way it was organised so quickly, as if they were well used to fires, that made the situation lose any sense of urgency: as far as she could see, the only person showing any real concern was Beinir.

'That's right, more buckets!' he cried, beating at the flames with what must have been Aslak's leather door curtain. The fire, Sigrid thought as her hands automatically seized and relinquished bucket handles, must have started further back in the house – the cooking fire, almost certainly, perhaps with a spill of oil? – and Aslak must have been between the fire and the door. Aslak was standing, shivering and shocked, to one side, not even looking at his burning house. Sigrid broke out of the chain with care, and unhooked her back cloak to fling around his hunched shoulders.

'You need to be careful, or you'll be ill,' she said firmly. 'Are you hurt? Burned at all?'

Aslak shook his head, staring past her. She was not even sure he had heard her. She gave him a little shake, seizing him by the arm. 'Was it the cooking fire? Your supper?' She tried to remember if he lived alone. 'Was there anyone else in there?'

'He lives on his own,' said Beinir, passing just then. 'Do you want to take him down to my house? He doesn't look well.'

'He'll come to my house,' said a tall man, suddenly appearing behind Beinir. Sigrid could not see his face: his head, with thick, long hair, was scribbled against the flames of Aslak's burning roof. Beinir turned at once.

'Oh! Vali! Well, of course, if you have the room …'

'Of course Vali has the room,' snapped someone from the bucket chain – oh, yes, Gillaug. Sigrid had not yet found any reason to like the woman. 'Just get out of the way, Beinir, and let us get on with putting the fire out.' To be fair, Sigrid thought, Gillaug laboured as hard as any of the others, swinging heavy wooden and leather buckets as if they were dripping with feathers instead of water. Her face was flushed, though it may have been the reflected firelight. Beinir, too, seemed reddened.

'Well, someone had better take him,' Sigrid said sharply, for it was clear that Aslak himself was not going to ask for help, or go to find shelter. She pushed him forward a little, into Vali's field of vision. 'Will you, or shall I?'

'I shall, of course,' said the tall man, and the firelight outlined his raised eyebrows. 'Aslak, come with me.'

Aslak, shoulders slumped, drifted over to Vali and walked in front of him, resigned, down the hill. Sigrid had the strangest impression, just for a moment, that Aslak was under guard. Then her freezing fingers reminded her that she had work to do, and she rejoined the bucket chain.

But already the fire was diminishing: people were bringing torches to see if anything needed to be sorted out before the morning. Hamthir emerged from the darkness to untie and lead away a skittish goat, and the hens, which had evidently made their own way to safety as soon as the door was opened, were rounded up and chivvied across the hillside by someone Sigrid was fairly sure was Katrin's mother. There seemed to be a collective decision that any inanimate valuables could wait until morning when the wreckage would be cooler, and the people dispersed again to their own longhouses, Hamthir taking the goat.

'I hope you slept well after our little excitement!' Beinir greeted Sigrid when she rose the next day. He was already at the doorway, writing on one page of a bundle, though the wind was flicking at its corners. Sigrid wrapped an extra shawl about herself against the cold air, and scuttled past him to go to the privy.

Back, washed and dressed, she took a seat near him, also benefitting from the daylight to work with her weaving tablets.

'Will Aslak be all right? Did he really live on his own?' she asked, thinking it had been a largish house for one man and his goat.

And the hens.

'His parents died last summer. No doubt he has plans for marriage, though I don't know to whom.' Beinir frowned, probably concerned that he had not been informed. 'So yes, he was there on his own.'

'Will you be asking him how it started?' She knew Thorfinn would want to know, if it had happened on the Brough.

'I shall, of course,' said Beinir, 'but I am writing an account of the event into the annals first.'

'Oh!' Sigrid tried to squint at the writing but it made no sense. All those curly bits! And joined together in a long line, like wool that someone was trying to pull out straight. And that was never a good idea: tugged wool just became worse. She tried to concentrate on the writing. Was she in that, somewhere? 'You keep annals?'

'Of course: would you like to see?'

'Oh, yes please!' She disentangled the weaving quickly from her bare toe, and tugged her hose and boot on. But Beinir only led her to the far end of the longhouse, next to his own bed – what Sigrid thought of as the loom place in an ordinary longhouse. Here, though, was a strong set of hanging shelves, close to the wall, covered with a cloth. Beinir lifted the cloth.

'Here we are. I'll show you,' he added kindly. From the row of maybe ten or twelve books – ten or twelve books! Tosti would keel over in delight – he slid one, easing it gently out of the lipped shelf. The cover was plain brown leather, quite fine. She wondered who on Shapinsay worked leather so well. But Beinir paid little attention to the cover. He opened the book across his broad palm, leafing through the pages with a delicacy that, just for a moment, sent a shiver down Sigrid's spine.

'Here, this is an account of the vart and how we keep it ready,' he said, running a finger down the writing.

'Oh, yes, I'd heard there was a vart here ...' She had not seen much of the island yet, but higher ground had not been obvious.

'Oh, yes, of course,' said Beinir. 'Shapinsay is in an important strategic position. If someone wanted to threaten Thorfinn, they would undoubtedly take Shapinsay first.'

Or Rousay, Sigrid thought: it would be closer to the Brough and easier to defend if Thorfinn made a counter-attack. She opened her mouth to make her case but something about the certainty in Beinir's face made her let the subject drop.

'So has the vart ever been fired?' she asked. For a moment Beinir did not reply. Perhaps he was checking the account in the annal – reading that strange tangle, taking some kind of meaning from it. She pressed on. 'Has it? I imagine that would have been quite a moment for the annals.'

'Ah, there was an incident a few years ago – an error.' She struggled to interpret the look on his face. Embarrassment? Anger? 'Of judgement. It was a mistake. A few ships were despatched, but they were able to return to Birsay without trouble.'

'Oh, I think I remember something about that!' said Sigrid suddenly. 'This was when Thorfinn was away in Rome? And Einar was in charge?'

Beinir's lips were curling, his expression even more strange. Perhaps it had been his mistake. But Sigrid was flung back two years, more, to when her husband was still alive. He had been Einar's man, but he was already a cripple. He wanted to hurl himself into Einar's longships, to go with the men to whatever drama the vart had signalled – she remembered the light, low on the horizon, the women standing and pointing, grim-faced, and her husband's anger at his own inability to go and fight. Her husband's anger had never been a good thing.

Beinir was closing the book and slipping it back into place, but he did choose another one and pull it gently out. It was from a lower shelf, and as it swung a little Sigrid noticed something behind the books – a box of some kind, decorated with odd, coloured panels.

'Is that your treasure hidden behind there, then?' she asked with a chuckle. Most people hid their most precious things under the floor, but Beinir's eyes glinted.

'If you don't tell anyone,' he said in a low voice, 'I'll show you. Though in a fire I would rescue the annals first, of course.'

'Of course,' she agreed, wondering why. Beinir reached round the side of the shelf, and pulled the box out. It was half-wrapped in an unbleached cloth, rough work, but inside could not have been a bigger contrast.

The colours Sigrid had glimpsed were not paint nor cloth, but enamel panels, set into the sides and top of the box. And the box was of a glowing yellow metal that could only, really, be gold. Delicate, detailed figures adorned the panels, tall and thin as if they had been stretched, white-bearded, haloed in shell-white, draped in robes of such unearthly beauty that Sigrid barely even aspired to them. The colours were subtle, not the bright reds and purples and greens that she was used to working with: they drew in the eye and challenged it even while they delighted.

'Pretty, isn't it?' Beinir remarked, and Sigrid realised she had not breathed since he had drawn back the cloth.

'Where did it come from?' Sigrid did not dare even touch it.

'I found it in Miklagarth, years ago.'

'You were as far as Miklagarth? I had no idea!'

He laughed.

'When I was young,' he said.

'What's inside it?'

He reached for the catch.

'I think it might have been made for a relic, perhaps? A holy thing. There's nothing now. I'm afraid I think someone before me looted it for the box, and threw the relic away.'

'It did happen,' Sigrid agreed, remembering things she had seen for sale in Heithabyr. The covers of books, with no books inside them: those had stayed with her. Beinir pulled out a cloth bag to show her the empty interior, glowing gold.

'I thought of keeping my gold and silver in it, but it didn't seem right,' he said, 'so I wrapped it in a bag first. I have, you see, a bit put aside, Sigrid: our children would inherit a comfortable sum.'

She felt herself blush, cross at him for bringing the subject up when she wasn't ready for it, but what could she expect when she had asked to see the things he valued most?

She was relieved when at that moment there came a knock at the door.

'Beinir?'

'Hello there! Who's that?'

Hamthir edged through the doorway, flecked with snow.

'Vali sends his greetings, and asks if you'd come along to his house to talk about last night. Aslak's still with us, see.'

'Oh! Of course.' Beinir turned to Sigrid. 'Katrin's already gone to fetch her parents.'

He closed the box gently and set it back behind the books on the shelf, then drew the cloth back over all the books. Then he brushed down his shirt, and seized his kirtle to fasten it on, looking smart. He flicked his fingers through his hair.

'There, do I look the part?' He smiled at Sigrid. He looked every inch the head man of the settlement. She nodded. 'Then would you like to come? You can meet Vali properly now.'

'Of course,' she said, and set her tablet weaving aside. She was about to follow him when Hamthir held out a bundle to her.

'Your cloak,' he said. 'You lent it to Aslak last night.'

It smelled strongly of smoke, but she hooked it over her shoulders nonetheless: she would not be keen to go out without it.

As it turned out, there was quite an assembly at Vali's longhouse.

Vali himself sat in the chair, and by the firelight and the slithering snowlight from the roof Sigrid could see that he was not as young as she had assumed last night: he was upright, and well-built, but his face was lined, and there was grey in amongst his thick fair hair – or perhaps fair amongst the grey would describe it better - tracing the weaving of the neat plaits that held it against his head. Presumably his age allowed him to summon the head man, and not offer Beinir his seat: at any rate, Beinir seemed not to find it unusual.

Hamthir led them in, and fetched wine for them himself, bowing to Vali without words. Ingvar, his poor brother, followed him about trying to help. Aslak, subdued but washed clean of all soot, sat by the fire, not meeting the eye of anyone else. Opposite him sat the delightful Gillaug, spinning industriously as she sat, and a serious looking man who, from his proximity, was likely to be her husband. Gillaug glanced up as Sigrid and Beinir entered, raised her eyebrows almost into her headcloth, and subjected Sigrid to the kind of look that implied she thought Vali had higher standards for his guests. Sigrid made herself smile brightly in return, though her jaw clenched.

Next to Gillaug's husband again were Katrin's mother and presumably her father, short and dusty from his pottery. Katrin, too, sat by her mother, watching Hamthir as he tended to the guests. Hamthir paid her little enough attention, though, for someone he was expected to marry. He concentrated on pouring wine - there must be no womenfolk in the household, Sigrid noted. Nearer the door, on Aslak's side of the fire, giving an air of being slightly reluctant to be there at all, were Leif and Hervor, who at least looked pleased to see Sigrid and Beinir.

Ingvar, at last recognising Sigrid, came over and flopped beside her as she sat by Hervor. He pointed at the fire, grunted, and grinned happily into her face.

'Nice and warm, isn't it?' said Sigrid encouragingly. She held her free hand out to the fire, then rubbed her other arm with it, smiling at him. Ingvar nodded enthusiastically, then pointed to Aslak, grunting with excitement. 'Ah,' said Sigrid, thinking she understood, 'yes, that wasn't such a good fire, though, was it? Poor Aslak.'

'Slak,' Ingvar managed, shaking his head. It was the first understandable thing Sigrid had heard him say.

'Aye, sometimes you almost think there's something in there,' said Hervor, fondly sad. 'Such a shame.'

'Was he born like that?' asked Sigrid. Ingvar had found her free hand and was holding it close between both of his own, though he seemed otherwise to have forgotten she was there.

'No, he fell when he was a bairn, hit his head on a rock. He was fine before that.'

'Oh, yes, so Hamthir said.' Sigrid squeezed Ingvar's hands, and he turned in surprise, eyes wide, then made a face and bounded away.

'Now,' said Vali, silencing the house effortlessly with one word. 'Let us talk about last night's events. Aslak's house is no longer habitable, though the contents for the most part were secured, I believe.' He spoke with easy authority: Sigrid wondered if he were related to Aslak, taking him in so readily last night and now talking about his circumstances like that.

'Yes, we need to sort out how it started,' said Beinir. He leaned forward to look more clearly at Aslak. 'What do you think, Aslak? Was it oil spilled on your cooking fire?'

Everyone looked at Aslak, then away. Hm, thought Sigrid, that's interesting. Was he drunk, or something? The room had grown tense and still.

Aslak cleared his throat, something that seemed to require unusual effort.

'Aye, that's right, I think. I had my back to it, but I must have nudged the pot by the fire.'

'In any case,' said Vali smoothly, 'the cause is behind us. Aslak can stay here – with his goat – until the house is sorted out, which will have to wait until after the snow. I believe you have his hens, Asta?'

'That's right, Vali,' said Katrin's mother, with an odd little bow of her head.

'Then we need to remove anything else that will be spoiled by the weather, as soon as possible.'

'I was just about to say that,' said Beinir. 'We'll put together a chain, now that we're all together here. What have you got, Aslak – blankets and pots and so on?'

Aslak glanced at Vali, then nodded.

'Then unless there is anything else to say, let's make a start while the snow's lighter.' Beinir rose to his feet, and, after a moment's hesitation, the others followed, Vali included.

It did not take long to poke out and remove Aslak's few belongings from the ruins. Sigrid found herself somehow in the forefront of the search, feet sensing just a little warmth still from the stone flags of the floor. The pots were easy to find, around the fireplace, along with a couple of wooden spoons that had only been singed along the edges. But at the far end of the house, where she thought the storage space might be, the damage was greater: the blankets must have been very dry. The charred skeleton of a loom stood only up to about her hips, the top spars burned away completely.

'Oh,' said Katrin's mother, working beside her, 'this is my husband, by the way – Hoskuld.'

Sigrid smiled at the dusty little man.

'Good to meet you, Sigrid,' said Hoskuld, raising a hand before he shifted a carved board out of the wreckage – presumably part of a bed. 'This is not such a good welcome, though. Aslak will never learn.'

'Has he had accidents with the fire before, then?' Sigrid asked. There was a basket of wool at the foot of the loom, perhaps left when Aslak's mother died.

'That's an awful shame, that wool,' said Asta, Katrin's mother, quickly. 'Such a waste. His mother made a nice bit of cloth in her day. You'd have got on well with her, Sigrid.'

'I'm sorry not to have met her,' said Sigrid.

They had the place cleared as well as could be done before the women headed off to start making the midday meal, and Aslak watched the last of his smoky possessions – the ones that were worth saving - vanish into Vali's longhouse. He had said almost nothing all morning: Sigrid wondered if he might still be in shock. But thinking back to her short acquaintance with him, it was not far from his usual manner. Perhaps he was behaving perfectly normally. If she took Aslak and maybe Hamthir as examples she might think that the men on Shapinsay never spoke at all – but then she remembered Leif's welcome, and

Hoskuld just now, dusting the clay from his hands, and Beinir himself –
and even Vali. No, so far things had not been too bad. Though if Gillaug
decided to leave, Sigrid would not weep.

She walked slowly back down to the path by the shore with
Hervor, Leif's wife.

'It's not always like this!' said Hervor. 'Very little ever happens
on Shapinsay, you know.'

'So they tell me,' said Sigrid. 'If Katrin cooks another good
midday meal, I shall want to sleep after it. Last night was far too
eventful!'

'Come for a gossip with me instead,' said Hervor. 'Old Osk is
not the chattiest person on the island, just sitting there, and of course she
goes nowhere so she never has any news of her own. Oh, no, not today,
though – I have to go and help Gillaug with some dried herbs. Come
tomorrow!'

'I'd like that,' said Sigrid, and thought that actually, she
probably would. Hervor was easy company, and Osk was barely there.

'I'll see you then!' Hervor waved farewell, and disappeared
inside her own longhouse. Sigrid walked on, wondering where Beinir
had got to.

But Beinir was already in the doorway, adding to his annal,
while behind him Katrin stirred something that smelled very good
indeed. And instead of gossiping with Hervor after the meal, Sigrid sat
and wove alongside Katrin, and the day was not exciting, but it was
pleasant.

At first Sigrid thought, if she thought at all, that the smoky smell
from her cloak and the events of the previous night had made her dream
again of fire. But then, like a horrible echo, came the shouting. She was
up and out of her bed before her feet were ready: staggering across the
floor she pulled on boots and cloak, and ran outside, Katrin and Beinir
along with her.

'It's Leif's house!' Beinir shouted, and Sigrid's heart sank.

Somehow – perhaps it was lack of sleep after last night –
somehow it was all much more chaotic than the bucket chain at Aslak's
house. The sea was nearer, and that meant that people ran with their
own buckets, stumbling and bumping into one another in the dark,
spilling water before it could ever reach the blazing house. And how
was it blazing like that? Flames roared around the doorway, and licked

out through the roof holes, tearing and gobbling at the turf of the roof as it burned the wooden rafters inside. They had hardly started to make a difference to the flaming door when there was an awful groan of sagging timber, and a shriek, cut off and smothered. The roof collapsed, and the fire bulged in the doorway, pressing up against them, sending them fleeing. Flames danced tall from inside, now, too, up behind the walls.

'Beinir!' she cried, seeing him scooping snow into his bucket to fling at the door. 'Beinir! The fire is at the door – how could it have gone so far? It's all at this end of the house. Look at where the timbers have collapsed!'

'What do you mean? What are you saying?'

'It's not from the hearth, that's what. And Beinir, Aslak's house didn't burn from the hearth either.' The realisation was sudden: all those burned blankets, the burned loom. Beinir stared at her, then spun to look again at the burning longhouse. She was wasting time: she ran back down to the sea to fill her bucket once more.

Then, in the midst of the confusion, she heard Beinir's ominous voice.

'We are invaded! We must alert Thorfinn! Light the vart! Light the vart!'

IX

They were to take a small, fast boat around the coast to see what was happening on Shapinsay.

Thorfinn seemed to think it urgent they find out, though not, perhaps, of great significance. Asgerdr did not think it necessary for it to be Ketil who went.

'What about me?' she said, coming as close to a pout as she had done all week. Ketil pondered a reply but Thorfinn rounded on his daughter.

'Would you have the islands lost because you thought yourself more important? For I can tell you, my girl, I would not!'

Asgerdr opened her mouth to respond to this, then stopped, looking suddenly uncertain.

At that point Ketil reckoned that he should probably go and see if Skorri and the others had the boat ready. He reflected that from all he had heard of life on Shapinsay, it would not have surprised him in the slightest if, for want of a bit of excitement, Sigrid had lit the vart herself to see what would happen. He therefore agreed with Thorfinn that a small investigative expedition might be best to set off first, and to send clearer word on the situation back to Thorfinn. And as for being part of that small expedition himself, well, it was his job. And a few days away from Asgerdr and her strangely clingy behaviour was an added bonus. He was not sure that he should feel like that about his affianced wife, but that was something he chose not to examine too closely.

'How fast do you think light travels?' asked Alf, as he sorted out the oars on the beach. Geirod had gone off to fetch something unspecified: Ketil hoped he would hurry up. The days were short enough as it was.

'Light?' said Skorri. 'Travel? Don't be an idiot, boy: light doesn't travel anywhere. It's all around us. It's just there.'

'It won't be for much longer,' said Ketil. 'What has Geirod gone for?'

'But the light is in Shapinsay first,' said Alf, in slow contemplation. 'Then it reaches – what's it called? Redland? Then Greeny Hill, and we see it here. They don't light all the beacons at the same time, do they? It's one after the other.'

'Sometimes quite a long time after,' said Ketil, remembering other vart chains – and Tosti's tale of the drunken vart warden on Shapinsay.

'Especially if there's a dozy beggar like you in charge,' added Skorri to Alf. 'Get those oars inside. Will you be going up to say farewell to Thorfinn, sir?'

Ketil blinked.

'I had not particularly thought of it, Skorri. I assumed Thorfinn might come down here to the harbour.'

'You wouldn't expect Asgerdr to troop down here in the snow, though, would you?' Skorri said reasonably. Ketil had to admit that he had barely considered the matter, but that no, probably he ought to go up to the Brough and make his farewells. It was a strange feeling, something he had barely done for years. He had had no one in particular to say farewell to.

By the time he returned – and he had not taken long – Geirod had also come back, along with Tosti and a man of Thorfinn's, Skafti, who would carry news back to the Brough when they had assessed the situation. That must have been what he was going to fetch.

'Right, let's get going,' he said, and Tosti helped them shove the boat down across the shingle into the water, hopping aboard as nimbly as the others. Ketil had seen him at a skirmish and had no qualms about taking the priest with them into an uncertain situation, even if Skorri and Geirod gave him odd sideways looks.

The boat was lightly loaded and skipped over the waves as soon as they were able to raise a sail.

'It'll still be dark before we get there, though,' said Geirod. He was his usual miserable self, but Ketil thought he noticed something else about him: a slight tension, perhaps. Excitement at the thought of a bit of a rammie, which would be welcome for all of them. Winters could be dull when you were used to fighting. He looked around his men, Skorri at the tiller, the others perched amongst the few bundles they had brought: they were all a little on edge, he thought. Casually, he looked over the bundles: some food, their own spare clothing, a bit of fuel in case they had to light their own fire – and a bundle he could not quite remember seeing come on board, wrapped in a blanket. He glanced at Skorri. Of all of them he was the one most likely to accumulate possessions as he went, something fancy here and there, but he was also wise enough to have left them safely at Thorfinn's hall.

'So do you think it's an invasion?' asked Alf, lifting a hand to attract Ketil's attention. Tosti shifted slightly, too, obscuring the bundle a little.

'Who knows?' Skorri answered instead.

'The vart was once fired by accident,' said Tosti, and repeated what he had said to Ketil earlier. 'It could be the same thing again.'

'Surely they wouldn't be stupid enough to do it twice?' demanded Geirod, who nevertheless seemed to think they might well be.

'Well, if it's that, then it won't be long till we're back at the Brough again,' said Alf comfortably. Ketil hoped it was something that might detain them a little longer.

'I'm here till midwinter, anyway,' put in Tosti, 'unless it really has been invaded, I suppose.'

Snow began to fall again as they sped along: the flakes seemed to hover about them as they slid over a sea of grey and white, like a pool of moving hacksilver. The lumpy ruined tower at Gurness loomed high on their right, the ghost of Rousay in the snow on their left, and if it had been possible to see any distance at all they should by now have been able to see Shapinsay in the distance, though the light was fading fast.

'Aye, you said we should have set out earlier,' said Skorri to Ketil. 'Maybe you shouldn't have bothered going back up to the Brough at all.'

Ketil said nothing: it was done now.

'We'll just make it, I think,' said Tosti, peering into the white-flecked dusk. 'Is that not the vart fire?'

Ketil looked where he was pointing. Below a low red glow, if you squinted hard, you could just about see a haphazard jumble of what were probably torches down near the waterline. On the whole he reckoned it was a good sign that the vart was still burning, if that was the vart – if it had been lit by some drunken fool again, no doubt they would have tried to put it out as soon as possible. Assuming that anyone else had noticed. That fire was very low down, though, for a beacon fire. What if it was hostile burning, and not a vart at all?

'Right,' he said, keeping his voice low, 'we'll go in quietly, see if we can assess the situation before anyone knows we're here.'

'They should be looking out for us if they fired the vart,' Geirod objected.

'All the more reason to be careful – we want to make sure it's friendly Shapinsay people looking out for us, not invaders. The harbour's on the mainland side of the island. We should almost be able to see by now if there were ships there that shouldn't be, but they might have landed elsewhere and come overland to the settlement. If we can slip past, just outside, and take a proper look, then we can land perhaps on the other side of the harbour. It's a long bay.'

There were few more words after that, though the wind just now would be likely to carry island noise to them rather than the other way around. Whatever the fire was it continued to glow red with the occasional flash of orange as if someone had tossed on another lump of fuel, or the wind had snatched it up – or a dragon had snarled. It would have been lit nearly a whole day now. They could see no sign of hostile activity at the small harbour: boats were pulled up innocently on the shore, and even in the dusk Ketil could recognise the sturdy little craft that Hamthir had brought to the Brough with Beinir and Aslak. It appeared undamaged. He pointed to where he wanted to land, and with practised, stealthy movements they manoeuvred into position, slipping from the boat on to rocks to land more quietly. Skafti and Tosti agreed to stay with the boat for now, and a twist of emotions slipped across Geirod's grumpy face.

'Bear in mind,' said Ketil quietly to him, 'that I'm aware it's Margad's yellow dog under that blanket.'

Geirod jerked back as if he had been slapped. Skorri, Tosti and Alf all exchanged a look of resignation, and Tosti tugged the blanket back to show the bewildered face of the dog. He fondled its ears gently.

'Come on, then,' said Ketil – but almost at once he heard voices ahead. He flattened himself on the rocks, waving a quick hand to his men behind him, and slid forward until he could just about see two figures, standing by a torch outside the end of a longhouse. The man's face was intermittently lit, the woman's more obscure. But Ketil knew her voice.

'So it's not an invasion, then?'

'No …' said Beinir, looking, if anything, a bit disappointed. Ketil for once sympathised.

'Well, that's embarrassing,' he heard Sigrid say tartly.

'Why's that?'

'Well, we fired the vart.'

Beinir looked at her, face as blank as a wet flagstone. She shifted, and Ketil could see part of her face now, clearly wondering how small the words needed to be. 'We can't exactly unfire the vart, can we?'

'Mm?' Beinir had a look of shock to him, Ketil realised. So something had really happened. But Sigrid was ploughing on with her assessment of the situation.

'So in a few hours, no doubt, Thorfinn's longship is going to run up that beach and his whole hird of warriors is going to leap ashore, axes out, looking for something to repel. It's a wonder they're not here already. Oh, Thor, it's winter, too: they'll have been bored stiff when the signal came through. They'll all want to come.'

Ketil rose resignedly to his feet, and stepped forward, unreasonably gratified when Sigrid jumped.

'So why was the vart fired, then?' he asked. He could smell smoke, cold smoke though, on the air.

Sigrid looked past him. Skorri, Alf and Geirod rose from the rocks and arranged themselves behind him.

'Where are the others?' she asked.

'Well, Tosti and the dog are in the boat,' said Ketil.

'Oh,' said Sigrid, and he could tell she was struggling between anger that so few had turned up to rescue them, and relief that there would be so few witnesses to whatever stupidity had been displayed here this time. But then there was the shock on Beinir's face.

'There must have been some reason for doing it.'

'There was,' Sigrid admitted. 'There was … some reason, as you say, to think that there had been some kind of invasion.' She glanced at Beinir, as if she were sorry now she had been harsh. 'But it looks as if it was just – well, you can't say 'just', can you? And it was horrible …'

Now that he could see her more clearly, he realised that she, too, was hollow-eyed with shock. And that smell of smoke – that was not coming from the vart, or from a cooking fire. Dragons …   Beinir cleared his throat heavily.

'It seems to be a case of deliberate house-burning,' he said. 'A bad one. Three people are dead – the whole family.' His throat caught again, and he choked to a halt.

'When did this happen?' asked Ketil.

'Last night – no, early this morning,' said Sigrid. 'Almost dawn. We've spent all day just – trying to put the fire out, trying to find them, trying to rescue -' Her voice, too, broke, and suddenly a trail of tears lined the smoky grubbiness of her face.

'Show me,' said Ketil. He did not want to see Sigrid cry.

Beinir and his men followed, too, but Ketil turned to Geirod and sent him back to bring Skafti, Tosti, dog and baggage from the boat. Geirod scuttled away with uncharacteristic humility into the darkness. Beinir carried the torch ahead, leading them along the shore path to where, until recently, a longhouse had stood, almost with its end wall on the path – but the end wall was nearly all there was left. The smell of cold burning was strong.

'Who lived here?' Ketil asked, stepping carefully to the doorway. Much of the roof must have burned before it fell in: you could still see parts of the inside, a bed end, a loom, an axe head with the shaft burned almost away.

'It's Leif's house,' Beinir said.

'And his wife, Hervor. And an old woman called Osk – was she Hervor's mother or Leif's?' she asked.

Beinir shrugged.

'I'm not sure. She'd always been here.'

'Anyone else? Servants? Children?'

'No,' said Beinir. 'No one who would have been there at night.' He drew a shuddering breath. 'We've found two bodies, anyway. They're laid in my house.'

'The priest, Tosti, is with us,' said Ketil, still examining the remains of the longhouse from the doorway.

'Oh, good,' said Beinir at once. 'We can give them a proper burial.'

'You'd best wait,' came a new voice. Ketil turned slowly to find a man about his own height, wrapped in a blue cloak, his hair fluffed white with snow. Beinir raised the torch, perhaps so they could see each other better, and Ketil noted the boatman, Hamthir, gripping his brother's arm, just behind the new man.

'Why is that?' asked Ketil politely.

'Ketil, this is Vali,' Sigrid explained. 'Ketil is – he's from –' She broke off. 'Are you really all that Thorfinn sent?'

'For now, yes,' said Ketil. 'Think of us as scouts. We responded to the vart fire,' he explained to Vali. Vali nodded solemnly, but Ketil could see anger in his eyes.

'That vart may have been a little premature, but this is certainly a mystery.'

'Aye,' said Beinir, 'two fires in a few days!'

'Two fires?' Ketil turned to him.

'You remember Aslak, who had the fight at Thorfinn's hall? His house burned a couple of nights ago,' said Sigrid. Vali gave her an odd look.

'Toofus!' The sound, barely a word, came unexpectedly from Hamthir's brother. His eyes glittered in the torchlight. 'Toofus!' He shook his head weightily.

'Hello, Ingvar,' said Ketil. 'Hamthir. Good to see you. Was Aslak killed?'

'No, he escaped, with his animals. I don't think Leif and Hervor had any animals here in the house, did they?'

'No,' said Beinir, 'they're up in the byre, up the hill a bit. I sent Eyolfr to feed them this morning, when we'd sort of finished putting the fire out.'

Ketil noted the sense of exhaustion amongst Beinir, Sigrid and Vali, that drained feeling after the rush of a battle. The fight to put out the fire, the failed rescue of their friends, the search for and recovery of the bodies – all that was over now. They needed hot food and a warm fire, and wine if there was any. He turned as Geirod appeared with Tosti, and, like a ghost behind them, Margad's yellow dog.

'Skafti's seeing to the boat,' said Geirod.

'Isn't that Margad's dog?' asked Sigrid. 'What's happened to Margad? I thought he was going to be all right?'

'He is,' said Ketil. 'This is Geirod's new dog.'

'It looks a bit like Margad's,' said Geirod hurriedly.

'Must be related somehow,' Tosti added, with an expression that a saint would have been modestly satisfied with.

'Probably Caithness blood in it,' added Skorri. Alf patted the dog on the head.

Sigrid gave the dog a stern look, then shrugged and wiped at her eyes with the heels of her hands, smearing soot over her forehead.

'I think we need hot food,' she said, echoing Ketil's thoughts. 'Do you think Katrin has anything ready?'

'Let's see,' said Beinir, weary.

'Wait,' said Ketil, still trying to take in quantities of new information, 'Vali, why did you say the burials should be delayed?'

'Oh,' said Vali, who had also turned to go, 'Gillaug – she lives nearby – she said there are kin on Hoy, and in this weather I think we should wait for them to come. If we sent a message tomorrow, they could be here within the week.'

'I see,' said Ketil. 'Tosti, what do you think?'

'What do I think about what?' Tosti asked.

'Sorry: there have been deaths in this fire. The bodies are at Beinir's house. Vali here is suggesting the burials could be delayed until kin arrive from Hoy.'

'I don't see why not,' said Tosti at once. 'Had they kin here?'

Vali shook his head.

'None on Shapinsay,' he said.

'Then it seems even more fitting to wait for the ones they did have,' said Tosti.

'You're the priest, then? From the Brough?' said Vali.

'Tosti, yes.'

'You are welcome,' said Vali, with a short bow.

'Come,' said Beinir, 'Sigrid's right: we need something hot inside us.'

The girl Sigrid said was Katrin had a large pot of stew cooking: it smelled wonderful, but at the sight of all the visitors she gave a squeak and began adding more ingredients. The longhouse needed rearranging: six new guests, who would obviously stay with the head man, meant that with Tosti's supervision and with great care the fragile, charred remains of Leif and his wife had to be moved, on the hurdle on which they had been placed, to an outhouse. Tosti offered to sit with them, at least for now, and pray. It would grow very cold later in the night. Ketil helped move the bodies and took the chance to raise the cloth that had been laid over them. Each had been found on their side, it seemed, with clenched fists and bent limbs that he had seen in other fires, as though the victims could somehow have punched their way to safety. Their faces were patchily preserved, disturbing in their desperate expressions, a wild eye here, a gasping mouth there. He laid the sheet back down, thoughtful. They looked like fire deaths to him, with no sign of knife wounds or of any blow that would have brought on unconsciousness before the fire struck.

He nodded to Tosti and walked slowly back to Beinir's longhouse, considering. From the ruins he had seen, it looked as if the fire had burned most fiercely around the doorway of the house, and not, as one might expect, around the cooking fire. He wondered if the same had been true at Aslak's. If so, how had Aslak and his animals managed to escape?

In the longhouse, things were bustling. Skorri had already settled his bedding as close as he could reach to Beinir's own place, and was conversing with him deferentially. Alf was sitting dreamily in a corner, looking at nothing in particular. Sigrid was helping Katrin with dishes and with turning bread, baking on the hot stones by the fire. Ketil was impressed that Sigrid seemed to have found a good cook: that would certainly help her future prospects, for no man would have been wooed by Sigrid's cooking. He watched the women for a moment, seeing the fire lick around the base of the cooking pot, the subtle arrangements of chains to lift the stew to a cooler level, the neat construction of the fireplace. Around the longhouse, shadows were dispelled by pools of light from small oil lamps, hanging from the roof posts, just like the little one Tosti had with him in the outhouse. Care was usually taken with them, everyone aware of how many were lit and where they were placed. Accidental fires in longhouses did happen: even here in Orkney, bereft of timber as it was, there was enough for a blaze to consume. But it was rare for a fire to start in the early morning, away from the hearth, near the door. Could the man Leif have lit a lamp to light his way to the privy, and dropped it? But even if Leif could not speak for himself, Aslak, who had survived, should be able to say how his fire had happened. He would talk to him in the morning, if he could. After all, the vart had been fired, Thorfinn's men had been summoned, and there was, if not an invasion, at least a mystery to be solved. He was keen to stay and solve it.

Geirod had sorted out a bit of space nearly opposite the door, with the yellow dog cushioned beside him: he had already found him a piece of scraggy meat, presumably begged from Katrin. The dog nosed it as if unsure the treat was really meant for him. Ketil thought about Margad, and the whipping – of the dog by Margad, and of Margad by

… presumably Geirod. He considered. Would Margad accept compensation for the whipping? And then, would he also accept compensation for the dog? Ketil was a truthful man, but if telling Margad what had really happened to his dog meant that Margad would claim the dog back, Ketil would rather swear to him that Odin had appeared in his travelling cloak and ordered his twin ravens to carry the dog off to Valhalla.

He began to sort out a bedspace for himself near the door: he did not plan to sleep deeply that night – caves and dragons had hovered, hot and fierce, around his dreams for several nights now - and he was keen to be aware of anyone coming or going. He laid everything out with brisk efficiency, the habit of a thousand nights slept in a different place from the night before, and he had just finished when Sigrid called,

'Ready.'

The men were not slow to gather around the hearth and Katrin swiftly scooped stew into their bowls, then took another bowl to fill for Tosti. Sigrid helped herself, and sat back, then nearly dropped her bowl.

'Osk!' she cried.

Ketil spun round. Behind him, emerging from the shadows, black with soot, an old woman appeared silently and sat by the hearth, holding out a bowl for her share of stew.

X

'Osk, you're alive!' cried Sigrid, unable to resist placing a hand on Osk's arm, testing to see she was not an illusion. The cloth was rough and greasy. Osk ignored her, simply sitting by the fire and holding out her bowl. Sigrid scooped stew into it, and sat back. 'Are you all right? Are you injured?'

Osk said nothing, but sat eating the stew.

'Shock?' Sigrid ventured, glancing about her at the others. She felt quite taken aback herself.

'This is the third person from the burned house?' asked Ketil, surprising Sigrid with his recollection of the details.

'That's right – she's Leif's mother. Or Hervor's. Or something. Isn't she, Beinir?'

Beinir nodded, but without much conviction.

'I believe she's one or the other. Aren't you, Osk?' They all waited for her to speak, but she was intent on eating. Beinir made a resigned face. 'I've never actually heard her say anything,' he admitted. 'I mean – it's sort of easy to forget that she's there. Sorry, Osk,' he added, though the old woman did not react. The stew was disappearing fast.

'We thought you were dead!' said Sigrid, reaching out to her again, though she felt a bit reluctant to touch the greasy sleeve. 'You – you know that Leif and Hervor are dead, don't you?'

Osk held out her bowl for more stew. The loss of her family – however they might be connected to her – was clearly not her first priority.

Sigrid served her again and sat back. Katrin reappeared at the door, and screamed.

'Where did she come from?'

Sigrid was not quite sure how to answer. Katrin seemed more shocked than pleased.

'She was sort of in the shadows,' she said. 'We must have missed her – she must have come in while we were all out at the fire, I suppose.'

'You know what she's like,' Beinir added.

'I thought she was dead! Like poor Leif and Hervor.'

'I think we all did,' Sigrid agreed. 'She doesn't seem to have eaten all day.'

'I don't think I've ever seen her eat,' said Katrin, apparently recovering. 'She just sits there, doesn't she?'

'Presumably whoever we're waiting for for the burial will take her home,' said Sigrid, still watching Osk for any kind of reaction.

'Waiting for for the burial?' Katrin queried, refilling the old woman's bowl once more. She went on to serve the men again: Sigrid noted how quiet they had been in the face of Osk's appearance. A strange welcome for a boatload of warriors come to fend off an invasion: a fired house, a silent old woman, and a peaceful longhouse with supper and bed readily available. Not much call for battle cries and axe blows. She cast a surreptitious glance around them: the tall, thin one, Alf, was in a dwam, staring ahead of him as if he might be writing skaldic verse in his head. He looked harmless, and Sigrid wondered what use he was to Ketil. Skorri was enjoying being the guest in the head man's home, admiring the fine features of the longhouse: Sigrid had noticed, when he was at Thorfinn's hall, that he always brought a rather good cup and knife to the meals. Geirod, the grumpy one, was fishing bits of meat out of the stew and feeding them to the yellow dog with his fingers. It was an unexpected moment of tenderness: otherwise Geirod looked like the kind of man you avoided after dark, or after a drink. She did not look at Ketil.

'Vali wants the burial held back until their relatives come from Hoy,' Beinir explained to Katrin. 'In this weather it should not be a significant problem.'

'Won't the snow make it harder for them to travel?' asked Katrin.

'Maybe, but the bodies – Leif and Hervor – they'll not … they'll be slower to start, ah …' Beinir tailed off, too delicate to talk about decay and its effects. Katrin frowned, puzzled. Sigrid looked at Beinir. She was still astonished at the fact he had caused the vart to be fired. If she had not known him to be the figure of importance on Shapinsay that he was, she would have said he had panicked. Was he just too soft for his position? But the authority was there: as soon as he had given the order, Aslak had gone running down the snowy path, the flickering torch in his hand the only sign of him in seconds until, eventually, they saw the vart fire surge on the low hill to the east.

No, it was a surprising overreaction to a house burning.

And yet … and yet, there was definitely something wrong. Two houses burned down in only a few days. And Leif's house had burned from the doorway, and Aslak's from the back, about as far away from the hearth as could be. It looked as if someone had set fire to both houses, and that meant that Leif and Hervor had been murdered, and that someone had tried to kill Aslak, too.

But an invasion? Well, what invader sneaked in and burned one house at a time? It was certainly not the normal way of doing things, unless fashions had changed considerably since her late husband's raiding days. She would have to ask Ketil later.

The stew was finished, and people had scraped the last taste of it from their bowls with the flatbread she had helped to make (well, had turned when it was starting to burn). Geirod had his eye on Beinir, toying with his empty cup, watching to see if any further wine might be forthcoming, but the others all seemed ready to turn in. They would have to squeeze up a bit to make space for Osk. Katrin, good servant that she was, was already tugging down blankets to make the old woman comfortable, finding a cosy spot between her own space and Sigrid's. Sigrid had not slept in such a crowded longhouse since … well, probably since she was a child in Heithabyr. The thought did not make it any more charming, though at least they would not be cold.

Subdued but warmed and nourished, they all prepared themselves for bed, and within a very short time the lights were blown out. Sigrid was not sure about the others, but she could not rid herself of the notion she could smell smoke. It was probably soaked into everything in the house, but it did not make for a restful night.

She rose early next morning, fuddled with the unaccustomed warmth of the house, and sat for a moment in the churned blankets rubbing her eyes and face and scalp. When she emerged from behind the bed curtains, Ketil's space was already empty and tidy. Sigrid found such unwarranted neatness disturbing, if not suspicious. She skipped past the empty space to the door, and when she returned from the privy, she found him on the path outside, staring across at Leif's ruined longhouse.

'How's Bolla?' she asked at once.

'As you left her.'

'Still not speaking?'

'Not a word.'

She waited for more, but nothing was forthcoming.

'Asgerdr will be missing you,' she said. 'I'm surprised she let you come here so close to the wedding.'

Ketil was expressionless.

'I'm sure the preparations will continue in my absence,' he said. 'You seem to be settling in well here. Two fires and two deaths – how many days is it since you arrived?'

'I think Beinir over-reacted,' said Sigrid, keen to clear that straightaway. 'Mind you, I think Thorfinn under-reacted, just sending you five. And Tosti.'

'And the dog,' added Ketil. 'Thorfinn was sensible. There was a misfiring of the vart before, a couple of years ago.'

'I know: I remember. While Thorfinn was away. Einar sent ships, and someone had lit it when they were drunk.'

'So Thorfinn sent us to see what was happening.'

'And that might not be such a bad thing,' said Sigrid, moving slightly closer to him and lowering her voice. But he was quicker.

'Because the longhouse was fired at the doorway, not at the hearth?'

Sigrid shut her mouth sharply, and nodded. That was irritating. But she had her other information.

'Aslak's house was burned from right at the back. His mother's loom was cinders.'

'Was she all right?'

'Both his parents died last summer, they tell me,' said Sigrid. 'He lived alone, but he had animals in the house. Everything escaped, not even a hen lost.'

'Fortunate.'

'He wasn't even burned, I think.'

'Where is he living?'

'Vali took him in. And his goat.' Sigrid nodded up the hill to Katrin's parents' house. 'Katrin's family took the hens.'

'Is Vali kin?'

'That I don't know. But he seemed happy to order Aslak to go to his house.'

Ketil gave a very small smile.

'I'm disappointed in you. Why don't you know everything about your neighbours by now?'

'I'm working on it,' said Sigrid. 'And Leif and his wife were nice: I thought they might even be friends. If I stayed.'

'And are you going to stay?'

The question was lightly put – almost. Sigrid hesitated – and in that moment, Tosti emerged from the outhouse where he had spent the night.

'Good day!' he called across, and then tramped through the snow towards them.

'Were you warm enough last night?' Sigrid asked, anxious but not quite in the role of hostess.

'Yes, thank you, Sigrid: Katrin brought me blankets and stew and a hot stone later. She's a lovely girl.'

'She is,' Sigrid agreed. Tosti looked at them both.

'Well, I assume it wasn't some drunkard lighting the vart this time?'

Sigrid gave a laugh.

'No, it was Aslak, under Beinir's orders. Beinir thought we were being invaded.'

Tosti's eyebrows rose, but then he glanced back at the outhouse where he had watched the bodies overnight.

'But?'

'But it's the second house in a week,' said Ketil, with a sigh, 'and neither of them looks like an accident.'

Tosti's eyebrows performed further acrobatics.

'Whose was the other?'

'Aslak. No one was hurt.'

'Poor Aslak, though.'

'He's not saying much about it, but then, he doesn't,' said Sigrid, a little tartly. 'I mean, there are a lot of people here who don't seem to say much.'

'It's a small place,' said Tosti. 'They've said most of what they're going to say.'

'Out loud, yes,' Sigrid agreed. 'But there still seems to be talking going on under the surface.' She was not quite sure why she had said it: who had she meant? A picture of Vali flashed into her mind – Vali and Hamthir, and then, oddly, Beinir himself.

'So,' said Tosti to Ketil, after digesting that, 'you're staying to investigate?'

Ketil looked out across the water to the mainland.

'I think I have to. It's not the kind of situation that Thorfinn would like me to leave un… uninvestigated.'

This time Tosti and Sigrid met each other's eyes. Sigrid was relieved to catch the light of a laugh on the priest's face. He was a kind man: he would not be mocking either of them, so whatever humour he was finding in the situation must be genuine. She felt suddenly awkward.

'I'd better go and dress properly,' she muttered. 'No headcloth and talking to a priest out in front of the house – what would Beinir say?' She meant it as a joke, but somehow it came out gravely, as if she really cared what Beinir might say. Feeling her face flush, she hurried indoors and hid behind her bed curtain.

The next time she emerged, the longhouse was awake and busy. Geirod, Alf and Skorri, almost as prompt as their captain, had red up their bedspaces as if they had never been there. Skafti and Geirod had already gone to their boat, so that Geirod could take Skafti to the mainland to return to Thorfinn with a report. Alf was helping Katrin bring in water in buckets, and Skorri was about to head out into the snow.

'Good morning, Sigrid!' he called. 'Ketil wants us out looking at your neighbour's longhouse. What's left of it.' He made a face and waved. She waved back and greeted Alf and Katrin, taking her wool to work at the door. She wished Ketil well of the ruined longhouse: she had seen enough of it yesterday.

But the light was better today – he might be finding things she had not seen yesterday.

So what? What on earth might he find that would be of any use? The house had burned, Leif and Hervor had died, Osk had escaped and that was that. She adjusted the arrangement of the weaving tablets, and skipped the weft through the new shed of wool. She flipped them on to another combination, and returned the weft thread.

Yes, but who knew who else might be there, taking a look? Eyolfr and Gillaug, maybe, or Vali and Hamthir? Or Katrin's parents, or Aslak? They had all been there yesterday, of course, but yesterday Thorfinn's representatives had not arrived. They could be telling Ketil all kinds of things, and what might he make of it?

She wove a few more inches of braid, flicking the tablets round and back without thinking about them. The pattern grew under her fingers.

People talking to Ketil … Well, really, Ketil wasn't good at getting people to talk. He always needed help. He might be missing information, instead of misinterpreting it. Would Skorri or Alf be of any help? Big fighting men, more interested in the sharpness of their axe blade than the sharpness of their minds? No, of course not.

She looked down hard at what she had woven. Then she sighed, slipped the loop off her toe and set the work carefully aside, then pulled her hose and boot back on and went back to her bedspace for her cloak. Obviously Ketil needed her help.

When she reached Leif's ruined house, it looked as if a minor Thing had been called. Ketil, Skorri and Alf were in conversation with Eyolfr, Gillaug's relatively quiet husband, Hamthir the boatman, and Katrin's dusty father, the potter Hoskuld. All the men were wandering about the ruins, inside or out, poking at interesting bits with the toes of their boots or knocking snow off something they thought might be worthy of further examination. It was slow work, and as far as Sigrid could see, simply something to do while they were talking. It was far from systematic, and did not seem to be getting them anywhere useful. Geirod's yellow dog, that looked so like Margad's, sat watching in Alf's care, but even he did not seem that interested.

Nevertheless she was not sure she should interrupt, and sidled up to an outhouse not quite in order to eavesdrop – she would never eavesdrop, not unless it was really necessary – but just to be unobtrusive. Men, in her experience, did not always talk the same way when they knew women were present. She could jump in later when required.

'So what was he like, this Leif?' Skorri was asking. 'Was he rich? Important?'

Eyolfr snorted, but just a little. Hamthir shrugged.

'He was just Leif.'

'He was a good man,' added Hoskuld, lifting part of a storage pot from the wreckage and examining it. Sigrid wondered if it had been his own work. 'Everyone liked Leif.'

'He'll be missed, right enough,' Hamthir acknowledged. He gave the yellow dog a curious look, but said nothing about him.

'But it looks as if he was killed,' said Ketil. Eyolfr, Hamthir and Hoskuld jerked their heads up suddenly, as if they had all been pulled by the same string.

'Don't be ridiculous,' said Eyolfr. 'Who would have killed him?'

But Hoskuld was looking about the ruins with fresh eyes, brighter, perhaps, than he seemed.

'You mean the fire was – you mean it was – he did it deliberately?

All right, thought Sigrid, maybe not quite that bright.

'Or someone else did,' said Ketil, calmly.

'No,' said Eyolfr. But he, too, was scanning the wreckage anew. 'You mean the way the fire started over at the door, by the looks of it?'

'How do you know?' asked Hamthir. Eyolfr was impatient, and for once Sigrid was in sympathy with him.

'Look, can't you? Much more burning there. Roof gone. Door gone. And that would have stopped them getting out, wouldn't it?'

'Oh. Right.' Hamthir looked more closely, then shuddered and looked away. He coughed, and pointed. 'Is that not Margad's dog? Margad from Caithness?'

'Looks a lot like him, doesn't he?' said Ketil briskly. 'So Leif had no enemies, then?'

'I'd be surprised,' said Eyolfr, a little dismissively, as though it took a slightly superior man like him to have an enemy or two.

'No one he had offended, even accidentally? No one wanting land he claimed? Animals he might have said were his?'

It always amused Sigrid when Ketil pretended to know about farms and farming. Hamthir looked at Hoskuld, and Hoskuld looked at Eyolfr.

'I can't think of anyone,' Hoskuld said. 'He was a nice man.'

'Had he someone who might inherit from him?'

Hoskuld shrugged.

'There's a daughter on Hoy, married a man there. I suppose she would be the heir.'

'What about his wife? What was her name?'

'Hervor,' said Eyolfr, with a promptness that made Sigrid glance up at him. 'No one would have killed her, either.'

Eyolfr needed to examine his own logic, Sigrid thought: he could see how the fire had been lit at the door, but could not accept that someone had done it to kill Leif and Hervor. How else could it possibly have happened?

'Had they other family nearby, either of them?'

Again, the Shapinsay men exchanged glances, hesitant.

'Well,' said Hoskuld eventually, 'there was Osk. She would have been in there too, though.'

'And who was Osk?'

Sigrid opened her mouth to interject, then suddenly realised that for once Ketil was being clever. There was no sense yet, when one of these men could have set the fire, in telling everyone that Osk had survived. It would come out eventually, of course.

'Osk?' Hoskuld looked at the others once again. 'The old woman? She was Hervor's mother, wasn't she?'

'Leif's, I thought,' said Hamthir.

'No, his aunt,' said Eyolfr, authoritatively. 'She was very old indeed.' But Sigrid wondered if any of them really knew. Osk herself was certainly not telling, for now.

'Did they find her body?' Hamthir asked.

'There would have been nothing left of her,' said Eyolfr. 'She was skin and bone anyway.' Sigrid was surprised he had bothered to notice.

'There are two bodies, both badly burned,' Ketil said. 'It could be that she is one of them and that either Leif or his wife is still missing.'

Sigrid grinned to herself: that was pure mischief. She would not have expected it of Ketil. But if one of those men had fired the longhouse – and it was a possibility that had to be faced – then it was no bad thing to let them think suspicion might fall on Leif or Hervor, rather than on them. Ketil seemed to be acquiring some kind of wit.

'But if it was deliberate,' said Hoskuld, slowly now, 'and somebody did it – deliberately, I mean.' He looked across at Ketil, perhaps to check that Ketil was keeping up with this complex argument, 'then who could it have been?'

'Well?' Ketil prompted. Hamthir and Hoskuld exchanged glances but of such little significance that Sigrid dismissed them at once. Eyolfr snorted. 'Yes?' said Ketil. 'Eyolfr, isn't it? You seem to have some importance around here – who do you think it might have been?'

Eyolfr seemed about to deny all knowledge, then reconsidered – and it was not just Ketil's flattery, Sigrid thought. Something serious was now troubling Eyolfr, and he drew breath to speak.

But at that moment, there was a cry of annoyance from the lane by the shore, and in a second Eyolfr was seized from behind and jerked backwards with such violence that Skorri and Alf both laid hands on their axes. But the voice that accompanied the sudden attack was so familiar, already, to Sigrid that she only looked on with irritation at the interruption.

'Eyolfr! What are you doing talking to these men?'

It was Gillaug, bright-faced in the cold, eyes like binding needles.

'I was only –' Eyolfr tried to explain, and choked, hands flying to his collar which she was twisting. He squirmed free. 'I was only discussing the deaths of these poor people – Leif and Hervor, if it was them – with Hamthir and Hoskuld. You know them, Gillaug.'

'We don't know them, though.' She gestured viciously at Ketil.

'Ketil Gunnarson, at your service,' said Ketil at once. 'I am here at Earl Thorfinn's bidding.'

'There you are,' said Gillaug, barely acknowledging Ketil. 'Men here from Thorfinn. Now what will happen? You don't think, do you?' She shook her husband like a puppy – Geirod's yellow dog seemed to shake with him, though Sigrid may have imagined it – and let him go, a dropped rag. 'Anyway, what do you mean, 'if it was them'? Who else was it likely to be?'

'Osk,' said Eyolfr, in a moment's bravery he seemed at once to regret. Hamthir and Hoskuld exchanged another look, this time warning each other to stay clear.

'Osk?' Gillaug stopped, taken aback.

'Leif's grandmother – mother – Hervor's mother – you know the one I mean.'

'Wasn't she found?' Gillaug demanded.

'Two bodies were found,' Ketil put in politely, 'but of course they were very badly burned. Have you any information about the woman Osk? Or anything that might lead us to understand better the deaths of any who died in this fire?'

'Osk was Hervor's mother's sister, as she told me,' said Gillaug stiffly, as if the words might come out of her only on slices of whalebone. 'Whoever died in this fire was burned to death, no doubt in an attempt to escape. The fire was the cause of their deaths. I cannot quite see,' she went on, drawing herself up for a glare at Ketil, 'what else there is to understand about the circumstances, nor, indeed, what business it is of yours to seek to know it. Eyolfr, you are needed at home.' She turned, and made her precise way back to the lane. She did not look back: she knew that Eyolfr would follow, as indeed he did.

Skorri let out a breath he had evidently been holding for a while, and Hoskuld and Hamthir too seemed to relax. Hoskuld even shook himself, as if he could dispel the thought of Gillaug.

'Aye, she's likely right,' said Hamthir, clearing his throat and spitting. 'No one would have killed Leif and Hervor. It was an accident – maybe they left a light burning by the door. It happens.'

'That'll be it,' Hoskuld agreed. He slipped the fragment of pottery into the pouch on his belt and nodded at Ketil. 'I'd better be getting back to work. There are pots to be fired.'

'Aye, and I told Vali I'd see to the sheep,' said Hamthir. 'Good day to you.'

With almost indecent haste, both men hurried off in their different directions, Hoskuld up the hill and Hamthir back along the shore path in Gillaug and Eyolfr's wake. Ketil turned and looked straight at Sigrid, as if he had known she was there all along. But then, she had not been eavesdropping.

'Nothing,' he said to her.

'True,' she agreed. 'But I wonder what it was that Eyolfr was about to say, when Gillaug so unfortunately interrupted him?'

XI

'So, then,' said Ketil, strolling across to where Sigrid had evidently been listening in to the whole conversation. If he did not include her, she would probably sulk. 'as a long-standing resident of this island, what do you think?'

'I think Eyolfr knows more than he told you,' said Sigrid, not rising to his bait. 'But what Hoskuld the potter and Hamthir said to you is right, as far as my first impressions are concerned: Leif and Hervor were lovely. They were welcoming and friendly, and hospitable, and I had thought perhaps Hervor and I might become friends.'

'So you said.' He considered, watching Hoskuld climb the last few paces to his workshop up the hill. Hamthir had vanished beyond the neighbouring longhouses. 'What about Aslak? Is he popular?'

'It's hard to say,' Sigrid admitted. 'You saw what he was like on the Brough: a bit grumpy, argumentative. He's the same here. His house is a little apart from the others, up over there.' She pointed, and he turned to look. Another ruined longhouse, higher up the hill, if you could call it a hill, from the settlement down by the shore, higher than Hoskuld's house and much further to the west. It did look set aside.

'His parents' house, didn't you say?'

'That's right. They died last year, I think.'

'No other family?'

'None in the house: none that I've heard of elsewhere.'

'Did his father have a trade? Does he?'

'I don't think so: just farming.'

Ketil was a little surprised: sometimes distance like that from the other longhouses meant that you were involved in dyeing, or leatherwork, that made for unpopular smells. But either of those would have been nearer the shore, too. Perhaps Aslak's parents had been as grumpy and argumentative as he was, or perhaps growing up all the way over there had contributed to the man he was now. Why had he been selected, or opted, to come to the Brough with Beinir? Ketil had assumed they were friends, or that Aslak represented some aspect of Shapinsay life.

'People really hurried to put out the fire at Aslak's: they had a bucket chain going and everything organised before we even got there,' Sigrid was saying. 'Aslak and the animals were already outside. Katrin's mother was rounding up the hens and taking them back to her place. I remember thinking how well organised they all were – and then Vali hurried up and took Aslak back to his longhouse – Aslak looked very shocked, I mean, by the fire, not by Vali – and the goat, too. But when Leif's house went up, well, I suppose we were all still tired from Aslak's. People were slow, and the fact that the water was so close to the house almost made it harder to form a chain, if you know what I mean?'

Ketil nodded.

'But in any case, the fire would have been between them and the door, here. At Aslak's things were different.'

'We'd better go and look.' He paused, then said, 'Will you come?'

Sigrid opened her mouth, and closed it again, then shook her head.

'I'd better help Katrin with the midday meal. Beinir will want his guests treated well.'

'Of course.' He was relieved: he would prefer not to have Sigrid's opinion forced on him before he had the chance to form his own.

He and Skorri took to the shore path, followed by Alf and the dog. The dog trotted along contentedly at Alf's heels, and of the two Alf seemed more unsettled, checking, smiling, every few seconds to see that the dog was still there. That was another reason for not rushing back to the Brough. Though Thorfinn, dog lover as he was, would almost certainly allot the dog to Geirod if Ketil asked him the right way, Margad would want compensation. Geirod could probably not afford to pay it, and in any case Ketil was reluctant to let Margad get away with his treatment of the dog – or be given the means to buy a new one. And then there was the beating Geirod had given Margad – Margad might have made a bit too much of it, but he would certainly demand payment for that, too.

'Quiet place, this, isn't it?' Skorri commented. Skorri did not like to leave too much space for silence.

'When they're not burning down each other's longhouses, yes,' said Ketil. 'I think this is our path.'

The path was gently sloped upwards from the harbour, between the last house and a bathhouse: once the house nearest the harbour was past, there was a walk of some two hundred paces to the charred remains of Aslak's longhouse. The bucket chain would have had plenty of room.

It was the far end of the house that had suffered most damage, Ketil could see, just as Sigrid had described it. The door stood ajar, though, and he stooped through the doorway, finding himself in a half-house, the roof intact at this end, and part collapsed, part burned away at the other. He could see parts of furniture under the snow that had tumbled in where the roof had been, including the loom that Sigrid had mentioned. The far wall, as far as could be seen, was black and sooty, and the place still reeked of burning. From the footprints in the snow, a few people had been in since it had last fallen, perhaps collecting what could be rescued.

'Big house, for one man,' said Skorri. 'No servants, even?'

'Apparently not.' Ketil peered into the animal section, where the goat and hens would have had their sleep interrupted. He was reminded of Sigrid's longhouse. It was big for one person, too.

Skorri stood in the middle of the place, and sighed, fists on his hips.

'Well, if you ask me, it's not an invasion.'

Alf, perched on the end of what had been a bed, rubbing the dog's head, gave a light laugh.

'But it is a mystery,' said Ketil. 'One which Thorfinn would no doubt prefer to have sorted out.'

'Right,' said Skorri, not sounding too enthusiastic. 'Is that not Beinir's job, as head man, sir?'

'I doubt Beinir has had much experience of such matters,' said Ketil. 'But you're right: in the first place we should offer him our services.'

'Right …' said Skorri again. 'And how long do you think we might be stuck here, then?'

'As long as it takes.'

'I see, sir. Only … well, I was looking forward to Yule at the Brough.'

Ketil said nothing. All other events aside, Yule at the Brough was not something he had thought much about, and if he had, it had not been with any sense of anticipation. Feasting, and singing, and silly competitions. Sorting out Geirod and Margad and the yellow dog. Marrying Asgerdr. He could think of things he would rather be doing.

But for now, he needed to go and talk to Beinir.

He strode out, as he often did, leaving Alf and Skorri behind, allowing himself time to think. But there was not much form to his thoughts yet: he had been bombarded with information, but he did not know enough. Aslak was a grumpy argumentative person with no relatives, Leif and Hervor had been wonderful and had a daughter on Hoy – and Osk, whoever Osk was. Who would attack both households? And in such a way that Aslak lived, but Leif and Hervor died? Had the attack on Aslak's house been a warning? But if so, why? No, he knew nowhere near enough so far.

He rounded the longhouse that marked the corner of the settlement, down by the harbour. Outside, impervious to the snow, Hamthir and Ingvar were sorting driftwood, watched by the tall man he remembered from last night, Vali. He did not often meet a man, particularly an older man, as Vali seemed to be, who could look him in the eye. Vali's hair had been white with snow in the lamplight last night but he could see now that it was closer to grey, though it had been fair and was still thick, bound back to restrain it. Vali stood by the longhouse end, his hands wrapped about the head of a staff, though he did not seem to need it for support. Hamthir organised the driftwood into pieces large enough for building or furnishing and pieces only fit for the fire – an important job, Ketil knew, in these islands with barely a tree. It seemed to be something Ingvar could manage, too: he pounced on the little pieces unerringly, like an eagle stooping, and flung them on to the kindling pile so quickly you would have thought they were straight from the fire.

Vali's role appeared to be supervisory, and certainly he had something about him – not quite the air of a captain of men, but still a leader of some kind. Ketil could not see him in a ferocious attack, but he had an air of authority – a senior priest of some kind, perhaps? Ketil had met a senior abbot before, and there was indeed something the two men shared. In some way he elevated Ketil's opinion of this little settlement just by being part of it: there must be something to the place if Vali chose to live here.

He was about to raise a hand in greeting when Vali caught sight of him and called him over – Ketil might not quite have said 'summoned', but it was very close. He went.

'Thorfinn's man, yes?'

'That's right, sir. Ketil Gunnarson.' He felt himself bow.

'Here at the summons of the vart fire?'

'Yes, sir.'

'Yet presumably Thorfinn did not think we were being invaded?'

'We were not entirely sure, I admit. It seemed best to send a scouting expedition first.'

Vali's eyes smiled.

'You could have brought all your longships racing to Shapinsay, then return to find Rousay had been the real invasion point!'

Ketil nodded, lips pressed tight.

'Are you Earl Thorfinn's second in command these days, then?' Still Vali's eyes seemed to be laughing. Ketil hastened to deny it.

'Not at all, sir. Just one of the hird.'

'A trusted man, though.'

'That is for Thorfinn to say.'

Vali laughed out loud this time, but softly. Hamthir looked up, a little too far away to have taken part in the conversation.

'This is the fellow who stopped Aslak's fight, Vali,' he said. Vali frowned, and looked again at Ketil, a much closer scrutiny than before.

'Is it indeed?' After a moment, he adjusted his hands on the long staff, and somehow indicated that Ketil was dismissed. 'But you'll come for supper this evening, won't you? You can bring your men, too.'

'Thank you, sir.' Ketil bowed his head, and continued along the path. When he had gone twenty paces, it occurred to him that he had not even thought to question Vali about the fires. That would have to be rectified – perhaps at supper.

At Beinir's longhouse, Beinir was not at home. Osk was seated at the end of her bedspace, staring at nothing in particular.

'Beinir's gone to see if Leif's animals are all right,' Sigrid explained. 'And Katrin has gone over to let Tosti get out of the outhouse and stretch his legs a bit before his dinner.'

'She seems a pleasant girl,' Ketil said.

'She is – pretty, too,' said Sigrid, giving the dinnertime broth a stir. 'Katrin tells me she has an understanding with Hamthir – you know, the boatman.'

'I've just seen him, outside Vali's longhouse. And Ingvar, and Vali.'

Sigrid sat back.

'Were they able to tell you anything useful?'

Ketil shrugged, not willing to admit that he had forgotten to ask.

'Not yet, but the men and I are invited to supper there this evening.'

'Vali's a generous host. You'll get a good meal.'

'Katrin cooks well, too.' He sat opposite her, a little to one side. He did not want to look as if he were interrogating her. 'Those men we saw this morning – Hoskuld and Eyolfr. What can you tell me about them?'

Sigrid puffed out a breath.

'Not much, yet. Hoskuld is a potter – well, you'll have noticed the dust – and he's Katrin's father. They took in Aslak's hens when his house burned. They seem good-hearted: the mother, Asta, is a bit of a gossip, I think. Hoskuld I haven't met so much, but Katrin seems fond of him.'

'And Eyolfr?'

'Married to Gillaug.' He knew the way she snapped her mouth shut. Sigrid was terrible at hiding it when she didn't like someone.

'What has Gillaug done to offend you?' he asked, almost smiling. She flashed him a look.

'She told me an odd thing,' she said. 'Apparently Beinir was betrothed before, but the woman died. A couple of years ago. He hadn't mentioned it to me.'

'Well, people do die,' said Ketil reasonably. 'And perhaps he was going to. You haven't known each other that long.'

'No …'

'What else have you found out about the woman, then?' he asked, knowing she would not have left it there.

'She came from the south, maybe Hoy, maybe South Ronaldsay. It was Asta, Katrin's mother that told me and she was a bit vague. Felt that a couple of years ago was long enough to have forgotten everything, but she said the girl was nice, and fell ill, and died. And that Beinir was upset and didn't look for a wife again for a while. Though as I say, two years seems to be considered a long time around here.'

'Where nothing ever happens,' Ketil said automatically.

'That's what they say,' said Sigrid, but she looked less sure about it than Ketil would have expected.

'People fall ill and die,' he said. 'You know that.' Then he stopped – Sigrid's husband and son had both fallen ill and died – less than two years ago. He bit his lip. But she seemed more concerned by Beinir's lost love than her own family, just now.

'Gillaug made it sound as if there were more to it than that,' she said obstinately.

'It sounds as if Gillaug is a mischief-maker.'

'Well … maybe. But still.'

'Have you asked Beinir about the girl?'

'No.'

'Then there you are. You need to ask him.'

She frowned, and seemed about to reply, but at that there was a noise at the door and Katrin appeared. Katrin's face was pleasingly flushed by the cold air. She was indeed very pretty, Ketil thought.

'Skorri, Geirod, Alf and I will be at Vali's for supper,' Ketil told her. She glanced over.

'Thank you, sir.' She checked that Sigrid had not ruined the cooking, and took up her spinning, settling beside Sigrid. Ketil noted that it was the first time he had seen Sigrid cook while someone else did the woolwork. Shapinsay was in danger of changing her.

In a few minutes, Skorri and Alf appeared at the door, followed almost at once by Beinir, and the household gathered for the midday meal. Beinir was gracious as host.

'It's a delight to see the old house full up with people!' he remarked, patting the yellow dog on the head. He made no comment about its resemblance to his acquaintance Margad's dog: Ketil assumed he was biding his time, perhaps intending to send word to Margad.

'We hope not to impose on your hospitality for too long,' he said, with his best Trondheim court manners. 'But I know that Thorfinn will be keen to have this interesting situation sorted out as soon as possible, and as we are here we are of course at your service. It would not be the first time that we have solved problems of this kind for Thorfinn.'

Beinir, who had seemed on the point of refusing their services politely, stopped to rethink. It was clear he appreciated Ketil's manner – though Ketil could see that Skorri was on the point of laughter – and the fact that Beinir would have the help of the men who had similarly helped Earl Thorfinn also had its appeal. He nodded his handsome head slowly and thoughtfully.

'No doubt you will be of much use,' he agreed, 'for I cannot say who might have wished to kill Leif and Aslak. Unless they tried the wrong house first, and Aslak was lucky?'

'It's true that Aslak's house looks like a bit of a failure,' said Sigrid, unable to stop herself joining in. She seemed oblivious to Beinir's raised eyebrows. 'Fired at the wrong end, and the man escapes – and then the brennumad, the arsonist, learns, and fires Leif's at the other end. It could be that the person is learning.'

'Ha!' Beinir leaned back in his chair dismissively. 'Sigrid, what would you know of such things? And you make it sound as if the brennumad is setting out for a career in burning!'

Ketil braced himself for a sharp response from Sigrid, but, though she blushed, she said nothing. He wondered what it cost her in restraint: did she really think Beinir was worth the effort?

At this time of the year, nearly midwinter, the midday meal was warming but quickly done so that there was time for some more work before the sun set. Ketil had his plans, and as soon as the meal was over he pulled his cloak about him, jerked his head at the men, and led them out and along the shore path to the east, away from the harbour.

'Where are we going?' he heard Alf ask.

'We're going to take a look at the vart,' Ketil tossed the words back to them. The bulk of Shapinsay lay before them, glowing white in the low winter sun. The waters lapping at the stony shore to their right were pale green within the bay, tended by a few startling white swans, but beyond the low holm that formed the harbour the sea was the richest of dark blues.

At the very head of the bay, where a lazy stream ran peaty between muddy banks, there stood the smithy and a small, smelly leatherworks. Neither displayed much activity today. Ketil despatched Skorri to question the two households, for this was by way of being the gateway to the settlement where the fires had happened. He and Alf and the dog continued onwards, carving an inland path for themselves through the snow. From the coast below them, forming part now of a broader, more exposed bay, the land eased upwards, a gentle rise, punctuated here and there with the rolled-up bundle of a longhouse, smoke trickling from the roof holes, and occasionally with the crumbled ruin of some building left by the old people long ago. Sheep the colour of parchment had cleared a way down to the thin grass and were too busy drawing what nourishment they could from that to bother lifting their heads even at the yellow dog's approach. The dog paid them about as much attention.

'Hardly worth building a vart up here, is it?' asked Alf, when they came upon the stone platform. 'I mean, even the word 'up' is a bit misplaced.'

'It gives us a good view of the rest of the island, though,' said Ketil. 'Look down there: that's Veantro bay. If I were to invade, I'd come in there, not straight to the village bay. You could attack the village from above, and cut them off from the vart before they knew you were there. Can you see any ships?'

Alf scanned the broad bay to the north. From here the island looked as if it were lunging out to the east, one long arm stretched north-east, fringed with unwelcoming rocks, but a lesser arm reached north from the west of the island. The bay was broad, with a fine beach for landing and no close collections of longhouses as there were in the settlement. And it was comfortably concealed from the mainland: Eday and Egilsay were much further away, and a fleet slipping in through the dusk might never be noticed. But there was nothing there: Shapinsay at least was free from invaders.

'So whoever did the burning is a local, then,' said Alf.

'It looks that way,' Ketil agreed. He waited.

'And maybe even within the settlement,' Alf went on, focusing on the matter. 'You would need to be determined, in this weather, to tramp through the snow and set fire to someone else's house.'

'If the motive was strong enough, they might do it all the same,' said Ketil. 'Aslak's house was fired just at the end of the day, and Leif's just before dawn, unless it took a long time to catch: it's not quite the same as going about in the middle of the night.'

Alf nodded thoughtfully. The yellow dog, which also displayed sense when allowed, was sitting off the snow on Alf's feet. Ketil surveyed the vart platform.

'Someone has already been up to replace the fuel here. It's well-maintained: they must come up every couple of days. Look, there's even a lamp lit ready to fire it quickly – all you would have to do is pull that rope, and the whole thing would tip out on to the fuel.' He turned to look at a small hut close by. 'The warden could shelter in there in perilous times, but I doubt he lives there all the time.' The snow around the hut was pristine indeed.

'Where would you get a light from to fire the houses?' Alf asked. 'I mean, you could bring a torch, which would help finding your way in the dark, but it makes it more likely that you'd be seen.'

'Whereas if you brought a flint, you would be there for longer and more likely to be caught. That's an interesting question, yes.'

He glanced at the sky to the north. A flat blanket of dark cloud, furred at the edges, was sliding towards them. If he looked closely he could almost see the snow already falling from it over the sea.

'Aye, more snow,' said Alf.

'We'd better go. Don't want to be sitting soaking in Vali's longhouse.'

They turned and began the easy descent again, following their own footprints while they still could. The hill was bare, with no one else about. Yet why was it, that when Ketil cast a glance back at the vart platform, he could not shake the feeling that they were being watched?

XII

Much to Sigrid's relief, the invitation to supper at Vali's was extended to her and Beinir, which would save her interrogating Ketil about it afterwards. She was not entirely surprised, for Vali seemed like the kind of man who enjoyed filling his house in the evening, and in any case it would be odd to invite the head man's guests and not the head man himself. She hoped that Ketil would manage to work some information out of someone in the course of the night's conversation, but she certainly intended to find out one or two things herself. But what? They had so little to start with. Two houses were destroyed, two people were dead, two survivors knew or were telling nothing. No one would say anything against Leif and Hervor, so she knew of no reason they might have been killed. But what about the survivor at the other house?

She had happily reverted to woolwork after the midday meal, braiding a complex pattern with her weaving tablets. Katrin was suitably impressed.

'Do you think you could teach me?' she asked. 'I've done a very simple one before, but I've never done anything like that.'

'Here,' said Sigrid, resigning herself to sitting on her hands while Katrin ruined her pattern, or at best worked it so slowly Sigrid would want to scream. She took over Katrin's spindle to keep herself occupied and issued some instructions. Katrin, concentrating so hard Sigrid could see her lips go white, set to. Sigrid knew that people often talked more when their hands were occupied and their eyes fixed on their work, so she took her chance abruptly. 'What's Aslak like?'

'Aslak? Well, you met him in Birsay, didn't you?'

Sigrid said nothing, watching Katrin's fingers hesitantly spin the tablets a quarter turn. Katrin tried a run of the weft, examined the result, and seemed satisfied.

'He's not very friendly,' she said eventually, trying to work out which way to turn the tablets next. 'He lives on his own – well, he did, anyway. I suppose because of that he's given odd jobs like maintaining the vart. He doesn't need company for that: he just stamps off over the hill and does whatever he does to it. Oil and stuff.'

'His parents died last year?'

'Yes, that was sort of sad. His father had been ill for a long time, and his mother nursed him, and when the father finally died everyone thought well, at least poor old Ella can have a rest now, but she had a seizure and died just after the funeral.'

'Were they friendly?'

Katrin looked away from the weaving, down at the floor, trying to remember.

'I think his mother was, but then she just stayed in looking after his father for so long, and his father was not a very nice man,' she finished, a little primly.

'I suppose they are almost your nearest neighbours, with both longhouses so much further up from the shore than the others.'

'Mm.' Katrin focussed hard on the tablets again. First two left, next two to the right … Sigrid flicked the spindle around, feeling the fibres lengthen and bind between her finger and thumb – second nature. Nearly every girl did it from the moment they were tall enough to get a good length on the thread. It was taking Katrin a good deal more effort to work out the braid pattern. Once again her lips were pressed white.

'Is he thinking about marriage? Anyone caught his eye?'

'How would I know?' Katrin snapped, then flushed red. 'Oh, I'm sorry, Sigrid! I shouldn't have spoken to you like that! That was really bad of me!'

'Not at all, not at all,' said Sigrid, as soothing as she could manage. 'I take it there's something going on here? Or something that went on?'

Katrin dropped the weaving in her lap, and sighed.

'I'll never work out how to do this,' she said. 'You'd better give me back my spindle, before I make a mess of this. Yours is so beautiful.'

Sigrid disentangled both pieces of work, handed Katrin the

spindle and watched it fall naturally into her hand again. She began to sort out the weaving, saying nothing.

'When his parents died, Aslak came to talk to my father,' Katrin said at last, once her hands were busy again. 'You know, asking to marry me. I don't know why: if you'd asked me I'd have said he didn't know I existed. Father was pretty interested, because that would mean the two lands could join up – I don't have any brothers or sisters either, and Aslak's land is good. He works hard,' she added grudgingly. 'Probably because he has no friends to distract him.'

'So was the marriage arranged?' Sigrid prompted. Presumably not, if Katrin was now interested in Hamthir, but she wanted the whole story.

'I said I didn't want to, but of course that doesn't count for much if the parents agree. And Mother was keen, because it would be a rich farm and because I'd only be across the hill, I think. But then Father spent a bit more time with Aslak and he decided the man was not really … well, I don't know what men talk about when they get together. But anyway, he said that if I didn't want to marry Aslak he certainly wouldn't make me, and in fact he said – I mean, Father doesn't usually say anything really important, so this sticks in my head – he said that he would rather I didn't marry Aslak. I don't know what it was, but whatever he told Mother, Mother was happy too and I didn't have to marry him. Which was good, because it's Hamthir I want to marry.' This time the blush was less ferocious, and came with that pretty smile.

'And they're happy with Hamthir? Your parents, I mean.'

'Oh yes! Well, once he's made a bit more money. He's Vali's nephew, after all, but he'll share Vali's property with Ingvar. Not that Ingvar will know what to do with it.'

'Who's his father? I suppose his parents are dead.'

'Mm,' said Katrin. 'He's Vali's only relative – well, he and Ingvar – so he'll inherit when the time comes, but that could be years away. We'd live at Vali's and that would be good because there's no other woman living there so I could run the household myself, not have some mother-in-law telling me what to do!'

'So you could!' said Sigrid. 'That's very often an advantage. And you're more than capable, to judge from this place. The food is good, the house is clean, the animals are healthy – what more would any man want?'

Katrin smiled again.

'Mother taught me well,' she said. 'But she maybe left out tablet weaving!'

'That's all right,' said Sigrid, 'with luck you'll never have to earn your living by it!'

When darkness fell, Ketil and his men returned from whatever fiddling round they had been doing – including Geirod from the harbour, happily reunited with his dog - and Beinir came back from seeing to Leif's animals and his own. There was a queue for hot water as they all changed their shirts and smartened themselves. Beinir took the chance to make a few letters in his book.

'You'll remember to take some food to Father Tosti, won't you?' he said to Katrin.

'Of course, sir.' There had been regular visits to Tosti in his vigil, letting him stretch his legs frequently, which was just as well, Sigrid thought, with the amount of food that Katrin had been taking him.

She herself, not wanting the men to make her look shabby, retreated behind her bed curtain and pulled her best overdress from her bundle of clothes: it was old, but did not look too worn. An extra string of beads added some more colour, though none of them was particularly valuable. She shook out her headcloth, folded it for the morning and found a slightly better one, then brushed her hair for a moment or two and wound the fresh headcloth around it, hoping it would stay in place. How was it that some women could wear a headcloth all day, perfectly settled and flatteringly shaped, while she always looked and felt as if she were being attacked by a blown-away sail?

It had snowed again while she and Katrin had been working, and the depth made the short walk to Vali's longhouse a high-stepping struggle. Beinir gave her his arm, gracefully, and that helped, as well as passing on some warmth, but as soon as they entered Vali's house they both seemed to let go in one slightly embarrassed move. She could feel Ketil watching them, probably laughing to himself. Well, that was fine: she hadn't seen any hesitation on his part when Thorfinn offered him Asgerdr. Whereas she – and perhaps Beinir too – were still at the not-quite-sure stage. She wondered how long it would last.

She hid her dismay when she saw that Gillaug and Eyolfr were already seated by the hearth: Gillaug was the only other woman there, so she supposed she ought to be gracious and respectable and sit beside her, though the few leaden paces to reach the seat next to Gillaug were almost as hard as the path through the snow to get here. She made herself smile.

'Good evening, Gillaug! Nice to see you.'

'I heard you'd been invited,' Gillaug responded, which Sigrid reckoned was probably the closest she could come to being welcoming. I heard you'd been invited, and I still didn't turn and leave. Thank you, Gillaug.

'Good evening, Eyolfr!' Sigrid, now bound to friendliness, called across the fire. Eyolfr jumped, and stared at her as if he had never seen her before. Beside him sat Aslak, whom Katrin's father would not make her marry (why? Sigrid wondered to herself. What was wrong with Aslak that a good farm would not balance?), then Beinir. Alf slid in beside Sigrid, and the rest of Ketil's men arranged themselves around the foot of the hearth space, facing Vali in his chair at the top. Ingvar was playing with wooden kubb pieces on one of the grand beds, bouncing on the mattress and making them talk to each other in gabbling voices, and Hamthir, acting in place of the woman of the house, crouched at Vali's feet putting the finishing touches to the food. It smelled very good.

'Gillaug's fine cooking,' Vali remarked, watching Hamthir. 'So good of you, Gillaug, to take the time from your own household to look after a house of men like this one.'

Sigrid turned to Gillaug, trying to hide her surprise, and found that Gillaug had an extraordinary expression on her sour face – a kind of simper. It was very disturbing.

'I'll look after it now, Hamthir,' Gillaug said sweetly, as if she had just been waiting for that acknowledgement before she would take on her role.

'May I help?' asked Sigrid quickly. It was better to offer than to be told. But Gillaug shot her a filthy look and shook her head.

'You are a guest,' she said, quite as if it were some kind of curse. Sigrid glanced over at her husband Eyolfr – was he proud of his wife and her cooking? It was hard to say: Eyolfr was glaring into the fire, apparently oblivious to the conversation. Vali was smiling generally.

'How are you, Beinir? I'm glad you could come this evening.'

'Thank you, Vali, I am quite well, and pleased to see that you are, too.'

Again Sigrid was puzzled at how the two men addressed each other almost as equals. She wondered who had been the head man before Beinir: could it have been Vali? But if so, why had he given it up? He looked hale, hearty and intelligent. It was a small question, perhaps, but it might help her work out how this place fitted together, if she were to live here.

She scanned the room as Hamthir helped Gillaug serve the food. Hamthir, Vali's nephew – his sister's child, apparently. But who was his father? Katrin had skipped past that one. Hamthir had little of the stature of his uncle, anyway – his looks maybe came from his father, but he reminded Sigrid of no one. Nor did his brother Ingvar, now trotting over for his bowl of soup and bread. Hamthir sat with him to help him manage his spoon without too much mess.

The sister was dead. Had Vali ever married? Had he children of his own somewhere? They could be anywhere – like Leif and Hervor's daughter on Hoy. But no: Katrin had said that Hamthir and Ingvar were Vali's only relatives.

As if Beinir had partly read her thoughts, he said,

'Has anyone sent word to Leif's daughter yet? We'll need to have a funeral.'

'Who would have gone?' asked Vali. 'No, nothing's been sent yet. I thought perhaps you were organising it.' The smile took any criticism out of it.

'I thought I should make sure no one else had done it first – two messengers would be a waste, and embarrassing,' said Beinir. 'I'll send someone tomorrow. After all, we don't know how long Father Tosti can spare to be with us – no doubt he will want to return to Birsay before Christmastide.'

Hamthir looked up from his brother's soup, and cleared his throat.

'In this weather you might not get holes dug before then. We might have to wait till spring.'

Vali and Eyolfr nodded agreement, but Alf, who it seemed paid little attention to social conventions, spoke up against his hosts.

'I don't think the ground's that hard, under the snow. It hasn't really frozen. I'll give you a hand, if you like. If that's all right,' he added sideways to Ketil.

'We'd be happy to help when the time comes,' Ketil confirmed.

'You'll still be here?' asked Beinir in surprise. 'I thought you were just going to find out what happened that caused the houses to burn.'

Sigrid caught the look of shock on Aslak's face – clearly Ketil had not managed to talk to him yet. She frowned at Aslak: shocked, certainly, but also not at all pleased.

'That could easily take a little while,' Ketil was explaining.

'Though we have to be back at Birsay by midwinter, too,' added Skorri, deferentially. Sigrid doubted that the deference was aimed at Ketil, but from what she had seen of Skorri on the Brough he was probably impressed by both Beinir and Vali. Then she remembered with a jolt that Ketil was to marry Asgerdr at midwinter.

Anyway, she told herself, that was not relevant. If Ketil was ever to get back in time for midwinter, with the mystery solved, then he would need help. Who could have wanted to fire the houses of both Aslak and Leif's family, and were they by any chance seated around this hearth?

Vali – surely not. He was the beneficent father of the settlement, even if he were not the head man. Look at him there, smiling kindly at Beinir, who was talking about the services he was hoping Tosti might be able to lead during his stay. No one commented on the list: no doubt they would abide by Beinir's decision, along with Tosti.

What about Beinir? No, she was pretty sure he was in the house when both fires were discovered. He could not have been out lighting them, surely.

Oh, but only when they were discovered – if he had set something to burn slowly, then he could have done it and been asleep in his bed when the alarm was sounded.

Actually, she found she did not want to think about that. Sharing a house with a brennumad? That was really not a comfortable idea. But she would have to keep an eye on Beinir. Sharing a house with him as a temporary arrangement was one thing, but marrying an arsonist was certainly not the way she had pictured spending her old age. If she were allowed to have one. But the thought of a slow-burning fire was important: it meant that not even anyone asleep in their bed with three witnesses when the fires were discovered could be above suspicion. She almost growled in frustration.

She looked around again, checking to see that no one was expecting her to be part of the conversation. Eyolfr, across the hearth, certainly did not. He was barely talking either, watching his wife refilling people's cups and bowls.

Well, then, Eyolfr. What did Eyolfr think about things? Did anyone know, or did Gillaug perhaps tell him what opinions to have? It did look a little like that. In that case would Gillaug have told him to burn the two houses? Why would she? But Sigrid barely knew either of them: she would again have to pay more attention to them. She would be delighted to find Gillaug was guilty of brennu-mal. But at least just now Gillaug was allowing Hamthir to take a seat and enjoy a cup of wine.

What about Hamthir? She glanced over at him, trying to take him in without his noticing. He was dark-avised, a fringe of black curly hair half-hiding eyes that looked as though they ought to sparkle with laughter, though she had never seen them do so. Perhaps Katrin had. Away from his boats he dressed respectably in bright colours, as befitted the nephew of a man like Vali: he had a rather good brooch at the neck of his tunic, and what she could see of his boots was fine and free of salt. Even sitting by the fire he had a nimble look, ready to spring up again and help serve the wine.

She was not sure if she felt drawn to him as a character, or not. Though he talked about as much as Aslak did, he seemed a little less surly than Aslak. He was attentive to his poor brother, and Katrin wanted to marry him, which were real points in his favour from Sigrid's perspective. He was a hard worker, building up his boat business, and seemed to live in harmony with his uncle. In fact, Sigrid knew nothing against the man. He must be about an age with Aslak, though: could there have been some rivalry between them as they grew up? But Aslak had lost out when it came to Katrin, at least, so what would be the point in Hamthir burning Aslak's house?

Hamthir and Aslak sat side by side, but Aslak was talking to Alf – or rather, Alf was talking to Aslak across the hearth. When Alf began talking he seemed not to notice if his companion was actually responsive in any way – where did Ketil find his men? Aslak's fringe was long, too, but it was a dull red, and flat, as though he had some kind of board to hide behind. His snub nose seemed repressed by it. Below that his mouth, framed by equally straight and unlustrous whiskers, was set in a permanent downturn. His elbows were propped on his knees and he seemed to grind his feet into the stone floor. Whatever he did to feed himself, his hands were just as workworn as anyone else's – and there were traces of burns on one, presumably from where he had tried to pull things from his blazing house.

But what about Aslak as a perpetrator? He could have set fire to his own house – and perhaps that explained the look of shock on his face when Beinir had mentioned that Ketil was to investigate the fires. But why would he have done that? And then why would he burn Leif's house? Or … there was a thought. Could Leif or Hervor have burned Aslak's house and he had taken his revenge?

But why would Leif or Hervor have burned Aslak's house? And done it in such a way that he was likely to escape, whereas their house had been burned with every apparent intention of trapping them in there to die?

She resisted the urge to set down her dish and put her head in her hands: she knew almost nothing about all these people, and Ketil knew even less. And then there were others in the settlement – Katrin's family, and the smith, and the leatherworker, at the very least, and no doubt more islanders. How would they ever discover who had lit the fires? Would anyone say anything negative about Leif and Hervor, or had her instincts about them been accurate? Would anyone hint at a motive? Or an opportunity? Only Aslak lived alone, so who might know that someone had been out of their house and wandering about when the fires were lit? But then she thought again about slow burning, and realised it was going to be very hard to determine that, anyway. Ketil would never get back to the Brough before Christmas. The wedding would have to be postponed. Or much more likely, Ketil and his men would have to leave Shapinsay with the mystery unsolved, and her still there, wondering if another house might be fired. A feeling of despair swept over her, and she did set down her bowl and take a deep swallow of wine, resisting a sudden urge to cry. It was not like her at all, not in public, anyway. She prayed that it was not obvious to the others around her. Blinking hard, she looked about, pretending that nothing was the matter, and found Ketil watching her. She glared, and he looked away.

'Well,' said Vali, across the general conversation as Gillaug oversaw the clearing away of the food, 'Hamthir, will you see that everyone's cup is full?' He glanced behind him, and saw that Ingvar had gone back to playing contently. Hamthir passed around the jug of wine dutifully. Beinir straightened, and made sure his kirtle was neatly arranged, and out of the corner of her eye she could see that Ketil and his men had very slightly tensed in response to Vali's words. Vali saw that everyone was waiting. 'Now we are comfortable, shall we discuss the matter of the tragic deaths of Leif and Hervor? Whatever you know, and whatever you suspect, now is the time to share it with the others.'

He sat back in his chair, and waited for the contributions to begin.

XIII

Apart from the fire, and the gentle humming of Ingvar in the background, the house fell silent. Ketil watched. As far as he could see, no one was meeting anyone else's eye. Vali watched them, then smiled to himself.

'Beinir,' he said. 'You know the business of this place well. What do you think happened to Leif and Hervor?'

Beinir frowned, a mixture of sorrow and concern.

'I have to believe it was an accident. I cannot see why anyone should have wanted to kill Leif. Or Hervor.' He folded his hands neatly on his lap: he had spoken. There was a slight release of tension around the fire, but Ketil thought it was only because none of the rest of them had had to go first. Vali considered Beinir for a moment, then turned to Eyolfr.

'Eyolfr, what do you think? You live close to Leif's longhouse, too.'

Eyolfr jerked in surprise, as if he had not considered the dangers of such proximity.

'I didn't see anything, Vali. I was asleep until the shouting woke me.'

'But you have an opinion, do you not?' Vali asked kindly.

'Of course.' Eyolfr thought quickly. 'I think it must have been someone from outside the settlement. Someone from the other side of the island, maybe. That's most likely.' He nodded firmly towards Vali, then towards each of the other men in turn. His wife, Gillaug, emitted a distinct snort. Ketil saw Sigrid beside her suppress a laugh, but no one else seemed to notice except for Alf, who glanced at Gillaug over the top of Sigrid's head, puzzled.

Vali acknowledged Eyolfr's reply, and moved on.

'Hamthir? What do you think?'

Hamthir fiddled with his cup for a moment.

'I'm not sure, Uncle,' he said eventually. 'I don't think it looked like an accident – sorry, Beinir, but it doesn't – but I agree with you that I can't think of anyone who would want to kill Leif. Or Hervor. They were both nice people, weren't they?' There was a consensus of murmurs around the fire. Ketil noted it, but thought to himself that even nice people could be killed, if they happened to be in the way of something someone wanted badly enough.

'They were indeed good people,' Vali agreed. 'Yet they are dead. Aslak, what do you think?'

Aslak had clearly not expected to be asked. Hamthir had to nudge him, and then repeat Vali's question into his ear. Aslak blinked and stared around the company, gathering his thoughts.

'Well,' he said, clearly, 'I should say it's Hoskuld.'

'Hoskuld?'

Ketil had met him: the dusty potter. Katrin's father. He had been busy looking about the ruins of Leif's longhouse, and took away a piece of pot in his pouch. Where did he live? Up on what passed for a hill?

But around him others seemed disturbed by what Aslak had said.

'He's not here to defend himself,' said Hamthir.

'No one said we had to accuse someone in this room,' snapped Gillaug. 'That would be very restrictive. After all, my own husband thinks someone came in from the other side of the island, apparently, just to fire a longhouse.'

Two longhouses, Ketil corrected her silently. Eyolfr looked reprimanded. Ketil wondered why the idea was so unlikely. He would have to find out about relationships with other settlements on Shapinsay, about outlying farms nearby.

'But why Hoskuld?' Vali was asking Aslak. 'Tell me why you should name him.'

Aslak looked uncomfortable, but then he had hardly seemed at his ease all evening. Ketil could have drawn the shape of the tension around him when they came through the door.

'None of you will believe me,' he said. 'You asked me for a name and I gave you one. I'll say no more.'

'Aslak,' said Beinir, in a well-pitched voice, 'you must tell us why you name Hoskuld. If there is good reason then he must be questioned, and if guilty fined.'

'And prevented from doing it again,' Vali added mildly.

'And that,' Beinir acknowledged. Aslak burrowed his head down between his shoulders, sulkily defiant.

'No reason,' he said, though Ketil was sure he had one.

'Then you should not have named him,' said Vali. He looked about the room, and at last his gaze fell on the two women. Ketil thought he had been avoiding them.

'Gillaug,' he said. 'I think perhaps you don't agree with your husband Eyolfr – perhaps you have good reason? Will you give us your opinion?'

Gillaug preened, but shook her head.

'I should prefer,' she said, lowering her lashes modestly, 'not to speak in front of the whole company. May I tell you later, Vali, before we leave?'

Vali hesitated fractionally.

'Of course,' he said. His eyes flickered around the rest of the room suddenly, involuntarily, Ketil thought. He believes she means to accuse someone here. But which one? Beinir looked particularly uncomfortable, but that could just have been the effect of watching Gillaug treating Vali as the man in charge.

Everyone jumped at a sudden crash from behind Vali. Ingvar had leapt from the bed, hurling his kubb pieces before him.

'Turn! Turn!' he called, grinning, and shambled over to his brother Hamthir.

'He thinks we're playing a game,' Hamthir explained apologetically. 'He wants his turn.'

'Of course,' said Vali. 'Well, Ingvar, who would you like to name? Who do you think lit the fire?'

Ingvar frowned terrible.

'Fire,' he said, as if considering his reply. Then he grinned again. 'Dragon! Dragon fire!'

Everyone laughed, and Hamthir clapped him on the back. But Ketil saw the expression on Gillaug's face: she looked furious.

Dragon fire. For a moment, he was back in his nightmares, staring into the flames.

'Ketil?'

He glanced up.

'Yes, sir?'

'Do you have any questions you would like to ask the company?'

'Thank you, sir. Perhaps one or two to start with. Who raised the alarm when Leif's house was burned?'

Beinir opened his mouth to reply, then hesitated. The others were looking around, eyebrows raised.

'Beinir?' Ketil prompted.

'I heard a voice shouting "Fire!" and I went outside – I mean, I could smell the smoke anyway, but it was the shouting that woke me up.'

'Me, too,' Gillaug offered an unexpected agreement.

'You were both already there when I came out,' said Vali thoughtfully. 'I think I heard you shouting, Gillaug. Aslak, you were already awake, weren't you? Hamthir?'

'Yes, I woke you,' said Hamthir. 'The whole place smelled of smoke by then. And I thought,' he added, looking round at Aslak, 'that as we came out I saw Hoskuld and Asta running down towards the shore.'

'So it may be, in fact,' said Ketil, when they all seemed to have made their contribution, 'that it was Leif and Hervor themselves who managed to attract everyone's attention.' Too late, he added to himself. 'Thank you. Now, was any one of you up and awake when the shouting began? Vali, sir, you were clearly not if Hamthir had to waken you.'

'That's quite right,' Vali agreed. 'I was sound asleep. Unusual, perhaps, for an old man, but I find in the winter I do sleep better.'

'Aslak?' Ketil asked. Aslak shot him a filthy look.

'I woke up when I heard the shouting.'

'Hamthir?'

'Me, too,' Hamthir agreed. 'It was very early.'

Ketil nodded.

'Gillaug?' he asked.

'I was awake, of course,' she said with an air of superiority, 'lighting the hearth to start the day. Eyolfr was still asleep, though,' she added, unable to resist a little kick of spite in the words.

'So no one here was outside?' Ketil scanned them. 'No one was in a position to see anything happening?'

Gillaug seemed about to say something, but then she glanced up at Vali and changed her mind.

'No,' she said, speaking for them all.

'No,' said Beinir, speaking for the settlement.

'No,' said Vali, summing up for Ketil. 'It does not look as if anyone here saw anything useful. I fear, Ketil, you are going to have a difficult task here. But if I can be of further assistance to you, you need only ask.'

'Thank you, sir.' He realised he was addressing Vali as if he were head man of the place. But there was undoubtedly an authority about him. He wondered if he had been head man before Beinir had taken over – but then why had Beinir taken over, when Vali still seemed so capable?

But there was something behind the serene authority, too, and Ketil saw it when he looked into Vali's eyes – Vali was angry. Now why would that be? Because he cared for Leif and Hervor? Because two fires and two deaths meant that his settlement was out of his control? Though again, Ketil realised, he was thinking of the settlement as Vali's.

'One more question just now, if I may, sir,' he said quickly.

'Of course.' Vali sat back in his chair, the soul of patience.

'I have not travelled about Shapinsay, nor do I know much about local politics or enmities. But is there anyone specific outside the settlement who might have committed an act of brennu-mal against you? Might it have been in someone's interest, or another community's interest, just to pick a house – two houses - in this settlement, and fire them?'

'What a thought!' said Vali, then raised his eyebrows and looked into the fire, clearly working his way around the island in his mind. He shook his head. 'No, there is no one. We are a friendly people on Shapinsay.'

He seemed quite definite, and Gillaug and Eyolfr shook their heads, too, but Ketil noted that Hamthir looked a bit more dubious. He would talk to him later, away from company. And he would talk to Aslak, too.

The evening was clearly over: Gillaug rose like the mistress of the house and stood, smiling, at Vali's side as the men and Sigrid scrambled to their feet from their places around the hearth, even Hamthir, who might have considered he had a right to stay where he was. Beinir waited to escort Sigrid, already holding his arm out to support her, and Ketil made sure Skorri and Geirod preceded them into the darkness. There was no guarantee that whoever was setting fire to houses was not behind them in Vali's longhouse, and who knew what an arsonist might do when first he had burned two people to death? He took up the rear with Alf, and glanced behind as they left: Gillaug was still smiling, half-turned towards Vali. Aslak and Hamthir were clearly itching to head for their beds, and Eyolfr stood, as much use as a second rudder on a ship, halfway to the door, watching his wife.

A second night with little sleep would do him no harm, Ketil thought, but that his sleep had been so broken for the past days. While Beinir was contentedly making for his bed, and Sigrid, Katrin and Osk sorted themselves out behind their own bed curtain – who knew what that bed would be like? - he split the men out into watches, and left Skorri to take the first, responsible man that he was, while he unrolled his bedding and told himself to sleep. Before he did so, though, he touched the cross that he wore on a chain around his neck, and prayed that the arsonist would also sleep well tonight, and not feel the urge to set anything on fire again.

It worked. He woke in the morning with Geirod's hand tapping his shoulder and the yellow dog licking his hand. Remarkably refreshed, he made his way out to the privy, and noted with pleasure that there was no smell of smoke other than the faint morning scent of newly lit hearths. No other house in the settlement had been burned during the night. Perhaps in normal circumstances it would be an odd thing from which to take satisfaction, but he did.

Tosti was emerging from his vigil in the outhouse, relieved by Alf, and smiled when he saw Ketil. It was still, by most people's assessment, dark, but it was not early: one had to stretch the winter days into dusk and dawn or they were too short for anything. And the late winter sunrise would not be too long in coming. Ketil watched for it, the dim shadows of the snowy island sidling out of the night against the tentative light. Tosti came to join him, and guided him a little further from the longhouse door.

'I thought I should let you know,' said the priest quietly, 'we had a visitor last night.'

'Oh, yes?' His men had said nothing.

'Someone was around the outhouse,' Tosti explained. 'At least twice. I don't know what they were looking for. Slow, of course, in the snow and the dark, but I'd say they were being quite thorough.'

'Yes, but thoroughly doing what?' Ketil scowled, angry that he had allowed himself to sleep. But the outhouse was some distance from the longhouse: he would probably not have heard if the intruder were as slow and careful as Tosti said. He would have to get the men to extend their patrols. 'I take it there was no fire?'

Tosti grinned.

'Once I heard him leave I checked right around the outhouse. Believe me, if there had been fire you would have heard about it!'

Ketil allowed himself a small smile.

'Why would anyone be interested in the outhouse?' he asked. 'Everyone in the settlement would know that the bodies are in there – and that someone would be sitting with them. A thief from somewhere else?'

Tosti shrugged.

'Maybe. But they didn't try the door, whoever they were, so if they had come all the way here for theft, they didn't make much of an effort.'

'Any idea when this was?'

'Well, I heard all of you come back from your supper, and it would have been less than an hour after that, I believe.'

'The beginning of the night, not the edge of morning,' said Ketil, half to himself. 'So someone was up late, not up early. I wonder who?'

'I'd hoped I might be able to make something out,' said Tosti, 'but no, not really. Whoever it was was just another shadow.'

'Is he gaining in confidence, I wonder? Did he mean to strike again?'

'But why only an outhouse?' Tosti asked. 'If he were gaining in confidence, surely he would attack another longhouse?'

Ketil bit his lip. He had no idea.

'Are you going to discuss it with Sigrid?' Tosti tilted his head back towards the longhouse. 'You know she sometimes sees things that other people don't.'

Ketil sighed.

'When it comes to the women, perhaps,' he said, knowing he sounded grudging. 'But today I want to talk to some of the men, on their own, if I can get them. Hamthir the boatman, Aslak, and the potter Hoskuld. She'd be no use with any of them.'

Tosti said nothing, and Ketil felt vaguely ashamed of himself. He nodded sharply at the priest, and went indoors to dress and tidy his bed.

He was out of the house again with his men before Sigrid and Osk had appeared. Katrin was sorting out the fire with drowsy cheerfulness. Tosti had vanished back inside the outhouse, and Ketil eyed it with concern. He told the men about the night time intruder.

'They could have set the priest on fire!' cried Skorri in alarm.

'I suppose we need to be watching out for where he strikes next,' added Geirod, as glum as ever.

'But why an outhouse?' asked Alf.

'Maybe,' said Skorri, 'he likes the fires, but he didn't like the fact that he'd killed someone. An outhouse would be safer, if all he wants to do is watch a building burn.'

Ketil knew there were people like that, drawn to fire, to the heat and the destruction. He had not yet seen that in anyone here.

'Anyway,' he said, 'from tonight we'll patrol, instead of just watching. Pairs: Geirod and Skorri, you do first watch, and Alf and I will do second.' Alf was least likely to send him mad by talking too much or too little.

'And what about today, sir?' asked Skorri smartly.

'Today you and Alf will go and talk to the people at the smithy and the leatherworks, along the shore. I want to know how much they see of anyone going past, and who they remember on the path. Of course people can come over the fields, too, but in the dark you would be sensible to stick to the path.'

'Aye, sir,' said Skorri. Alf was still pondering.

'Am I with you, then?' asked Geirod, not entirely enthusiastic.

'No, Geirod, you're off in the other direction, north. Nothing specific – see what you see, see who lives where, and ask whoever you meet about fire, grudges, strangers in their midst – you know the kind of thing.'

'What will you be doing, sir?' asked Skorri.

'I'm going to have a more private conversation with Hamthir and with Aslak, and then, if there is still time, I shall go to see the potter Hoskuld.' He dropped his voice: he had no wish for Hoskuld's daughter Katrin to overhear and warn him. He had heard someone at the longhouse door behind him. He glanced around, but it was Sigrid.

'If you're going,' she said, and took several steps to close the gap between them so she could lower her voice. 'If you're going to see Aslak to ask him about what he said last night – about Hoskuld – then there's something you ought to know first.'

'Really?' Ketil asked, then regretted his tone. If the men had not been there he might have corrected it.

'Yes,' she said, giving him an odd look. 'After his parents died last year, Aslak asked Hoskuld if he could marry Katrin. It was considered, apparently, but Katrin wasn't keen and in the end Hoskuld, according to Katrin, found out something about Aslak that made him turn Aslak down anyway. He told his wife Asta what it was, again that's what Katrin says, but he didn't tell Katrin.' She glanced to the hearth, making sure Katrin was not listening. 'I don't think Katrin cares what it was, because she's set on marrying Hamthir, when his business is good enough,' she finished apologetically.

'So Aslak's naming of Hoskuld might only have been revenge,' Ketil confirmed. 'I'll bear it in mind. Thank you, Sigrid,' he added, stiffly.

'I could come with you, if you like,' she said. 'I mean, if you think I could be of any help.'

'I can manage, thank you,' said Ketil.

'Have you any ideas yet?' she persisted. 'Any ideas of your own, I mean – that selection they offered us last night was a bit useless.'

'Do you think so?' asked Skorri, though Ketil thought he was watching the conversation a little too closely.

'Well, of course. It was just vague – a passing stranger, a secret name that only Gillaug knows, an accident,' she said bitterly, repeating Beinir's offering. 'And a dragon! Well, bless the lad, but only Aslak named anyone, and that, as I've told you, needs taking out and looking at in the broad light of day.' She tried a smile, but it looked uncomfortable on her face and swiftly fled, like a cat on the wrong lap.

'As I said, I'll bear it in mind,' Ketil repeated.

'And no one asked Vali what he thought. I'd say there was little around here that happens without Vali knowing.'

'Or Beinir?' he could not resist asking. She stopped, midbreath.

'Well,' she said, tugging her shawl tightly around her shoulders, 'I'll leave you to it. Good luck.' She marched back into the longhouse, leaving a silence behind that almost, for a moment, hurt.

'Right,' he said, 'you know what you're doing. Off you go. Back by dark. I want us ready to patrol as soon as the household retires.'

Alf and Skorri headed off along the shore path to the east, Alf moderating his loping stride to Skorri's shorter legs. As Ketil and Geirod turned the other way, Beinir appeared at the longhouse door, and waved, before setting off up the gentle slope inland. Ketil waved back.

At Vali's longhouse, Geirod grunted farewell and headed onwards to investigate the curve of land that they had sailed around to reach the harbour: there were one or two houses there, Ketil remembered. He himself glanced at Vali's door, already open, but instead headed for the harbour. A man building up his business for marriage would most likely be at that business, on this fine, bright, freezing morning.

The waves had been greedy this morning, licking the snow from the stony beach where several boats were pulled up ready for use, and a few others lay higher up, resting in the winter months. Ketil looked about for Hamthir's boat, but he could not immediately see it. Instead he followed the sound of scraping, just audible over the swish and suck of the waves. Along the shore, behind a small, rounded vessel, he found Aslak, rubbing down the edges of a new piece of wood inserted into the side of the boat. He looked up as Ketil crunched towards him.

'Your boat? Hit a rock?' Ketil asked.

Aslak shook his head, and pointed at the repair.

'Making myself useful,' he said. 'Hamthir did the new piece, but I'm trusted to make it tidy.'

'Where is Hamthir?'

'Out,' said Aslak, this time nodding at the sea. 'Taking Beinir's messenger over to the mainland so he can go along to Hoy and find Leif's daughter.'

'I'll catch him when he comes back, then,' said Ketil, leaning against the battered keel. The rock had scraped as well as punctured: someone had had a bad day. It was a fat little boat, he thought, eyes running over its lines: comfortable, slow, just for pottering about the coast, or a gentle trip with a sheep or two from island to island.

'Whose is it, then?'

Aslak pursed his lips, maybe with his own opinions about the boat.

'It's Beinir's.'

Ketil had a vision of Sigrid squatting in the boat with the sheep, Beinir rowing placidly along the low Shapinsay coast. She would be fairly safe, anyway – and she could help Beinir look out for rocks.

'So you're not usually a boatman, then?'

Aslak shook his head.

'Farming,' he said. 'I mean, that's mine there,' he pointed to a slightly more slick, but still practical, boat a little along the beach. It was well maintained, but nothing fancy.

'Sheep?' Ketil prompted, trying to sound as if he knew what he was talking about.

'Mostly. The usual. A goat, and hens, and a few fields.' It seemed an effort for him to speak even about ordinary things, so Ketil decided he would just plunge in with the harder questions.

'Last night you said you thought Hoskuld had set fire to Leif's house. Why was that?'

Aslak ran over the rough edges of wood again twice, three times, and Ketil thought he had cast him into complete silence.

'He's nearest,' he said at last. Ketil glanced up at the village. Actually, Leif's three nearest neighbours were all about the same distance away from him, Hoskuld inland, and on either side Eyolfr and Beinir.

'What reason would he have had? Had he quarrelled with Leif, or with Hervor?' Or with Osk, he thought belatedly, but no one thought about Osk.

Aslak shrugged.

'I don't know.'

'Did you maybe name him because he wouldn't let you marry his daughter?'

Aslak flashed Ketil a filthy look from under his dead fringe.

'Who told you that?' When Ketil said nothing, he turned back to the boat, anger fast subsiding into surliness. 'You know nothing. This is nothing to do with that. And the man's a fool: it would have been a good alliance, the two farms together.'

'That was all it was, an alliance?'

'Of course. What else would it be?'

'Well, she's pretty. And a good cook.'

'Marry her yourself, then.' Aslak spat, but Ketil was not wholly convinced. 'Anyway … you wanted to know if we'd seen anyone out that night. And I was out – going to the privy – and there was no light anywhere in the settlement – except for one. And that was up between Hoskuld's house and Leif's. So there.'

Ketil allowed his eyebrows to rise.

'Is that a fact? Perhaps I should go and talk to Hoskuld, then.'

'Perhaps you should,' said Aslak, a nasty smile on his grim face. 'Only you can't.'

'Why not?'

'Well, he's the messenger Beinir has sent to Hoy.'

XIV

The good thing about spinning, basic household craft as it was, was that whatever your mood, it turned out pretty much the same. Every woman had done it for so long that the motions were natural, the lumps smoothed, the rhythm steady. The bad thing about tablet-weaving, as Sigrid knew only too well, was that if you were distracted – for example, by thoughts of resentment at the attitudes of an old acquaintance who had needed your help before and would certainly benefit from it now if only he had the common courtesy to admit it and not be drawn away, presumably, by idle thoughts of the undoubtedly pretty wife he had waiting for him back on the Brough (here she paused, and deliberately drew some deep breaths) the bad thing about tablet-weaving when you were distracted was that it went wrong, and you forgot which tablet had to be turned which way how many times. Which was all right with the kind of basic braid that lots of women did to edge their husband's cloaks or their children's tunics, but Sigrid's living was made from these braids, these intricate, delicate, expensive braids that no ordinary housewife would have time to complete or skill to design, and she was making a complete mess of this one.

She set it aside, ignoring Katrin's curious glances, and instead took out some fine nailbinding she was doing for one of Thorfinn's unmarried men: he was to pay her in hacksilver, which was handy when usually she was paid in bread or chicken or beer. She liked variety. The wool slipped easily around her thumb, twining and turning off, and she allowed herself to relax again.

Had Ketil even listened to what she had said? She was fairly sure he had been paying no attention at all. How could he hope to be back on the Brough in time for his wedding? And being late would not please Thorfinn at all – not a good way to start a marriage, annoying your powerful father-in-law. Ketil should have the sense to know that. So he should have the sense to take any help he could get.

She was binding faster and faster, tugging the wool tight. She ignored the scrape across her thumb. Ketil would go and question Aslak and take what he said as unbiassed, no doubt, and then he would go off and ask Hoskuld all kinds of hostile questions, assuming that Aslak was telling the truth. That was no good. And then even if Ketil realised he was wrong he would have made an enemy of Hoskuld and he would never get any useful information out of him. How long would it take him to talk to Aslak? She frowned. How long had he been gone, anyway? She might be running out of time.

'Ouch!'

She cried out involuntarily: she had rammed the nailbinding needle under her thumbnail, and blood was beginning to ooze from the wound. She tore the wool from her thumb and sucked hard on the injured nail, cursing to herself.

'Are you all right, there, Sigrid?' Katrin asked, concerned.

'Yes, yes,' she said, pulling her thumb out of her mouth and pressing it hard between her fingers. She made herself tidy the wool away neatly with her other hand, resisting the urge to kick it across the floor. At least she had not bled on it. 'I thought of going out for some fresh air,' she said. 'Can I pick anything up from your mother? I think I'll head up that way.'

'Today's flour would be good, if you don't mind,' said Katrin.

'Of course.'

Fumbling with her sore thumb, Sigrid hooked on her back cloak and tidied her headcloth. She would catch Hoskuld before Ketil had a chance to turn him against any questioning.

But she was only halfway up to Hoskuld's longhouse, slithering in the snow, when she met Beinir coming in the opposite direction. He greeted her with every appearance of pleasure.

'Good morning, Sigrid! A fine morning, and no burnings last night! No doubt it was some accident, though it is a real shame that it was poor Leif and Hervor who died.' She watched his gaze flicker and thought perhaps it lighted briefly on the longhouse of Eyolfr and Gillaug. If it did, she felt inclined to agree. Though, she remembered guiltily, it was not for mere people to question whom God took and whom He spared. After all, if she were God, she would have put off Gillaug's death for a good long time, just in case she made it to heaven.

'Have you been off seeing to the sheep?' she asked, 'or to Leif's animals?'

'Both,' he said. 'And before that I went to see Hoskuld.'

'Oh yes?'

'Yes: I've sent him off to Hoy, to break the sad news to Leif's daughter. I think I saw Hamthir setting out with him a little while ago: they'll have a smooth crossing today, anyway.'

'Oh.' Sigrid was disappointed, but there were other things she could do. 'I'm going to see Asta.'

'I'm glad to see you getting to know the neighbours,' said Beinir. 'It has no doubt been a strange introduction for you to the island, but now that things have settled down again I hope you will like it when you are more familiar with it.'

He smiled at her, and she was deeply aware of how handsome he was, standing there with his face fresh from the cold air, his hair bright, his eyes kind. She found herself smiling back. After all, she could do worse, couldn't she?

'I'm sure I shall,' she heard herself saying. 'Um … I must go on: I am to fetch the flour for Katrin.'

'Of course: and I have my writing to do! I shall see you at the midday meal.' He raised a hand in farewell, and strode on down the slope. She watched for a moment, admiring the set of his broad shoulders. Had things really settled down, though? She was fairly sure that they had not.

She turned and continued up towards Hoskuld's longhouse. Well, if she couldn't question him, then at least Ketil couldn't, either. But how long was he going to be away? She should have asked. Maybe Asta would know.

Asta's servant was grinding the grain for both their household and Beinir's when Sigrid arrived at the door.

'Come in, sit down!' said Asta, laying aside her spinning to fetch hot wine. 'We're all behind this morning. Beinir was here only a little while ago, asking Hoskuld to go over to Hoy to tell Leif's poor daughter about her parents. Well, he was right to send Hoskuld, for at least he'll break it gently to the girl. But who knows how long he'll be, at this time of the year? Look at that snow – I've never seen it lie so long. And the girl might not be able to leave her own family straightaway to come back, and she'll make it slower on the way back anyway … Here you are, Sigrid! Comfortable?'

'Yes, thank you,' said Sigrid, grateful for the pause. The wine was good, too. 'So you wouldn't expect him back for what, two or three days?'

Asta paused, clearly tracing a journey in her head.

'More than that, I think, in this snow. Have you ever seen snow lie so long?'

'Never, here,' Sigrid agreed. She glanced about the longhouse. It was completely ordinary: you could have taken a note of it to tell a young housewife how to set things up. Bedcurtains, with one bedstead of plain design; a loom at the back, with a plainish weave on it and a basket of wool at its foot; hanging shelves holding food up and out of the way; square soapstone dishes by the fire, ready for the midday meal – Hjaltland soapstone, not the finer stuff from further north - a space for a cow and some hens, presumably including Aslak's, at the lower end. Plain and sensible, nothing fancy – no books, for example, but nothing embellished with complicated braid, either. If Sigrid stayed on Shapinsay, she doubted that Asta would be much of a customer for her woolwork.

'Was Leif a particular friend of Hoskuld's, that Beinir sent him?' Sigrid asked.

'A particular friend? No, not really,' said Asta. 'But of course they got on well. Everyone liked Leif, and Hervor. You met them, didn't you?'

'Yes, a couple of times,' Sigrid agreed. 'I liked them, too. It seems impossible to believe that someone killed them.'

'Someone killed them?' Asta was startled. 'But Beinir said it was an accident!'

'Others don't agree. Ketil Gunnarson, for instance – have you met him?'

'Ketil who? Who's he?'

'He's one of Thorfinn's men. Four of them came when the vart was lit, to see what the matter was.'

'But Beinir said it was an accident!'

'I know, but …' She looked at Asta, who seemed genuinely distressed – and now she was here on her own with the serving girl for a few days. Sigrid decided not to press it further just now.

'But if it had been right,' she could not resist a different angle, 'if Thorfinn's man – I know, he's an outsider and what does he know? But if he had been right, is there anyone who had fought with Leif? Or with Hervor? Anyone who might just have wanted to frighten them, or to damage their house? Maybe whoever burned Aslak's house, too?' Surely, surely, it must be the same person. Unless it was revenge, one attack for the other. Otherwise it made no sense.

'Well, now, Aslak …' Asta glanced at her servant, and lowered her voice, leaning closer to Sigrid. She was a broad woman, and Sigrid resisted the urge to move back to make room. 'I mean, if you asked me if anyone round here might have done a stupid thing like that, set fire to anyone's house, then Aslak would be the top of my list.'

'Why's that, then?'

'Well, if anyone is going to do anything that stupid … he'll have been drinking, of course. That's what causes it. He drinks too much, he can't hold it, and he goes and does something he shouldn't.'

The fight in Thorfinn's hall flashed into Sigrid's mind. Was that an example? But many men fought when they had taken a bit too much. Then a thought struck her, and she tilted towards Asta for closer confidences.

'Is that why Aslak was – why your husband would not let him marry Katrin?'

Asta hesitated, but only a little.

'That was part of it – that was the start of it, really,' she said. 'When Aslak came over to ask for Katrin, well, Hoskuld thought it would be a good idea, for the lands join and Aslak's not short of wealth – I mean, he's not Earl Thorfinn, but his wife would be comfortable enough. We knew he'd been in a few fights when he was drunk, but that's a thing that young men grow out of, more often than not, don't they?' She nodded, agreeing with herself.

'So what happened to change his mind?'

'Hoskuld went over to Eday, taking some of his pots to sell – there's no potter there just now so every now and then he goes across to some of the other islands, spends a few days travelling about, taking orders sometimes.' She was clearly proud of him. 'Well, it hadn't been that long since Aslak had been away, too, up in Westray, and it so happened that Hoskuld met a man from Westray on Eday. And they got talking, and the Westray man said he had a low opinion of men from Shapinsay, because it had been a man from Shapinsay had got his girl drunk and taken her, and got a child on her, before he'd even touched her himself. And Hoskuld of course asked the name of the man, and you'll never believe it!'

Sigrid pretended to have no idea.

'Aslak! The very one that lives over there.' Asta jerked her thumb over her shoulder in the approximate direction of Aslak's ruined house. 'Aslak had done it, and gone and never even made compensation! That's what he's like, see: when he gets drunk, men get thumped and women get – well, more than they bargained for. Now,' she sat back, satisfied with the evidence she had presented, 'what man would want a fellow like that marrying his only daughter?'

'Or any daughter,' Sigrid agreed. A horrible thought had occurred to her – was that what had happened to Bolla back on the Brough? Was it Aslak she had met, and not Margad at all? And hadn't it been a Westray man that Aslak had fought in Thorfinn's hall? Maybe there had been much more to it than she had realised at the time. She should tell Ketil – if he would listen. She wondered if Bolla was yet able to speak, but shook herself – she had to concentrate now on what was happening here.

'Do you think Aslak might have set fire to his own longhouse, too, when he was drunk?'

There was the smallest hesitation, then Asta said quickly,

'Seems more than likely, doesn't it? I mean, what else could have happened? And then,' she went on, easier now – Sigrid tucked her brief discomfort away in her memory to think about later – 'then maybe Leif said something to him about it, probably just as a joke, and the next time Aslak was drunk he set fire to Leif's house. He probably didn't even think of how they might get out alive.' She rubbed her hands over her face. 'Oh, poor Hervor! And poor Leif. They never did anything to deserve that, I can tell you! Good, kind, gentle people.'

'I haven't heard a word said against them,' Sigrid said. 'Were they really that perfect?'

Asta frowned for a minute, considering.

'Well, Hervor wasn't the best baker you could find on the island.

But I'm struggling to think of anything else. Leif was very proud of his ram, and would never let anyone say a word against it. But even then, he laughed at himself about it. No, they were just nice people.' She sighed weightily.

'Can you tell me a bit more about the island?' Sigrid tried a little flattery. 'You seem to know everyone and a bit about them, and it seems to me that that kind of knowledge will be important in finding out whether or not it was Aslak that set fire to Leif's house.'

'Oh, it was, I'm quite sure! Who else would it be?' But she thumped her fists on to her knees and pushed herself to her feet. 'Come on, then, if it's not snowing: we can go up the hill a bit and take a look.'

Asta's boots and cloak were thick and solid, and it crossed Sigrid's mind that they might be Hoskuld's old ones. The serving girl sat back from her grindstone and smiled goodbye as they went. It occurred to Sigrid that she had not seen many servants or slaves around the settlement: perhaps the bulk of them came from somewhere else when the farms needed more workers.

She followed in Asta's large, rounded footprints past their own outhouses and up the easy hill beyond the longhouse. The path was broad, edged by bushes busy with finches and clamouring with waxwings, stealing the last of the berries.

'It's not the highest point on the island, but we get a good view from here,' said Asta, puffing terribly as she reached the top. Nevertheless as Sigrid looked about there was only one point higher, and that, from what she could see, was the vart hill over to the east. Beyond that, on a spit of land pointing north-east, was another irregular rise, probably where some building left behind by the old people was half-hidden by the snow. On the eastward slopes of the hill on which they stood the snow was rough and pierced with blackened stalks, and a bold flock of horra geese had landed to root through the snow.

'Boggy ground,' Asta remarked, nodding towards it. Her arms were bundled into her cloak and she was beginning to catch her breath. Sigrid understood, and turned slowly from east to west. To the north, where the dark grey sea's fringes fiddled at the island's shores, she could see a couple of little ayres, pools of water cut off from the sea by the thinnest strip of snow. Most of the longhouses she could see were by the shore, only one or two raised up on the gentle slopes. There were more on their south side of the island than she could see on the north, spread between the two natural harbours, the one she had arrived at and a bay she could see to the east end. Another building had been left by the old people on the headland, where it seemed they had liked to build.

'We don't see the people from the north side so much, not in the winter, anyway,' Asta explained.

'Any reason for that? Are there any feuds between the settlements, or between families?'

Asta giggled – such an idea was clearly daft.

'No, not that I can think of! It's just that we're busy enough on this side, and they do whatever they do on that side. My husband goes over in the spring to take orders for pots.' She made it sound just as much of an expedition as it would be for Hoskuld to go to Eday. Sigrid wondered how many good woolworkers they had on the north side.

Asta looked down the hill at the settlement from which they had climbed.

'You know whose house is whose here, don't you?' The two broken and burned longhouses were even more obvious from here, despite the snow's attempts to swathe them. A movement caught Sigrid's eye: Gillaug, Eyolfr fluttering in her wake, striding off to Vali's longhouse, marching inside as though she owned the place.

'Yes, Katrin pointed them all out when I arrived,' said Sigrid.

'Of course she has her eye on Hamthir,' said Asta, sighing a little. 'He's a good man, and he works hard: it'll be a fine household for her, if he asks her.'

'Oh, I thought there was already an understanding?' said Sigrid.

'Hm.' Asta's amiable face creased with a scowl. 'Well, as to that … I'll say this for him, he's not pushing her into anything.'

'Not pushing enough, perhaps?' Sigrid suggested.

'Aye, maybe. Hamthir's very interested in wealth. Which is no bad thing, except that I don't think he thinks that wealth and a wife go together. He told Hoskuld one day that he wouldn't rush into marriage where a wife would bleed him dry.'

'Ah, but maybe he'll see reason with Katrin. She's a sensible girl,' said Sigrid. 'She runs Beinir's household beautifully.' She glanced towards it, and noted that Gillaug, Vali and Eyolfr had emerged, and were in intense conversation by the longhouse door. Whatever it was, it looked serious. Sigrid's curiosity was aroused.

'Aye! Oh, and I've that flour to give you before you go back.'

'Oh, that's right. I'll collect it now, shall I?'

It had turned cold, and it was no wrench to hurry down the hill towards Asta's house. Inside she quickly picked up a jar filled with flour, and handed it to Sigrid.

'Here we are,' she said. 'It was good to see you – I like a gossip! Come again, any time!'

Sigrid thought she might well, as she turned and hefted the jar carefully down towards Beinir's longhouse. She was almost at the outhouse where Tosti guarded the bodies of Leif and Hervor when Gillaug, Eyolfr and Vali suddenly rounded the corner from the shore path, and rapped on Beinir's doorpost. Some instinct made Sigrid duck behind the outhouse instead of hurrying forward: she had vanished before Gillaug's sharp look could have pinned her. She leaned back against the outhouse wall, wondering why she had hidden: she would have to go inside soon, for it was really chilling fast.

She crept around the back of the outhouse, trying to decide what to do. Someone had been here before her since the last snowfall yesterday, someone who had carelessly scuffed their footprints as they went. It was hard to make out the shape of the prints, but she stared at them, following them with her eyes as she wondered how long Gillaug might be inside. One print, right at the corner, was less distorted: whoever it was must have slipped, one foot sliding backwards into a small drift of snow. It couldn't be Beinir, anyway, she thought: surely his feet were bigger than that? It might be the right size for Tosti, but she had no idea if he wore boots with such a pointed toe – not very sharp, but not as rounded as most people. She stretched one of her own feet towards it, and noted that it was a good fingerlength longer than her own boot. But she was wasting time, and growing cold: she would have to go into the longhouse.

Still clutching the precious flour, she stepped carefully down to the longhouse door, pushed aside the curtain, and stepped inside. Gillaug and Vali were seated on either side of Beinir at the hearth, while Eyolfr stood back, fidgeting, by the door. Ketil stood, too, a hand on his sword hilt, a strange look on his face. Katrin was holding a jug, presumably having just served the visitors. At Sigrid's entrance, all conversation fell silent, and everyone turned to stare at her.

Refusing to be intimidated, Sigrid stamped the snow off her boots and went straight to hand the jar of flour over to Katrin, setting it at the foot of the hearth.

'Good day to you, Gillaug, Vali – oh, and is that Eyolfr? Good day to you, too! I trust you are all well?'

The jug wobbled in Katrin's hands, but she steadied it, glanced at Beinir, and poured a cup of wine for Sigrid. Sigrid unclipped her cloak, and sat by the fire, waiting to see if any of them would say anything. Anything at all: apart from Katrin they seemed to have frozen.

Of course it was Gillaug who recovered her tongue first. She smiled at Sigrid, a smile of what – pity? – then turned back to Beinir.

'As I was saying, I have pointed out to Vali,' she bowed her head slightly in Vali's direction, 'the obvious thing. We had no fires in this place until a few days ago. Until, that is, just after she arrived.' She turned, and observed Sigrid like some kind of farm animal that might or might not be for sale. 'So the obvious thing, as I say, is that it was that woman who set fire to Leif's longhouse.'

XV

Sigrid opened her mouth, but for once no words came out. Ketil coughed, pointedly, and waited until he had the attention of at least Vali and Beinir.

'Where is your proof?'

Gillaug, her satisfied gaze still fixed on Sigrid, did not bother to look up at him.

'It's enough that the fires only happened after she arrived.'

'No,' said Ketil firmly. 'No, it is not. You need more than that.' He found he was standing straight and using his best Trondheim court voice. He was here to represent Thorfinn's justice. 'Even if her arrival and the fires are somehow linked, it need not be that she lit the fires. But the chances are that the two things are unconnected. Why would she set fire to the house of someone she had barely met?'

'She's probably mad,' said Gillaug, finally looking away from Sigrid. 'She looks mad.'

Ketil heard an indrawn breath from Sigrid and, suppressing an urge to laugh, he quickly talked over whatever she might want to say.

'More investigation is needed, and no trial can take place until that investigation is complete. Send word to Thorfinn if you wish, and he'll say the same. I hold his authority here in this matter.'

He was aware of Sigrid turning and staring at him, but he did not look at her.

'She should be kept under lock and key, then, while you're investigating,' said Gillaug, turning the last word into a hiss. It struck Ketil that she was going out of her way to be unpleasant, and he wondered why.

'I'll keep an eye on her,' said Beinir anxiously. He reached out a hand towards Sigrid and she turned back towards him, though they were either end of the hearth. Ketil could not see her face. 'And Vali, I've sent Hoskuld to fetch Leif's daughter.' He smiled at Vali, anxious to please.

'Already?' Vali started. 'But –'

'Not you,' said Gillaug sharply. 'You can't guard her, Beinir. You brought her here. We'll -'

'She will be in my charge,' said Ketil. Gillaug's jaw snapped shut so hard it was audible.

'That seems fair,' said Vali, frowning still at Beinir. Ketil asked himself how much of this was Vali's doing, and how much Gillaug's. 'I think you'll have to accept that, Gillaug.'

Gillaug had clearly had other ideas, but Ketil was pleased to see that she subsided under Vali's look.

'Now,' said Ketil, one hand casually still on the hilt of his sword, 'unless you have any useful information to offer, I think you had better be going and allow me and my men to continue my work.' It was not his place to order Gillaug and Vali – oh, and Eyolfr, who only seemed half-there anyway – out of Beinir's house, but as Beinir did not seem to be doing it Ketil was happy to help him. Vali rose at once, eager to depart: Gillaug looked as though she might well resist but Vali reached out a hand to help her up, which she could not refuse. Eyolfr was already at the door, breathing the fresh air, as if the whole thing had smothered him. Ketil watched them go. The longhouse seemed suddenly twice as large.

Sigrid still sat at the foot of the hearth. Beinir slumped in his chair at the other end.

'What am I to do?' he asked. 'Gillaug can be very determined!'

'Does she base her argument on a wish to discover the truth?' Ketil asked. 'Or is there some reason why she seems to have taken against you, Sigrid?'

'I haven't done anything to her!' said Sigrid at once. 'The first time I met her she made unpleasant remarks about – about the last woman who was betrothed to you, Beinir.'

Beinir looked up in shock.

'She did what?'

'She said your last intended wife had died.' Sigrid's face was a muddle: Ketil could see embarrassment there, but also keen curiosity. 'I was going to ask you, but … well, it's not an easy conversation to start, is it?'

'You've started it now,' said Beinir, but without rancour: he looked more concerned than angry. Ketil, still standing, did his best to disappear into the shadows – Katrin, too, quietly continued forming flatbreads from her mother's flour, concentrating on their perfect circles. Sigrid stayed silent, too, but her gaze was fixed on Beinir's face. Beinir shifted, his empty wine cup forgotten in his hand. Ketil could see the brownish stains of ink on his fingers.

'It was a couple of years ago,' Beinir started, looking into the fire '- a bit more, for it was summer. Ingigerd was her name. I met her on Graemsay when I was there on business. I … it wasn't maybe a good marriage, not in terms of wealth or status, but oh, she was pretty! But of course we barely knew each other, and so, a little like you, Sigrid, she agreed to come here to see the place and so that we could become better acquainted. I would not like to make a mistake in such a serious matter.'

No, thought Ketil, you might have thought her pretty, but you are a careful man, nevertheless.

'Things were arranged with her uncle – her father was dead – and she came here with her maid Ali. And … she died.'

'How?' Sigrid's voice was a whisper.

'An accident.' Beinir licked his dry lips, and cleared his throat. He seemed to hope that that would be enough, but after a moment of silence he went on. 'She drowned in Vasa ayre. It's a little ayre north of here.' He lapsed for a moment into his desire to educate and inform. 'Brackish, you know, cut off from the sea by a narrow strip of land.'

Sigrid nodded, as if she knew the place he meant.

'Was she alone?'

'She was, yes. She went missing early one morning, and we found her there the next day. I don't know why she went there.' His voice was wracked with remembered pain. 'She just went out: I didn't even see her go. I had my work to do, you know? And the summer light was good for writing …'

Ketil glanced at Sigrid. She was stony-faced, but he could see from her eyes that her mind was working hard.

'That's very sad,' she said, after a moment. 'You must have been much affected.'

'I was!' he cried. 'She was so pretty! Such a sweet, lively girl! I had no idea what to do with myself. I had to go and tell her uncle – he could not read so I could not send him a message. That was an awful day. An awful journey to have to make.'

Sigrid nodded, thoughtfully sympathetic.

'How long had she been here when it happened?'

Beinir stared at her, as though he did not at first understand the question. Then he shrugged.

'A few months. Spring, she came, and it would have been late summer when – when she was found. We were growing so close, so dear to each other …'

Ketil was sure he saw Sigrid shiver. Had she been growing dear to Beinir, too? And he to her? He was not sure how they had wandered down this side path, drifting away from the longhouse fires, but for the moment he was happy to let it go. It was all more information about Shapinsay. And about Beinir.

But Beinir seemed to have run out of things to say on the matter of his late sweetheart, lapsing into melancholy, and Sigrid did not appear to be on the point of asking another question, not yet, anyway. Not doubt she was formulating more for later. For a moment they sat in silence, the only sound the hum of the fire and the light scrape of Katrin scooping flatbread from the baking stones and turning it. Ketil wondered how long it would be until his men returned from their tasks for their dinner. He had in a sense handicapped himself by offering to guard Sigrid, and he was sure she would not be happy if he passed her on like baggage to Alf or Skorri. And she could run rings around Geirod, no doubt.

But in any case what was he going to do next? He could not question Hoskuld, not for several days. Hamthir would probably be back by dark, but then he would be tucked up in Vali's house, and Ketil wanted to speak to him on his own, as he preferred with anyone prominent in the settlement. He could go and talk to Gillaug and Eyolfr, but all they would offer him at the moment would be their opinions on Sigrid, and that would not get him any further. Only when – or if – he had proved Sigrid innocent would it be worth discussing the matter with them again.

Beinir roused himself, shook his head as if he were waking up, and went to a covered hanging shelf at the back of the longhouse, near his own bed. He came back with a book and a box, and made for the door, settling himself just inside it. The draught of cold air as he shifted the door curtain to give himself space and light made Sigrid shiver. She stood to go and help Katrin with the meal. Ketil drifted over to watch what Beinir was doing.

The box contained a pen, a fine knife, and a jar of ink, and another jar, equally well sealed, which Beinir left alone for now. Ketil squatted down to see more clearly, and Beinir glanced over at him, angling the heavy book so that Ketil could see better.

'Can you read and write?' he asked kindly. Ketil shook his head.

'Only runes. And one or two letters.'

'Which ones? K, I suppose!'

'T and S, actually,' said Ketil, quite proud. It was useful to know the letters that started the names of one's lord, even if the sounds were different from the runes. Beinir clearly did not make the link, and gave a puzzled frown, but he found a scrap of parchment in his writing box and made two shapes on it, one angular, the other more curved.

'Gunnarson, aren't you? This spiky one is K, and the other is G, K for Ketil, G for Gunnarson.'

Ketil stared at the two shapes, wondering how they could mean those sounds. The same way runes did, he supposed. In fact, the K was not far from the rune for the same sound, now he looked at it. But the G was not shaped like any sound at all.

'What are you writing?' he asked.

'The events of this morning,' said Beinir. His earlier discomfort seemed to be forgotten, and he paid no attention to Sigrid, accused of arson and murder and his guest. 'I do it every day, morning and evening, so I have a full report for Thorfinn when he asks for it. I shall note down Gillaug's accusation of Sigrid, of course.'

Ketil dropped his voice, glancing over at the hearth and the two women working. They did not seem to be listening.

'Do you think she might have done it?'

Even as he asked the question he felt bad. Sigrid was his friend. He was sure, in his heart, that she had not done anything like what Gillaug had said. But still, she had been here, and as Gillaug had said the fires had not happened until she arrived. He would not be doing his duty to Thorfinn if he did not at least make sure he could confirm Sigrid's innocence. And anyway, he thought, justifying himself, it would be useful to know what Beinir thought – it would tell him more about Beinir.

'Oh, no, I shouldn't think so,' said Beinir, almost at once. 'It must have been an accident. Why would anyone kill Leif? And Sigrid in particular had only just met him. She had known Aslak a little, I suppose, but still … Thorfinn never said anything about her doing anything like that when he suggested the match.'

Many wouldn't have, Ketil thought. Here, what about marrying this woman? She has a bit of a habit of setting fire to other people's houses, but she's harmless enough. Anyway, he knew very well that Sigrid did not have a habit of setting fire to anything. Why would she have started now? And, most tellingly, the accusation had come from Gillaug. Gillaug, a woman who seemed determined to do damage, and had no evidence. If it had been anyone else, he might have been more suspicious. Though there was the question of why Gillaug had picked on Sigrid. Was she just convenient, or had she, in the short time Sigrid had been on Shapinsay, taken a dislike to her? There was certainly a nastiness in Gillaug's accusation that implied it was something personal. Ketil scowled at himself: he was able to believe that Gillaug could develop a grudge against Sigrid in such a short time, but not that Sigrid could have one against Leif and Hervor. Could he be wrong? Sigrid was not good at hiding her feelings about people.

'I hope Hoskuld comes back soon with Leif's daughter,' Beinir said. He was probably writing a bit about sending him off to Hoy. 'I'd like Father Tosti to be able to carry out the funerals, and then he can do some other things for us.'

'You've never had a priest living here?' Ketil asked.

'No, not yet. It's such a privilege to have one now. He will be able to set us up for Christmas, though I know he will have to be back on the Brough before then. I wonder if Thorfinn would find us a priest of our own?'

'The settlement must be excited to have Tosti here,' said Ketil. 'Will people be coming from around the island?'

'Oh, I expect so,' said Beinir. 'I expect Father Tosti will be very busy.'

Geirod appeared in the doorway with the yellow dog, almost tripping over Beinir's long legs. In a moment, Ketil saw Alf and Skorri approaching from the direction of the smithy and the leatherworks, Skorri chattering away as usual while Alf seemed to drift a finger's length or two above the snow. Beinir finished his brief account of the morning's doings, took the other sealed jar from his writing box and scattered fine sand over the ink to dry it, then packed everything away at the back of the longhouse. The men went to wash before the meal, and when they returned Katrin and Sigrid had the food ready. Ketil had never seen Sigrid so involved in cooking. Perhaps she was trying to impress Beinir. He was not yet convinced that Beinir deserved it, however clever he was at reading and writing.

After the meal, Ketil went outside with his men to hear their reports on the morning's work. Geirod had little to say: he had walked around the west coast as far as a small ayre and had come across no people and no longhouses, though he could see some in the distance beyond the ayre. Ketil nodded, wondering if it was the same ayre where Beinir's sweetheart had been found drowned. Geirod had walked back up the low hill behind the settlement, and had seen ahead of him Sigrid, with another woman, but had not caught up with them.

Skorri and Alf had little more. The smith had a large family and several servants, and the leatherworks was small but busy. The smith had seen smoke at dawn the morning that Leif's house had been burned, and had sent a servant to ask what the news was, but had no other source of information: neither household had seen anyone recently passing either east or west along the shore. But then, they were mostly indoors at night time. Ketil sighed: he had not expected much more than that, but it was not much for a morning's work for three men. He told them how Sigrid had been accused, and was pleased to see that they seemed to find it as unlikely as he did.

'She is under our guardianship now,' Ketil explained, 'so between us we must not let her out of our sight. If another longhouse is burned, and we are not completely sure where she is, it will add fuel to Gillaug's accusation.'

Skorri nodded solemnly, and reinforced the order, like a good second in command, with a look at Alf and Geirod.

'What do you want us to do with the rest of the day, then, sir?' he asked.

'I'd like you to go back down to the harbour, Skorri, and tell me when Hamthir returns from the mainland,' said Ketil. 'If you see Aslak, have a chat with him. Not questioning – I did that this morning – just idle conversation. What Sigrid told us about him wanting to marry Katrin is right, but he denies it meant much to him that he was turned down, and he's still accusing Hoskuld. See if he says anything else when his guard is down.'

'Aye, sir.'

'You two, let Father Tosti have a break from the outhouse, let him stretch his legs for a while. Then a swim before supper.'

'Aye, sir,' said Alf. Geirod scowled, but that was his standard reaction to any orders. The pair wandered over to the outhouse, and Skorri hesitated.

'Why do you think they've accused Sigrid?' he asked, low-voiced. Ketil knew that what he meant was 'Do you think Sigrid did it?'

'Because she's a newcomer, perhaps, nothing more than that. It is beginning to look as if someone in this settlement, not an outsider from elsewhere on the island, is most likely to have burned the two houses: no one wants to think that their old, trusted neighbour might do such a thing.'

'Aye, sir,' said Skorri, nodding. 'Well, I'll be going.' He turned and tramped down to the shore path. It was almost clear of snow now with the passage of feet, but when Ketil looked up at the sky he was sure there would be more to come. Was he right? Was it really someone from this small settlement? He thought so, but was that just a feeling? At a loss, he went back into the longhouse.

Beinir had gone out.

'Who knows where?' Sigrid shrugged, settled by the door and weaving. 'And Katrin has gone to see her mother. Asta, up the hill.'

'Hill?' he queried, sitting and propping himself against the other doorpost.

'Not a big one, I admit,' Sigrid conceded. 'But I quite like the place. Well, I'll see what it's like when the snow goes – it can't lie much longer, surely. I hear the land is good.'

'You're thinking of staying, then?' he asked, but found he did not want to hear the answer. 'Asta is Hoskuld's wife, isn't she?'

'That's right. I happened to be visiting her earlier.' If Sigrid was pleased at the turn in the conversation, she hid it well. 'Beinir has sent Hoskuld off to Hoy to fetch Leif's daughter.'

'He has. Not exactly convenient.'

'No, not after last night.' Sigrid flipped her weaving tablets to make some intricate change to the pattern. He had long ago given up understanding the process, but he watched in silence for a moment.

'Sigrid, you know I have to ask you –'

'I suppose so.' She did not look at him. 'Go on, then.'

He drew a deep breath.

'Did you set fire – to either longhouse?'

'No. Of course I didn't.'

'Thank you.' Of course she would say that, he thought, but he was happy to believe her. 'And then Aslak – I spoke to him earlier. He claims he was only interested in Katrin for the advantages of the connexion.'

'I don't know about that,' said Sigrid at once. 'I can't think why he would have accused Hoskuld so readily if he didn't have a grudge, but I suppose the grudge might be something else. Come to think of it, Katrin said she was surprised when he offered for her, for she had never thought he knew she existed before then.'

'Hm,' said Ketil. Perhaps in that, at least, Aslak had been right.

'But listen, there's more,' said Sigrid, finally meeting his eye with a degree of her old friendliness. 'I asked Asta why she and Hoskuld had turned down Aslak's offer, and she told me that they had found out that for one thing, Aslak fights men when he's drunk.'

'Well, we knew that, didn't we?' Ketil remembered that evening in Thorfinn's hall. 'And many do.'

'Yes, but it's what he does to women when he's drunk that is more to the point,' said Sigrid urgently. 'Listen, because it raises more than one question.' Then, clearly concentrating on remembering accurately, she went on. 'He makes women drink, then rapes them. Sound familiar?'

'Bolla,' he said grimly.

'It fits, doesn't it? Maybe Margad actually tried to save her, and Aslak attacked him. And Geirod only took the dog,' she added, slyly.

He sighed. His chances of hiding the identity of Geirod's new dog had never been good.

'Don't tell me you haven't even asked Geirod what happened?' Her jaw dropped in mock amazement.

'I only knew he had the dog when he brought it with him in the boat,' he admitted. 'There hasn't been a good moment.'

'Margad beat the dog, didn't he? Thorfinn won't like that.'

'My thoughts exactly. But Geirod couldn't afford whatever compensation Margad demands.'

'Between them, though … I take it the others knew before you did?'

He cast her an unfriendly look, then slumped a little.

'Even Tosti knew before I did.'

She was kind enough not to smile.

'Well, you'd have had to tell Thorfinn if you had known. They were just protecting you.'

He decided to reflect on that later.

'Do you think Aslak is guilty, then?'

'Asta reckons he's more than capable of setting fire to his own longhouse when drunk,' she said. 'But the thing is, I went up to talk to him outside his burning house, and there was no smell of drink. He was deeply shocked, I would have said. But I could almost see him bearing a grudge against Leif and setting fire to Leif's house. Or, perhaps, Leif had found out something about Aslak that he didn't want people knowing. If he did attack Bolla, and he attacked the girl on Westray, does he make sure he does these awful things away from home, to hide them? Then Leif perhaps finds out and threatens to tell ... Beinir, I suppose.'

The light had gone, and she unhooked her weaving from her bare toe and wound it up carefully. He rose and followed her back towards the hearth and its warmth, waiting while she put the weaving away by her bed. They sat next to each other, staring into the fire, not speaking for a moment. He was always taken aback at how comfortable he felt in her company.

'Did you find out anything else useful?' he asked at last.

'I think I saw the ayre where Beinir's – where that girl died,' she said.

'Geirod seemed to have come close to it, too. He saw you in the distance.' He paused again. 'Are you relieved to have had him tell you about her?'

'A bit,' she said after a moment. 'A bit. But don't you think it sounds a bit strange, all the same?'

Ketil gave a small snort of laughter.

'Not every odd death is suspicious,' he reminded her.

'I know … but it was her death that Gillaug taunted me about when I came here. Just straightaway, as if it was the first thing in her head.'

'Two and a half years ago, or thereabouts,' said Ketil

thoughtfully. 'What were you doing then?'

'Oh!' she snapped, 'you're not going to let her accuse me of that, are you?' She glared at him, but he waited, smiling slightly, and at last she grinned, briefly.

'Thorsten was still alive,' she said, 'but he was a cripple. I remember – I had forgotten - when the vart was lit here, the time it was lit by accident, or whatever it was, Einar took his ships round to find out what had happened, and Thorsten was furious that he couldn't go with them. So that's where I was.'

Ketil had some idea, from things she had said before, that Thorsten's fury was likely to have resulted in some kind of violence.

'The vart was lit, and Beinir's betrothed died in an ayre. An eventful summer, that year.'

'And they say that nothing ever happens on Shapinsay,' she said, managing a smile of her own. 'But Beinir has books full of what happens here, you know. Perhaps that summer was nothing out of the ordinary.'

'After all, you've only been here a few days and already –' he began, when they were interrupted by a shout from outside.

'Fire! Fire!'

XVI

Sigrid was up and at the door almost as quickly as Ketil – how did such a tall man move so fast? – but she had to elbow past him to see what was going on when he stopped in the doorway. No need to ask where the fire was: they could almost feel the warmth from where they stood, and the light from the flames was nearly enough for her to take her weaving out again. Beinir's outhouse, where Tosti was keeping watch over Leif and Hervor's bodies, was blazing, long tongues of flame licking upward almost from the top of the snow. There was a strange smell of cooking fish.

Sigrid could not help yelling 'Fire!' again. Ketil was already running forward, and she seized a bucket from beside the doorstep and scooped up snow, where it was still thick enough, and ran after him. Who had raised the alarm? It was hard to see: the pattern of dancing flames had seared across her eyes and even the darkness around them flickered and jumped. She edged as close as she could and hurled the snow towards the doorway. Where was Tosti? The outhouse was small: could he possibly be trapped? Surely he could have reached the doorway before the fire caught hold? What if he had been asleep?

She scooped another bucketful, and it hit the flames, hissing but useless. What was that smell? Someone took the bucket from her hands and handed her another one, full of water this time. She glanced back.

'Vali!'

'I was passing and saw the fire just as it surged up!' he yelled at her, for the flames were shouting, too. 'Where's the priest?'

'I don't know!'

Ketil had been shouting beyond the outhouse and returned now at a run, with Alf and Geirod and more water. Alf was stationed nearest the outhouse and threw the water with remarkable accuracy.

'Where's Father Tosti?' Katrin slithered and stumbled towards Sigrid.

'We don't know! Get another bucket, help Vali!' Sigrid called. Was this what living on Shapinsay was going to be like? She would have to have a pair of leather gloves made, to save her hands from the bucket handles, or she would never be able to work fine wool.

'Here,' said a different voice, handing her the next bucket. This time when she half turned she saw, to her immense relief, Tosti in the line behind her. 'Can't a man even go to the privy?' he objected breathlessly, managing to make a joke. Sigrid laughed abruptly, then gasped.

'Was anyone in there for you while you were away?'

He shook his head.

'No, I sneaked out,' he said. 'Too much ale with my dinner.'

The two-pronged effort began to have some effect. Slowly, the flames died down, but the shape of the building they outlined was much changed. The outhouse had burned almost to the ground.

'What's that nice smell?' asked Tosti. 'I noticed it just as I left earlier.'

'Fish oil,' said Ketil, his face blackened and grim. 'Someone wanted the place to burn fast, and burn down. What else was in there, besides you and the bodies, Tosti?'

'A rough table – just a couple of boards on some stones – for the bodies, and a cloth to cover them. You know there was not much left. And a stool, which I sat on. That was about it.'

'You're sure?' asked Vali, concerned. Tosti smiled.

'I've sat in there long enough to take notice. It was not a big building.'

'Anything of your own?' Vali pushed. This time Tosti made a face.

'My bag,' he said, mouth downturned. 'But my gospels are in my pouch. There was nothing else of value.'

'Nevertheless you'll receive compensation – from the community, if we do not find who did this. And you are uninjured?'

'Yes, quite.'

'Did you see anyone outside when you came out?' Ketil asked. Sigrid saw that Vali had had his mouth open to ask something else, but

Ketil had beaten him to it. Where was Beinir? It was his outhouse.

Others had appeared now, too: Asta had followed Katrin more sedately down the hill, and Skorri had appeared from somewhere behind the longhouse. No doubt, Sigrid thought, Gillaug would be along in a moment to check Sigrid's hands for burns. She decided she wanted to be inside and in some comfort when that happened.

She went to the barrel to wash her face and hands first, the ice already broken by the urgent buckets. She was the first in the queue: Tosti appeared after her, and others were moving in the same direction. He edged up beside her.

'It was deliberate, wasn't it?'

'I think so,' she agreed, her voice as low as his. He looked more puzzled than anxious, though he had been lucky.

'Who would want to burn a minor priest and two dead bodies, already badly burned?' I'm going to say a blessing over the ashes, for there will be nothing left to bury after that fire.'

'There was really nothing much left of them? Nothing that could have been … I don't know, used to identify them? Used to identify their killer? Some jewellery or something that might have survived the first fire?' But Tosti was shaking his head.

'There really wasn't anything. You could tell one was a man, for part of his neck was preserved – tucked under, I suppose, and there was some beard. Beinir said it was the right colour for Leif. The woman was a sort of woman's shape, and therefore, given where they were found, of course they said Hervor. But no clothes survived, and when Beinir and I examined them we saw nothing else. We just laid them out as best we could.' His eyes were full of sorrow for these people he had never met, and yet had kept vigil with these last hours.

She heard footsteps behind her, but it was Ketil. He drew her away from the busy barrel, and Tosti went to make what prayers he could over the ruins of the outhouse.

'Of course I know you didn't do that,' he said, before she could begin. 'But if you had wanted to it would have been convenient, so close.'

'Very close,' she agreed. 'And why only an outhouse this time? Why not someone else's longhouse?'

'A warning?' he suggested. 'We'll keep good watch tonight, just in case.'

'And very early, too,' she said. He looked at her, and she

explained. 'Both other fires were either later at night or early in the morning, when you would not expect people to be about. Is the fire raiser becoming bolder?'

'Or there was something urgent about this one, perhaps? Come on, let's go inside: it will be a while before people have finished here.'

They turned back towards the longhouse door, and heard a cry of alarm.

'What's this?'

It was Beinir, trotting along the shore path from the east, his face white in the light of the lantern someone had lit by the door.

'What on earth has been going on?'

Vali stepped forward, consoling arms out.

'It's just the outhouse, mercifully, nothing else and no one hurt.'

'The outhouse? With the bodies? Where is Father Tosti?'

'I'm here, Beinir.' Tosti emerged from the dark shadows by the ruin.

'What are we going to do? What about the bodies?'

Tosti shrugged.

'We'll have to see in daylight, Beinir, but I don't think there's anything left.'

'What's that awful smell?'

'It seems someone splashed fish oil on the building to make it burn,' Vali explained, his very voice calming.

'Fish oil? Fish – then this was deliberate, too?' He shook his head ferociously. 'No, no. No, how can this be happening? Who is doing this?'

'He's not taking it well,' said Sigrid quietly to Ketil. 'Let's get him inside to the warmth. Not that it's that cold standing by the outhouse, but that smell would make anyone unsteady.' She sniffed. 'Very rich. Herby.'

She trotted over and seized Beinir by the elbow, the first time she had laid hands on him herself. He blinked down at her, unrecognising. Vali took the other arm and between them they drew him into his home, set him in his chair, and held him still while Katrin quickly prepared spiced wine. Beinir gulped at it like a lifeline, swallowed noisily, and shook himself. Sigrid and Vali backed away, letting him settle.

'Why would someone burn my outhouse?' he asked, sounding more like himself. 'What an extraordinary thing to do! Were they trying to kill my animals?'

'I don't think anyone knows, Beinir,' Sigrid offered. He ignored her.

'Tell me, Ketil! What is going on here?'

Sigrid stepped back. The house seemed full, suddenly: Katrin by the hearth as usual, Ketil and his men, Vali, Asta, Tosti looking serenely concerned, and there, inevitably, in the doorway, Gillaug and Eyolfr. If they had Hamthir, Aslak and Hoskuld the entire settlement would be in the house. She had a great desire to throw herself behind her bed curtains, draw them fast, and hide in her bed.

The bed she shared with Katrin and Osk – but where was Osk? When was the last time she had seen her? First thing this morning? Sharing a bed with Osk was a little like sharing a bed with a dead tree, the branches poking and stiff, the twigs prickly. But she said nothing: she still felt that it was not a bad thing, for Osk's sake, that people forgot she existed. It was possible that whoever had set fire to Leif's house had not wanted anyone to survive to tell the tale – not that Osk was saying much.

'Where was she?' Gillaug's voice was shrill before she had even reached the hearth. 'Where was that woman when this happened?' Sigrid found it hard to resist slapping her face and telling her to pull herself together, though at the same time the woman's persistence began to frighten her. What if others did believe her? What if she were tried for brennu-mal? She could not possibly afford compensation, not even for Beinir's outhouse, let alone two longhouses and two lives. What would she do? Would she be exiled? A woman on her own? That never ended well.

She found she was shaking, and made herself sit calmly by the hearth, near Beinir. After all, she was here under his protection. But it was Ketil who moved towards Gillaug, almost imperceptibly until you suddenly noticed the presence of him, and Gillaug shifted backwards.

'Sigrid was with me – as I had undertaken – when the outhouse was fired.'

Gillaug swallowed audibly.

'And anyway, Gillaug,' said Beinir unexpectedly, 'Sigrid is my guest. Why would she try to destroy anything of mine?'

She glanced up at him, grateful, but he was staring at Gillaug. There was a tap on her shoulder and she half-turned to find that Katrin had brought her a cup of hot wine. Her gratitude swung round and they exchanged a smile.

'As this firing has taken place virtually in daylight,' Ketil went on – how did he do that? Everyone stopped to listen to him: it couldn't just be that his men were casually close to the doorway, 'it should be easier than on the other occasions to establish who was where. Gillaug, perhaps you would like to take the opportunity to start?'

'Me? Why me?'

'Because I shall be asking everyone and I am paying you the courtesy of asking you first. How did you hear about the fire?'

'Eyolfr told me,' she answered, unsteadily. 'He came in and said there was a fire. He said it was at Beinir's, and so of course … Well, after the last two, we hurried over to see if there was anything we could do.' From somewhere she summoned a kind of smile: it looked unnatural on her face, as if she were chewing something awkward.

'And where were you when he told you?'

'I was at the hearth, making dinner,' said Gillaug virtuously. 'If it wasn't her,' she added, 'then presumably it's an accident. That priest probably fell asleep and tipped over a lamp.'

'I didn't, sorry,' said Tosti at once.

Ketil nodded.

'Eyolfr, presumably you were outside, then?'

'Was I?'

Sigrid restrained a snort of derision. Was Eyolfr really stupid, or had he depended on his wife for too long to have any knowledge or opinions of his own? Ketil seemed more patient.

'Where were you when you heard about the fire?'

'I heard people shouting,' he said. 'They were up by Beinir's longhouse – you know, here. And I could see flames, if I stretched a bit.'

'So where were you? Up behind your house, or out on the shore path?'

'The shore path,' he said confidently, then glanced at Gillaug. 'Or, no, no. I was up behind our house. That's where I was.' He finished with a nod. Sigrid did not remotely believe him. She, too, sneaked a look at Gillaug: she did not seem pleased with her husband.

'Beinir,' said Ketil, satisfied for now – Sigrid hoped he was not stupid enough to take Eyolfr at his word – and turned to his host. 'You arrived late, though you may have seen something useful. Where had you been?'

'I had been up on the hill, checking on my sheep,' said Beinir. 'It grew dark just as I was finishing, and I came back and saw the outhouse on fire. Well, dying down by then. And the smell!'

'What smell?' Gillaug demanded at once. 'You mean someone was burned again? Who?'

'No one living,' said Ketil, cutting her off. Then a thought seemed to strike him. 'Gillaug, may I smell your hands?'

'What? Eyolfr, are you going to permit this?'

'Yours too, Eyolfr.' Ketil stepped towards both of them, and lifted Gillaug's shocked, unresisting hands to his face. He nodded, then did the same to Eyolfr. Sigrid had to set the wine cup down before it tipped: she was convulsed with silent laughter. But Ketil was still solemn. 'Father Tosti, what did you see?'

'Nothing of note,' said Tosti humbly. 'I needed to visit the privy, so I left the outhouse and noticed a strong smell, but thought nothing of it. I assume whoever left it must have been waiting for me to leave. Which means they had no desire to kill me, which I find quite comforting.' He smiled around the company.

'Vali, sir, may I smell your hands, too?' Ketil asked, rather more respectfully than when he had spoken to Gillaug and Eyolfr. There was definitely something about Vali that commanded respect. He extended his palms gracefully, and Ketil bent to inhale, again nodding. 'Thank you. You raised the alarm, sir: what were you doing so near?'

'I was coming to see Beinir,' said Vali at once, 'to ask him how he was after Sigrid was accused. I assumed he would be somewhat unsettled by events.'

He must have been very concerned, Sigrid thought. He had come with Gillaug earlier, and again before the fire. Sigrid had had the impression that it was more common for Vali to summon than to visit, but perhaps she had been wrong.

'Skorri,' Ketil continued, 'has Hamthir returned?'

'Aye, sir, I was just coming to tell you.'

'And Aslak?'

'I had a chat with him at the harbour earlier, then off he went, said he had to see to his sheep.'

It's a popular pastime, Sigrid thought. She hoped Gnup was keeping a good eye to her own flock.

'Has anyone here seen Hamthir or Aslak this evening?' Ketil asked generally.

'Hamthir is only just back from taking Hoskuld over to the mainland,' Vali said quickly. 'I haven't even seen him myself yet. And I did see Aslak heading up the hill. Perhaps you saw him, Beinir?'

Beinir looked startled at this.

'No, no, I don't believe I did. But then my sheep tend to go east, and Aslak's are further to the west, usually. And Hoskuld's and Eyolfr's and Leif's in the middle, so there's no reason ...' But he still seemed puzzled. Sigrid felt sorry for him: it was clear that events were taking their toll on him. He looked tired and worn.

'And Hoskuld is away,' said Ketil, turning to where Katrin and her mother were quietly working on the dinner preparations. Sigrid was sure Ketil would not remember Asta's name. 'Asta, isn't it?'

'Aye, sir,' said Asta, half- standing. He waved her down.

'You came running down with your daughter – what did you see?'

'I'd come to the door just to see Katrin off back here, and at once we saw the fire. I thought it was the longhouse first! I must have screamed like a pig!' Her eyes wide, she looked about her, shaking her head. 'As to seeing anything, once I'd seen the flames that was all I looked at! I ran down here after Katrin, to help put it out, then I saw it was the outhouse but I knew that was where the Christian priest was and so I was still frightened something might have happened to him, too, for Katrin says he's a lovely man and very kind,' she grinned and nodded at Tosti, 'but then someone said no one had been hurt but what about the bodies? That's no way to go, is it, unless you're intending it. I mean, what's the point in burning dead bodies in a shed?' She stopped to draw breath, and Ketil held his hand up, acknowledging her contribution. She subsided. Sigrid squinted at Ketil, wondering where he had found this authority: he had never been like that as a boy. Maybe carrying a sword helped.

'Right,' he said, 'I think that's enough for now. Vali, may I speak with you in the morning?'

'Of course: any help we can offer to Thorfinn's man ...' Vali bowed his head graciously, and, perhaps as Ketil had intended, he swept Gillaug and Eyolfr before him out into the night. Asta, however, as the other outsider, turned to Beinir.

'Please, Beinir, can I stay here tonight? I don't want to be up there on my own!'

'Mother, you have the serving girl,' Katrin reminded her, casting a glance over at the bedspace that was already shared by her, Sigrid and Osk. Sigrid, not relishing the thought of sharing it with Asta as well, realised belatedly that Osk was sitting in it, silent as ever.

'Oh,' said Asta, 'that's true. And the animals – as well as Aslak's hens. I didn't think of them.'

'We'll have patrols tonight,' Ketil said, 'and I'll make sure they go about your house as well as this one. Yes, Skorri?'

'Aye, sir.'

Asta looked impressed.

'Patrols? Well, then …' She rolled to her feet, and kissed Katrin on the head. 'In that case I'll be off. I don't want to miss my own dinner!'

She headed out. Before she closed the door, they could hear her tutting at the burned outhouse once again. A waft of the fishy smell fingered the air before disappearing up to the roof vents.

Sigrid stood to go and help Katrin finish the work on the supper, passing Ketil.

'Aren't you going to go and talk to Hamthir and Aslak?' she asked quietly. 'If you leave it till tomorrow who knows what might have happened to them?'

'I mean to go after supper,' he said.

'What about their hands?'

'None of them smelled of fish oil, anyway,' he said. She almost thought she caught a smile on his face. 'But it proves little: whoever did it could have protected themselves.'

'And who do you think did it?'

He sighed.

'I don't know. And to tell you the truth, I don't trust any of them.'

'Not even Beinir?' She asked it almost to tease him, but he looked down, straight into her eyes.

'Not even Beinir,' he agreed. She blinked, and shivered.

Supper was a quiet meal. No one seemed inclined to say much: Ketil and Skorri withdrew afterwards and seemed to have a conversation about Hamthir, but Sigrid did not even feel much like butting in and finding out what they were saying. Again she felt like crawling into her bed and pulling the curtains around, blocking out Gillaug's accusations, Beinir's polite distance, Ketil … But then Osk and Katrin would join her, anyway. Osk had eaten two plates of meat and bread at dinner, making an exhibition of chewing both lengthily with the selection of teeth left to her. To judge by her astuteness when it came to food and to seizing the best bit of the bed, there was nothing wrong with her mind. No one had cut out her tongue – she had made that fairly obvious – so was there some other reason that she could not speak, or had she decided not to? Did she know who had burned down Leif's house, her own home?

Ketil glanced over and caught her eye, then moved away from Skorri towards the door. Summoning her, eh? But she lacked the energy to resent it. She scrambled to her feet and went over to him. He was watching her, a hint of concern in his face.

'I'm off to see if I can catch Hamthir and Aslak,' he said quietly. 'Is there anything else you've heard about either of them that might be useful?'

'I've told you all I know about Aslak,' she said, thinking hard. What had she heard about Hamthir? 'I don't know much about Hamthir, except that he's Vali's nephew, his mother, Vali's sister, is dead, and Asta and Katrin both slid past my question about Hamthir's father. But Asta and Hoskuld seem to think he's suitable husband material for Katrin – and we know they won't just give her to anyone with a bit of money …' She tailed off, trying to remember – the mention of money had set off something in her mind. That was it. 'But Asta did say he was wary about marriage – he seems to think that wives are expensive.'

'I'm sure they are,' said Ketil.

'He'll be saving up,' Sigrid said.

'Katrin strikes me as a careful girl,' Ketil remarked, casting the servant a glance over Sigrid's shoulder.

'I think she is. I'm not sure I would like a husband that did not trust me with the household money – that's the way things are supposed to work, after all.'

There was a slight pause.

'Do you think Beinir would trust you?'

She drew a breath.

'Yes, I think he would. He has shown me his treasure and its hiding place.'

'Has he?' Ketil's pale eyebrows rose. 'I see. Good.'

He must have thought she had nothing else to say: he turned, and went outside, disappearing into the night.

For a moment she stood at the door. It had snowed again – extraordinary. The wind had dropped and all she could hear, as his muffled footsteps faded, was that empty, dull snow sound, the sound of nothing.

XVII

As Ketil stamped through the snow along the shore path, he tried to make sure his mind was occupied with the conversations to come. Would he be able to coax any further information out of Aslak, or would Aslak be as unco-operative as before? If nothing else, he needed to find out about Bolla and Margad. And then what was he going to ask Hamthir? He needed to talk to the two men separately, anyway.

But despite his efforts to concentrate on Hamthir and Aslak, he kept going back to the fire in the outhouse. He was ashamed of himself. How could he have hesitated, when Tosti – Father Tosti, whom they all regarded as a dear friend – Tosti might well have been inside there, burning with the already burned corpses? His mind danced away from the thought, but he knew he should have done better. The relief he had felt when Tosti came up behind them was immeasurable. Even so, when he closed his eyes he was back in his nightmare, flames bounding up before his eyes, the smell of burning flesh hot in his nostrils. How could you dream a smell? But when he woke each time he remembered it, as sharp as if it were real and alight in front of him. His skin tightened with horror at the thought, and at what Tosti might have suffered. He sent up a prayer, not his first in the last hours, a prayer of thanksgiving and of repentance – sorry, sorry, sorry, but thank you, thank you, thank you. Thank you that nothing worse had happened. Thank you that, this time, no one had died.

Even on his long legs the march through the snowfall was hard work – he wished he had brought a pair of Thorfinn's old skis. But at last he reached Vali's prosperous-looking longhouse, with its neat outhouses outlined in the light from his torch. He wondered briefly if anyone would have the nerve to set Vali's house alight, and knocked at the doorpost.

His request, made politely to Vali, to talk to Aslak and Hamthir separately, did not seem to come as a great surprise to Vali. All four men, poor Ingvar included, were sitting about the fire, supper over: Hamthir and Vali still had cups of wine by them while Hamthir worked at some kind of peg with his knife, no doubt part of a boat. Aslak, with no wine, was splitting old rope into fibres for stuffing the gaps between a ship's boards. Ingvar was helping him – it was a mundane but useful task and no doubt mindless enough for this time of the night. Ketil hoped Aslak was not drunk, but in fact he could smell no wine on his breath at all as the pair of them headed out into the night to find private shelter in the doorway of a cattle shed. Aslak looked as if he would rather be splitting old rope.

'I know why Hoskuld turned down your request to marry his daughter,' Ketil begin, seeing no point here in blandishments. 'You raped a girl on Westray.'

'Is that what you heard?' Aslak struggled to be defiant, but he lacked the wit.

'And it makes me wonder,' Ketil went on, 'about what happened at the Brough during your recent visit there.' He stood a little warily: he was taller than Aslak by some way, but tall men were always vulnerable to a small man with a knife and a grudge. Stomachs were ill protected by nature. But Aslak chose to look confused. 'Let's start with the fight in Earl Thorfinn's hall. A man from Westray, wasn't it?'

'He started it!' Aslak objected at once.

'He might have thrown the first punch that night,' Ketil agreed, 'but perhaps he knew you? Or was acquainted with those who did – who knew, perhaps, the girl you raped and left with no compensation?'

'How do I know?' Aslak said sulkily. 'Westray men all look the same to me. They never comb their hair, you know. They're probably half-troll.'

Ketil had never particularly noticed any common traits in the Westray men he had known, and scowled at Aslak's time-wasting.

'Then there's Bolla,' he said. It was Aslak's turn to scowl.

'Who's Bolla?'

'Serving girl in Earl Thorfinn's hall. Pretty maid, dark hair, nice smile. We're all fond of Bolla.' His voice hardened. 'We were all very upset when we found out what had happened to her.'

'Oh,' said Aslak, and Ketil knew he had been right. 'Oh, her.'

'Yes. That was Bolla.'

'I thought she was just a servant,' he tried, but Ketil could hear in his voice that it was a desperate attempt. 'Ahh – what are you going to do?'

'That depends,' said Ketil. 'To start with, I'll be taking you back to the Brough when I go, and you can explain yourself to Earl Thorfinn.'

Aslak gave a grunt – it almost sounded like relief. Ketil must be mistaken.

'I can't afford much compensation,' Aslak said.

'Then you shouldn't go around injuring people,' said Ketil, unsympathetically. 'Now, that's Bolla. What about Margad?'

'Margad?'

'Don't pretend you don't know who Margad is,' Ketil snapped. 'You and Hamthir and Beinir spent your time at the Brough with him.' Aslak made a noise of reluctant agreement.

'Margad from Caithness – stuck up fancy man,' he muttered with a degree of ferocity.

'That's the one,' Ketil was quite prepared to concur with that. 'What did you do to him?'

Aslak sighed.

'He came round the corner with his dog just as I was finishing – what did you say her name was?'

'Bolla,' said Ketil coldly.

'Yes, her. Of course he knew me. I didn't want word getting back … I didn't want people finding out. So I floored him.'

'And the belt marks?'

'Belt marks?'

'On his back,' said Ketil patiently, though he suddenly had a feeling this was not going to go quite as he had expected. Aslak in the torchlight was blank-faced.

'I don't know,' he said. 'I just hit him on the head. And his dog paid no attention to me, so I left him. I wasn't going to hang around doing things to his back – why would I do that?'

Why indeed? Ketil wondered. But he was fairly sure he knew who might do it.

'Right,' he said. 'I need your word that you'll be staying here in the settlement until I need to take you to the Brough.'

'Aye,' Aslak sighed. 'You can't take compensation from me that I don't have. But I'll come with you when you go. It can't be much worse …'

Much worse than what? Ketil wondered. But he sent Aslak back to the house with orders to ask Hamthir to come and replace him.

He had not seen much of Hamthir here or at Birsay, and he half-wondered what to expect. Vali's nephew, as he approached the outhouse, seemed equally uncertain. Ketil nodded to him.

'Thank you for coming out here. I had hoped to talk with you earlier but you had already departed with Hoskuld for the mainland.'

Hamthir, reassured by this friendly start, relaxed a little and gave a short laugh.

'Yes, that's right: poor Hoskuld is the one sent off to find Leif's daughter on Hoy. I offered to take him round by sea, but he thought he might be quicker going overland to Hamnavoe. Ah, well!' he finished, confident that Ketil would agree that Hoskuld had made the wrong choice.

'Is your business building well? Surely most people here have their own boats.'

'Oh, aye, most,' Hamthir agreed, 'but they're not always fit for crossing to the mainland! Beinir's, even, I wouldn't trust further than the other side of the sound here.' He jerked his head into the darkness. 'And then sometimes people want to take friends or family or a few animals, and I have the bigger boat. Then there's repairs, and a bit of building new … Yes, it's not too bad.'

'You live with your uncle? You have no land of your own?'

Hamthir shook his head.

'No, but I'm my uncle's heir, or one of them, anyway. Ingvar, of course, but he'll need looking after. And a few kin in Hjaltland.'

'Your parents are dead, I gather?'

'That's right. My mother, Vali's sister, died when I was born.'

'Ingvar is older than you, then?'

'No, he's younger. I've always looked after him – even before.'

'And your father?'

Hamthir said nothing for a moment.

'He paid little attention to me.'

'Your parents weren't married?'

Hamthir paused again.

'No. They weren't. And … and Ingvar's father was not my father, I believe. His father was in Hjaltland, and I understand he's dead.'

'Well … Thank you for telling me that.'

'Vali said we were to tell you anything you needed to know,' Hamthir said, suddenly looking rather young.

'Very sensible.' Ketil covered his surprise. 'And I gather there are possible arrangements for you to marry Katrin, Hoskuld's daughter? So presumably you get on well with him.'

'Yes …' Hamthir hesitated again. 'Yes, I'll marry Katrin. Eventually. When I've made more money, to be on the safe side.'

'You're not going to wait until Vali dies, are you?'

'No! No, not at all.' He cleared his throat. 'No, Katrin's worth going for, and I shouldn't keep her waiting.'

Ketil nodded, as if agreeing.

'Anyway, about these burnings, Aslak's house, and Leif's house, and Beinir's outhouse …'

'Yes, I heard about the outhouse! That was strange!' He heard his own words, and clarified: 'I mean, the whole thing is strange, but when you've burned down a longhouse, why burn someone else's outhouse?'

'So what do you think is going on?' Ketil asked. 'Where were you each time?'

'This evening I was only home a little while when I heard about the outhouse, so I suppose I was at home by the time of the fire, or nearly. Vali told me later he'd found the fire: he was out when I got back so I suppose that's where he was. Leif's house … I was in my bed, for it was early in the morning. I mean, in the summer I'd have been up and out, but there was nothing urgent to be done and it was dark, so there was no point. If Ingvar's asleep on a morning like that you don't wake him, because once he's up he's always on the move!'

'I can imagine. You share a bed?'

'Always have.'

For a moment, Ketil imagined Ingvar's disappointment when Hamthir came to share a bed with Katrin instead. Would he understand?

'And when Aslak's house was burned?'

'Aslak's? Oh – yes. That was late evening. I was, um, I had gone to bed, but I wasn't quite asleep, I think. I remember smelling the smoke, and commenting on it,' he went on, sounding more sure of himself, 'and that was when we all got up and went out to see what was going on.'

'And of course you were with Vali, then, both times?'

'Yes, that's right.'

'Can you think of any reason, any reason at all, why anyone should want to burn both these houses? Why anyone might have wanted to kill Leif and his wife?'

'Leif and Hervor were lovely,' Hamthir said at once, and in the torchlight Ketil caught the least glimpse of moisture in Hamthir's eyes. 'I can't think why anyone should want to burn their house, or them.'

'And Aslak?'

'Ah, well,' Hamthir said, his voice at once lighter, 'Aslak is a different case! I can think of a few people who might want to give him a fright! Would you like a list?'

'What about what happened before you left Birsay?' Ketil asked.

'That girl? And Margad from Caithness? Oh, was that Aslak, too? Ha!' he said, 'I might have guessed! I should have guessed,' he added, more seriously.

'I wish you'd said,' said Ketil. 'It might have caused a great deal less trouble.'

Hamthir shrugged.

'Nobody asked me,' he said reasonably. 'Ha, another one. He needs locking up, Aslak.'

'It might well come to that,' said Ketil, grimly.

The air outside Vali's warm longhouse was soft and bright with snow. Ketil took a moment to consider all he had learned – such as it was – allowing the downy flakes to settle on his head and shoulders. His head was full, and the prospect of returning immediately to Beinir's busy hearth was not one that appealed to him. He hesitated, then lit his hissing torch from the lamp at Vali's door and turned right, away from the settlement, away from the harbour, turning inland and feeling the slight incline under his feet. It was hardly a difficult climb, even in the snow, and in a few minutes he had drawn level with the shadowy remains of Aslak's burned longhouse. In the flickering torchlight the broken roof glowed yellowish, crossed with black where the snow had not been able to settle. Only the faintest scent of burning remained. He paused, and swept a look over the wreckage once again. It was obvious that the fire had started at the back, just as Sigrid had pointed out. Either Aslak had set fire to the place himself inside, or someone had perhaps stuck something burning into the roof from outside. Either way, he had had a good chance to escape, taking his animals safely with him. Leif and Hervor had not been so fortunate. And what about Tosti? Had the arsonist waited until he came out of the outhouse, or had he, too, been blessed with good timing? And that fish oil … was the arsonist learning more about making the fire sure, or was he in a hurry because it was so early in the evening? And why had it been so early?

One fire late at night, one early in the morning, and one in the early evening. One intended to spare, one intended to kill, and one ambiguous. What was going on? Was the arsonist learning as he went along – well, that was probable – but to the extent of changing his method each time? Or had he a different purpose each time? Had he really intended to kill Aslak but only realised afterwards the chance he had given Aslak to escape?

But who? Who wanted to kill Leif and Hervor? Who wanted to attack Aslak? And who wanted to destroy Beinir's outhouse? More to the point, who wanted to do all three? He could see no sense, no pattern beyond the fact of burning buildings. If he had to guess he would almost say that different people had set out to light these fires. And of course he had been saying, in his mind, 'he' and 'him', but setting fire to a building was certainly not beyond the strength of any woman he had met on Shapinsay, even Osk.

He turned back to the path, or as far as he could tell where it was, and continued up the gentle rise where he had sent Geirod earlier. He was heading roughly north west, and the ground soon levelled even further. He could see little beyond the pool of torchlight, no reassuring expanse of silver-grey sea, no dazzling sweep of ice-white land. The snow grew thicker, and he began to reconsider straying too far from the settlement. He gradually swung his path north, then north east, veering around the upper reaches of the infields. He decided he would circle the whole settlement perhaps until he reached the stream by the smithy and the leatherworks: it would be hard to miss the stream, even in the snow, and he would know he had not wandered too far.

He passed the broad end of a longhouse tucked into the slope below him – Hoskuld's, presumably. All seemed quiet, and when he looked out for the promised patrols he saw no one. That was annoying, but then there were only three men, with quite an area to cover. He should be back helping them. He would not be much longer.

He strode on as smartly as he could in the conditions, wary of tripping and dropping his torch to certain extinction, torn between his duty and his reluctance to return to the company of others yet.

His mind went back to Birsay, to poor Bolla and Margad: he wondered how they were doing. Would Bolla make some recovery if he were able to tell her they knew the truth now? If he managed to drag Aslak back to make reparation? Though it might be that seeing Aslak again would be even more upsetting for Bolla: perhaps the reparation could be made to Thorfinn instead. Satisfying enough for Ketil, punishing enough for Aslak, and kinder to Bolla … The first thing would be to get him back to the Brough, though the thought of being in the man's company even for so short a journey was repellent. He was glad that Hoskuld and Asta had found out about him before allowing him to marry Katrin.

He stopped, and glanced back at Hoskuld's house behind him. Even if Hoskuld had attacked Aslak's house – and why would he, since he and his daughter had had a lucky escape? – why attack Leif? And Hoskuld could not have set fire to Beinir's outhouse, even if he had had a reason. He was not even on the island.

Hoskuld's house … Asta must still be awake. He could see a dim light at the roof vents, perhaps from the hearth below or from some lamps … Or from someone setting fire to it.

He stood, heart beating hard. Was it? Was the house on fire?

And if it was … He had hesitated at the door of the outhouse. He should not hesitate now.

He could smell smoke, suddenly, as a light wind lifted it towards him. Too much smoke for a hearth and a couple of lamps. Before he really knew what he was doing, he found he was running, slipping and sliding, back to the longhouse.

He had walked further than he had thought, lost in his

ponderings. Now he had to make up for it. Sure he could see flames, he sped up, slipped and fell, and lost the torch. Rolling to his feet he ran on, strong boots supporting his feet and ankles. Then, on the edge of the rising wind, he heard a scream.

He began yelling for help as soon as he thought anyone would hear, but he was almost at the house by then. He heard, distantly, a door open somewhere, and yelled again, then he crashed into the longhouse door. It was warm to the touch already.

'Stand back!' he cried, and thumped his shoulder into the thick wood. It shifted slightly. He stepped away for a moment, trying to see the roof, trying to judge where the worst of the fire was – he should have looked before. Somewhere towards the back? It was hard to tell. Then he drew breath, took a step back, and launched himself at the door again.

The lock gave almost at once, and he had to shelter his face as a flock of hens flustered out past him, feathers flying.

'Asta!' he called. 'Asta!'

'I'm here!' came a voice. 'Oh, and Ali, and my cow ...'

'Hurry,' he urged her. He could hear people approaching, running, questioning, and in a flash there was a bucket of snow in his hand. Asta grabbed it before he realised what it was, and hurled it towards the back recesses of the longhouse.

'More!' she cried. She handed the bucket to a small girl who shoved past Ketil with surprising strength, and in a moment she was followed by the cow. Ketil was pinned against the door post, while more people handed him buckets.

'There's a chance of putting it out,' he called to whoever was outside. 'More buckets!'

Inside, Asta was a mighty shadow between him and the fire. He passed her bucket after bucket, edging forward with her as the fire receded, forcing it into its corner, the very back of the longhouse. There were the fragments of a bed there, under the smoking eaves, and a hole in the roof now above it where the snow offered its assistance in turning the very last of the flames into damp smoke. At last she sighed, and sat down heavily on the bed platform by the hearth. He could smell smoke and charred wool and, from both of them, the tang of fresh sweat. For a moment there was silence as the crowd by the door gradually took in what had happened, realised there was no more need for buckets just now, blinked in the smoky air. Ketil sank down beside Asta.

'What happened? Did you see anything?'

'I woke up coughing,' she said, 'just over there.' She pointed to a bedspace away from the burned bed. 'I never sleep in the bed if Hoskuld's away: Ali and I shared that one, keeping cosy.' Cosier for Ali, Ketil suspected: she was a fraction the size of Asta. 'The flames were already coming through the roof. I think someone had shoved a brand into the turf, near a rafter. It's a good dry house, this – and is that oil I smell?'

Ketil sniffed.

'I think it's pitch,' he said. She opened her mouth to disagree, then nodded.

'I think you're right.'

The quiet spell broke, as Beinir bustled in, carrying a torch.

'It'll be crowded,' he said, 'but bring whatever you want to rescue and come down to my house for tonight, at least. Tomorrow we can look at the damage.'

The little serving girl was behind him and for a second Ketil saw her face by the light of Beinir's torch – she glanced up at him, with what could only be called extreme distaste. An odd expression on the face of someone else's servant, he thought, and then he was too busy to think about it again that night.

There was reorganisation to be done in Beinir's house, bed spaces reallocated, the cow and the hens settled in with Beinir's own animals. Katrin chivvied the hearth back to life and made hot drinks for everyone who had been out in the cold, and there was once again a queue for water to wash the worst of the smoke off their faces and hands. He had to have a word with his men to find out just where they had been patrolling and what, if anything, they had seen. According to them, very little. Ketil sighed, which turned into a yawn, and rubbed the heels of his hands hard into his eyes.

His gaze fell absently on Asta, Katrin, Sigrid and the little serving girl clustered around the fire, Asta repeating her accounts of the night to anyone who would listen, or listen again. Osk was of course already in bed, defining her share of it, and again Ketil wondered how Asta's size was going to be accommodated – if he had been Sigrid he would have volunteered to sleep on the floor, just to be able to breathe. He wondered if Katrin would end up as round as her mother: it was hard to believe.

Katrin was not paying her mother much attention just now,

anyway: she and Sigrid and the maid were working around her, quickly toasting flatbreads for the rescuers.

'Ali, pass me that spoon, would you?' he heard Katrin say to the maid.

'Ali?' Sigrid repeated. He knew that voice: all her attention had been caught. But why? 'Ali? You weren't, by any chance, Ingigerd's maid, were you?'

XVIII

The girl nodded. Sigrid looked at her more closely: she had taken her for ten or twelve, but now she saw she was a few years older than that, but colourless, mouse-like, eyes darting away from whoever was looking at her.

It had never occurred to Sigrid that Ingigerd's serving maid might have stayed on Shapinsay after Ingigerd's death. Despite the fires and Gillaug's accusations, she had not been able to rid her mind of teasing thoughts of Beinir's first sweetheart, and of the death that he seemed to regard as tragic but perfectly ordinary. If she had thought at all of the maid he had mentioned, she had probably thought he had taken her back to Graemsay when he went to break the news to Ingigerd's uncle. No, no, that was not true. She had not thought of the maid at all. It was a wonder she had recognised the name.

Sigrid glanced about the busy house: there was no room to talk now, and everyone was tired. Asta and Ali still smelled strongly of smoke, despite their efforts at the water barrel. She would have to wait until the morning. And in the meantime, no doubt, her thoughts would dance between Ali's possible story and wondering who, now, might have selected Asta's house – Hoskuld's house – for the next fire. At least she could be sure it had not been Beinir – or Tosti, or Osk, if she had even once suspected either of them, or Katrin.

Once again, how could Asta or Hoskuld have caused offence to anyone, except Aslak? And Ketil had been off talking to Hamthir and Aslak, so surely he knew what they had been doing when the fire was set. She looked over at Ketil: he and his men had not rolled out their bedding, and seemed ready to head out again on patrol. She picked up a few hot flatbreads and bundled them in her hands, taking them over to the men at the door.

'Here,' she said, 'to start you warm, anyway. But do you really think whoever it is will do more tonight?'

'I don't know,' Ketil admitted, 'but he seems to be speeding up.'

It was true: the ashes of Beinir's outhouse were barely cold, and now another longhouse was in ruins.

'Are you all going?'

He gave her an odd look.

'No, Skorri is staying. One of us has to keep an eye on you, remember?'

She let that go for now, and drew a deeper breath.

'So, does this one let Aslak out of it?'

'Aslak? Why would that be?'

'Weren't you talking with him and Hamthir?' She read the hesitation in his expression straightaway, and felt dismay hit her. 'Oh, you weren't, were you? Where were you?'

'I left them a while ago,' Ketil said. 'I walked around the top of the settlement. I'd passed Hoskuld's longhouse and was heading for the smithy when I turned back and saw the light.'

'Well, I suppose that was something useful,' she acknowledged. 'Asta is certainly singing your praises over there. If the story grows much more you'll have carried her out bodily through the flames, which is something I'd have liked to have seen.' She looked up at him, and thought for a second she saw his eyes flinch – at the thought of carrying Asta, perhaps? But she was not sure. She lowered her voice still further. 'What did Aslak say about – about the Brough?'

Ketil edged her away from his men: he must not yet have told them.

'He admitted attacking Bolla.'

'Oh.' She had expected as much, but the fact still hurt. For a moment she longed to be back on Birsay, holding Bolla, hoping her tears would help Bolla cry, too. Was she any better? She had heard no news at all. She blinked hard now, and gave herself a moment before she met his eye again. He was watching her closely.

'He also knocked out Margad, but when I asked about the whipmarks he looked blank – no reason why he should not have admitted it by that stage. So someone else found Margad and took their chance.'

'Geirod?' she murmured, only just loud enough for him to hear. He made the slightest of nods. 'For the dog?'

'And in revenge on behalf of the dog,' Ketil added.

'Good.' She swallowed. 'Thorfinn would be pleased.'

'I think so.' The slightest smile twitched his lips. He hesitated, and his gaze flicked over her shoulder – well, over the top of her head. 'So that's Beinir's sweetheart's maid?'

'You heard?' She had not thought he was paying any attention to the women around the hearth. 'Yes, so she says. She's older than she looks.'

'It was only a couple of years ago, wasn't it?'

'To hear people round here that's a hundred years ago,' she said. 'I'm going to ask her about it tomorrow, if she'll tell me anything. She doesn't seem to say much.'

'I'm sure if she has anything to say you'll dig it out,' he said, and that smile twitched again. She scowled at him.

'You don't have to wave axes at people to make them talk. That's just laziness.'

'Laziness is lingering in here,' he said, his voice a little louder as he straightened. 'We'll have to go. Come on, you two,' he added to Alf and Geirod, who had the yellow dog close at his feet and a hand on the dog's soft head. 'Skorri, keep an eye on her, eh?'

He gathered the other two and strode off into the night. The door closed with a slap of cold air. Skorri gave her a slightly queasy smile. She returned him a look.

'I'm going to bed,' she said clearly. 'I have no intention of wandering off anywhere at this time of the night. Sit by the door if you want, and prevent me leaving, but any closer eye will not be made welcome.' She turned on her heel, and made for the bedspace she was going to have to share with … no, she decided, she would take her blankets and a fur, and sleep on the floor.

It was not the worst night's sleep she had ever had, in the end: her busy head finally allowed her to sink into unconsciousness and she slept dreamlessly for what must have been most of the dark hours. Katrin and little Ali must have slipped past her to rouse the cooking fire and the longhouse was warm from the hearth and fresh with air from the wide door when she allowed herself to open her eyes. She must have wriggled in her sleep and her head was pressed against the foot of Beinir's precious hanging bookshelf: she told herself she was unconsciously drawn to the place in the house where a loom would usually stand, and smiled. She would need space for a loom, if she were to live here. Then she thought of what she was going to ask Ali, and the smile faded into a frown of concentration.

Asta was up and organised surprisingly early. Sigrid was pleased she had already given her spare shift to Osk, for she dreaded to think what the bulk of Asta would have done to it: Asta was just having to make do with what she had been wearing when she was rescued, and Ali the same. But when they all ventured outside and looked up towards Hoskuld's longhouse, the prospects seemed less bleak than they had done last night.

'It's barely burned down this end,' Asta said in awe.

'You've been blessed,' said Ketil. She turned and elbowed him, and Sigrid saw him brace himself against the blow.

'Blessed by you! If you hadn't been passing I don't know what we'd have done – been burned to ashes!'

She said it as a joke, but at that they all glanced, as if pulled by strings, at the remains of Beinir's outhouse, where the ashes of Leif and Hervor mingled with those of the driftwood walls. She went a little pale, and for once fell silent. With a few thoughtful coughs, everyone began to pace up the hill to inspect the damage.

It really was not as bad as they had all feared. Asta seized a wooden box with delight, and opened it to display clean linen, completely undamaged. The outside of the box was charred, at most. The bed she usually shared with Hoskuld was destroyed and the roof above it would need work, but it was nothing more than Hoskuld and a few neighbours could do – or, judging by the murmurings amongst Ketil's men, nothing more than they could do that day and have the longhouse back to normal before Hoskuld even reappeared. She was impressed at their enthusiasm on so little sleep, but they could probably find Hamthir and Aslak, if not Vali, Beinir and Eyolfr, to give them a hand, too. Add in the men from the smithy and the leatherworks and it would be done before the midday meal.

Asta entered into negotiations with the men about the work even as they began to clear the snow-soaked wreckage of the bed back from its space to give themselves room to see what needed to be done. Asta would never notice if Sigrid drew her serving girl away and had a little chat, would she?

Sigrid edged to one side and just as Ali looked as if she were about to step forward and help, Sigrid cut her off and with what she hoped was a friendly smile gestured to invite her outside. Poor Ali also still smelled heavily of smoke: it would be unfair to keep her out here for long, but at least she had a warm blanket around her. It almost looked too heavy for the size of her thin frame.

'I was surprised to hear what you said last night,' Sigrid began. 'You really came here from Graemsay with Ingigerd? As her serving-maid?'

'A couple of years ago, that's right,' said Ali. Her voice was mouse-like, too, soft, with a breathy squeak to it.

'Had you been her servant for long? I mean, before she came here?'

'I was in her uncle's household, where she lived,' said Ali, and something about the tone suggested she had not much enjoyed the situation.

'And she needed someone with her to come to Shapinsay.' Katrin would not have been working at Beinir's house at the time, of course, and so there would have been no one to stay and protect Ingigerd's honour, from the local gossips if nothing else. Sigrid was fairly sure Beinir would not have done anything improper.

Ali nodded.

'How long was she here?'

Ali frowned, remembering.

'I think it was maybe a couple of months?'

'Is that all?' Ali looked shocked at her response, and Sigrid toned down her voice. 'That's very sad.'

'I suppose …'

'Did you like her? Was she friendly? Confiding?'

Ali shrugged.

'Sort of,' she said. 'She was never cruel to me.' She seemed to be taking each part of Sigrid's question separately. 'Sometimes she told me things.'

'Was she pleased to be here?'

'Oh, yes. She didn't like her uncle either …' The last word faded as if she had realised she had given herself away, but Sigrid was not likely to take her back to Ingigerd's uncle and accuse her of disloyalty. 'And Beinir's very good-looking,' she added, a little emboldened. 'She was quite excited, at first.'

'At first?' Sigrid prompted, after a moment.

'Well … he's a bit dull.'

'And Ingigerd wasn't?'

Ali looked at her out of the corner of her eye.

'Ingigerd thought there might be more to the world than just Beinir and Shapinsay. She – she was wrong about Shapinsay. Well, I mean, I like it. I like Hoskuld and Asta and Katrin, and I like living here. But I don't think it would have suited Ingigerd for much longer.'

'Hm.' Sigrid reflected for a moment. Was that like her? Would she, in normal circumstances (without someone burning buildings every night) find it very dull? She might not want to visit the Brough every day, or the busy harbour below it, but it amused her to have it nearby her little longhouse in Birsay. And it was good for business. But if she were not contracted to marry Beinir and were free to leave, as indeed Ingigerd had been, there would be no need to seek consolation in the waters of a brackish ayre, would there? Unless Ingigerd thought her only option would be to return home, and she really didn't like her uncle …

'So, then,' she pulled herself back to the present and the little creature next to her – she made Sigrid feel like an ogre by comparison. 'How was it that Ingigerd died?'

Ali looked about her for a moment, her eyes quick as if the little mouse had been told there was a fierce cat around. But there was no one nearby, and most of the people from Beinir's house were still in Asta's house, helping to tidy up. No one was paying them any attention.

'I think it began with the – the big fuss.'

'With the what?'

Ali flinched, and Sigrid tried to make it plain she was not cross, only confused. It was a delicate skill, talking with Ali. She was glad Ketil had not brought his axe.

'I call it the big fuss. No one else ever really talks about it.'

'Well, then, tell me!' said Sigrid, with a deliberate smile.

Ali cast another quick, careful look about, and drew a shaky breath.

'One day I woke up and I couldn't find Ingigerd. Beinir asked where she was and I pretended she'd gone out for a walk in the dawn – it's the kind of thing he likes women to do, I think. But she hadn't slept in the bed and I had no idea where she was. But before Beinir could really miss her there was a terrible noise from the harbour, and everyone ran there, and I'd never seen anything like it! There were warships everywhere! I screamed and ran, but I bumped into Asta and she said they were warships from Birsay and I shouldn't worry. But I was worried because everyone was running around and there was a very tall thin man called Einar who was in charge of the warships, and he and Vali and Beinir went into Vali's longhouse looking very serious, and lots of big men with axes and swords stood around looking cross.'

'I can imagine,' said Sigrid. She had begun to realise what this incident was – the one she had seen the other end of, where her husband had raged to go with Einar's ships and find out who had invaded Shapinsay.

'And Gillaug soon had the news – Einar said they had seen the vart fired, I mean they had seen the other varts in the chain and had come to the rescue, and of course none of us knew what had happened because no one had given the order for the vart to be fired, so they thought the invaders must be on the other side of the island. So the ships split, and half went one way and half the other, to catch the invaders. But Vali and Beinir wanted to see what was happening at the vart so they went up there, and I don't know why, but I followed. They walked awfully fast, for they're both big men, and I don't think they even noticed me.' Probably not, thought Sigrid, suddenly sad. I don't suppose many do.

'Did you go all the way to the vart with them?'

'Behind them, yes. I wouldn't have known where to go – well, except that you could just see the fire in the sunshine. And when we got up there, Vali and Beinir were furious.' She shuddered at the memory.

'What did they find?' Sigrid found herself whispering.

'Aslak, the vart warden, drunk and asleep by the signal fire. And Ingigerd with him, with her shift all everywhere and the pair of them … no wonder Beinir was so angry!' Ali breathed, overawed even by the memory. 'Vali took Aslak and shook him, and Beinir covered Ingigerd and pulled her to her feet. He was white!'

'She could only have been here a few weeks. They could barely have met,' said Sigrid, her eyes wide. But then, who knew how innocent Ingigerd might have been? But Aslak had taken Bolla quickly, too, and against her will. Who knew how long the girl on Westray had required?

'Aye, well, it wasn't long after that that … Beinir told her to stay in the house, but Ingigerd was not the kind to take telling,' said Ali. Nor am I, thought Sigrid – though I'm probably too old to interest Aslak. 'It was early morning again that I found she had gone in the night.'

'Had she taken anything?'

'Just her dress and her back cloak,' said Ali, 'and she must have pulled on her dress when she went outside, for I never heard so much as a bead rattle.' She was into her stride now: in Asta's house she probably never had a chance to say a word.

'So she was not running away?'

'No … no, I wouldn't have thought so. And I think it was because of that that Beinir went looking for her. If she had run away I don't think he would have – would have taken the trouble. He went off to see Aslak, but Aslak must have said he knew nothing, and the search – well, everyone in the settlement went out, but it was someone from along the coast found her, and brought her here.' She sniffed, but Sigrid did not think she seemed too upset. 'And then Beinir cried. But I suppose it was sad, really.'

'So there are several possibilities here,' Sigrid mused, then saw the blank expression on Ali's thin face. 'Several things that could have happened. Either she went for a walk – maybe to meet someone, maybe just to get out of the house – and she slipped and fell into the ayre. Is it deep, do you know?'

'Not very. But I suppose … well, if she'd fallen and hurt herself …'

'Good point, Ali. So she could have drowned by accident. She did drown, I take it?'

Ali shrugged.

'She was very wet.'

'No one tried to see if water was inside her? Turned her on her side?'

Ali looked appalled.

'No!'

'All right. Well, two years ago, we're past that now. So she fell in by accident and probably drowned. Or she threw herself in, ashamed of what she had done, or of what Aslak had done – or frustrated that Beinir was keeping her in.'

'That's the most likely,' said Ali at once. 'I don't think Ingigerd was ashamed at all. She was only cross they'd fallen asleep and been caught.' There was an edge to her voice now, and Sigrid wondered if Ali were slipping away a little from the truth. Surely Ingigerd had felt some shame: she could not imagine Beinir wanting to marry someone as wild as that.

'There is of course another possibility,' she went on, an eye on Ali for her reaction this time. 'She went to meet someone, or someone followed her, and they were the ones who pushed her into the ayre. Either she was unconscious, or they held her under.'

Ali's eyes gaped: the thought had evidently never struck her. But as she absorbed it, Sigrid could see acceptance creeping in, recognition of something that might be all too probable.

'That, too,' she said, nodding firmly. 'An accident, or that.'

Sigrid tried to imagine the scene at the vart: Ali creeping behind, while Vali and Beinir pounced on the sleeping couple. Vali taking responsibility for Aslak again while Beinir dealt with Ingigerd, the woman he now said he had cared for so deeply. Vali and Aslak …

'Ali,' she began, 'what is the connexion between Vali and Aslak? Aslak moved into Vali's house when his was burned. Vali picked him up, you said, at the vart. Are they related?'

Ali laughed.

'No, they're not, as far as I know,' she said. 'It's just Vali's responsibility, isn't it?'

'Why Vali? Why should he take the responsibility?'

'Well, because he's the head man, of course!'

Sigrid blinked. Wasn't it obvious?

'But,' she had to say, 'but what about Beinir?'

'Oh, Beinir's not the head man,' said Ali, and actually tossed her head. 'He just thinks he is.'

XIX

His men seemed unexpectedly keen to fix Asta's roof, Ketil thought. He did not mind: it kept them busy and active, particularly as they would have to find and prepare materials in the snow. But he had more urgent work to do.

He could be fairly sure now that last night's fire had not been set by Beinir, nor Katrin nor Osk (if he had ever suspected either of them), nor his own men (whom indeed he had never suspected). Sigrid of course was innocent. He wished he had paid more attention to what was ahead of him before he had turned at the smell of smoke – could there have been someone out there with him, someone from the smithy or the leatherworks? The light from his torch had not spread far, so it was possible. And someone seeing his torch, if they had wished to work in secret, would have known to avoid him. He walked away from the busyness of Asta's longhouse, out past where, a little distance away, Sigrid was talking with that little maid. Was she worried about Beinir's past? Ketil considered the man: the worst he could think to say of him was that he was harmless. If Sigrid married him, she might be bored to death, but she would be under no other threat, he was sure.

Beyond Hoskuld's infield, where the wind whipped snow from the tops of walls and rearranged the drifts, he had to squint to try to find any trace of comings or goings last night, but of course it had been snowing even as he had run back to the burning longhouse, and the land lay bare and white, prickled only with the few black spikes of reeds, all the way down to where smoke rose peaceably from the roof vents of the longhouses by the stream. Perhaps it would not have been a good path to take, with boggy ground beneath the snow. Perhaps even someone coming from there to go to Asta's longhouse, for whatever reason, would go by the shore path. And not only would the snow have obliterated their tracks there, but there would have been others along the path already this morning, no doubt, and between Beinir's house by the path and Asta's further up the whole contingent of those who had spent the night in Beinir's house – apart from Osk – had tramped up through the infields to investigate the damage. No trace could have survived all that.

He thought he should go to the leatherworks and the smithy later and see what they had to say – it seemed more pertinent now, for Asta's longhouse was the closest to theirs. Someone who had easily set the first few fires unnoticed might now wish to act more cautiously. But first he would go once again and visit Vali, and talk to him and Hamthir and Aslak. He sighed. Perhaps they would confess all to him just so they did not have to see him again.

Inevitably the first people he met on the shore path were Gillaug and her silent husband Eyolfr. She started her attack before they had even met.

'Are we all to be burned in our beds?' she shouted at him. Ketil thought he saw Eyolfr wince.

'Where were you last night, then?' Ketil countered.

Gillaug's hooped mouth dragged even further down as she straightened her back to give him the full benefit of her glare.

'We were in our house, weren't we, Eyolfr? At our own hearth as we should be.'

'Well,' said Ketil, 'of course I would not expect you to say anything else.'

For a moment she looked pleased with herself, and then the implication sank in.

'And where was that Sigrid? Where was she? Out wandering about, no doubt, doing whatever she pleases! It's about time she was married and under the control of a good husband. But not Beinir! Oh, no: poor Beinir has suffered enough! Let him well alone and get back to

Birsay. Doesn't she know what happens to wilful women here? Doesn't she?' She seized Eyolfr by the sleeve and marched him past Ketil who stood braced against this new outburst. 'I've warned Beinir. He needs to get rid of her,' she tossed over her shoulder.

He stood and watched them stride off, Eyolfr lagging a little as Gillaug tugged him along. They passed Beinir's house and he waited to see they were not about to turn back to it before he walked slowly on towards Vali's longhouse.

Sigrid was with everyone else at the moment, and Skorri knew to keep an eye on her. She should be safe. But he wondered: what did happen to wilful women here? And did it have anything to do with the death of Beinir's old sweetheart Ingigerd? And, more to the point, was Gillaug in any way responsible for what happened to wilful women?

As he walked on he could see Hamthir and Aslak down by the harbour, with Ingvar sitting in one of the boats fiddling with ropes. He decided to go into the longhouse first and see if Vali was alone in there.

He was, and looked up with polite pleasure as Ketil appeared in the doorway. Ketil was surprised to find that he was chopping vegetables. Vali shrugged.

'We need a new maid,' he explained. 'The last one left. And the young men have their work to do outside, so here I am!'

Ketil sat carefully opposite him, and watched the process.

'I always understood there was more to cooking than it appeared.'

'Perhaps,' said Vali. 'I'd certainly be reluctant to invite anyone to supper at the moment, unless one of the guests brought the food.'

'Like Gillaug the other night?'

'Exactly.' Vali sat back, assessing the quantity he had chopped. 'I don't know if that's enough or not. Some things swell up in the cooking pot, while others shrink away to nothing.' He looked across at Ketil, but Ketil shrugged quickly, not willing to take any responsibility in the matter.

'I met Gillaug just now,' Ketil took the chance, 'and she said something quite strange.'

'What was that?' Vali dug out a few more roots from a sack, and began slicing again. There was a pleasant smell of herbs, anyway, Ketil thought: he had always reckoned that the herbs were the tricky bit.

'She asked me if I knew what happened to wilful women here, and told me that Sigrid should go home and leave Beinir alone.'

'Did she?' Vali looked quizzically once again at the quantity he had cut, then pushed it to one side in a neat heap. He sat back. 'I shouldn't be surprised if Sigrid did leave,' he said. 'It has barely been much of a welcome for her, all this tragedy and mess. But I suppose that will depend on Beinir and how they both feel about the match. And if she should decide to stay and become one of us then she will of course be most welcome. I don't know what Gillaug is thinking about.'

Ketil let that sink in for a moment, waiting for anything more that might be added, but Vali only drew out a piece of salt fish from a small barrel nearby, and began to cut it into pieces. Ketil had a feeling he had seen people soak salt fish overnight before using it, to take out some of the salt, but perhaps he was wrong.

'You heard what happened last night?'

'What?' Vali looked up at him, concerned.

'Hoskuld's house was burned.'

'What? Oh, no.' His head sank between his shoulders, his pale, thick hair spilling out to each side. 'Oh, with Hoskuld away … how are we to tell him when he returns? His loss will be terrible.'

Ketil cleared his throat.

'He hasn't lost too much. Only, really, quite a good bed and some blankets.'

Vali looked up.

'But Asta? Katrin?'

'Asta and her serving girl escaped,' said Ketil, 'and Katrin is of course staying at Beinir's house. The fire was spotted quickly and fortunately there is little damage done. My men are at present helping to repair it. If Hoskuld returns as early as tomorrow morning, all he will find wrong, I hope, is a broken bed.'

'That … that is a great deliverance,' said Vali, unsteadily. 'You said the fire was spotted quickly – that was good. Whoever spotted it, did they see who lit it?'

'No, unfortunately,' said Ketil. 'He was concentrating more on dealing with the fire.'

'Of course … that makes sense, but it is a shame. We need to find out who is doing these dreadful things, Ketil.' He gathered strength, it seemed. 'They must be stopped.'

'They? You think there is more than one of them?'

'No,' said Vali at once, 'that is not what I meant. I meant rather that a woman could have done this just as easily as a man, do you not think so?'

'Yes, I agree,' said Ketil. 'And I'm inclined to believe it is someone in this settlement, not someone coming in from elsewhere each time.' He watched Vali carefully as he said this but saw neither dismay nor disagreement: Vali seemed to have accepted the idea. 'You are very much at the centre of this settlement,' he pushed on quietly. 'What do you believe is happening?'

Vali gave the question careful consideration, or seemed to. Ketil waited patiently.

'I am not sure that I know,' he admitted at last. 'I don't like not to know.'

'I'm sure you don't.'

'I should have said, with everyone here, that Leif and his wife had no enemy in the world. I should almost say the same for Hoskuld and Asta, though you'll know that Asta talks ... But to burn someone's house for that? It makes little sense.'

'And Aslak?'

Vali dropped his gaze, and one long hand smoothed the other briefly.

'Aslak can be awkward, especially when he is drunk,' he stated.

'He made himself unpopular on Birsay – and there was more he did while he was there that was not known at the time.'

'Was there?' Vali looked at him again. 'Let me guess – a fight? Or a girl?'

'Oh, both,' said Ketil. 'He seems to have left no opportunity untried.'

Vali bit his lower lip.

'Will he be punished? You said he did more than was known at the time.'

'The girl – he will have to come back with us and answer to Thorfinn for that.'

'I see.'

'Is it at all possible, do you think,' said Ketil, 'that Aslak might have set fire to his own house, either accidentally or deliberately, then gone on to set fire to the others? Could he have borne a grudge against either household?' He left out Beinir's outhouse for now – something about it bothered him, and it did not seem to occur to Vali to add it into the discussion, even though he had been the one to find it.

Vali nodded, as though he had already considered the

possibility.

'He might have,' he agreed. 'I hope not, for I have always thought that perhaps something in him could be a better man. You think he might have fired his own house deliberately as a distraction?'

'I had considered the idea, yes.'

'I sleep very soundly,' Vali said, with a sigh. 'I should never have heard him leave here, either that morning or – or when was Hoskuld's house fired? Last night?'

'That's right.'

Vali shook his head.

'No, I heard nothing,' he said firmly. 'Nothing at all.'

And it was clear that that was all Ketil was going to be given, to believe or not, as he chose. He gathered himself to stand up.

'What are the herbs? They smell good.'

'Herbs? Oh … just a bundle of dried leaves the servant left when she went. I hope she wasn't trying to poison us! But they were with other cooking things.'

'That's reassuring, then,' Ketil agreed, and went outside. But he had noted the uneasy flutter of Vali's fingers when he mentioned the herbs.

He sighed as he approached the harbour once again, where Hamthir and Aslak were fitting a new panel to the side of a boat. It was a sharp little craft, like a small boy looking for a fight with his elders and betters. Aslak, his back to the sea, glanced up and glared at him.

'Oh, aye, here he comes. Where were you last night when you were out setting fire to Hoskuld's stinking longhouse?'

Hamthir, taken by surprise, dropped his hammer and swore, then turned.

'Morning, Ketil! Sorry – delicate bit.'

'Sorry I disturbed you.' He surveyed the boat end to end, liking the lines – up to a point. He recognised it from another day. 'Yours, Aslak?'

'What's it to you?'

Ketil shrugged.

'So where were you both last night, then? Did you see anything odd?'

'Last night? Not this morning?' asked Hamthir.

'What did you see this morning?'

'Oh, nothing!' Hamthir grinned and shook his head. 'I was just making sure. But I was in my bed both times anyway. You were too, weren't you, Aslak? I didn't hear you go out.'

'I was,' muttered Aslak.

Ingvar popped his long head over the gunwale suddenly.

'Night?' he asked, tilting ominously to one side.

'Last night, Ingvar, that's right,' said Ketil with a smile. 'You were tucked up in your bed, no doubt, weren't you?'

'Cold!' said Ingvar, and hugging himself he wriggled from side to side. 'Brr!'

'He does like fires,' said Hamthir fondly. 'If there isn't a fire going he thinks it's too cold.'

'Your uncle has the fire going,' Ketil told him.

'Oh! Don't say that! He's out here with us while Uncle gets the dinner on! No servant at the moment, you see,' he explained before Ketil could say that he knew.

'That must make for hard work, even in the winter.'

'We manage between us,' said Hamthir philosophically, though Aslak looked less pleased. No servant had been mentioned at his house, either. In fact, when Ketil came to think of it, the settlement was remarkably short of the usual type of serving girl who would help the housewife with the cooking and cleaning and spinning – there was Katrin and there was the one at Asta's … Ali? He should go back and see what Sigrid had found out from her. What if the death of Beinir's sweetheart had something to do with all these burnings? But that seemed a fanciful idea – what on earth could the connexion be?

He was not going to find any more information here at present, he was sure. He found himself waving back at Ingvar as he left, heading once more along the shore path back to Beinir's. He hoped he would not meet Gillaug again.

Instead he met Alf, drifting along, with Geirod and the yellow dog marching to catch up.

'We've been sent to see if Hamthir has something that would do to brace a roof beam,' said Geirod, as if it had been the last thing he had wanted to spend his morning doing. Ketil nodded.

'I didn't have time to tell you last night,' he said. 'I found out something interesting about what happened back on the Brough – remember, the night that Margad was attacked?'

'Oh, yes?' said Alf, bringing his focus slowly back to Ketil. Not for the first time, Ketil wondered how he ever survived a battle, let alone proved himself more than useful in them. Geirod, somehow suddenly a little behind Alf, bent to attend to the yellow dog.

'Aslak's fight might have been more than random: he had attacked a girl on Westray.'

Geirod looked up, surprised.

'Had he, indeed? Those were Westray men he was fighting.'

'Yes, they were. And then … remember the girl Bolla? We found her outside near Margad, unable to speak.'

He felt, rather than saw, Geirod tense. Suddenly the man was a bowstring, arrow nocked and ready to fly.

'Bolla, yes,' said Alf calmly. 'Pretty girl, very nice.'

'It was Aslak attacked her, too.'

'Aslak?' Alf queried. 'Not Margad?'

Ketil shook his head.

'Not Margad. Was it you that whipped him, Geirod? Before you stole his dog?'

Geirod looked up at him, eyes burning.

'He did the same thing to the dog!'

'Yes, but …'

'There he was, lying there. And that poor girl. And this poor dog. I – it needed to be done.'

Ketil had seen Geirod in a rage before: he knew what he could be like. All concern for the girl, the dog, all that focussed into a wild, savage attack.

'Did it occur to you to help the girl?'

'Of course it did,' he spat. 'But you came round the corner. I knew she was safe. I knew.'

'You'll have to pay compensation when we go back to Birsay,' Ketil said. 'For the dog, and for the whipping.'

'I can't afford that,' Geirod gasped out in a whisper.

'You need to learn to keep your temper, Geirod. But I'm glad you took the dog.' He looked along the path: he felt a sudden need to discuss everything with Sigrid, to sort out his thoughts, everything that had happened. She had better be somewhere between Asta's and Beinir's, or he would have Skorri whipped, too. He was angry with Geirod, angry with Margad and his self-righteousness, angry with Aslak and his stupid violence. 'We'll deal with it all on the Brough,' he said, and strode off, leaving the pair of them standing there with the dog.

'How is it that things seem to be moving so fast when we aren't getting anywhere?' Sigrid asked. She was spinning, propped against one of the infield walls, arms reddened by the wind reaching from the shelter of her cloak. For one thing, out here they could see anyone approaching. For another, Asta had taken up a post by the hearth in Beinir's house while the men finished in her own house, and there was no peace to be found in there. Even Osk looked more bewildered than usual.

'What's been moving fast for you?'

'The story of Beinir's sweetheart – this young Ingigerd,' she said, and her voice was rich with disapproval.

'Drowned in an ayre,' Ketil said.

'That's right – after what young Ali – though she's not as young as she looks – calls 'the big fuss'.'

'A fuss? On Shapinsay? Surely not,' said Ketil, though he was beginning to wonder if there were an island in the archipelago where more happened than on Shapinsay.

'Oh, yes!' There was a distinct glint in Sigrid's eye, the kind of glint that is only fed by discovering the failings of one's predecessor. 'You remember the tale of the vart being fired by accident, a couple of years ago? While Thorfinn was off on his journey to Rome.'

'Yes, Tosti told me about it. The vart warden had got drunk and set it off.' Drunk, he thought. 'It wasn't Aslak, by any chance, was it?'

'It was,' said Sigrid, 'but not on his own. When Vali and Beinir went up to the vart to find out what had happened, they found Aslak blind drunk – and Ingigerd with him!'

'Also blind drunk?'

Sigrid nodded.

'And in a state of disarray. Ali followed Vali and Beinir up the hill: according to her, she saw it all. Then Beinir told Ingigerd to stay at home, but in a few days she vanished in the early morning, and was found in the ayre.'

'She threw herself in,' Ketil said. 'Ashamed of what she had done.'

'Ali reckons not,' said Sigrid, unexpectedly. 'Ali says she was not the least bit ashamed. She might have feared being sent back to her uncle on Hoy – they were both pleased to be getting away from him – but she was out to enjoy herself. Given the options, Ali reckons she either tripped and fell in, or was pushed and held down. The water is pretty shallow, apparently.'

'Did she drown?'

'Ali didn't know.'

'She could have been dead before she reached the water.'

'She could.'

Ketil considered for a moment.

'Was that all she had to tell you?'

He thought Sigrid hesitated, but she said,

'Yes, that was all. And then,' she hurried on, 'there was last night's fire. Now, of course, we know of a reason why Aslak might bear a grudge against Hoskuld, but Hoskuld wasn't there –'

'The fire began at the back of the house again,' Ketil pointed out. 'It might be that no one was intended to die. As with Aslak – if he did not set fire to his own house – it may have been meant as some kind of warning.'

'It was you that found it, wasn't it? Did you see anyone?'

'No: I'd walked past a little and happened to look back. It was dark, and as I ran back I slipped and dropped my torch.' He waited for the usual sarcastic remark, but none came.

'Beinir and Osk and Katrin were all inside with me, and Skorri, of course,' she said. 'Geirod and Alf were out on patrol. What have you found out about everyone else?'

'No one is admitting to being outside, no one is telling me that they heard or saw anything suspicious.'

'Four fires in less than a week, stories of an old scandal and death, and we barely have anyone to suspect apart from Aslak.'

'Trying to prove it will be difficult, if it is true,' said Ketil.

'That's what I mean about everything going so fast but we're getting nowhere.' She sighed, and gave the spindle a quick twist, helping it on its way.

'I think we might get somewhere with part of it,' said Ketil, slowly. He was not even sure himself yet, but something had been bothering him for a while.

'Part of it?' she queried.

'Yes,' he said, and tipped his head gently towards the wreckage of Beinir's outhouse. No one was quite sure what to do with it yet, not with the ashes of Leif and Hervor still inside. Tosti was standing near it, looking thoughtful, hands tucked into his sleeves. 'The outhouse fire. Does that seem to you as if it fits with the others?'

'Oh!' she said, and he had the gratifying feeling of having thought of something before she did, and not had it immediately dismissed. She stared at the ruins.

'The fish oil, certainly,' she said. 'As if someone wanted a quick fire, up and over with. And it was almost in daylight, with people still about.'

'I know. Somehow different.'

'Yes,' she said, 'I agree. But why?'

XX

'I can't think,' Sigrid admitted, after struggling to come up with something clever. 'I can't even see why anyone would burn down an outhouse that had been empty, or that had a priest and two dead bodies in it. Everyone swears there was barely anything left of them to destroy but charred flesh. It can't have been a question of making sure that there was nothing there to connect the killer to the fire, can it? It makes no sense. And who would want to kill Tosti?'

'No one, I hope,' said Tosti cheerfully, overhearing as he walked towards them from the outhouse ruins. 'If it would be of service for me to lay down my life then, well, I suppose one must. But just to be burned in an outhouse because someone has taken against you – that seems like a waste of time and effort.' He smiled, as serene a potential murder victim as one might be likely to meet.

'We're just saying that the outhouse fire feels different from the others,' Sigrid explained. 'Ketil says it even smells different.'

'Well,' said Ketil, 'did you smell fish oil at any of the other fires?'

'No ... Tosti, there wasn't fish oil stored in the outhouse, was there?'

'I'd have noticed,' said the priest at once. 'It was not a large space. And I did smell it when I came out to go to the privy. I remember thinking it must be someone's supper cooking.' He tipped his dark head to one side. 'I wonder if it was the same person who was walking around the outhouse before that?'

'When was that?' Sigrid snapped. She had a strong feeling that whatever was happening here was slipping between her fingers and running away, and it did not help that Ketil was not telling her everything. She had not told him everything, either, but that was less important: he was not the person who would put everything together.

'The day before yesterday,' said Tosti, hesitantly.

'I was at the back of the outhouse yesterday,' said Sigrid, scowling at Ketil before he could even say,

'Why were you at the back of the outhouse?'

'I saw Gillaug heading for Beinir's door,' she said, happy that that was quite enough of an explanation. 'I walked round the outhouse and noticed that someone had been scuffing through the snow – I thought they were just bored and had been fiddling about. Maybe they were.'

'No footprints, then?' Ketil asked.

'Well, that's it – at one corner I did find a footprint. Quite pointed, not the usual stub-toed boot.'

'A woman?' Tosti suggested.

'It could be,' Sigrid agreed. 'Not Asta, though: her boots look as if she has borrowed her husband's. Gillaug wears a pointed boot,' she added, trying to sound as if it hardly mattered.

'Any of the men?'

She had to think: she had not been paying much attention to the feet of the men around her. At that evening in Vali's house she had taken a good look at people around the hearth, but for the most part their feet had been hidden.

'Vali, perhaps?' she suggested. 'And Hamthir likes to dress up when he isn't working. But I couldn't swear to either.'

'I'll keep my eyes open,' said Ketil.

'So you're making good progress?' Tosti asked brightly. 'Thank the Lord Asta and Ali were not injured.'

'Indeed,' said Ketil.

'It was Ketil who spotted the fire,' Sigrid said, without intending to. After all, it was pure luck. Or God's grace, she reminded herself, glancing at Tosti. Either way, all Ketil had done was run to the rescue.

'So – not many left, then?' Tosti said helpfully. Sigrid and Ketil stared at each other. She had not considered that, and nor, clearly, had he.

'That's true …' she said quickly. 'Just Vali, Gillaug and Beinir left. Do you think someone is trying to wipe out the settlement?'

'I've not really had the chance to see much of it,' Tosti admitted. 'Is that likely?'

Ketil shrugged.

'There's not a great deal of evidence of any coming and going between this settlement and the rest of the island,' he said, 'not in this weather.'

'Boats?'

Ketil shook his head.

'I thought of that,' he said. 'The thing is, again, whoever it is would have to keep coming and going so often. It's hardly as if it's the weather to wait around the coast and come back the following night. And I sent Geirod to check in one direction, and Skorri and Alf in the other: no sign of any boats about apart from the ones in the harbour along the way. And most of those are in for repair.'

'Does Beinir have a boat?' She could not help asking.

'He does.' She saw Ketil's lips twist a little. 'It's in for repair, too.'

She would have to go and look at some point. You couldn't judge a man by his boat, not entirely, but it helped. And in Beinir's case, she wanted more information: from outside, not from him.

'Well, I'd better go and talk to the leatherworker and the smith,' said Ketil at last. 'I've been meaning to – and Asta's house is one of the closest to them.'

'Apart from Beinir's, you mean?' asked Sigrid. He looked down and met her eyes.

'Be careful, Sigrid,' he said.

'Because Beinir's house might be next?'

'That. And something Gillaug said to me this morning. She said that wilful women needed to be careful – and I think she meant you.'

'Me?'

'Well, whether you're wilful or not, it's clear she doesn't like you. Make sure you're with Skorri or me, or with Father Tosti here, all the time.'

'But surely she doesn't still suspect me –'

'Please,' said Ketil, and she fell silent. She felt him still watching her for a moment, then he turned away. 'I'll see you later, Tosti.'

'Sunday tomorrow,' Tosti said. 'I'll take a service before the midday meal – perhaps on the beach at the harbour?'

Ketil nodded.

'I'll be there.'

He strode off, long legs sweeping over the snow as if it had melted away. Sigrid watched him go.

'Want to talk?' Tosti asked softly. She drew a deep breath.

'Yes, if you have time.'

'Nothing else to do,' he shrugged. 'Except to put the word around about tomorrow. Beinir should be pleased.'

'He will be.' She stopped, but felt that Tosti was waiting. 'You've not seen much of Shapinsay so far, have you?'

'Not much, no.' He made a rueful smile. 'Though Katrin has been very attentive, and Ketil's men made sure it was not too dull.'

'When Beinir came to Birsay, it was as head man of Shapinsay, wasn't it?'

'That's what he said, yes.'

'And here ... doesn't he look like a head man?'

'Well ...'

'Tall? Authoritative? The one that people turn to when something goes wrong?'

Tosti smiled.

'I'm sure he doesn't have to be tall – or handsome, either,' he said, raising an eyebrow at Sigrid. She felt herself blush. 'And I haven't seen much of him.'

Sigrid drew another deep breath.

'I'm told he's not head man at all. That Vali is.'

'Really?' Both of Tosti's eyebrows rose now, and he blinked fast. 'But why would that be?'

Sigrid sighed.

'It seems all too likely,' she said. 'Even Ketil treats Vali with more respect than he does Beinir. Vali has the authority, he's the one they all consult – and yes, he's tall!'

'Then why –'

'Ali, Asta's servant, told me that Vali is the real head man, but that Beinir believes he himself is.' She paused, preparing herself. 'Tosti, can he really read and write?'

'Oh, yes,' said Tosti at once. 'No need to worry about that.'

'I don't think Vali can,' Sigrid went on. 'Maybe that's ... maybe he does the reading and writing, and Vali does the authority?' It sounded unlikely even to her. 'Tosti, I don't understand!'

'Have you mentioned this to Ketil?'

'Don't be silly. He'd laugh.'

Tosti pressed his lips together, but said nothing to that.

'Does it matter?' he asked quietly. 'If he isn't head man, I mean?'

For a moment, Sigrid tried to find words that would not make her look like a girl dazzled by glory. But this was Tosti: somehow one had to tell him the truth.

'Yes,' she said. 'It makes a difference. To me, anyway. I don't want to be an old, poor widow.'

'Then this difference is enough to make you reconsider your plan to marry him?'

'Oh! I don't know that that plan was ever a very firm one anyway!' She rubbed her face hard, blinking back something a bit like a tear. 'It's not as if he has lied to me, or I don't think he has. Once Ali told me, it was sort of clear. He thinks he's the head man: he goes about checking on people and things, taking responsibility, and he writes it all down in his annals –' a little burst of frantic laughter left her as she saw the look of dismay on Tosti's face – 'and, you know, goes off to Birsay like that, with all the other head men, and I don't even believe that he realises that everyone else turns to Vali, does what Vali tells them. I don't think I would even talk about it with Beinir: I think it might break his heart if someone said it to his face. But he is not the head man.'

'But why would Vali let him do it?' Tosti asked. She rubbed her eyes with the heel of her hand and looked at him.

'That I don't know,' she said. 'I can't even begin to understand this place. Even without four fires in a week, it makes no sense to me. But my fear is that I am going to be burned in my bed, and not even know why. It's ridiculous! Isn't it?'

'Well, the fear of being burned in your bed seems, just at the moment, perfectly reasonable,' said Tosti, though somehow he made it sound reassuring. 'So does all this mean you don't intend to marry Beinir?'

She eyed him, anxious.

'What do you think I should do?'

Tosti grinned.

'I don't think you've ever asked me for advice before! And now you come along to ask about something I know very little about – I don't think marriage is going to be an option for me.'

'You know people. You know me.'

'Nevertheless,' he said, 'you must decide for yourself.'

'You mean you don't know, either?'

'I mean I don't want to be blamed if it goes wrong – either way!' He paused. 'Have you talked to Ketil about it? He's a good judge of men.'

But at that Sigrid pushed away from the wall and gathered up her spindle.

'Now,' she said briskly, 'it looks to me as if there is more snow on the way, and I can see your nose is blue – why don't we go inside? I think I can just smell a hint of dinner, and Katrin's cooking is not to be missed!'

'That is very true,' Tosti conceded, and she hoped he had not noticed her speedy change of subject. Why on earth would she talk to Ketil about Beinir? 'Even staying in the outhouse was no great hardship with meals like hers.'

They walked together down to the longhouse door and went inside, instantly warmer out of the wind. Sigrid felt her face burn on one side and her eyes water, but once they had cleared she saw they had a visitor. Katrin was working by the hearth making dough for the flatbreads, and beside her sat Hamthir, more attentive than Sigrid had so far seen him, yet, she thought, they had not disturbed anything too intimate as she and Tosti came in. There was a reasonable distance between the pair, though Hamthir was turned towards Katrin who was smiling prettily. Hamthir's face, too, had a contented look to it, comfortable sharing a hearth with the girl. He had a kind of stolid dignity about him, and a handsome appearance – no wonder Katrin was pleased with him, and her parents, too.

Sigrid and Tosti joined them by the fire, and Sigrid at once began helping with the dough. Goodness, she thought, at this rate she might even be able to bake a little bread successfully when she went home – or when she became the woman of this household. Just at the moment, the latter seemed much less likely.

'I came to ask if I could help mend Hoskuld's longhouse,' Hamthir explained, ostensibly to Sigrid and Tosti but with an eye still on Katrin. 'Geirod and Alf came to ask me for wood, so I know what's involved. I've brought my tools!' He laid a hand on a large and lumpy cloth bag lying beside him.

'We're all going up again after the meal,' said Katrin, flashing a smile at Hamthir. 'Everyone's coming down here to eat. I hope Mother's going to bring some more flour, if Ali's had time to grind the grain.'

'It'll be a squeeze!' said Sigrid. 'Every day we seem to add more people to the household!'

'I love it,' said Katrin. 'I've always lived in a quiet household. I think it's exciting when there are plenty of people about, helping and eating and talking.'

Sigrid looked up, smiling, and caught a fleeting frown on Hamthir's face. Perhaps this was not something he enjoyed – he must like a quiet life. Ah, well, it was a simple thing to sort out, surely.

And anyway, Hamthir seemed to enjoy the meal as much as everyone else. There was a feeling of camaraderie Sigrid had not previously seen in the settlement. She overheard Vali talking to Skorri: Vali had appeared along with Aslak and the wood.

'It's hard to know what to do about the fires,' he was saying, 'but when someone has survived and we can fix the damage, that makes us all feel better.'

Even Beinir, who had been supervising at least until Vali had turned up, was flushed with the exercise and the sense of achievement.

'The beams are perfect,' he was telling Hamthir. 'We're ready to lay turves on them – even the turves are cut, though they might not be in the best condition, half-frozen. But they'll do for now!'

'If it's good,' said Asta, handing him soup and a hunk of bread, 'I'll get you to do the rest of the roof while you're up there!'

'What about your bed, Asta?' asked Gillaug, who seemed to have done nothing up at the house but had joined them for the meal. 'What are you going to do about that?'

'Oh, that I'll leave till Hoskuld gets back,' said Asta comfortably. 'He made that one, no doubt he'll want to make the replacement. I daren't ask anyone else to touch it!'

After the meal, people were keen to get started again, to do what they could before the light went. The wind was still strong – when was it not? - but there had been little further snowfall during the day. Beinir led the way back to the longhouse, with Asta puffing along behind, and while Gillaug vanished again the women in a body went to turn and sniff the cloths and furs that had been laid out earlier to air, trying to drive out the stink of smoke. Inside the house everything was disarranged, anything that could be shifted moved back from where the men were working, the hearth cold, the hanging shelves down and stacked out of the way. But it was orderly disarrangement.

'Where have you two been?' Asta called, pretending severity. Hamthir and Katrin drifted up the hill a good while after everyone else, Katrin a little pinker than usual. At her mother's words she flushed scarlet, and everyone turned to laugh.

'We're here now,' said Hamthir with a grin. He hurried off to help the other men carry turves from where they had been cut, leaving his bag of tools by the wall of the longhouse. Katrin, eyes down, went as far as she could from where her mother was working, and set to to help with the blankets laid out on the cleansing snow.

Ketil was still away – avoiding the hard work, Sigrid thought – but she stayed within sight of Tosti and Skorri as she had been instructed. For the moment she was quite happy to: she found herself sorting Asta's wool and fixing the work that had been disturbed on the loom, and she could have worked contentedly at that all day, if required. But it did not take long, and soon she was out with the blankets and furs, too, with the others. The men, carrying loads of turves up the hill from the edges of the bog, were scarlet in the cold air: they had worn a dark path down the hill where their digging had scarred the snow black. The turves would be very wet when they warmed up, but with luck – and some extra supports the men had inserted between the beams – they would last till spring, anyway. There might be a damp patch on the roof but at least the rain and snow would not be able to penetrate.

She turned blankets with Katrin, examining them for scorches or tears, sniffing them bundled between her hands. Katrin had not spoken a word since she and Hamthir had appeared late, and Sigrid's thoughts wandered. She glanced down past the scarred snow to the smithy. Presumably Ketil was still down there. It had been good to talk with him earlier, now he had shed that odd stiffness he had brought with him from the Brough. But to be fair, she had been odd herself since she had come here. She had not been herself, more timid and subservient and quiet than was her habit. What had she been doing? Was she trying to pretend to Beinir that she would be a nice, suitable wife? After all, it would be much more pleasant to reject him, if it came to it, than to have him reject her.

But was she a bit in awe of him, even now? Even when she knew he was not the head man? She had certainly never been in awe of Ketil, which was why it was so much easier to talk to him. But Beinir ... was it - could it just be - the writing?

Yes, it was. That and the reading.

Would he ever teach her to read and write? He had shown Ketil the marks for his name, but he had not shown Sigrid hers. She was almost too nervous to ask him, afraid he would say no.

She cleared her throat.

'Katrin,' she said, low enough that no one else working near them would hear, 'you know Beinir can read and write?'

'Of course,' said Katrin shortly.

'Do you think – if I asked him – do you think he would ever teach me?'

Katrin looked at her in amazement, her half-smile anticipating a joke.

'Why on earth would you want to read and write?' she asked. 'You don't need anything more than a few runes to run a household, do you?'

'I suppose not,' Sigrid conceded, a little cross. She had managed up to now, after all.

But she still wondered if the reading and writing was the key. Was that why Vali allowed Beinir to act like the head man, when it was really Vali who was in charge? And how had this situation come about? She tried to think back to things she had heard Vali say ... was there a hint there that he and Thorfinn did not, perhaps, get on? There had been perhaps just a little too much politeness when Ketil had announced whose man he was – or was she imagining it? She would have to speak to Vali: not something that the meek Sigrid, prospective Beinir-wife, would do, she felt, but the ordinary Sigrid would not be intimidated by anyone. Well, not usually, anyway.

But as a compromise, she wanted to catch Vali outside somewhere, or at least not in his own house. If anyone was looking for authority they only needed to look at him, sitting in his high chair at the end of the hearth, surveying his guests. For someone who had spent a few days being intimidated by Beinir, it was not a place to start with

Vali. She needed him off his own territory.

Even as she considered this, Katrin tapped her on the arm.

'We're starting to take the blankets back in,' she said, nodding at the house. 'I think the men have finished, and it's getting dark.'

'I hadn't even noticed,' said Sigrid. 'Here, give me that one when you've folded it, and I'll take both these in.'

Katrin folded the blanket in practised flips, and handed it to Sigrid. She turned to the house, and was just in time to see Vali calling farewell to the people still inside, and turning to go.

She hurried over to the doorway, and made herself take the blankets inside and lay them neatly on – on something or other of which she took no notice. Then she whipped back out into the dusk, and followed Vali round the corner of the longhouse. He was already beyond the building, striding across the snowy infields. She hesitated for a moment, then trotted after him, ducking into shelter for fear – she was not sure why – that he would see her following him.

But as she rounded the corner of the privy, tracing Vali's footsteps, she heard voices ahead. Vali had met someone. Praying it was not Gillaug, she dropped back behind the corner. The voices were close.

'Vali, I need to ask you –' She recognised Beinir's voice – not Gillaug. But her relief, as she was about to step forward again, was suddenly knocked back by his tone. 'Please.'

'Beinir, I know what you're going to say …' Vali was patient, but weary.

'Please. He's my responsibility – let me take it on. And when I'm married – which I hope will not be long – it will make perfect sense, won't it?'

He hopes will not be long, does he? Sigrid thought sharply. But she was trying to pay attention to what Beinir was saying – what he was asking for. What was it?

'He's settled where he is,' Vali said. 'There's no reason for him to move.'

'But he's my responsibility, you know that. Let me have him. Let him live with us. Please, Vali …'

His pleading was hard to hear. Sigrid longed to see Vali's face, to see how he was reacting. But who was Beinir asking about? It could only be Aslak – his responsibility as the head man he thought he was. How could Beinir marry her and then bring that man into the house? She turned away, leaning back against the cold stone wall of the longhouse. He certainly took his duties seriously. But would Vali let him?

'Beinir, there is no need.'

'Please!'

'No.' She heard movement, and the determined footsteps of Vali, striding away. She could not follow him now. Nor could she turn the corner and meet Beinir, for from where she was hiding, appalled, she could clearly hear sobbing.

XXI

On the whole, Ketil would rather have spent an afternoon sorting out a broken roof, though the idea of working in a team of cheerful strangers did not wholly appeal. Particularly cheerful strangers who might include someone who burned down other people's houses in the night.

But he had not been to see the smithy and the leatherworks, and though he had sent Skorri to visit them and there had been nothing suspicious to report, he himself had focussed so completely on the settlement and its few inhabitants that he felt it was only right to take himself outside it for a bit, and give himself a sense of perspective.

He avoided the bog – not least because digging had started there for turf for the damaged longhouse roof – and took the shore path. The bay was a tight one, turning almost back on itself, but he did not have to walk all the way to the steep little headland that marked its far end. The stream that entered the sea halfway round was fed by the bog, as far as he could tell in the snow, and the tanned water it provided enabled the smithy and the leatherworks to do their business.

Neither was a large concern. Two longhouses snuggled on the far side of the stream, with their outbuildings and infields, presumably where the ground was usually drier. On the near side he came first upon the smithy, a stone-built hut with a roof of flags, melted clear of snow, and hardly room for anything inside but the furnace and a fairly basic stone anvil, as well as a flag bench where the smith's tools lay. The man himself was cleaning and ordering them, and it looked as if the fire was dying down for the day.

'You're finishing early,' Ketil said by way of greeting. 'Not so much work about?'

'Work enough,' said the big man easily, 'but none of it urgent, and it's Sunday tomorrow.' He eased his leather jerkin where it rubbed around his armpits. His thin black hair was scraped back into a ponytail, and his bare arms were brown, and smattered with old burns.

'You've heard there's a priest to celebrate, back there?' Ketil nodded at the settlement. The man's face lit up as though he had stood too close to his furnace.

'A priest? Of the new faith?'

'That's right. Tosti is his name: he's visiting from Birsay.'

'That's a fine thing to hear,' said the smith, shaking his head with a smile. 'I'll be along tomorrow, surely. You're visiting from Birsay yourself, I suppose?'

'Yes,' said Ketil, 'but I'm no priest.'

The man's eyebrows rose, perhaps taking in Ketil's close-cropped head.

'I'm Thorfinn's man. I'm looking into these house burnings.'

'I heard there was another one last night,' said the smith, and crossed himself.

'Asta's house – Hoskuld's house – but no one was injured, and there was little damage,' said Ketil, watching the man with care. The smith looked more relieved than anything.

'Aye, Hoskuld the potter. I'm glad everything's all right. Well, not as bad as it might have been.'

'As it was more to this end of the settlement I thought I'd come and ask you again – I know my man has been here before – did you hear anything out of the ordinary last night? See strangers? See people who were not strangers, but had no reason to be out and about?'

'Huh, last night!' said the smith, shrugging, though he was still smiling. 'We were all out and about last night. See over there?' He pointed with some kind of delicate hammer towards the longhouses across the stream. 'That's my neighbour's place – he does the leather here. Not today, mind! Ha!' He waved the hammer towards the leatherworking shed and pools, which Ketil could now see were quiet and shut up.

'What happened?'

'His wife went into labour. He ran out and called my wife to come and help – it's their first – and she went running out to go to her, and he came on to our house to fetch me – I don't know what use I would have been, but he was that excited he spun round on our doorstep and knocked himself out on the wall. So I had to pick him up and take him home, and in the end all of us spent the night in his house, and the baby was born at dawn!'

'And he's all right?'

'No stupider than usual! Ha!' The smith chortled happily to himself for a moment or two. 'No stupider than usual, eh?'

'So what you're telling me,' said Ketil, 'is that you saw nothing out of the ordinary going past here.'

'Not a thing!' said the smith cheerily. 'Wish I had: it's not a good thing, these burnings. How many houses are left there by the harbour? What happens when he runs out – will he come here?' For once he frowned horribly, and the tiny hammer in his hand seemed more like a viable weapon than it had before.

'You'll know the people there well, no doubt – who do you think is setting the fires?'

'Me?' The smith blinked, bewildered, and laid down the hammer, adjusting it so that it sat in exactly the right place. 'I don't know. Aslak, maybe? He's always been trouble.'

'He's never set fire to anything before, though, has he?'

'Not that I know of.' His shrug was massive. 'I don't know.'

Ketil stood for a moment, and glanced across at the leatherworker's house. Was it even worth the short walk to go and ask him the same questions?

'So when's this service tomorrow?' the smith asked.

'Dawn, I think, or just after. Before the midday meal.'

'That's grand. I'll look forward to that.'

'Thank you for your help,' said Ketil, turning anyway towards the leatherworker's house. It was better to be thorough.

'You're welcome. Thank you for the news. That'll be Beinir's doing, no doubt,' the smith continued even as Ketil was walking away. 'The rest of them over there all stick to the old ways, bless them.'

Ketil had walked five paces before what the smith had said had sunk in.

Beinir had brought Tosti so that the settlement could have some

Christian services before Christmas, but the rest of the settlement was not Christian …

He walked on slowly to the longhouses, examining the matter in his head. Did that, perhaps, explain what had happened to the outhouse? He would have to think about it.

The leatherworker and his wife could tell him nothing more than the smith had – less, perhaps, as the baby was demanding all their doting attention. The leatherworker had a wonderful dent in his forehead, almost worthy of an axe blow, and happily confirmed to Ketil how he had acquired it.

'A bit of a night, eh?' he finished, beaming, and Ketil had to agree.

He walked back along the shore path towards the harbour settlement, puzzling over everything that had happened, trying to fit it all together. It was drawing on to dusk, though the light lingered on the snow. He could almost imagine he was back in winter Trondheim. There was a time when he would have preferred to have been there, when he had no desire ever to see these islands again. But now? Now he was, at least, used to them. He would need to be content, if he were going to marry and settle here.

His mind danced briefly over the thought, then skated quickly away. He had to sort out the problems here first.

At Beinir's place, as he arrived, people were drifting back down from Asta's house towards Beinir's door.

'All done!' said Skorri brightly when he saw him. 'They can be back in tonight. Asta's lighting the hearth again.'

'Good work,' said Ketil. 'Where is Sigrid?'

For a second, Skorri's face went blank, then Tosti appeared with Sigrid just behind him.

'She's here, Ketil, don't worry.'

'I know you pine away when you don't see me,' added Sigrid.

'At least you can't get up to anything stupid when you're with Tosti,' said Ketil.

She made a face at him but he had the impression there was more on her mind than just teasing him: she even let Tosti steer her inside the longhouse without making a reply.

He waited until everyone had gone inside, then stepped over to the wrecked outhouse. It was hard to tell in the dusk, but there really seemed to be nothing left of the bodies, just as Tosti had said. He sniffed warily: the smell of fish oil was still quite strong. But that was not all. Tosti himself had said how pleasant the oil had smelled, how it had made him think of a good supper. He sniffed again, closing his eyes. Herbs, he thought. Someone had added herbs to the oil. Why would they do that, just to help a fire to catch? And where else had he smelled herbs like that recently? He straightened, staring out across the bay, as two or three broken pieces fitted together in his head. He smiled, very slightly, and went back over to Beinir's longhouse.

There was plenty of time before supper: Katrin was only just coaxing the fire back to life to start cooking. Alf was bringing more fuel for it, and Skorri had gone to fetch water for her. Katrin was in danger of civilising his men, and Ketil cast a glance at Hamthir to make sure he was not angered by this attention to his intended bride. But Hamthir was relaxed, talking with Beinir, not even looking at Katrin. Beinir seemed to be listening to him intently, but if anything, Hamthir's attention seemed more focussed on Sigrid. Ketil watched him for a moment. What was it that had caught Hamthir's attention? Was he pleased that his young sweetheart seemed to be teaching the older woman how to cook? Or was he genuinely interested in something about Sigrid?

Ketil caught Sigrid's eye, and gestured to her. She rose, making a face, and went to join him near the door, as far from everyone else as could be.

'I'm not one of your men, you know,' she said, as soon as she reached him.

'I thought you'd be interested to know what I found out today,' he said, 'and what I worked out from it.'

'You worked something out? All right: that might be worth crossing the floor to hear. Go on,' she encouraged him, folding her arms.

'I mentioned to the smith down by the river,' he said quietly, watching over her shoulder to make sure that no one could overhear, 'that Tosti was going to take a service tomorrow, and he was delighted. Then he said that would be Beinir organising it, because everyone else here follows the old religion.'

Her jaw dropped gratifyingly. Then he thought he could see something in her eyes – this, she was realising, fitted with something else she already knew. Something she had not yet told him. He waited.

'That's … interesting,' she said at last. 'And I wonder …' She frowned, then her brow cleared and she drew breath. 'I found out something too, and I wonder if they go together. I mean, it should have been obvious. It was obvious, but when you're told something … You see, Beinir is not the head man here. Vali is.'

'But Beinir –'

'Beinir believes he is the head man. And Vali seems happy to let him think so. And if Beinir's the one who has to go and meet Thorfinn and talk to him about Shapinsay, maybe that suits Vali very well – what with Thorfinn wanting everyone to be a Christian.'

That made sense. Thorfinn would not want the head man of any of his territories, let alone a strategically important island, to follow the old religion. Not nowadays.

'But I can't see how any of that helps with the burnings,' she said.

'I think it helps with one of them,' said Ketil. 'Beinir's outhouse.'

Sigrid gasped.

'They tried to kill Tosti!'

'No,' said Ketil, glancing around again to make sure no one had heard. 'No, they seem to treat Tosti with respect. They waited for him to leave. But they wanted the bodies to be burned properly, with as much ceremony as they could.'

'That smell, with the fish oil.'

'Some kind of herbs,' Ketil confirmed. 'I smelled it at Vali's house this morning. And Vali claimed to be the first to find the fire – presumably after it had done what they wanted it to do.'

'And he and Gillaug and Eyolfr were in their best clothes,' she said, remembering. 'But they didn't want Leif and Hervor to have a Christian burial. Of course.'

'I think that's it, yes.' He paused. 'But it doesn't mean that any of them burned anything else, does it?'

'No …' She thought, then shook her head. 'No, I don't see how that would fit with any of the others. But it doesn't mean that any one of them might not have set fire to the houses.'

'No.'

'So we still have the same possible burners – Aslak,'

'The smith thought he was a good candidate.'

'Everyone does. Are we overlooking the obvious here?'

'I don't know. List the others.'

'Aslak, Vali, Hamthir,' she started again. 'That's one household.

Why don't they have a servant, I wonder?'

'Vali said she left recently.'

Sigrid frowned briefly.

'Eyolfr – too weak, unless Gillaug told him to. Gillaug herself, if she would get her hands dirty.'

'That's the next household.'

'Beinir,' she whispered.

'He couldn't have fired Asta's house.'

She nodded, and swallowed.

'Katrin, Osk, me.'

'Again, none of you could have been at Asta's.'

Sigrid nodded again, acknowledging that.

'Asta herself, and Ali – if Aslak could have set fire to his own house, then she could have, too. And are we sure that Hoskuld went, and is not back?'

'Hamthir took him, and left him on the mainland.'

'So no, we're not sure. We might have to think about that.'

He looked down at her as she screwed up her lips in concentration.

'Does it matter to you?' he asked suddenly.

'What?' She glanced up, then away.

'That Beinir is not the head man?'

'What do you take me for? Do you think I'd marry a man just because of his status?'

He did not reply, and after a moment she said,

'He takes his responsibility very seriously, you know. He does what he can. He wanted to take Aslak in here, you know, because his house is a wreck. I heard Beinir asking Vali – almost begging him. So you see, he knows where his duty lies.'

'Even if it's actually Vali's duty.'

'They must divide it between them. Vali can't read or write, anyway. He can't keep all the records that Beinir does.'

'But everyone does what Vali tells them.'

'I know …'

He reached out and touched her arm, lightly.

'I'm sure he's a good man, Beinir. He'd do his best to make you happy.'

She pulled herself up straight and gave her head a little shake, as if clearing it.

'I'd better help Katrin. Lots of people to cook for. It looks as if Hamthir's going to stay and eat, so she'll want to make a good impression.'

She marched back across to the hearth, taking her place at Beinir's feet as though she was already his wife. He watched her go, still wondering. Would Beinir's best be good enough?

After supper, an amiable meal after all their work together during the day, Ketil instructed Alf and Geirod to take a nap while he and Skorri began to patrol. As they began along the shore path towards the harbour they walked Hamthir back to Vali's longhouse, cloaks hard-wrapped against the wind. At Vali's door they stood to see him inside, and Ketil glimpsed Aslak and Vali settled by their own hearth, looking over at the door at Hamthir's arrival. Ingvar waved frantically, grinning. Ketil raised a hand in greeting.

'We're patrolling,' he called over, 'but I'd recommend you kept an eye open anyway.'

'You can't be everywhere,' Vali agreed. 'But surely he would not strike again tonight?'

'He moves quickly,' said Ketil.

Vali nodded sadly.

'He does. We'll be watchful.'

Ketil and Skorri walked on towards the harbour, taking a look in case any strange boats were hauled up on the beach, but all looked as it usually did in their torchlight. Ketil turned up the path that led to Aslak's longhouse and over the hill towards Vasa ayre, where Ingigerd had been found dead. Ingigerd and Aslak, infuriating Beinir and Vali. Aslak's house burned, and Ingigerd died.

Skorri, beside him, was also reviewing the wreckage of the longhouse.

'If it's deliberate, he was given a good chance to get out,' he said. 'And the burned bit doesn't smell of fish oil, it smells of pitch.'

Ketil was not quite ready to share his ideas about the outhouse fire yet. Skorri was too chatty.

'I think the reason was different. And pitch is easy – take a torch,' he raised his own slightly, 'and thrust it into the eaves. Anyone who's been raiding would know what to do.'

'That's not so many people these days,' said Skorri, a little mournful.

'Or anyone who has heard stories of raiding.' He lowered his torch and took a look across the settlement. From here, with all the doors facing east, there was barely a light to be seen. 'Come on,' he said, moving off again, 'we'll get a better view from up the hill.'

He led the way back up to the route he had walked the previous night, moving a little faster than he had then. If he could find any new fire as quickly as he had found the one at Asta's, they might be all right – and with two of them, one could raise the alarm and fight the fire while the other quartered the area for the arsonist.

Below them, Vali's house stood, a torch set at the door, perhaps their way of taking his advice to watch out. Next, after the intervening infields, Eyolfr's longhouse, silent and dark. He was about to pass on when Skorri stopped.

'Do you smell smoke?'

Ketil sniffed. Did he? He was not sure, but Skorri was following the scent on the wind, and now Ketil caught it, too. It could be a late-lit hearth – or it could be a torch rammed into the eaves of Eyolfr's longhouse. They began a slow progress over the complicated infields, walls, hurdles, furrowed ground, conspiring to trap them or trip them, but the smoke as they went grew no thicker, at least. They reached the end wall of Eyolfr's longhouse, and examined the eaves with care, carrying on around the back of the house, on to the shore path and, gingerly, past the door and along the front. Their unspoken agreement not to rouse Gillaug unless it was absolutely necessary caused a tight smile to pass across Ketil's face briefly, but at least there was no sign of excess heat or smoke.

'What do you think you're doing there? Eyolfr, I've found the arsonists! Come quickly!'

They both spun round as Gillaug shot out of the doorway, an axe in her hand.

'It's us, Gillaug,' said Ketil wearily. 'Skorri and Ketil from Birsay.'

Eyolfr appeared, bare-legged and wrapped in a blanket, peering around the doorpost.

'Are you the arsonists?' he asked, looking confused.

'Of course we aren't.'

'Prove it,' snapped Gillaug.

'How? By not setting fire to your house?' Ketil sighed. 'I'm glad to see you're on the alert, but just go back inside now. We're on patrol.'

'Well, that makes me feel so much better,' said Gillaug, though at last she let her axe arm fall. Ketil noticed that unlike her husband, she was still fully dressed. Was she indeed on watch, or had she been out somewhere?

'I still smell smoke,' said Skorri. 'Is your hearth still lit?'

'At this time of the night?' Gillaug demanded. 'Why, are you looking for hot wine?'

'It's coming from behind us – isn't it?' Skorri went on. Ketil turned. The longhouse behind them was Beinir's.

And Beinir's house was burning.

'Fire!' Skorri bellowed. 'Fire at Beinir's! Bring buckets!'

But already Ketil was staggering and slithering along the shore path, his eyes only on the burning house. Burning, he saw, at both ends. And beginning, like the dragon in his dream, to roar.

Distantly he heard shouts, some from the house, some from behind him – clattering of buckets, thud and scrape of feet running after him. He seized the sharp corner of the longhouse and spun to the door. It was closed. He shoved with his shoulder, already feeling the heat of the wood. The door held, and he squinted in the dark – there was a board somehow caught under the latch. He kicked at it and it fell free, then he beat at the door again, burning his fingers on the metal latch. The door gave way, and he fell back. Flames were eating at every pillar. They licked up the rafters, and danced around the hearth. The curtains around the beds were alight.

'Fire!' he yelled, in case anyone was still asleep.

'Aye, we spotted that,' gasped Geirod, as he pushed the yellow dog out through the doorway. Alf was there, too, bundling a confused Beinir towards the door.

'Here,' he said briefly, coughing.

'Get out, you two. Who else is in here? Sigrid? Tosti?'

'Aye,' Alf bent over in the snow, hands on his knees, catching his breath. 'And the old woman.'

'Katrin went to her mother's,' said Geirod. 'Here's Tosti.' The two of them staggered out together, and Alf grabbed them and rolled them in the snow, beating out the flames that clung to Tosti's back. Ketil looked back into the blazing house. Dragons, dancing, their eyes alight. He took a last breath, and ran inside.

Above and around him everything burned. He felt the hairs on his head tingle, his skin singe, and he could smell burning flesh. Where was she?

'Sigrid!' he managed, though the air scalded his throat. But then he saw her.

He knew her even in the weird dragon light – for one thing, she was clutching her bag of braiding. He seized her around the waist and somehow was back at the door in a single stride. He threw her out in front of him, and turned to go back in for Osk.

'She's here!' cried Alf, realising what he was about to do. Osk stood silent at the back of the group near the house. How had she escaped? Skorri, sensible Skorri, was pushing them all back from the doorway, away from danger, allowing his chain of bucket carriers access to the flames. Ketil wiped his forehead on his sleeve, and swallowed, and spat, and swallowed and spat again.

'Come up here before you catch your deaths!' came a voice, and it was Asta with Katrin and Ali, and Ketil pushed Sigrid towards them. Osk was already halfway up the hill.

'Beinir, you need to go and sit down in Asta's house,' Ketil shouted above the clatter and roar. 'Go on!'

But Beinir stared at the blaze framed by his doorway for what seemed an eternity. Then, with a cry that nearly outdid the fire, he plunged back into the house.

XXII

Sigrid heard the cry and spun on her heel. What new horror had happened now? She was just in time to see Beinir vanish into the house. Dropping her wool bag, she sped back towards the door. The heat blared at her.

'What's he doing?' Skorri cried. 'The man's a fool!' The bucket chain, briefly interrupted, began again. Sigrid pictured them throwing water over Beinir. Ketil was at the doorway, ready to go back in. She seized him by the arm.

'No!' she shouted. 'Look!'

Beinir was black against the flames, yet he carried flames with him.

'What's he doing?' Skorri yelled again, but they all backed quickly out of the way. Beinir staggered to the doorway, and out into the night, falling forwards into the drift of snow opposite the door. Ketil and Sigrid were beside him at once, scooping snow over him and over the bulky object he was hugging close to his chest.

'It's his annals!' Sigrid realised suddenly. 'His books - he went back to rescue them.' Her own hands began to hum with the cold and she noticed, unconcerned, that the palms had been burned. That would hurt, she thought absently.

'Come on, Beinir, let's get you up to Asta's,' said Ketil. He pulled Beinir to his feet, not without difficulty. Beinir would not let go of the books – perhaps could not. His sleeves and the books' leather covers were a mass of crinkling black. 'Sigrid, will you take him? Get yourself inside, too: this is no weather for bare feet and a shift.'

She glanced down at herself, and instantly felt the chill she had not noticed till now. Ketil flicked his cloak free of its brooch and slipped it around her shoulders. She hugged it close, then took Beinir by the arm and drew him, stumbling, across the infield towards Asta's longhouse. Thank goodness it had been repaired, she thought, her mind still wandering freely, her eyes blinking against the shadows imprinted on them. Their progress was slow: her bare feet had begun to ache, and Beinir still clutched his annals to his chest with both arms, still in the shelves of their hanging case, and stared over them at nothing at all.

When they drew close, Asta popped back out of her house and hurried forward to help.

'Come on, now, Beinir, you can put those down for now. Or give them to me.'

He gave a kind of sharp grunt of refusal, tugging the books away from Asta's grasp. She shrugged.

'Oh, all right, then. Here, Sigrid, can we take an elbow each? He's soaked through but he's hot!'

Between them, and Sigrid barely knew how, they pushed and pulled Beinir into the longhouse, where Katrin sat encouraging the hearth fire into life and Ali was finding blankets, all still a bit smoky too, to warm their refugees. Osk was already sitting by the fire wrapped and stiff, and Sigrid had no doubt that she would manage to get the first available cup of hot wine on offer. Osk appeared to be a survivor.

Beinir thudded down into what was Hoskuld's high chair, the annals still in his embrace, on his lap. He still stared straight ahead, and Asta looked carefully at him before turning to Sigrid.

'Did he catch a bump on the head?'

'I don't know.' Sigrid went to look, and gasped. Beinir's face, his hair and his shoulder – his left arm, even as he held the annals close – she swallowed hard, and swallowed again, the back of her hand pressed to her mouth. There was a cry from behind her – either Ali or Katrin must have caught sight of it at the same time.

'Thor's hammer,' breathed Asta, coming to see what was the matter. 'I have a salve …'

'How much do you have, though?' asked Sigrid on a gulp.

'Snow would help,' said Asta, trying to sound brisk. 'I'll get some. See if you can get him to put those things down.'

Sigrid laid a hand on Beinir's good shoulder, and began to murmur to him, as if she were soothing her old cow or a sickly sheep.

'I'm just going to take these, now, Beinir, just to put them down over here. You'll still be able to see them – to touch them, even. I can put them next to your foot, just here.'

But when she laid her hands on the books, they crumbled to ash. The shelving, just so much charred rope and fragments of wood, fell to the floor and the ash fell like soiled snow over his arms and legs, down the front of her skirt, dotting the flags of the floor. Beinir did not even notice.

Asta appeared in the doorway with two full buckets, and Sigrid ran to help her. They padded handfuls of snow on to Beinir's face and head, his shoulder and down his arm. He barely winced.

'I have willow bark in my bags,' said Sigrid.

'They'll be burned,' said Asta. 'I have some, too.'

'I don't know how we'll get him to take it.'

'Katrin, can you make some bark tea? We'll try, a bit at a time.'

Ali, who had been standing and staring, ran to fetch the bark.

Sigrid felt Asta look at her, assessing.

'Are you all right yourself, there, Sigrid?'

'I think so.' Then she remembered her hands. 'Just this, I think.' She held them out, and Asta, still scooping snow on to Beinir, examined them.

'The snow will help you, too. I can use the salve on you later before you go to bed.'

Sigrid went on scooping and padding the melting snow around Beinir, while Asta fetched a blanket to warm his other side. A great puddle formed on the floor at her feet, and she was vaguely aware of feeling chilled and wet, but Asta fetched two more buckets from outside. As she returned, others followed her: there was a thrum of voices, weary, pained, in a state of shock. She did not turn around. She seemed to lack the energy.

'How is he – oh!'

Tosti was beside her, gaping, though he quickly shut his mouth.

'Are you all right, Tosti?' she managed, though her voice sounded very far away.

'Yes, I was lucky. In fact, I think we all were: Geirod's lost some hair, but apart from that even the dog is fine. But ... Beinir, can you hear me?'

'I don't think he can hear anything,' she said. 'He doesn't even seem to know he's hurt.'

'What are all the bits of wood?'

'It's what's left of the hanging shelf that his annals were on. They – they just crumbled in my hands. Oh, Tosti!' Dropping the snow, she fell against his shoulder and felt his reassuring arm come about her, heard a murmuring close to her ear. A prayer? She would take that, she thought, as even that sound was drowned by her own sobs.

But before she was quite ready to, she forced herself to calm down and shift away from Tosti, then wiped her eyes hard. That was enough of that. There were things to be done, and next to them she noticed with a shock that Beinir was moving his good hand, blinking his good eye.

'Asta!' she cried. Asta seized the bark tea from Katrin and, using a horn spoon, lifted a little of the liquid to Beinir's lips. It dribbled down his chin, but at least he seemed to know what she intended, and tried to sip.

'Can you get some warm water with just a drop or two of wine in it, Sigrid?' Asta said. 'He'll be thirsty, too.'

She did as she was bidden. Asta used the spoon again to try to push a little liquid into Beinir's mouth, but succeeded mostly in wetting his lips. That was no bad thing either: they were dry and cracked. He could not seem to make them do what he wanted them to do, but at least he was trying. Sigrid looked away.

For the first time she took in who had arrived with Tosti: Geirod, whose high pony tail now ended in a charred tuft, was seated on the floor with his back to a pillar, his arm around the yellow dog. Alf was propped against the same pillar, coughing, his eyes tired and red. Ali was refilling their ale cups. Osk was of course still established in her comfortable perch by the hearth and now had a cup of wine. Skorri sat beside her, contemplating the damage to his sleeve and part of the front of his shirt which had burned away, though the flesh within was scarcely touched. He looked up, conscious of her gaze, and nodded to her, with an effort at a reassuring grin. She felt her lips half-twitch in response, but went on staring about her, slow to think. Where was Ketil?

She had drawn breath to ask, when he appeared at the door, apparently whole and unharmed. The man led a charmed life, she thought, a dart of waspishness flashing across her dull mind, then remembered that it was he who had appeared out of the dancing flames and seized her to drag her out. She could still feel the pressure around her waist.

He met her gaze, then looked past her, eyes widening at Beinir's injuries. He had taken one step towards them when he was struck from behind and, spinning, stepped out of the way. Sigrid stared. Gillaug had arrived.

'Have you been down fighting the fire?' Asta asked, but Gillaug shouted straight over her.

'Beinir! Beinir!' she cried. She darted around the hearth – the fastest Sigrid had ever seen her move – and flung herself down in front of Beinir's seat, oblivious to the ash and broken wood on the floor. She seized his good hand, tears streaming down her face. 'Can you talk? Are you in pain? Oh, Beinir!'

Sigrid stepped back, trying to take in the scene. Ketil was beside her in a moment.

'That might explain one or two things,' he murmured. 'I wonder how long that has been going on?'

'Do you think anything has been going on?' Sigrid countered, just as quietly. 'Maybe it was all one-sided. Otherwise why not marry?' She sighed, putting it away in her head to think about later. 'Is the fire out?'

'Yes, it seems to be. Gillaug and Eyolfr came to help. Everyone worked hard, but there's a lot of damage. It's much worse than this place was.'

'The fire came from both ends of the house,' she said, but he was already nodding.

'I saw that from outside. The door was blocked. I thought – I thought we might not get anyone out.'

'Blocked?' The image meandered through her mind, but she could hardly take it in. 'Then well done. But I don't suppose you –'

'Saw who lit it? No. Skorri and I were above the settlement. I assume whoever it was came along the shore path. We came down through the infields because Skorri smelled smoke but we thought it was coming from Eyolfr's house.' He yawned widely.

'Who's going to patrol for the rest of the night?' she asked.

'You're all exhausted.'

'Patrol?' Gillaug must have caught the word, and sprang to her feet. 'Patrol? You said you were on patrol, and you let this happen! My Beinir! My Beinir!' She launched herself at Ketil, punching his chest and arms, trying for his face, too. Sigrid caught at one arm, and Alf and Skorri came and pulled the woman back. Asta caught her.

'Come on, now, Gillaug, I don't think all that is going to help. Look, poor Beinir's face! It's hurting him to frown.'

The name was enough to drag Gillaug back, and she did not even notice when her husband Eyolfr arrived at the door.

'Has anyone seen – oh.' He sank into himself, but Sigrid hurried over to him.

'Come on in, Eyolfr. Gillaug's safe here for now.'

He let himself be led to the hearth. He was as grubby and smoke-stained as any of them, eyes as red. Sigrid sat down beside him and handed him the cup of wine Ali gave her. He took it, but his eyes never left Gillaug.

'It looks serious,' he said quietly. 'Is it?'

'You know as much as I do,' said Sigrid, 'but yes, it looks serious.'

'It was always him,' he said. 'He was never interested in her, as far as I could see. I think she threatened to marry me to get his attention, but it went further than she meant.'

'And you?' Sigrid asked softly. Eyolfr's face hardened.

'I got her money. What more did I need?'

Sigrid sat back sharply, feeling as if she had been slapped. She said nothing more but stood and left him. Gillaug and Asta were in dispute over Beinir's treatment. Sigrid looked at him. His good eye looked pained, but more, she thought, at the quarrel than at any sensation from his burns. It would have to hit him soon, surely.

His fingers twitched on his lap, as if he were trying to find something. She went over and knelt beside him.

'What is it, Beinir? What are you looking for?'

'Sigrid,' he hissed, only half of his mouth working properly. 'Sigrid, tell me. Where is box?'

Box. She scowled, thinking. But then she remembered.

'The enamel box?' she asked. 'The one you showed me?'

He tried to nod, but his movements were shaky, uncontrolled.

'Yes.'

She looked about, as if the box might have been missed in the fragments of the hanging shelf. But of course it was not there.

'It must have fallen,' she said. 'It must have dropped from the shelf as you ran.'

'Find it …' he breathed. She paused, thinking of what the house must be like. It would be hot still, surely. But his fingers were agitated. She stood.

'Of course. I'll go and look.'

'Sigrid …'

'Yes?'

'What's wrong - me?' he managed. 'Can't move …'

'You got a bit burned,' she said briskly. 'But Asta and Gillaug will look after you. I'll go and look for – for what you've lost.'

He drew breath, jaggedly, and seemed to rouse himself for one more effort.

'Only fools hope to live forever by escaping enemies,' he whispered, his good eye wandering past her and back again. He subsided.

She shivered, and moved away, rubbing her eyes. Even she was not sure if she was crying again or if it was still the smoke. She went back to where Ketil had at last been given a cup of ale.

'How hot do you think the ruins might be?'

'It's snowing again,' he said. 'Maybe not too bad, by now.' He gave her a look. 'Why?'

'He's lost something,' she said, tilting her head towards Beinir behind her. 'It's making him uneasy.'

'I'll go and look,' he said at once, setting down his cup.

'You won't know what it looks like. I'll go.'

He pressed his lips tight.

'Then I'll come with you. Remember, Gillaug still thinks this is all your own work.'

'Surely not now?'

'You still think Aslak might have set fire to his own house,' he pointed out. 'And anyway, whoever did set fire to Beinir's might still be around out there.'

It was a fair point. Sigrid had been going to march out into the dark and get the search over with, but she had not thought of who else might be there.

'Well, then,' she said, 'bring a torch.'

Outside the cold struck her hard, even though, she realised, she was still wearing Ketil's cloak. She was halfway down the path before she remembered her feet were bare. Ketil, in his shirt and kirtle, seemed unaffected by the snowflakes falling about him, spitting through the torch's flames, flattened in the wind. She had had no idea that the snow had returned: it was thick and wild, disorientating immediately. Ketil put a hand around her forearm, holding her steady and ensuring they did not lose one another. Beinir's house loomed sooner than she had expected, somehow, though it was as broken and blackened as she had feared. The doorway was clear, the door flung back to allow the rescue, but the roof above it sagged badly. Ketil would have had to stoop anyway, but Sigrid too bowed to enter, anxious in case any touch might bring the timbers down completely. But at least within the walls they were more sheltered from the wind, and could hear each other speak. The heat oozed from the walls.

'What are we looking for?' Ketil asked.

'A box, with silver in it. A pretty box, enamelwork, with figures on it. It came from Miklagarth, if that helps,' she added, and was surprised when he nodded, as if he might know very well what a box from Miklagarth might look like. 'It was on the hanging shelf, tucked behind the annals.'

'Where was the hanging shelf? Was it the one in the far corner, near his bed?'

'That's right.'

'So if he seized it and ran for the door, and dropped it on the way, it must be somewhere along this line.' He gestured. 'Only Skorri and I came inside while we were putting out the fire. The rest passed buckets from the door. One of us could have kicked a box off this line, I suppose. What size is it?'

Sigrid took her turn to gesture, outlining the dimensions of the box as best she could remember them.

'I only saw it once. It was his treasure.'

'Why didn't he bury it under the floor, like everyone else? It would have been safe then.'

'Well, you can ask him,' she snapped back, then remembered that for some time Beinir might not be in a position to answer. How bad was he? She was worried that he couldn't seem to feel the pain yet. Was that the shock? 'He's lost his annals, Ketil. They all just crumbled away in my hands.'

He paused, and looked at her. The torchlight made his long face ominous.

'Maybe he'll be able to write them again.'

But neither of them really believed it.

They searched up and down the line Beinir must have followed to get to the door, then out sideways from it, knocking aside bits of roof and cooking pots still steaming a little. With a yelp of delight Sigrid found her boots, unharmed under the edge of a fur. She shoved her feet into them, knowing they were going to hurt when they warmed up. She tried to tidy the fur and the blankets next to it: some of these could be rescued later, aired and dried. Ketil was lifting and shifting bits of Beinir's bed, the mess of his mattress, and peering underneath, but eventually he stopped and straightened.

'It's no good,' he said, 'I can't see it anywhere.'

'No … But where could it have gone?'

'You're sure it was still there? When did you last see it?'

'When I first saw it. I suppose he always kept it there, but perhaps, having shown it to me, he moved it?' Her voice became uncertain. 'In case he couldn't trust me?'

'Seems sensible to me,' said Ketil. 'I wouldn't trust you.' He raised the torch and turned slowly in what they had cleared of the floor, giving the place a last, long look. 'No, it's no good. We'll have to leave it till the morning. Surely it will be safe enough here.'

'You'd think so, wouldn't you?' said Sigrid. 'But then, you'd also think you'd be safe sleeping in your bed.' She sighed. 'Has this helped to eliminate anyone else?'

'Gillaug and Eyolfr – well, Eyolfr, anyway.' He told her of their encounter outside Eyolfr's longhouse. 'Eyolfr had clearly come straight from his bed. But now I think about it, though Gillaug was up and dressed, her feet were dry.'

'She was on watch,' said Sigrid. She had been tempted to do the same herself – and wished she had, given the current state of her feet.

'I believe so. Handy with an axe, by the way.'

'I'll keep an eye out. Did you see? Did you hear Eyolfr?'

'What did he say?'

'He knew she loved Beinir but Beinir didn't love her, and Gillaug used him to try to make Beinir jealous but she ended up marrying Eyolfr which pleased him because she was rich.'

'It's as good as a saga,' said Ketil.

'But if they didn't do it … then it's really looking like being Aslak, isn't it? Someone from Vali's household.'

'Vali, Hamthir or Aslak, perhaps. Yes.'

'You walked along the shore with Hamthir, though, didn't you? You and Skorri.'

'We did. We saw Vali and Aslak inside. And Ingvar.'

'Ingvar?' She had almost forgotten the poor boy. But – but was it possible? She caught Ketil's eye in the torchlight. 'Ingvar?'

'Oh, come on, Sigrid, there's no harm in Ingvar.'

'But there doesn't have to be. He might just like fire.'

'If he did, then Hamthir would know and would keep an eye on him. He might not want to tell anyone else, but he would do his best to stop him.'

'You sound very sure,' she said, irritably.

'It seems most likely. And in Vali's household, too: Vali would have it under control.'

'Ingvar is Vali's nephew. He might be an indulgent uncle.'

'To the extent of letting Ingvar burn people in their beds? That seems unlikely. And anyway, the fires are making Vali angry. I could see it when I first arrived.'

'Because he doesn't have them under control? Or because he doesn't have his nephew under control?'

'Who do you think is more likely, Ingvar or Aslak?'

'But you know you can't just go back to Thorfinn with "he seems more likely". You need something more than that.'

'Oh, I know.' He fell silent for a moment, and she wondered if he were thinking of Thorfinn's daughter, rather than the Earl himself. But he pulled himself upright. 'Come on, we're tired: let's see if there's any chance of some rest tonight.' He reached out a hand to help her back over the steaming wreckage to the doorway, and continued to hold it as they pushed back up the hill against the wind. The abrupt shelter of Asta's longhouse was very welcome, and they hurried inside.

But the place had changed. Sigrid looked rapidly from face to face, Asta, Skorri, Katrin, Alf … Beinir. It took her a moment to realise. Beinir was dead.

XXIII

At first light on Sunday morning, when Tosti had thought of starting his service, Ketil, Skorri, Alf and Geirod left Asta's longhouse and returned to Beinir's infields. Asta had given them directions to the best place, and in an outhouse, one that had not been destroyed by fire, they found digging implements. They began to clear the snow, hoping the earth would not be frozen. The smith and the leatherworker, turning up in their best clothes for the service, quickly lent a hand and with the smith's might on their side, Beinir's grave was swiftly dug.

They had almost finished when Hamthir, breathless, appeared around the corner of the burned longhouse on the shore path.

'Beinir's house now! Why did no one call us? Is everyone all right?' He took in the collapsed roof and the damage, and his face turned frightened. 'That's a bad one!'

'Beinir's dead,' said Ketil, handing his shovel on and going closer to Hamthir. 'Everyone else is – all right.'

'Beinir's dead?'

'Will you go and let Vali know? Father Tosti will carry out a funeral this morning, once everyone is ready.'

'A Christian funeral?'

'Beinir was a Christian, wasn't he?'

'Well, yes … I'll go and tell Vali.'

He cast another glance at the house and at the new grave cut, tawny earth spilling out and staining the snow. Then he turned and jogged back along the shore path. Ketil saw him hesitate at Eyolfr and Gillaug's house, as if he were about to knock on the door and share the bad news, but then Hamthir took a moment to look up at the roof vent. He must have thought that the couple were not yet awake, with no smoke there. He would not know that they, with everyone else, had spent the night at Asta's, huddled about the fire, while Beinir's body lay burned and still and bound for burial. The sudden wake had seemed sensible. There was no one to wait for, and with everyone crowded into one house there was not much room for the respectful laying out of a corpse. You could not guarantee, thought Ketil, that everyone there had stayed awake all night: he knew that he had allowed himself to slip into darkness at some point, having let each of his men in turn have their sleep. Tosti had said his prayers over the corpse, and they – well, not Asta or her household – had murmured Amen, and then the little priest had tucked himself on to his knees beside Beinir's head and settled down for the night. There had not been much reminiscing about the dead man. He and his men – and Sigrid – had barely known him, and everyone was simply too exhausted and stunned by yet another fire. Only Gillaug, crouched by the bier, had sobbed and sobbed: the sound had become as rhythmic as the wind outside, as soft as the whispering of the fire, and prevented no one else from dropping off.

In the cold grey light of another snowy dawn, Tosti led the way while Ketil and his men carried Beinir outside and back down to his own infield. The smith and the leatherworker, the smith's wife cosy in Asta's house with the other women, waited with bare heads, and so did Vali, standing respectfully with Hamthir, his hand on Ingvar's arm, and Aslak, sour-faced and shivering. Perhaps, thought Ketil, he did not like to be confronted with the results of his crime – or perhaps he was simply thinking that, with a bit less good fortune, he might have been in the same situation as Beinir.

The service was not long – Tosti would not make them stand out unnecessarily in the cold – and all the Christian men quickly crossed themselves and backfilled the grave. Vali and his household stood back, but Vali caught Ketil's eye. When the grave was filled, Ketil brushed off his hands and stepped over to see what he had to say.

'I must convey my sympathies to the woman Sigrid,' Vali said. 'She has had a wasted journey, and an unhappy sojourn. No doubt she will soon go home.'

'No doubt,' said Ketil, though he was sure Sigrid would not like to leave any questions unanswered, if she could help it. He was interested to note that Vali and Hamthir were both wearing the good clothes they had been seen in on the day Beinir's outhouse had burned down – and that Hamthir's boots were indeed more pointed than blunt. 'May I ask, sir – are these the clothes you would normally wear to a funeral?'

Hamthir glanced down, but Vali held Ketil's gaze.

'Yes, generally.'

'For the funeral of Leif and Hervor, too, then?'

Vali was still for a moment, then relaxed.

'I thought you had realised that. Yes – you recognised the herbs, didn't you?'

Ketil remembered the scent when he had seen Vali preparing the meal.

'It helped,' he said. 'Would you like to claim responsibility for any other fires around here, sir?'

Vali smiled.

'I wish I could help you,' he said. 'But in truth, the best help I can be to you is to tell you to look elsewhere. I had no knowledge – to judge from the building, last night's fire was truly terrible. I am only glad to hear from Hamthir that no one else is seriously injured. But Beinir is a tragic loss.'

'Because he could represent you to Thorfinn? A good Christian, not likely to draw down Thorfinn's disapproval?'

Again Vali paused for an instant.

'It helped, yes.'

'But he thought he was the head man?'

'Beinir was not, perhaps, as clever as he thought he was. No doubt a dog could be taught to read and write, if it could hold the pen and tell us what it sees.'

'You have not learned, though, have you, sir?' Ketil could not quite help himself.

'I have seen no need before. Now, perhaps …'

Ketil shook his head, changing tack.

'Last night, after Hamthir returned home, did any of you go out again?'

'Cold,' said Ingvar suddenly. Vali smiled at him.

'That's right, Ingvar. No, it was too cold to be wandering about.'

'None of you thought to take a look, to see if any arsonist might be about?'

Vali and the others exchanged looks, as if to check, but they all shook their heads except for Ingvar.

'Cold!' he insisted.

'Oh, cold now! I see – sorry, Ingvar,' said Hamthir, stroking his brother's hand briefly. 'Yes, it's cold. We'll go up to Asta's and see Sigrid. You like Sigrid, don't you?'

The two of them led the way up the hill, not too fast. Vali followed, and Aslak scowled at Ketil.

'I suppose you want to claim I did this one, too?' he demanded, not quite loudly enough for Vali to hear.

'Why, did you?' Ketil was calm.

'Ha! No, I did not – and I can prove it, too!'

'Can you?' If he could …

'Vali can, anyway. Look,' said Aslak, thrusting his thumb under Ketil's nose. It had a bandage around it. Aslak pulled the bandage away, swearing briefly, and showed Ketil the thumb again.

'I ripped the nail off yesterday working on one of Hamthir's boats. Last night it was sore, and Vali gave me a drink to make me sleep. And I did, I can tell you! I took it just after Hamthir came home, and I knew nothing till Vali woke me this morning, when the news came of the fire here.'

'And do you think Vali will confirm this?'

'Of course he will! It suits him very well if I'm dead to the world, anyway: no doubt he would rather have me properly dead,' he finished, back to his usual surliness.

'What do you mean by that?'

'Never you mind,' said Aslak as they reached Asta's door. 'It's none of your business. Nothing that happens on Shapinsay is any of your business.'

He stamped into the house, leaving Ketil outside in the snow, thoughtful.

Asta's longhouse was even busier than before, with the smith and his family and the leatherworker talking earnestly with Tosti – Ketil caught the word 'baptism' – and every other inhabitant of the settlement all crammed about the hearth, perched on anything they could perch on like kittiwakes on a cliff. Asta had given Vali the high seat, and Gillaug sat at his feet, face still soaked with tears. Eyolfr was about as close to the door as he could be without actually leaving the longhouse completely. Katrin, Ali and Sigrid passed cups and plates back and forth, using up Asta's winter supplies. Ketil wondered if any food had survived from Beinir's stores: with Leif's household destroyed, too, the settlement might be a bit short of food this winter. He noted the tight-lipped expression on Sigrid's face, and wondered how upset she really was at the loss of Beinir: he knew she had cried, anyway.

He leaned back against the wall near the door, nodding at Eyolfr, and surveyed the room. If he and Sigrid were right, whoever was burning their houses was in here, enjoying the warmth of the hearth, the sweet smell of roasting geese, the spiced wine. Why could they seem to get no nearer to finding out who it was? If they could even work out why, it might help.

It could not be some kind of campaign against the Christians, for Leif and Hervor had been of the old religion, and as far as he could gather from this morning so were Aslak and Asta. Aslak and Asta had not been killed, though. Some kind of warning? Had they been threatening to be baptised? His lips twitched: he could picture Asta converting, perhaps, if Hoskuld did, but it was a struggle to see Aslak seeking the discipline of following Christ. But perhaps he ought to ask Tosti if either of them had said anything to the priest, even tentatively exploring the idea. But Leif and Hervor? Tosti had never even met them: he would be no help there.

He needed to talk it over with Sigrid again, see if there was anything else she had picked up in that useful way of hers. She had no shame when it came to listening at doors or around corners. He would have difficulty doing it himself – unless it might be for a military benefit – and of course she was smaller, and a woman, so it was easier for her to do it without being noticed, but it was certainly handy when she did it.

She was at the far side of the house at the moment, making sure that Ingvar and Hamthir had some food and drink. Ingvar looked overawed by the crowd, wide-eyed and clinging to Hamthir's sleeve. Could Sigrid be right? Could Ingvar be one of those people intrigued by fire, too befuddled to realise what he was doing? He supposed it was possible, but how could he leave the house without Hamthir or Vali seeing him? Surely they would not let him carry on, even if he managed it once.

Yet it seemed that things were circulating around that household – Vali, Ingvar, Hamthir and Aslak. And of those four, surely Aslak was the most likely, if only they could find a way to prove it?

He cast an eye around, looking for Aslak. Looking as if someone had spat in his drink, Aslak had pushed himself back from the crowd at the hearth, and his face was only half-lit as Asta absently refilled his wine cup, talking to the smith's wife as she went. Something flickered in Ketil's mind – Aslak, and drink. Not a good combination, surely? But Aslak was slightly behind Vali, and Hamthir was talking with Sigrid. Ketil decided to make sure an eye would be kept on him.

The curtain moved beside him and he shifted to let Alf and Geirod, accompanied by the yellow dog, return to the house. He had set a patrol while they were all in Asta's house, just in case the arsonist was not from the settlement and thought to take the chance of wiping out all of them in one go. He nodded to Skorri to tell him it was their turn, then turned to Alf and Geirod.

'Anything odd?'

Geirod shook his head briefly.

'Nothing. There's no one about at all.'

'There's a boat coming into the harbour, though,' added Alf. 'Or there was when we were passing. It was too far out for us to tell who it was.'

'I'll take a look,' said Ketil. 'By the way, don't let Aslak do anything stupid while I'm out, will you? He's been drinking.'

Geirod made a face.

'Better get the women out of the house,' he muttered. 'I'll make sure he doesn't take any more.'

Ketil watched him go, uneasy, but before he could stop Geirod, there was more flapping at the leather door curtain, and a small, weary-looking man appeared with an expression of wonder on his face.

'What is all this? Asta, what is going on here?'

Hoskuld had returned.

He could not really fault his welcome. Asta and Katrin leapt up and scrambled past the guests to greet him, and the hug with which Asta enveloped him would have flattened a weaker man. In a few minutes he was grinning and greeting the guests, as if they had gathered especially to meet him – something he seemed to find surprising but gratifying. It was only when he took his place in his high chair – graciously vacated by Vali – that he looked about and said 'Oh, here's Leif's daughter, by the way!'

Everyone turned to see a young woman in the doorway, hesitant in the face of so many people. Asta was at her side in a moment.

'Thora, here, dear, come in! Was it a good journey? How have you been? How are the family?'

Thora, swamped with questions, slumped down by the fire and took anything offered to her.

'Is it true?' she asked. 'Are my parents dead? Burned?'

'Yes, my dear,' said Vali, who had established himself next to Gillaug at the hearth. 'I'm sorry.'

'But who would have done such a thing?'

'We don't know,' said Vali, then looked up at Ketil. 'Yet,' he acknowledged.

'We passed their house,' said Thora. She was a plain girl, Ketil thought, but there was something warm about her, friendly, despite her grief. You could tell, looking around, that those who had known her were pleased to see her again.

'Aye, we passed Beinir's house, too!' said Hoskuld. 'Don't tell me there's been more!'

'Husband, I'd have been burned out of our own bed, if I'd been sleeping in it!' cried Asta. 'But the worst is that Beinir's dead. We buried him this morning.'

Hoskuld nodded solemnly.

'I saw a grave. Wondered. But who would burn him? Or us?'

'Poor Beinir,' said Thora, and began to sob a little. 'This is terrible!'

The room fell silent, letting the grimness of the situation hit them again. Ketil scanned them, hoping to catch someone looking more satisfied than alarmed, more excited than dismayed. But there was nothing, unless you counted Eyolfr's dagger eyes directed at his wife and Vali.

Gradually conversation began softly again, Thora answering questions about her husband and children, and asking for news about the people on Shapinsay. Hamthir wanted to know what boatman had brought Hoskuld back, and was it a good boat and a fair price. Gillaug and Vali, heads close, talked while Gillaug wept again. Hoskuld demanded information on the fire in his own house, which Asta was all too happy to provide and, as far as Ketil could hear, embellish. Aslak pulled himself to his feet, and made for the door.

'I need the privy,' he grunted at Ketil, shoving past him. Geirod followed a few paces behind.

'I'll make sure that's the only place he goes,' he said, as he passed. While Geirod was keeping watch on Aslak, it was unlikely that anyone would sneak up and set fire to the longhouse, anyway. Hoskuld was on his feet, examining the patchwork on his roof and nodding a considered approval.

'Thank you, everyone,' he said. 'It'll need redoing in the spring, of course, but it'll keep us going. For now, if there are no big storms, anyway.'

'Aye, Hoskuld, it's good to see your trip to Hoy hasn't dulled your sense of the fun of life!' Hamthir called, and there were chuckles.

'Hamthir! I didn't see you there!' called Thora. 'Are you married yet?'

'Not yet,' Hamthir looked awkwardly at the floor, then at Katrin, as if he knew he had to.

'Does no one have any news?' Thora complained, but then the leatherworker jumped in with the tale of his child's birth and the dent on his head, and the conversation turned again. Ketil began to wonder how long Aslak needed in the privy, but perhaps he was being unreasonable. Geirod would watch to see he didn't wander off. Ah, but Geirod … Geirod had not been alone with Aslak since he had found out about Bolla.

In a moment, Ketil was outside.

It seemed that Aslak had indeed finished in the privy, assuming Geirod had ever let him reach it. The two were locked in each other's brutal arms, foreheads pressed against each other, furious gasping the only sound as they each wrestled for a better grasp on the other's neck.

'Stop that!' Ketil shouted at once, but he might as well not have bothered. The two men were well matched, low and sturdy. And they loathed each other.

Then all of a sudden it was over. Geirod flicked a foot somewhere near Aslak's knee, and brought him down, landing hard on top of him. He seized him by his fringe, drew his head up and slammed it back against the privy wall. Aslak slumped, eyes rolling. The warm smell of piss answered at least one question.

Ketil strode across.

'Get up,' he said, and his voice was snow-cold. Geirod struggled to his feet, head low. 'Carry him indoors. Carefully.'

Geirod hesitated, but he stooped and hauled Aslak up and over his shoulder, head averted. Ketil followed him as he staggered back into the longhouse.

'Oh, what now?' cried Asta. It was clear that no one was as eager to tend to Aslak as they had been to look after Beinir. 'Who was he fighting?'

Geirod did not answer as he flung Aslak down where Beinir's bier had recently lain. It was not a soft surface, and Aslak's head bounced. Several people winced despite themselves. Asta sighed, and fetched more of her salves, waving to Ali to bring a blanket. Ali tilted backwards as she smelled him. Ketil took Geirod by the scruff of the neck and pushed him back outside.

'What was that for?'

'For Bolla.'

'You had a claim on Bolla?'

Geirod hunched his shoulders.

'I hadn't said to anyone, no.'

'Then you leave that kind of thing to those who have. Tempting though it might be.' He drew a long breath. 'Look at me.'

Geirod straightened, bracing himself. Ketil's cold fist struck him solidly on the bridge of his nose, and blood squirted haphazard across the snow.

'There's a limit to how many more times I'll tolerate this,' Ketil said. 'I suggest you don't try to find out what that limit is.'

He returned to the longhouse, leaving Geirod slumped against the infield wall, a scoop of snow padded on to his face.

The arrival of Aslak, unconscious, had brought an end to the wake for Beinir, and people were stirring. Aslak, too, seemed to be coming round: Asta and Ali had wrapped him in a blanket and left him on his side to recover on his own. Tosti had gathered himself up and was heading for the door.

'I'm off to baptise this man's baby,' he explained to Ketil as he went. The leatherworker grinned and nodded: he did not appear to have stopped grinning since Ketil had last seen him, even if it had dimmed a little for Beinir's funeral.

'Someone had better get out of Beinir's longhouse anything that's left,' said Asta, at last sitting down beside her husband. Ketil had barely seen her rest all day. 'And it'll get you all out of the way while Ali and Katrin and I make the meal.'

'If I find any food I'll bring it to you,' said Sigrid at once. Katrin nodded.

'I can help: I know where some things were stored. And the other outhouse has grain in it and a sack of carrots. And onions.'

'Life without onions would be dull,' Sigrid agreed, giving her a smile.

'Then Ali and Katrin can empty the outhouse and bring the stuff up here,' said Asta. It seemed fair – she had Beinir's household to feed, whoever might turn out to inherit whatever was left. 'Wasn't there salt mutton hanging up in the house?'

'There won't be any more, I suspect,' said Ketil. Asta's face fell.

'No, I suppose not. Hoskuld, will you go and help?' For a moment they held hands, then the grasp slipped and he came to the doorway.

Alf and Skorri came too, along with Sigrid and Eyolfr. Gillaug seemed to have taken up a permanent position by Asta's hearth, the last place she had seen Beinir alive. The salvage party was joined by Geirod, to whom no one said anything, though the yellow dog at once pressed against his legs. They began at the doorway, working their way into the house, throwing out the roof parts over the walls where they could and digging underneath them.

'I have the salt mutton,' Alf called over at one point, 'but it's a bit overcooked.'

'What a shame,' said Sigrid.

'Excuse me?' came a voice from behind them. It was Leif's daughter, Thora. Ketil crossed to talk to her.

'Yes?'

'I'm just –' For some reason, she looked nervous. 'I was wondering – my parents' bodies ...'

'They were burned. Vali saw to it,' Ketil said, as gently as he could.

'All of them?' Her voice was tiny.

'All but Osk.'

She met his eyes, her own bright with sudden hope.

'She's alive?'

'She's up at Asta's. She has a remarkable skill for not being seen.'

'Oh!' She turned to run back up the hill, but he called after her.

'Who is she, Thora?'

'My great grandmother!' she tossed back over her shoulder, and ran on.

'Ketil?'

He turned back to Beinir's longhouse. Sigrid was holding something cradled in her reddened hands.

'Osk is her great grandmother,' he said, astonished. He must have misheard.

'Look!' she said, apparently unimpressed. He went closer. In her hands was a box, the long pale figures along its sides beautifully executed in delicate, Eastern enamel.

XXIV

Sigrid did not know very much about enamel, but she loved this.

'It looks perfect,' she said. 'It mustn't have been damaged at all by the fire.'

'Where did you find it?'

'Well, that's the thing,' she said, frowning. She kept her voice low so that only Ketil could hear. 'It was just under that fur over there. The thing is, I tidied those furs last night, and the blankets.' She glanced up at him, making sure what she had said was sinking in. Sometimes he could be a little slow. 'So the thing is,' she went on, 'I don't think it was there last night.'

There was an uncharacteristic twist to his lips.

'You mean someone came to a ruined longhouse and put something valuable back in?'

'Well, it looks like it. And to judge from the weight,' for her wrists were straining with it, 'they didn't empty it, either.' She eased back the catch with her thumb, and lifted the delicate lid. Inside – well, she could not say for sure that every piece of silver was still there, but the box was certainly as full as it had looked when Beinir showed it to her, so few days ago. It felt like a lifetime.

But now she could leave Shapinsay and go home. She could see her sheep, and her cat, and Gnup, and sleep in her own lonely bed, and eat whatever her neighbours were prepared to cook for her in exchange for woolwork – she would miss Katrin's housekeeping, that was certain. But to have to put up with all those people in the house: that was interesting for a while, but she did like her own company.

'Sigrid?'

She jumped: Ketil was speaking. Not enough sleep, that's what it was.

'Yes?'

'Just to be sure, did you in fact marry Beinir? Or enter into any contract with him?'

She was shocked at the question.

'I think I'd probably have told you.'

'Would you, though?' he asked unexpectedly. Then he seemed to shake something off. 'I was just wondering who Beinir's heir is? Who gets this?' He brushed the box with a long finger.

Sigrid blinked.

'I have no idea. He's never mentioned anyone.' He had talked of the children they might have. That talk had died with him. Not that that was worth mentioning to Ketil.

'There'll be others here who will know, no doubt,' he said. They looked about, but just now it was mostly Ketil's own men here. And Eyolfr was not very approachable.

'Well, for the moment,' she said, 'we should get on with taking out what can be taken, for whoever it might turn out to be. But it won't be me, sadly.'

She handed him the box. Ketil removed his cloak and wrapped the box in it, tucking it safely into a niche near the doorway where it would not be disturbed or attract attention. Then they set to work.

After a few minutes more voices hailed them from the doorway. It was Hamthir and Ingvar.

'Sorry, it takes us a while to get moving sometimes,' said Hamthir, as Ingvar played in the snow. 'Can I help?'

'You can move these outside, and take them into the other outhouse,' said Sigrid, handing him folded blankets and furs. They were thick with smoke, but she had no enthusiasm for sorting them out just now to air. 'How is Aslak?' She had not asked Ketil what had happened, though she assumed it had been something between Aslak and Geirod. Geirod was in line for two prize-winning black eyes.

'Not quite back with us yet,' said Hamthir, a slight smile on his face. He lowered his voice. 'I take it he annoyed someone?'

'I assume so,' she said. Hamthir's eyes flicked towards Geirod, and away.

'Right, I'll take these.'

He worked on with them for a while, ferrying what they rescued into the outhouse and, from what Sigrid could see when she checked, stacking it neatly inside. She felt a responsibility for Beinir's things, particularly when she thought about his annals. The way they had crumbled in her arms ... all that writing, gone just like that.

'Is Vali waiting for Aslak, then?' she asked, the next time she and Hamthir met at the door.

'No, he's talking to Gillaug, trying to get her to go home.'

'Why did Vali let Beinir think he was the head man?' she asked, finding the words spill out before she had even thought of asking them. Hamthir laughed.

'I don't know that he ever did, deliberately. Beinir was happy enough to believe it and didn't need anyone else to help him.'

'But the writing ... Vali can't write, can he?'

'No,' said Hamthir, 'but who needs writing? You saw that – all Beinir's books, all gone. What use is that to anyone?'

'I know, but –' She broke off as Ingvar galloped over, seizing Hamthir's arm.

'Cold!' he cried, and pushed a handful of snow into Hamthir's face. He cackled, and Hamthir himself had to laugh.

'Yes, Ingvar, very cold!' He pushed the boy off playfully, shaking snow from the pots he was carrying. 'Ingvar doesn't like the cold, do you, Ingvar? He's always one for a nice warm fire.'

But Ingvar did not seem to mind the cold at all: he went straight back to where he seemed to be building something in a snowdrift, a broch of snow, perhaps. His tongue stuck out of his mouth in concentration.

'He'll be soaked,' said Hamthir. 'I'd better take him home, when I've taken these pots over.'

'Thanks for your help, anyway,' she said. She waited until he came back and urged Ingvar to abandon his broch, just as the old people had done all over the islands, then waved them goodbye.

'I think that's everything.' Ketil came to stand beside her. 'I hope whoever inherits is happy enough.'

'With that box and the silver inside it they certainly should be,' Sigrid said crisply. 'And I found my wool bag outside where I dropped it last night. Maybe we should put the box inside it for now, for safety?'

'A good idea.' Ketil unwound his cloak from the box, and slipped it into Sigrid's bag, where it tipped and nestled in the skeins of wool. She sighed.

'It is beautiful, isn't it?'

'Come on,' he said, 'I should think supper is ready.'

Vali and Gillaug, and Eyolfr, stayed for the meal, though Asta did not seem particularly pleased that Gillaug was still weeping at her hearth. Hoskuld's house was smaller than Beinir's, and if they were to accommodate Sigrid as well as Ketil and his men it would be cosy, to say the least.

'But you can all stay with me,' said Vali, 'of course. From tomorrow, rather than have everyone unsettled again tonight. Asta, you can't be expected to rescue everyone.'

'Will you take that fellow as well?' she asked, clearly trying to balance respect and gratitude towards Vali with a determination to be rid of Aslak.

'We'll do that,' said Vali. 'He'll come tonight, if someone can help me take him home. He is part of our household now, anyway. And it is not right that you should suffer just because we missed the fact that he was drinking too much.'

Sigrid caught the look he cast over at Aslak's curled body. Vali was not in control anymore, she thought. That would not suit him.

When the meal was over, she helped Katrin and Ali to clear up. Ali worked hard, tougher than she looked.

'It's a shame Hamthir had to go home early,' said Sigrid. 'Ingvar was chilled, though.'

'Hamthir saved my life,' said Katrin, face glowing.

'He did? How?'

'It was last night. He suggested I should spend the night up here with my mother, for she'd be scared after the fire the night before. Well, it was a good idea – and in the end, it saved me!'

'Well ...' Sigrid had no wish to besmirch Hamthir's reputation as a saviour, but she liked to be accurate. 'To be fair, only Beinir was killed. And that was because he went back in.'

'Still!'

There's no arguing with young love, she thought. Had she ever felt that way about Thorsten? She must have done, to follow him from Norway to Orkney. She supposed – it was hard to remember, through everything that had followed.

She watched out of the corner of her eye as Vali helped Gillaug into a cloak with Eyolfr looking on. Poor Eyolfr, a wretched third place after Beinir and Vali. But then he had only married her for the money. A rash decision: he must have needed money very much, surely?

Thora stood to say good night to those leaving. Sigrid thought she seemed a pleasant woman, instantly appealing, naturally friendly, like her mother Hervor: she had been sitting companionably with Osk, though Sigrid had not seen Osk speak to her. It seemed the old woman had no way of communicating – except when she was hungry. Thora helped to see Aslak fairly comfortably disposed with his arms around the shoulders of Eyolfr and Skorri. He was conscious now and, though unsteady, was at least able to move his feet in an imitation of walking if he were supported. From her expression as she saw to his arrangement, Sigrid guessed Thora had no fond memories of the man: she was much more affectionate towards the others, her old neighbours from before her marriage and departure for Hoy.

With Gillaug and Aslak and their escort gone, and the supper dishes washed and cleared, Sigrid managed to take a seat beside Thora, on the other side from Osk, and hand her a cup of wine. Thora had the same gift as her mother Hervor had had: Sigrid at once felt comfortable with her. She wondered how it was done.

'I'm so sorry about your parents,' she began. 'What terrible news for you.'

Thora nodded, a tear surging easily in her eye.

'It seems so strange to be here without them. I keep looking round for them. And to be here and not in their house, too – it feels very strange.'

'It must do. I had only just met them, but I was looking forward to being close friends with them. They seemed good people.'

'They were. They were good parents to me,' Thora agreed, wiping her eyes now. 'I'm sorry, I don't think I heard who you were?'

'I'm Sigrid. I live in Birsay, but I came here to stay with Beinir for a while to – to see if we might be suited.'

'Oh!' Thora's face wobbled with different emotions – surprise, pleasure, recollection, sorrow. 'Oh, that's bad. Were you?' she asked tentatively. 'Because that would be …'

'I liked him,' said Sigrid, 'but, I have to say, I'm not sure in the end that I liked him enough. But I'm sorry he's dead. Very sorry.'

'Me too. Why would somebody kill Beinir? He was harmless!'

Sigrid sighed.

'It makes no sense to me. Why on earth would someone have killed your parents, either?'

'I don't understand it at all,' said Thora. 'They hadn't an enemy in the world. And I'm sure they hadn't done anything to be punished, though even if they had it must have gone wrong.'

'Punished?'

'You know, your house fired. And that's another thing, because I'm sure Asta hasn't done anything wrong either. Why was this house burned? I mean, Aslak, you can understand that. What had he done this time? No,' she broke off, with a half-laugh, 'don't tell me. I don't need to ask: knowing Aslak, he got drunk and fought a man or assaulted a girl.'

'Both, actually,' said Sigrid, thinking hard. Aslak's house had been fired when he returned from Birsay, where he had indeed done both. He had survived his fire, standing outside in the snow, but had he really looked surprised at what had happened?

'Oh, that's awful! Who was the poor girl? Not –' She looked around quickly. 'Not Katrin?'

'No, no. It was in Birsay – a maid in Thorfinn's household.'

'Earl Thorfinn?' She stopped to take in the enormity. 'Oh, my. And who did he fight? Don't tell me he tried to fight the Earl?'

'Oh, no! No, he fought some visitors from Westray.'

'Ah,' said Thora. 'Well, he has a history on Westray.'

'So I've heard,' said Sigrid. 'Does he usually, um, go elsewhere to behave like that?'

Thora shrugged.

'No, not really. I mean, this place is notorious, thanks to him. We could never get a serving-maid to stay any length of time, whatever we did to try and protect them. And there was Ingigerd, too, she was betrothed to –' her gaze flickered suddenly towards Sigrid, but she continued, '- to Beinir, in fact. You'll maybe have heard. I was away by then but even I heard. Well, Vali must have lost patience with him again. But Vali wouldn't have done anything to my parents, and surely not to Asta and Hoskuld either. That's where my questions are. Who killed my parents? Because Vali doesn't seem to have any idea, and Vali usually knows everything.'

'I only wish I could tell you,' said Sigrid. And then I really could go home, and be at peace, she added, silently.

'I've just been talking to Leif's daughter,' said Sigrid.

'I noticed,' said Ketil. There was rarely anything he did not notice, Sigrid reflected. Nor did he follow by asking her what Thora had said, which would be gratifying. He just waited, and despite herself sooner or later she found she was telling him. It was not fair.

'She says that it looks to her as if Vali set fire to Aslak's house to punish him for what happened – for all that happened in Birsay. A deliberate punishment, not intended to kill or injure. She said Aslak's been trouble for a long time, and brought a bad reputation to the place.'

It was too cold to go outside to talk privately, but they were perched near the door, as far from the central hearth as they could be, while everyone else was sensibly somewhere warmer. She pulled her shawl close about her shoulders, and wriggled her icy toes.

Ketil did not seem bothered by the cold, and nodded slowly.

'I can believe that,' he said, 'but what does she have to say about the other houses? What about her parents?'

'No help. Except to confirm what I had already thought: they were good people, popular people, with no enemies. She was fond of them. And she can't see why Asta or Hoskuld might be punished, and she reckons that Beinir was harmless –' despite herself she heard a hint of bitterness in her own voice '- and no one would kill him, either. And they certainly wouldn't have been punished by Vali. She's a bit disappointed that Vali doesn't know what's going on, though.'

'I don't think it's a task for which Vali is suited,' said Ketil unexpectedly. She had thought he admired Vali, from the respectful way he addressed him.

'Why not?'

'Vali's a leader,' said Ketil. 'Men would follow him into battle – I'm sure they did, when he was younger. They'll do what he tells them to do. And in normal circumstances no doubt he has the wisdom to make the right decisions, so there is no reason for them not to.'

'Yes, I can see that.'

'But that doesn't mean he can reason out a problem. That's a different thing.'

'And that's where we have the advantage, of course,' she said brightly. 'Except that, of course, we don't seem to be able to do it, do we?'

He leaned back against the door post, pressing his spine hard against the wood. She wondered if his back was stiff. He had sent Alf and Skorri out on patrol first tonight, but he still managed not to look tired himself. She was sure she looked as if she had been up for a week: she felt as if she had. Nothing could rid her nose of the smell of smoke, either. But they should be concentrating on the matter at hand.

'Right,' she said. 'Who can't have done it?'

'We've been through that,' said Ketil. 'Gillaug and Eyolfr, Katrin, you, Beinir, probably Asta, Hoskuld ... Osk. I suppose.'

'Leaving us, as we said, with those living in Vali's household. Vali, Ingvar, Hamthir – and Aslak.'

'Yes.' He leaned towards her, which she took as a sign that he was prepared for serious debate. 'You say that Thora reckons Vali burned Aslak's house, or had it burned. And he burned Beinir's outhouse. What's to stop him having burned the other three longhouses?'

'You said he was angry about the burnings.'

'Maybe he was angry that they didn't go according to plan. Or didn't have some effect he desired. Maybe he hadn't intended to kill Leif and Hervor.'

She considered, trying to imagine Vali out at night with pitch and a torch, working out the best place to shove them.

'If he went out at night,' she said, 'would Hamthir or Aslak tell us? Would they just keep quiet because it's Vali?'

'Good point,' Ketil acknowledged. 'I think Hamthir would defend his uncle. But Aslak ... that's hard to say.'

'I don't think he's too happy living under Vali's supervision, do you?' She thought back – had she ever seen Aslak look happy, though? 'I mean, it's as if he's been a naughty boy and his father is keeping him indoors until – I don't know, until he says he's sorry.'

'It's true,' said Ketil, 'but that perhaps shows us that he wouldn't tell us if Vali was going out at night. After all, it's the force of Vali's authority that is keeping him in there, isn't it?'

'Right ...' Sigrid made a face. 'So we can't prove it isn't Vali. What about Hamthir?'

'Why would Hamthir burn any of those houses? Particularly

Asta's. There's no sign that he and Katrin's family have fallen out, is there? If anything,' he added, 'I'd have said Hamthir was the one being slow to wed.'

'Apparently he thinks wives are expensive,' Sigrid explained. Ketil raised his eyebrows and nodded.

'You said. And I thought it possible.'

She scowled at him. He'd soon find out for himself – perhaps he had forgotten.

'He might burn them at Vali's command,' he offered.

'Back to Vali again. Look … what about Ingvar? I know,' she held up a hand, 'I like him, too. He seems completely harmless. But what about him? Hamthir told me he doesn't like the cold, that he likes fire. And he's certainly been talking about being cold.'

'Yes, he's said it to me, too,' said Ketil. 'Being cold at night, I think. Look, as I said, I don't think he could do it without Vali and Hamthir knowing, and I don't think they would let him. Do you?'

'No, not really,' she said. 'It's just – it's sort of a better solution? Poor Ingvar wouldn't know what he was doing. It might explain why there's just – no explanation.'

Ketil's hand moved slightly and for a moment she almost thought he was going to lay it on hers, but it stilled again.

'So,' she said quickly, 'Aslak.'

'For whom no one has a good word.'

'No. But in a way, does that make him less likely?'

He raised an eyebrow at her. She drew breath.

'I mean, well, for one thing no one remembers him doing anything like this before, even when he was drunk. We think we know now he didn't accidentally set fire to his own house while he was drunk, even. What he does is he gets into fights and he attacks women. He's done it for years. And for another thing, if he's being kept in Vali's household as a punishment, wouldn't they be particularly careful that he didn't wander out alone at night? Wouldn't they be suspicious? And if it happened once, wouldn't they make doubly sure it didn't happen again?'

Ketil rubbed his chin – she could hear the faint crackle of stubble.

'Aslak says,' he said, 'that he couldn't have fired Beinir's house.'

'Why not?'

'Here's a thing,' said Ketil, slow enough to annoy. 'He showed me his thumb.'

'His thumb? Why on earth would that make a difference?'

'Listen. He showed me his thumb because he had torn off the nail - working on a boat, apparently. It was painful, last night, and he couldn't sleep. And Vali gave him a sleeping draught which knocked him out until this morning. Or so he told me.'

'Vali gave him a sleeping draught?' Her mind flipped sideways. 'Vali has sleeping draughts?'

'Apparently so.'

'So Vali could knock out his whole household and do whatever he likes in the middle of the night, and no one would be any the wiser?'

'Well – yes.'

'That,' said Sigrid, torn between crossness and intrigue, 'puts a whole new light on the matter, doesn't it?'

XXV

'And of course,' said Ketil, 'tomorrow we're all moving into his longhouse.'

He had a moment to watch concern spread over Sigrid's face, then the door beside them opened. It was Alf and Skorri, returned from their first circuit of the settlement. He had not realised it was so late: looking around, he saw that the rest of the household were making preparations for bed. Sigrid rose with a sigh, and went over to see where there was space for her. She had been looking chilled for a while. Ketil rose and stretched.

'All clear?' he said to Skorri. Skorri nodded.

'There's hardly anything left to burn.'

'But if by chance someone from outside the settlement is doing this, then there's more work for them to do. Not that I think that's the case,' he added.

'No. We'd have spotted something between the snow showers,' said Skorri. 'Footprints or whatever. And there's no odd boats about. You think it's someone in here, or someone at Vali's?'

'Someone at Vali's.'

'Anyone in particular?'

'What do you think?'

'Aslak,' said Skorri at once.

'Someone wants us to think it's Aslak,' said Alf, unexpectedly. Ketil and Skorri looked at him. 'People keep telling us how bad he is.'

'Which he is,' Skorri put in.

'Yes, he is. But I haven't seen anything that definitely points to him, and he's a very convenient excuse.'

'So who do you think it is?'

'Vali, of course,' said Alf, as though it had been obvious all along. 'Or maybe Hamthir, if Vali told him to.'

A similar thought to one Ketil had had earlier.

'It can't be Vali,' Skorri objected. 'He's the man in charge. Why would he need to go around burning people's houses?'

'Apparently he burned Aslak's, or had it burned,' said Ketil, and this time the others turned to look at him. 'A punishment for Aslak's behaviour in Birsay.'

'See?' Alf looked down his long nose at Skorri.

'Aye, well, that makes some kind of sense,' said Skorri. 'A punishment, aye. But why would he do Beinir's, or Asta's? Or the other one – that lassie Thora's parents? They weren't like Aslak. No one had a bad word to say about any of them.'

'Not enough to burn their houses, anyway,' said Ketil. He had heard one or two bad words about Beinir.

'Poor Aslak. Nobody likes him,' said Alf. Skorri gave him a look of disgust. 'Well, I know it's his own fault,' Alf went on, 'but he maybe can't help it. It's just him.'

'Aye, well, there's a way to fix that for him,' said Skorri.

'Not something we're supposed to take into our own hands,' Ketil reminded him. 'Not under Thorfinn's jurisdiction. Not unless there's an urgent need.'

'Right,' said Skorri. 'What was the urgent need that Geirod found, then?'

'I doubt what Geirod did will have had much effect on Aslak's behaviour,' said Ketil. 'Take a rest, the two of you, and keep an eye on things here. Geirod and I will walk around for a while.'

'Take the dog,' Skorri advised. 'It's more useful than he is – and a lot better-tempered.'

Outside, the sky had cleared, and you could taste the frost on the air, crinkling the starlight. The wind tore across the island, paying no attention to its shallow hills, but made little impression on the snow,

now frozen in place. The yellow dog huddled briefly around Geirod's legs, then decided it could cope. Ketil chose to turn left for a change, walking towards the smithy and the leatherworks, and the dog trotted along just ahead of the two men.

The starlight almost, but not quite, made the torches redundant. Casual conversation would have been difficult in the wind but in any case, Ketil had no particular wish to talk to Geirod at the moment. They walked in silence, concentrating on the angle of their torches, avoiding dancing sparks, and trying to keep their hands warm: it was enough to be getting on with.

All was quiet at the smithy, even the walls cool after a day's inactivity. At the leatherworker's house they could hear drowsy conversation from within – Tosti's voice, and the leatherworker's, coming to the end of a busy day that had presumably, for them, included a christening. Ketil chose not to disturb them. He looked at the ground for prints, found the only ones around the door led to the privy, and left it.

'Where's the vart from here?' asked Geirod, since they were in the shelter of the longhouse wall. Ketil pointed.

'Up over there. I think, in daylight, you might be able to see the hut for the vart warden.'

Geirod sniffed.

'Why?'

'Just interested.'

Ketil hoped he was not going to lay some kind of trap for Aslak. Not that Aslak seemed to spend much time up at the vart – perhaps only when invasion seemed likely.

'Right, then, back along the shore path and we'll walk to the harbour.'

Geirod knew better than to sigh. He followed Ketil back to the path, crossing the small stream, and set off with him towards the main settlement.

The approach to the settlement was grim now, with first the burned bulk of Beinir's house looming up, and then, another wave on a dark sea, Leif and Hervor's ruined place. Gillaug and Eyolfr's house was almost a relief after that. Ketil, keeping Geirod and the dog back, observed it from a slight distance, hoping not to disturb Gillaug's time on watch. She might be overwhelmed with grief, but she had not looked as if she would have hesitated to use that axe.

She would not have set fire to Beinir's house, he was sure of it. But looking back over all they had learned this week, he began to wonder: had she perhaps, a couple of years ago, followed Beinir's sweetheart Ingigerd to that ayre on the north of the island, and made sure she did not come back? Would she have harmed Sigrid?

He waited for a long moment on the far side of the shore path, watching Gillaug's silent, dark house. No one else on the island seemed ever to have thought of pursuing the matter of Ingigerd's death. Was there any point in going back over it now?

He switched his torch to the other hand and warmed the first one under his cloak, then jerked his head at Geirod. The dog obeyed the instruction before Geirod did.

The path was becoming far too familiar. Past Gillaug's house, past Eyolfr's infields, then Vali's infields, then, just beside the harbour, Vali's house, with the shadow of Aslak's place beyond it, pretty much invisible just now. But if they had expected Vali's house to be silent and dark like the others, they were wrong. Vali's door was open, and lamplight spilled over the snow-cleared, icy step.

'Hello there!'

It was Hamthir, on the doorstep, staring out anxiously into the night.

'Hamthir? Is all well?' Ketil stepped forward so that Hamthir could see who he was. Hamthir scowled.

'Is that Aslak? No, you're far too tall – oh, Ketil! Is that Aslak with you?'

'No, it's Geirod.'

Even as he spoke, Vali appeared in the doorway behind Hamthir.

'Is it Aslak?'

'No, Uncle, it's Ketil and one of his men,' said Hamthir.

'Come in, come in! Are you on patrol?' Vali asked, waving them inside, but Ketil hesitated at the door.

'Where is Aslak?'

'I don't know,' said Vali, still trying to usher them inside.

'That's why we were looking,' said Hamthir. 'I woke up and he wasn't here.'

'He'll be in the privy,' muttered Geirod. 'He was interrupted last time.'

Ketil nudged him and Geirod grunted.

'Have you looked in the privy?'

'Of course,' said Hamthir, a bit cross. 'That's what we both thought. But he's not there. You haven't seen him?'

'We haven't seen anyone,' said Ketil. 'But then, we were looking for people moving about, and for torches. If he saw us coming, he could have hidden until we had gone past.'

'I think maybe he took a torch,' said Hamthir.

'Right.' Ketil looked at their faces. 'How long has he been gone for?'

'Don't know,' said Hamthir. 'I woke up and he was gone, I said.'

'Has he done this before?'

'Don't know,' Hamthir mumbled again. 'Maybe.'

'I don't know. I told you I always sleep soundly,' said Vali, but Ketil could see growing realisation on his face. 'You don't think –'

'Is Ingvar safely inside?'

'Yes,' said Hamthir, glancing behind him.

'Geirod, stay here and keep an eye on the house in case he doubles back. I'm going back to Asta's.'

'It's quicker across the infields,' said Hamthir, trying to be useful.

'It is if you know your way,' said Ketil, already heading back to the shore path. 'I'll stick to what I know.'

He broke into a run as soon as he could. The snow was unsteady beneath his feet, soft in one place, then crisped over under his next step. His torch flame flared and flattened, but he held on tight to the stem. He was not sure what he was going to find, but he dreaded the worst.

Skidding past the corner of Beinir's longhouse, he began the cluttered climb up through the infields, past Beinir's fresh, dark grave, past the stump of the outhouse. Ahead was Asta and Hoskuld's house – Alf and Skorri, Thora and Osk, Asta, Hoskuld, Katrin and Ali. And Sigrid. He vaulted over the last wall, and slowed.

The house was dark and still.

He approached as quietly as he could through the crunching snow, though anyone could see his torch. He stepped slowly, making sure that if there were any traces on the ground, any hint of what might be happening, he would not destroy it. Clear snow lay around much of the longhouse. The path down to the shore was marked with several different footprints, his own and Geirod's among them. Between the door and the privy, again, there had been a small procession of feet. But from his left, from what Hamthir had pointed out as the quickest way from Vali's house – the complex but direct path over the infields – there was indeed a line of prints, crisp in the bright snow. He followed them with his eyes.

They came from the infields, just as he had expected. They skirted Asta's longhouse. They vanished for a moment into the muddy common path they had all used several times today. Then, to his surprise, they reappeared on the other side of the path, stamping relentlessly onwards, across Hoskuld's own infields. Ketil followed.

This was where he himself had run, in the opposite direction, the night he had seen the smoke rise from Asta's house. He knew the ground was uneven, probably carved up into plots for different crops. He tried not to stumble and clung tight to his torch, remembering that he had dropped one the last time he was here. But Aslak's footprints were steady, and firm. He had known exactly where he was going.

He had veered inland to skirt the marsh, Ketil saw with relief. He paused, and held the torch a little behind him so that he could squint into the distance, trying to see further ahead. The starlight sparkled on the snow like sharpened silver, carving the smooth curves of the island out of the darkness beyond. Smooth, empty curves – Aslak was nowhere to be seen.

There was no point in stopping for long in this spiky wind: Ketil could feel it already chilling him through his cloak. He used the torch to find the footprints again, and began to follow them downhill. Could Aslak have set out to fire a longhouse in another settlement? Surely he would know he would be missed? And how were Hamthir and Vali so surprised – had they honestly never noticed him go out at night before?

But Aslak was not heading for another settlement, nor even, as Ketil had feared, rounding the marsh to attack one of the houses by the stream, the smith's or the leatherworker's. Instead, once the marsh was passed, he began to climb again. Ketil had been here before. And now he knew where Aslak was going.

By the time Ketil reached the vart, the snow had been brushed off the wood laid ready to fuel the signal fire. But the fire had not been lit: instead, the footprints meandered around for a bit before heading, as expected, just a little downhill to the hut built for the warden's shelter. Ketil assumed that that was where Aslak and Ingigerd had had their drunken assignation two years ago – by the sound of it, one of Aslak's victims who had relatively willingly accepted his attentions. Poor Ingigerd, determined only on escape from her uncle. Poor Aslak, Alf would say – a victim too, of his own nature. Ketil was less sympathetic.

He skirted the little hut warily. It was stone-built, roofed with turf, with a small vent at the top to allow for the smoke from a warming fire. It looked the ideal refuge for someone like Aslak, not so fond of the company of others – except the occasional drunken girl.

He rounded the corner to the front of the hut again – then noticed, at once, an object shining on the platform of the vart. He took a step towards it, and something hard and heavy hit him on the back of the head. He tried to spin towards his attacker, but his cloak had been caught on something – what? – and before he could free himself or his sword, he felt a blade, scalding as ice, slide into his flesh.

Bright colours enveloped him, swirling faster and faster and then vanishing into black. He tried to remember how to move. The world quivered, uneasy as the flames on his torch – no, not his torch. He had dropped it, hissing, into the snow. For some reason he seemed to be down in the snow himself, breathing in the flakes. He must have been there for a while – most of the snow beneath him had melted. He was soaking. Something is going to hurt soon, he thought distantly. There's going to be a lot of pain.

It struck him that he was not alone, and he struggled to take in who else might be here with him. He had been following someone. Who? Why? He tried to swallow, but he was lying on his face.

Behind him, above him, he heard a chuckle. Something solid, pointed, connected hard with his ribs, then with his thigh.

'Not so clever now, are you?' came a voice. He found it vaguely familiar. His thigh and ribs began to hurt, a dull, thudding pain. Not long now and it would be his head and his stomach. Stomach – that was not good.

Someone grabbed him by his hood and pulled his face clear of the snow. There was a torch – not his – glaring in his eyes. And a face, dark, long-fringed …

'Aslak?'

'Needn't expect any help from me. Not when you were following me to take me back to Thorfinn.'

'Umm.' His head jarred as Aslak dropped it back into the snow. Yes, there we were: waves of pain, crashing on the shore of his mind, sucking the pebbles of his thoughts down and away and lost … He tried to focus. Who was Aslak? Why was he going to take him to Thorfinn? Thorfinn he remembered – that name made sense. But why would he want to see Aslak?

Footsteps, crunching about. There was a black shape nearby, coming and going in the torchlight. Hut, that was what it was. A shelter for … for the warden. Was Aslak the warden? Maybe.

It was hard to keep his eyes – well, his eye, for only one was free of snow – open, but he forced himself to stay awake, watching. Aslak had shoved the handle of the torch into the snow, and by its light he had laid out a cloth of some kind. It looked like sacking. Then he began to go back and forth to the hut, taking things out, laying them on the cloth. He was making up a bundle.

Ketil tried to roll on to his side, and discovered two important things. The first was that his hands had been tied behind his back – how long had he been swirling in blackness? The second was that the movement finally set off the pain in his stomach.

He rarely swore, but as he was a soldier all the words were readily available. For a moment he allowed himself to close his eyes, and concentrated on every expression of alarm, disgust, irritation and fury he had ever heard. When he had finished, the pain had eased very slightly: the cold of the snow, he thought, was probably helping.

But at least his head, sore as it was, was clearing. Aslak was making up a bundle. What was the stuff? Where was he taking it? He considered. He would lose nothing much by asking.

'It's my stuff,' Aslak replied. 'I'm no thief.'

'I never said you were,' said Ketil. It was not easy to talk, but he made himself press on. 'Are you going somewhere?'

'Away,' said Aslak. 'I'm going. I've known for a while it was all I could do.'

'You'd leave your community? Your land?'

'Pff – my community? They all hate me.'

'But your land?'

'It's not worth all I have to put up with from everyone.'

'Where are you going to go?'

'Don't know yet.' He tossed some tools down on to the cloth with a clang. 'Thanks to Hamthir I know a bit about repairing boats. I can do that anywhere.'

'Anywhere you haven't already made enemies.' It maybe was not the wisest thing to say, but it leapt into Ketil's head. But Aslak just made a snort of a laugh, and disappeared into the hut again. He came back with a long strap, and began the process of tying the bundle up so that he could wear it on his back. 'You've been setting things aside for a while, have you? Storing them up here?'

'That's right,' said Aslak. 'No one ever comes up here.'

'And once you had finished burning the settlement you could go. But you haven't finished, have you?'

Aslak paused and looked across at him.

'No,' he said. 'I don't think the job is finished at all, do you?'

He gave the strap a final tug and tucked in the tail, then hauled the bundle on to his back. He picked up his torch.

'I'd say I'll see you,' he said, 'but it's not part of my plan. Goodbye.'

He turned, and set off. The dwindling light of his torch marked his progress briefly, until he disappeared over the curve of the hill. He was heading back towards the settlement, then.

Towards the two houses he had not yet burned.

Ketil sagged into the snow, letting it wet his dry lips. Aslak had to be stopped. But how? Could he be sure that Geirod and Alf and Skorri would find him before he set fire to Vali's house – or, again, to Asta's? Or both? What was to stop him firing both?

For a moment as he lay there in the starlight the swirling lights returned, dragon eyes, surging with colour and fire. He could feel the heat of the dragon's breath, the ache in his head, the searing pain in his stomach. He prayed that the cold, a danger in itself, was holding back any bleeding, but if he moved it was likely to grow worse. But if he could manage to free his hands, at least he might be able to pad the wound. Maybe with snow. Maybe Aslak had left something in the hut he could use.

He lay still for a moment, collecting his strength – his strength, for a knot! Then he began to try to work his freezing fingers around, feeling the rope, following its curls. If he could lift his arms over his head it would be easier – not that he would be able to see the knot in the dark, but he could use his teeth. But when he tried that, and then, failing that, tried to pull his long legs back through the loop of his arms, the wound in his stomach turned to a dragon bite of agony. He worked on at the rope behind his back, and at last, after an age, his hands scraped themselves free.

Slowly, slowly, he tried to sit up. The world spun, and would not settle. He lay down again, but curled on his side this time, exploring the damage to his stomach with careful fingers. The knife had not gone all the way through: the wound was in his back, and felt sticky and hot. He scooped snow over it, holding a handful tight against it. He could not get back to the settlement like this, not without help. But what help was going to come at this time of the night, up here? If he stayed out here until morning, the chances were he would not see that dawn – and more importantly, Aslak would be free to do whatever he intended to do down at the settlement. And down there were his men, and Sigrid.

There was only one thing he could think of to do, and he might not even be able to do that. He began, with a mixture now of prayers and swearing, to crawl towards the vart.

Why had he ever thought this island was flat? Every step, on his hand or his knee or pushing himself along with his toes and elbows, every pace seemed like a mountain. And the vart was so far away. The cold stars were no comfort, only showing him the miles he still had to go, the pathetic trail he had left behind him – ominously marked with a black line that, in daylight, would no doubt show red. But he pushed on, concentrating on every limb, what it could do, how it could best be used. His breathing was ragged, the effort to ignore the pain draining him dry.

But at last he had one hand on the stone vart platform. Another hand up, and he thought he had exhausted his strength. But he hauled himself up and stretched to reach the oil, and the lamp – Aslak always had the place well maintained. He tipped the oil over the wood, and with a final flicker of determination he dropped the lamp on to the platform.

The fire caught. He sagged back, the blackness threatening again, but in the centre of it a raging scarlet dragon roared at the sky.

XXVI

Sigrid had fallen asleep almost immediately, her bag of wool snuggled against her stomach, hands folded over its long wooden handles. But it seemed only a little while later that she woke again, sweaty in the stuffy bed that she shared with Osk and Thora. Katrin and Ali were somewhere nearer the animal end of the house. Asta and Hoskuld, despite the absence of the bed that Hoskuld had constructed, slept where it had lain on a hastily assembled mattress of blankets. She was not sure about Ketil and his men: they had been coming and going, and there were probably one or two of them near the door, dozily guarding.

She turned, and enjoyed a drift of cold air falling from the roof vent on to her face. Osk had taken the central place in the bed as before, and Thora had been stuck against the wall. Sigrid was lucky, in her favourite position on the outside, where she could stick her feet out easily if she felt overheated. She tried to settle back to sleep.

But the smell of smoke was always there, tugging at her, like a small, dissatisfied child. Was it fresh? Was it from her clothing, laid nearby? Or was it simply stuck in her nose, not really there anymore but something she could not ignore? She turned over, pressing her face into a smooth section of woollen cloth, scrunching her eyes shut. Osk smelled of smoke, too, and of musty clothing rarely washed. Sigrid screwed around in her place again, trying not to disturb the others too much. With her back to Osk, she tried again to succumb to sleep.

What would they do when they moved down to Vali's in the morning? They would not be quite so cramped, she was sure: Katrin and Ali would stay with Asta and Hoskuld, but Tosti would no doubt be back from the leatherworker's house. But Vali's house was bigger.

Then she froze when she remembered what Ketil had said, just before he had headed out on patrol. Vali had sleeping draughts. What if he gave them all sleeping draughts and then set fire to the house? They would definitely all be burned in their beds! Except for some of Ketil's men: they were never all in the same place at the same time. It was dizzying watching them. But if Vali had drugged them … he could kill all of them.

But why would he want to? Why would he do any of this? To assert his power? Surely he didn't have to: everyone knew he was head man, everyone except poor Beinir. And Beinir was dead.

For a moment, tears rose again to her eyes, tears of pity for that poor, stupid, handsome man and his skills of reading and writing, that he would never now teach her. She suppressed a sob, keen not to waken anyone else. She bit her lip, and reviewed her memories of Beinir. They did not amount to much, and she was sure now that she would never have married him. But she was sorry he was dead, nevertheless.

Her mind, trailing the hem of its dress in sleep, wandered on. Would Vali drug them? How would they sleep down there? No doubt she would have to share with Thora and Osk again, at least until Thora left. Would she take Osk with her, back to Hoy? Would Sigrid return to Birsay only to wake up and find that Osk had moved in there? That was not a particularly pleasant thought. Sigrid had barely enough to feed Gnup and herself, and Osk, twiglike though she was, would eat anything put in front of her and hold her bowl out for more.

So yes, she would share there just as she was sharing here. She tried to remember what beds there were in Vali's house – three, she thought. Vali no doubt had one to himself. Then Aslak, Hamthir and Ingvar would be arranged somehow in the other two.

Poor Ingvar, complaining of the cold. She smiled at the memory of him playing in the snow, building his broch, dancing in the falling flakes when they arrived on the island. In fact, he seemed very much to like being out in the snow. When was he complaining of the cold, then?

She thought back, suddenly puzzled, trying to remember. It was when Hamthir mentioned night time, and sleeping. That was when Ingvar had started talking of cold.

Did Ingvar share a bed with Aslak? And if Aslak went out at night – for example, to set fire to someone else's longhouse – did Ingvar miss him, because it left him alone in the bed, and cold? If only Ingvar could talk a little bit better, they might have been able to ask him. But then, if he could have been a good witness, Aslak might not have slipped out and left him to notice his absence.

Her mind was waking further now, and tangling again with all the questions she had been asking herself over the past few days. Who was setting the fires, and if it was Aslak, could they prove it, or get him to admit it? Thinking of Aslak, why had Ingigerd run away that morning, and why had she died? Had someone killed her? If so, who? Could it be the same person who had lit the fires, or was that too distant a connexion? Why had Beinir been so fond of her? Why did Beinir think he was head man? How had he come to be able to read and write? She had never asked him. Had he been trading in Miklagarth, where the beautiful enamel box had come from? How had the box come to be in Beinir's longhouse when they went back in the morning, when she was sure it had not been in the same place the night before? Who returned treasure, instead of stealing it? It was a lovely box – she could feel its angular presence among the soft skeins of her wool, and hear, very slightly, the soft chink of the silver inside.

Had it been left in the ruins by accident, or by design? It must have been a risk to leave it there deliberately: anyone could have picked it up. Had someone taken it earlier, then repented and brought it back again for Beinir's heir to find and claim? It had been completely undamaged by fire, it seemed. Could someone have taken it before the fire, and brought it back afterwards? Why would anyone do such a thing?

Because it would be theirs, and they didn't want it damaged in the fire they knew they were going to light.

She sat up sharply in bed, and had to put a foot out to steady herself. Osk scrabbled at the covers and pulled them back around her, and Sigrid quietly slid down to sit with her back against the edge of the bed. Was she thinking straight? Or was this a night time fantasy? Could all the fires have been lit with the ultimate aim of killing Beinir, and inheriting his goods?

It made sense, in one way: it explained the urgency of the burnings. Whoever was doing it was anxious to have Beinir die before he married Sigrid – if he did – or had any children, to complicate things. Whether Leif and Hervor had been intended to die or not, the arsonist must have learned from that fire about setting it near the door. Asta's house had been fired from the back, so Asta and Ali had a good chance of escaping. But Beinir's house had been fired from both ends – they had been intended to die there, and would have, if Ketil's men had not been alert and capable. She shuddered.

The question was, then, who was Beinir's heir?

She felt about her, and found her boots and hose, and pulled them on. A little further stretching gave her her dress and cloak. She pulled the dress over her head, as quietly as she could, and attached the cloak, all without standing up. Then she seized her head cloth, and stood, easing out her skirts, and made silently for the door.

Outside, to her relief, starlight twinkled in an icy sky, bright enough to walk by. She did not wish to draw attention to herself with a torch. Though why she should hide she was not sure – for her own safety?

Well, at least no one could accuse her of being out to set fire to someone's house, if she had no fire with her.

For a moment she paused. The feeling that she should be up and doing and outside and going somewhere had been so strong that she had not stopped to wonder where exactly she was going, or why. Well, Vali would know who Beinir's heir was, so that was one thing. Whether Vali might want to be disturbed at whatever time of night this was was another question. But in any case, she might meet Ketil, and could tell him what she had thought. He had not been in his chosen, bare sleeping place by the door so she assumed it was his turn to be patrolling. But then, she did not remember seeing Alf and Skorri in the longhouse, either, as she left. Perhaps they were all out, dividing the work.

She tucked her hands into her cloak and trotted down as best she could to the shore path, checking as she passed that there was no one hiding in the ruins of Beinir's house. The settlement from here, under the starlight, looked peaceful, each longhouse a dark roll under the snow, only the shape of the roof showing whether it was fit for habitation or not.

But as she walked on, eyes darting here and there to see if she could spot the patrols, she came to the point where she could see around Eyolfr and Gillaug's house all the way to Vali's longhouse. There, by contrast, the door was open, light spilling out on to the snow, and people round and about it. What was going on? She took two quick steps, then stopped. Whatever it was, much as she wanted to know, it was possible that it was dangerous.

Oh, where was Ketil when she wanted to talk to him?

She edged to the landward side of the path, sheltering at the edge of Eyolfr's house, trying to see more clearly. Vali was there, and Hamthir, and she thought she could see Ingvar inside. Outside, at the door, apparently talking with Vali, were Alf and Skorri. As she watched, Geirod emerged from the house and joined the conversation. Was Ketil inside, too?

But if Alf and Skorri were there it should be safe enough for her. She stepped out from her shelter, and hurried over to the lit doorway.

'Sigrid! What's the matter?' Vali cried when he saw her. 'Is there a fire? Is it Asta's?'

'No, no, nothing like that!' Sigrid waved her hands. 'I wanted to talk to Ketil.'

'To Ketil?' Vali looked taken aback – presumably people who turned up at his door only wanted to talk to him.

'Ah,' said Skorri, 'There's a bit of a problem there. You see, Aslak has disappeared.'

'Aslak?' It sounded like an echo of Vali, and she reddened slightly. 'Where's he gone, then?'

'We don't know. There are no boats missing,' said Hamthir. 'I woke up earlier and realised he had gone.'

'I stayed here,' said Geirod, taking her by surprise – he did not often volunteer information, 'while Ketil went back up to Asta's to see if he was there, you know, setting fire to the place.' Sigrid could not help a shiver at the idea, and she thought perhaps some of the others felt the same way. She made her voice brisk.

'And I assume he didn't find him? I've just come from Asta's, and it was not, at that stage, on fire.'

'We don't know,' said Skorri, almost apologetically. 'Ketil hasn't come back.'

'How long ago was that?' Brisk, remember, brisk. Brisk holds the panic at bay.

They looked at each other, and she felt like shaking them.

'Well? Sunset? Moments ago?'

'A while …' said Hamthir.

'Long enough to be worried, I think. Alf and I aren't long down here – we woke and wondered why Ketil and Geirod weren't back to change over.'

'I was here,' said Geirod. 'Ketil told me to stay here.' The yellow dog had most of his attention: it was restless, drifting around the doorway. 'Then Hamthir said we'd better see if there was a boat missing, and we went to look. I mean, it's only over there, the harbour.' He pointed vaguely towards the sea, a shifting, silver-black surface in the starlight. The yellow dog seemed to take it as an instruction, and pottered off towards the harbour, paws delicate on the snow. Geirod followed with the least backward glance.

'And did the rest of you stay around the door, or in the house?' Sigrid asked, thinking about the harbour, and about the path around the top of the settlement, and the path that led down past Aslak's burned house to the harbour, round the back of Vali's house. 'Only, if I'd gone out and done – whatever Aslak went out to do, and I came back to find all of you cluttering up the doorway, waiting for explanations, I might try to think of another way out.'

Vali smiled.

'You have a lot to say for yourself suddenly, Sigrid! Did Beinir know you could be so forthright?'

Sigrid opened her mouth to retort, but then she remembered that to all intents and purposes she had tried not to be forthright with Beinir.

'Too late for that now,' she said instead. 'Has anyone –'

'There's a boat gone!'

Geirod came running back from the harbour, the yellow dog at his heels.

'Which one?' Hamthir demanded at once, setting off in the opposite direction. He peered over to the beach as soon as he was close enough. 'I see. That's a fast one, that, and seaworthy. How did he get past us?'

Sigrid contained a frustrated sigh.

'We'll need to get after him,' said Skorri. 'Is it just the one boat missing? Ketil's a handy man on the water.'

'Just the one,' called Hamthir over his shoulder. 'He's maybe taken Ketil with him, though. Knocked out, or something.'

Again, Sigrid opened her mouth to speak, and held back. Why on earth would someone who had knocked Ketil out go to the trouble of dragging him – nearly twice Aslak's size – down to the harbour and fling him – well, shove him, which would take ages when he would be anxious to escape – into a boat to take away with him? It made no sense at all, and however horrible Aslak was, and stupid, too, when drunk, he had never seemed insane.

But the men had lit torches and were all scurrying down to the harbour – men and boats! – and even Vali was following. Sigrid thought hard. Even if Aslak had escaped – and it was true that the missing boat seemed to show that – then Ketil was still about. He had gone straight to Asta's longhouse to see if Aslak had set fire to it, and had presumably found that he had not. What had Aslak been doing, then, between leaving Vali's house and taking the boat? That might prove clearer in the morning. For now, she had a bad feeling about Ketil. Aslak had left by boat, and Ketil had evidently not followed him to the harbour. So where was he?

She turned and surveyed the settlement, as much as she could see it, light and dark grey blotches in the snow. Clouds were beginning to cover the sky, and the air, she noticed, was milder, almost as if someone had thrown over her a damp blanket fresh from drying by the hearth. Her cold fingers ventured out from beneath her cloak, and pushed her hair back – she had not taken the time to tie up her headcloth yet. That would not have helped Vali to take her seriously. But now the men had forgotten about her and would not notice if she headed off. She lit a torch for herself, took the shore path again, and headed back towards Asta's.

If Aslak had escaped from Shapinsay, and had had time between leaving the house and sailing away, why had he not set fire to another house as he went? Again she asked herself what on earth he could have been doing. There was no sign of fire at Eylofr's house, certainly. Leif's house was dark, and Beinir's, too.

Poor Beinir: even she had deceived him, not showing her true character. On her best behaviour. How long could she have kept that up for? She half-smiled: she had been trying to live up to him, the head man, the writer and reader, trying to make a poor woolworker who could barely cook worthy of him. And he was not even the head man.

But he had taken his responsibilities seriously. She remembered again hearing him begging – and it was begging – Vali to let him have custody of Aslak. It had almost sounded as if he truly cared for Aslak, more than just taking responsibility for him. It was impressive, for no one else cared for Aslak.

Except, when she really thought about it, had Beinir ever mentioned Aslak's name?

She stopped, just short of Asta's house, mind leaping. Had she jumped to the wrong conclusion? Who was it Beinir had wanted to come and live with him?

Was there any chance that Ingvar, poor orphan, was actually the son of Beinir? Or Hamthir?

She leaned forward, propping her arm on the cold stone of the house wall, feeling the sharp edges of stone dig into her cold fingers. The wind caught drips of melting snow from the eaves, and tossed them down at her. The torch danced, casting odd shadows over the snow at her feet. She stared at it blankly.

Even if Vali's sister and Beinir had not been married, any child would have a claim on his property at his death.

Hamthir thought wives spent all a man's money. He liked riches, that much was clear. She had a sudden memory of him with his bag of tools, comfortably established by Beinir's hearth, talking to Katrin. What could you fit in that bag of tools – an enamel box?

'He saved my life!' Katrin had told her. Well, he would, she supposed. If he was going to set fire to Beinir's house, he would not want to burn Katrin.

She swung round, staring down towards the harbour. Hamthir should be there, heading out after Aslak, perhaps, with the others. Should she go down? But would they even believe her? No: she needed to find Ketil.

She turned back to the house and swept the torch around, examining the ground. The snow was starting to melt, she could see: the much-trodden path just outside the door was almost clear, wet stone. But beyond that, where the snow was thicker, she could still see two lines of prints. One was smallish, pointed. The other must be big enough to be Ketil's. She lifted the torch, looking for evidence of a couple of people climbing over the infield wall, crossing the field beyond. It was there: this was where they had gone. But where then?

Then she shifted the torch, and her eye was caught by another light. A red flare, high on the hill.

Someone had lit the vart – again.

It was a good enough excuse to rouse the household behind her.

Somehow she managed to persuade Hoskuld that they were not being invaded – she prayed she was right, but in her heart she knew that Ketil was up there. He was there and needed help. She added another prayer that they would get the vart fire out before anyone in Birsay launched anything they might regret, and urged Hoskuld, Asta, Katrin, and a very interested Thora, to leave their beds and come with her.

'Round the bog!' Asta shouted from behind her as she strode out in front of them beyond the last infield wall. 'Not straight ahead!'

Resentful, eyes still on the flaring vart, she hesitated and looked back to see where Asta was directing her. In a rough scramble they staggered through the increasingly soggy snow, sliding and slithering up the hill on the other side.

'It wasn't Aslak,' Sigrid tried to explain. 'But he's left, taken a boat and gone.'

'Good riddance,' said Asta, remarkable in her ability to climb and talk at the same time, even with her bulk. 'But who was it? Was it poor Ingvar?'

'Who is Beinir's heir?'

Asta reached out a hand to haul her up. They were nearly there. What would they find?

'Beinir's heir?'

'Hamthir,' called Thora. 'Hamthir's his heir. He's his son.'

Katrin let out a cry, and fell to her knees.

'Hamthir!'

'Hamthir,' Sigrid confirmed.

Then they crested the hill. They could feel the heat of the vart fire. Sigrid blinked, arm up to shield herself from the light of the flames. And then she saw him.

XXVII

The first thing he was aware of was the delicious scent of soup.

Onion soup, he thought. And he was warm and dry. Possibly dreaming.

Wait, though: onion soup. A wave of dread passed over him.

'Onion soup?' he tried to say. There was a little cry of surprise, and he felt a hand on his shoulder. He was lying face down, his head sideways on a pile of blankets. Above him was Sigrid.

'Yes, onion soup. You know why.'

'Oh ...' His eyes closed.

'You'll need to drink some, you know.'

He opened his eyes again to find a full spoon beside his face. He groaned, and managed – it seemed to take a week – to prop himself on one elbow. His head hurt, but it was as nothing to the pain across his lower back. With his head close to upright, he nodded, and she pushed the spoon into his mouth. It did taste good, he had to admit, and though it was slow he finished the bowl she was holding. He sank back down again, and slept.

The next time he woke, he felt marginally brighter. Asta was sitting by his bed, spinning.

'He's back!' she called. Sigrid appeared again, and he scowled at her.

'Not more soup,' he said.

'No, no need. There was no smell of it: he missed your stomach.'

He closed his eyes in relief, then opened them again.

'It was Aslak.'

'Yes, we thought so.'

'But I don't think he set the fires.'

'No, he didn't,' she agreed. 'Look, we've managed quite well without you, so just rest and get better. Thorfinn won't want a sickly son-in-law.'

Ketil closed his eyes again. That particular thought did not produce very happy dreams.

But he woke again, and slept again, and woke again, and by the time he could, just, see daylight through the roof vents, and feel a sweet, damp breeze come from the open doorway, he felt as if his mind might be working. He thought he might be able to turn on to his back, but as it turned out he was wrong, so he stayed prone.

'Ah!' said Sigrid, glancing up from her tablet-weaving. 'That looks more like you.'

He grunted. Some parts of him felt a bit too much like him.

'Well, go on, then. Tell me: I know you want to.'

Her smile was almost entirely one of deep satisfaction, but she made sure there was no one close enough to listen before she started.

'We're at Asta's, of course, and it's not a happy story for them. Particularly for poor Katrin.'

'It was Hamthir, then?'

'It was. And I suppose Gillaug was right in a way – it happened because I came here.'

He thought.

'Because you were going to marry Beinir?'

'Exactly that.'

He thought again. Hamthir with his tool bag, lingering around Beinir's house.

'He wanted to steal Beinir's treasure – the box, and the silver. So why did he put it back again?'

'He didn't want to steal it. He wanted to inherit it.' She waited for him to ask, but he was struggling. 'He's Beinir's son. It was Hamthir he wanted to have live with us, a happy family, when he had married me. Not Aslak – for that at least I'm pleased.'

'What about Ingvar?'

'Different father. Vali's sister seems to have been – unfortunate. She was expecting Hamthir when Beinir went to Miklagarth and points east for a few years. He knew nothing about it until he came back, by which time the woman was dead.'

'Unfortunate indeed.'

'Hamthir has had his share of misfortune, too. He didn't mean to kill Leif and Hervor. His plan was simply to fire a series of houses – he thought he knew what he was doing, because he'd helped Vali with punishment burnings, like Aslak's longhouse.'

'Fool,' said Ketil.

'Yes,' said Sigrid thoughtfully, 'he is a bit of an idiot. By contrast he did mean to kill Beinir, but he wouldn't have succeeded if Beinir hadn't run back inside for his books. But at least he made sure that Katrin was not in danger.'

Ketil met her eye. It was a small virtue in the face of the rest.

'Ingvar complained about the cold because he was left alone in his bed at night when Hamthir went out to light fires.'

'Did he use Vali's sleeping draught?'

Sigrid shrugged. Ketil wished he could do that. He knew how much it would hurt.

'I have no idea. Aslak's away, and Vali's – Vali's a broken man.'

Ketil tried to imagine it. That tall, authoritative man, lost in his own household, uncle to the destroyer of his community. He had enjoyed control, and he had lost it so completely.

'I thought he might come and see you,' Sigrid went on, 'but he just sits in Gillaug's house by the hearth. Poor Ingvar doesn't understand at all.'

'Aslak's away?' He was trying to take everything in.

'He took a boat, the same night he attacked you.'

'He said he was going to. He'd planned it – he had things in the hut by the vart. He said everyone hated him.'

'They did,' Sigrid said. 'But he didn't set any fires.'

'And Hamthir?'

'Hamthir is secured in one of Beinir's outhouses. He'll be a brennuvagr, a burning's wolf, outlawed for what he has done.' Her face was grim.

'Did he admit it all?'

'Eventually, yes. In fact, after a bit of – well, pestering,' she said, turning a little pink, 'he admitted that he killed Ingigerd, too, to stop her marrying Beinir.'

'So he could have killed you, instead of Beinir?'

'There's no need to look so disappointed!' She made a face at him. 'I suppose he could, but I think by this stage he was in more of a hurry. He did want to marry Katrin – he was prepared to take the risk that she would not ruin him, particularly if he had the additional wealth of Beinir's treasure.'

'I should have found him faster,' he muttered into the blankets.

'Don't be hard on yourself,' said Sigrid, generously. 'Hamthir may be a fool, but you're not too bright, either.'

He opened an eye to glare at her, but she was back concentrating on a tricky turn in her tablet weaving, a little smile catching her lips. Suddenly he was very glad she was not going to stay on Shapinsay.

'Thora's leaving!' called Asta. 'She's coming in to say goodbye!'

The cheery, friendly woman appeared as promised. Katrin, who had been working at the hearth, rose to embrace her, and Sigrid gave her a hug which seemed to surprise Sigrid more than Thora. Ketil smiled, and took Thora briefly by the hand she offered.

'Maybe I'll go to Birsay one day and see the Brough!' Thora said with a grin.

'Then I hope we'll see you there,' said Sigrid.

'Come on, Osk, we need to go!' Thora called. The old woman appeared out of a dark corner of the house, her bundle looking suspiciously as if she had slipped a few of Asta's food stores into it. She glided forward to join her kinswoman, then turned at the last moment to Katrin. There was a creak, and then, squeakily, words.

'You're a good housekeeper. You'll find someone better.'

She swept past Thora, and out into the bright daylight. Katrin's was not the only jaw dropped in shock.

Yule and Christmas passed quietly. Vali, Asta and Hoskuld, with Gillaug and Eyolfr, celebrated in their own way, and Tosti led services with the smith and leatherworker and their families before everyone joined in a somewhat subdued feast.

Skorri and Alf returned to Birsay with Hamthir, to report to Thorfinn – not an enviable job, but they set off with good heart – and the others waited, resting, while Ketil slowly recovered. As they had already seen, Asta was a good nurse, and Ketil was wise enough to be patient. A wound like this one could turn bad if he rushed things. Sigrid elected to stay a little longer, claiming that she had no wish to travel with Hamthir. Hoskuld ferried the men over to the mainland where they would hire a boat to take them around the coast to the Brough. Ketil could see that the arrangements might not appeal to her, though she claimed she was keen to get home.

Slightly before Asta was completely happy with the idea, Ketil declared he too was heading for the Brough, and began to walk about the settlement during the day, reminding his body what it was there to do. He felt horrendously weak, but the fresh, wet breeze soon slapped him back to life, and he was able to climb once more up to the vart and survey the island, yellow-green now in a steel-grey sea. Flattish, yes, but a fair place. The vart was blackened and burned out – they would have to appoint a new warden.

The journey back was not pleasant. Bracing himself in a small boat around the coast as the winter gales set in was quicker and smoother than travelling overland, but he had to fight not to show the pain on his face. Geirod hunched with the yellow dog by the tiller. Tosti and Sigrid both watched Ketil for any signs of weakness: he would not give them the satisfaction, either of them.

After that, even standing for so long reporting to Thorfinn was easier. Of course, most of it was old news to Thorfinn, though Hamthir's trial was still to happen when a proper Thing could be called to examine the case. Ketil went through the story in detail, Thorfinn nodding throughout, sitting alone in his high seat in the hall.

Ketil came to an end. Thorfinn was still frowning. Ketil wondered what more he could say, to try to explain how so much could have happened in so short a time, but then the Earl heaved a particularly heavy sigh.

'Look, Ketil, I've pardon to ask of you.'

'My lord?' Pardon for what?

'It's Asgerdr. I know she was promised to you.'

Ketil felt his heart begin to beat hard.

'But, see, well – she's married to Margad.'

'What?' Ketil's voice was faint, even to him.

'Yes, she's married to Margad. They're going to head back to Caithness shortly.'

Ketil struggled for something to say.

'That was – sudden.'

'Look ...' Thorfinn pushed his hands through his black hair, weighed down by domesticity in a way he never was by battle-leading, or land-governing. 'Look, there's something we should have told you from the start, Ketil. I wanted to but – well, anyway. You'd have found out soon enough. Asgerdr and Hakon – that man that came here last summer –'

'Yes,' said Ketil abruptly. He had no wish to remember Hakon.

'Well, she's expecting his child. She needed to marry – and we had no idea if you would recover. And Margad was very keen to take her off our hands – I mean, he seemed very fond of her.'

'Well, then,' Ketil was still finding words hard. 'Well, then, I hope they'll be very happy.'

'That's good of you,' said Thorfinn, on a great outbreath of relief. 'Very good. There'll be compensation, of course: you'll have been expecting land, as well as a wife. We'll talk about it when you're more rested.'

'Thank you, my lord. But may I ask for something in that regard?'

Thorfinn looked up, surprised.

'What?'

'One of my men stole a dog from Margad. He had reason: the dog was not well treated. I was going to make him pay compensation, but he can ill afford it – and now ...'

'I see.' Thorfinn scowled horribly at the mention of the dog's treatment. 'Yes, I think we can sort something out. Margad mistreated his dog, eh?' He lapsed into thought for a moment, then roused himself and stood. 'Off you go, now: make sure you get better soon. I have need of you!'

'Yes, my lord.'

He bowed, still feeling a twinge in his back as he did so, then turned and left the hall.

Outside, a smirr of rain washed against his face and the wind caught him. He felt so light he thought he might blow away. He was free.

Outlandish words in *Dragon in the Snow*:

Bygg	barley, the kind known now in Orkney as bere
Heithabyr	Hedeby
Hjaltland	Shetland
Kirkuvagr	Kirkwall
Kvarr	broad merchant vessel
Lervig	Lerwick
Miklagarth	Istanbul
Noust	boat shelter
Rammie	rough fight
Vart	signal fire

Shapinsay is never named in the Orkneyinga Saga and for years it was speculated that the island was not settled at that time – this would be odd for it's very accessible from the mainland and richly agricultural. Recent research by Louise Hollinrake has identified plenty of names of Norse origin around the island, and so the current theory seems to be that nothing ever happened on Shapinsay.

Thanks, as so often, to Jill, Kath and Nanisa, my valiant beta-readers, and to M and E, as always.

About the Author

Lexie Conyngham is a historian living in the shadow of the Highlands. Her historical crime novels are born of a life amidst Scotland's old cities, ancient universities and hidden-away aristocratic estates, but she has written since the day she found out that people were allowed to do such a thing. Beyond teaching and research, her days are spent with wool, wild allotments and a wee bit of whisky.

We hope you've enjoyed this instalment. Reviews are important to authors, so it would be lovely if you could post a review where you bought it!

Visit our website at www.lexieconyngham.co.uk. There are several free Murray of Letho short stories, Murray's World Tour of Edinburgh, and the chance to follow Lexie Conyngham's meandering thoughts on writing, gardening and knitting, at www.murrayofletho.blogspot.co.uk. You can also follow Lexie, should such a thing appeal, on Facebook, Pinterest or Instagram.

Finally! If you'd like to be kept up to date with Lexie and her writing, please join our mailing list at: contact@kellascatpress.co.uk. There's a quarterly newsletter, often with a short story attached, and fair warning of any new books coming out.

Murray of Letho

We first meet Charles Murray when he's a student at St. Andrews University in Fife in 1802, resisting his father's attempts to force him home to the family estate to learn how it's run. Pushed into involvement in the investigation of a professor's death, he solves his first murder before taking up a post as tutor to Lord Scoggie. This series takes us around Georgian Scotland as well as India, Italy and Norway (so far!), in the company of Murray, his manservant Robbins, his father's old friend Blair, the enigmatic Mary, and other members of his occasionally shambolic household.

LEXIE CONYNGHAM

Death in a Scarlet Gown

Knowledge of Sins Past

Service of the Heir: An Edinburgh Murder

An Abandoned Woman

Fellowship with Demons

The Tender Herb: A Murder in Mughal India

Death of an Officer's Lady

Out of a Dark Reflection

A Dark Night at Midsummer (a novella)

Slow Death by Quicksilver

Thicker than Water

A Deficit of Bones

Hippolyta Napier

Hippolyta Napier is only nineteen when she arrives in Ballater, on Deeside, in 1829, the new wife of the local doctor. Blessed with a love of animals, a talent for painting, a helpless instinct for hospitality, and insatiable curiosity, Hippolyta finds her feet in her new home and role in society, making friends and enemies as she goes. Ballater may be small but it attracts great numbers of visitors, so the issues of the time, politics, slavery, medical advances, all affect the locals. Hippolyta, despite her loving husband and their friend Durris, the sheriff's officer, manages to involve herself in all kinds of dangerous adventures in her efforts to solve every mystery that presents itself.

A Knife in Darkness

Death of a False Physician

A Murderous Game

The Thankless Child

A Lochgorm Lament

Orkneyinga Murders

Orkney, c.1050 A.D.: Thorfinn Sigurdarson, Earl of Orkney, rules from the Brough of Birsay on the western edges of these islands. Ketal Gunnarson is his man, representing his interests in any part of his extended realm. When Sigri, a childhood friend of Ketil's, finds a dead man on her land, Ketil, despite his distrust of islands, is commissioned to investigate. Sigrid, though she has quite enough to do, decides he cannot manage on his own, and insists on helping – which Ketil might or might not appreciate.

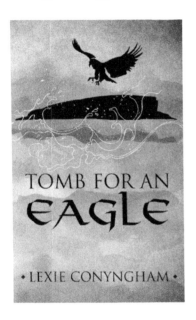

Tomb for an Eagle

A Wolf at the Gate

Dragon in the Snow

Other books by Lexie Conyngham:

Windhorse Burning

'I'm not mad, for a start, and I'm about as far from violent as you can get.'
When Toby's mother, Tibet activist Susan Hepplewhite, dies, he is determined to honour her memory. He finds her diaries and decides to have them translated into English. But his mother had a secret, and she was not the only one: Toby's decision will lead to obsession and murder.

The War, The Bones, and Dr. Cowie

Far from the London Blitz, Marian Cowie is reluctantly resting in rural Aberdeenshire when a German 'plane crashes nearby. An airman goes missing, and old bones are revealed. Marian is sure she could solve the mystery if only the villagers would stop telling her useless stories – but then the crisis comes, and Marian finds the stories may have a use after all.

Jail Fever

It's the year 2000, and millennium paranoia is everywhere.
Eliot is a bad-tempered merchant with a shady past, feeling under the weather.
Catriona is an archaeologist at a student dig, when she finds something unexpected.
Tom is a microbiologist, investigating a new and terrible disease with a stigma.
Together, their knowledge could save thousands of lives – but someone does not want them to …

The Slaughter of Leith Hall

'See, Charlie, it might be near twenty years since Culloden, but there's plenty hard feelings still amongst the Jacobites, and no so far under the skin, ken?'
Charlie Rob has never thought of politics, nor strayed far from his Aberdeenshire birthplace. But when John Leith of Leith Hall takes him under

his wing, his life changes completely. Soon he is far from home, dealing with conspiracy and murder, and lost in a desperate hunt for justice.

Thrawn Thoughts and Blithe Bits and *Quite Useful in Minor Emergencies*

Two collections of short stories, some featuring characters from the series, some not; some seen before, some not; some long, some very short. Find a whole new dimension to car theft, the life history of an unfortunate Victorian rebel, a problem with dragons and a problem with draugens, and what happens when you advertise that you've found somebody's leg.

Printed in Great Britain
by Amazon

78078183R00174